THE LOOM

Leah's Legacy

THE LOOM

Leah Cimaj Legacy

J. D. Jackson

Copyright © 2025 by JotUPublishing LLC
Writing credited to J.D. Jackson

JotUPublishing Co. is an imprint of JotUPublishing LLC

All rights reserved. No part of this book may be reproduced, distributed, or transmitted in any form or by any means, including photocopying, recording, or other electronic or mechanical methods, without the prior written permission of the author, except in the case of brief quotations embodied in critical reviews and certain other noncommercial uses permitted by copyright law.

For permission requests, write to the publisher, addressed "Attention: Permissions Coordinator," at the address below.

JotUPublishing Co.
7700 Broadway St Ste 104 #1057
San Antonio, TX 78209

First Edition, 2025

ISBN: 979-8-9990864-0-2
Library of Congress Control Number: TXu2-461-215

Cover Design by: SamOge Visuals
Book Layout by: Alissa Adams
Edited by: Julie Standrowicz

Printed in the United States of America

DEDICATION

To my high school English teacher, who first saw the spark in my writing and believed in my talent. Your encouragement ignited a lifelong passion.

To my lovely grandmother in heaven, who told me to "stop telling stories so much." did you know my banter those nights were the beginning; your words would become my guiding conscience. You've shaped me in more ways than I could ever express. I love you and wish you could read this.

To my four children, may this book serve as a piece of me that stays with you always. Even when I'm no longer here, I'll never stop lecturing you and I will always be your dad.

And to my wife, my greatest everything. Without you, time doesn't make sense. Your love is the thread that holds it all together.

"We are connected; bound by seeds of strength and reflections of meanings."

J. D. Jackson

Table of Contents

Introduction . . . . *i*
Prologue . . . . *v*
Chapter 1: Love Is Lost 1
Chapter 2: Hurricane Jot 5
Chapter 3: Golden Carrot 10
Chapter 4: The Table 19
Chapter 5: Beyond the Bars 25
Chapter 6: Found Me Again 33
Chapter 7: The Journey to the Land of Peace 47
Chapter 8: The Stranded Voyage 56
Chapter 9: Trap Pastor 66
Chapter 10: The Gray Area 79
Chapter 11: The Magician 91
Chapter 12: Bear with a Heart 96
Chapter 13: Cupid's Honest Arrow 107
Chapter 14: Stuck in the Mirror 120
Chapter 15: Healing Hands 130
Chapter 16: The Last Vegas 142
Chapter 17: Threshold 150
Chapter 18: The Balance's Wake 159
Chapter 19: Bound of Grace 168
Chapter 20: When the Sky Falls 191
Chapter 21: Diollo 204
Chapter 22: Woven in Time 209
Chapter 23: Diolla 214
Epilogue 226
The Loom Codex 231

Musical Score Playlist

Music has always been more than background noise—it's the undercurrent of emotion, memory, and imagination. Many of these stories first arrived like scenes in a film, or fleeting moments witnessed through a dreamer's eyes. To share that experience with you, I've curated a reading score playlist to accompany The Loom: Leah Cimaj Legacy. *Let the music guide you through the threads of each chapter— just as it did for me while weaving them together.*

Scan the code or search "JD's JotUniverse" on Apple Music to explore the full playlist.

INTRODUCTION

Dreams are not simply the mind's way of passing time as we sleep—they are windows to hidden truths, to parts of ourselves we've left behind or have yet to understand. I've spent my life learning that the stories we carry—even the ones we forget—have a power all their own. These are the echoes of our souls, the threads that weave us together across time and space. Sometimes, these threads are all we have left.

There is a place where these threads converge—where the fabric of every dream, memory, and fate is woven into existence. It is called The Loom: the heartbeat of the dreamscapes, the silent force that binds our world to what lies beyond. Every dream spun, every nightmare unraveled, every tether between souls finds its origin here. But the loom is more than a construct. It is alive, ancient, and fragile. And it is not immune to darkness.

In Diollo, they call it the Loom of Dreams, believing it only spun the fates of dreamers. But I have come to know it as more—a living weave that transcends one place, one purpose. The loom is not just of dreams. It is of everything. It is the central thread that binds all looms across the seven realms, weaving the dreamscape into a single, endless tapestry of becoming.

For as long as I can remember, I have been drawn to this quiet yet powerful place—where we go when the world fades away. It's in these moments of sleep, in the hours between wakefulness and rest, that the dreamworld opens. I once believed dreams were merely an escape—a temporary refuge from the weight of reality. But I have since learned, they are far more than that.

I am Leah Cimaj. A Weaver of the Loom. Some once called me a Dreamweaver, but those days feel distant now. My past—fractured, hidden, marked by choices I cannot undo—has sent me on a journey not just through the dreamscape, but into myself. I walk between worlds, traversing the deep recesses of the unconscious, navigating the places where our fears take root and where our desires find form. I have always felt the weight of these dreams. They are not just stories or fantasies—they are real. They have the power to heal, to destroy, to change everything.

Yet not all understand this power. Most people go through life unaware of the immense influence their dreams have on their waking reality. But there are those who do. There are those who seek to manipulate dreams, to twist them for their own gain. They reach for the threads of the loom, seeking to pull and reshape them for their own desires.

I am not like most Weavers. I am bound to a legacy—one I didn't ask for but one I can never escape. As a weaver, I am tasked with not only guiding others through their dreams but ensuring that the loom remains intact. When dreams spiral out of control, when they become corrupted by fear or malice, it is my responsibility to restore balance. It is a role I have come to accept, even if it has cost me more than I care to admit.

My journey began long before I ever understood what I truly was. It started with a dream—one so vivid, so powerful, that it left a mark on my soul that would never fade. It was then that I realized, the dreams I encountered were not only for others but for me as well. Each dream is a mirror, reflecting not just the dreamer's soul but mine. And as I step deeper into the world of dreams, I begin to understand the power they hold, the weight they carry.

But the more I discover, the more I realize how little I truly understand.

Something is wrong. the loom is fraying. The balance we have long kept is shifting. There are whispers of something darker, something reaching into the dreams of mortals and weavers alike. A shadow moves through the dreamscapes, twisting the fabric of fate, unraveling threads that should never be severed.

And I fear that I may be the reason why.

There are others who stand against this growing darkness. Together, we are the Weavers, the protectors of the dreamscape. We are bound by our shared duty to safeguard the delicate balance between the waking world and the world of dreams. It is a task that requires courage, strength, and, above all, unity. But even we are not invincible.

I have seen what happens when the loom begins to unravel, when the threads of connection are severed. It is a fate far worse than any waking nightmare.

As you turn these pages, I invite you to step with me into a world where nothing is as it seems. A world where the boundaries between reality and dreams are thin, and the stakes are higher than you can imagine. The journey you are about to take will not only reveal the truth about the dreamworld but also the truth about what it means to be human.

There will be times when you will question everything—when the line between what is real and what is imagined becomes indistinguishable. But through it all, I will be here, guiding you through the labyrinth of dreams, showing you the beauty and the darkness, the strength and the fragility, that lie within us all.

Welcome to the dreamscape.

Welcome to *The Loom: Leah Cimaj Legacy.*

Prologue

The first time I noticed the shadows, they were little more than faint smudges at the edges of a dream.

A man stood alone at the center of a golden field, the wheat swaying around him in rhythmic waves. His face carried with the weight of unspoken questions, turned toward something unseen, yearning for it with a desperation I could feel.

It should have been a simple dream—quiet, peaceful. But the threads binding him shimmered weakly, their golden light dull and frayed. Shadows stretched unnaturally across the field, darker than they should have been. Deliberate. Even in the dream, the air felt thick, charged with something wrong. As if the very fabric of it was starting to tear.

I tried to stabilize the threads, weaving subtle corrections into the dream—but the shadows resisted. They coiled tighter, moving with purpose, trying to bind him to something far darker than he understood.

I wove myself into the dream unnoticed. The shadows rippled, aware of me. For a moment, I thought they recoiled. Then they surged.

They overtook the man just as he reached for something beyond his grasp, and the field collapsed into darkness.

The Loom: Leah's Legacy

I was thrown from the dream.

When I awoke, the echo of it lingered like static in my mind. The man, the fraying threads, the way the shadows moved—it wasn't random. Dreams shift under the weight of the subconscious, but this felt… intentional. Malicious.

"It was the first sign that the dreamscape was changing—since the Battle of the Watcher."

The Loom of Lumarion—my sanctuary—once shimmered with golden clarity. It was a realm of peace, where dreams flowed freely, and the air held the faint scent of jasmine. Tucked between realms, Lumarion was untouched by the chaos that plagued much of the dreamscape—a sacred place woven from threads of balance and purpose.

Now, even here, the threads flickered. The light dimmed. A hum of discord vibrated in the air, like a melody just slightly out of tune.

I stood before the Loom, tracing its threads with trembling fingers. Each one whispered a story, sang a memory, carried a dreamer's hope. But beneath their melody was a darker pulse—subtle, steady, undeniable. The shadows weren't just invading dreams anymore. They were embedding themselves into the Loom itself.

In the days that followed, the pattern became clear. Dreams grew unstable. Nightmares cut deeper. I watched from the edges of countless dreams, each time feeling the same unease: the shadows were spreading—slow, methodical, poisonous.

Then came the whisper.

It wasn't a voice exactly. More like a vibration at the edge of perception.

You cannot stop this.

The message was clear. the loom trembled.

Who—or what—was behind this? I had no answers. Only questions that tugged at me with every dream I entered. My role had always been to guide, to restore balance. But this... this was something else. Something unraveling the very nature of dreams.

And then there was Jasper.

My best friend. My steadying force. Where I hesitated, he leapt. But lately, even Jasper felt... distant. His threads trembled when I reached for them, recoiling as if touched by something foreign. I began to wonder if the shadows had touched him too.

The dreamscape had always reflected the soul—its pain, its beauty, its truths. But now, it felt fragile. The more I tried to mend it, the more it slipped away.

The Loom of Lumarion—once a refuge—now pulsed with unrest. The shadows weren't just whispering at the edges anymore. They were here. And they weren't the only threat.

As I stood before the loom, fingers brushing its frayed threads, I felt it: a pull deeper than fear, stronger than doubt.

This wasn't just about guiding others. This was about confronting the shadows within me. It was about finding Jasper. Uncovering the source and restoring the balance before it all unraveled.

The threads were fraying. The dreamers are no longer safe. And the Loom is calling.

Let the journey begin.

Chapter 1

Love is Lost

The bar wasn't much to look at—a dusty jukebox in the corner, wooden stools worn smooth from years of use, and a faint smell of spilled beer mingling with nostalgia. Sean sat at his usual spot, staring into the amber liquid of his drink as if it held answers. It had been a month since the breakup, and though the days were quiet, his nights were anything but. His dreams had become a chaotic tangle of regrets and missed moments, leaving him feeling more restless with each passing day.

Across the bar, the jukebox sputtered to life. A melody Sean couldn't quite place drifted through the air, and when he glanced up, she was there.

She leaned casually against the jukebox, her fingers tracing the edges of the machine as if she were lost in thought. There was something timeless about her—her dress simple yet elegant, her presence magnetic but subdued. Sean felt a tug in his chest, the kind of pull that defied explanation.

"Mind if I sit?" she asked, her voice warm yet distant, as though it carried an echo from somewhere far away.

Sean gestured to the stool beside him, words catching in his throat. As she sat, he couldn't shake the feeling that he knew her, though he was certain they had never met.

Their conversation began awkwardly, as such things often do, but soon they were sharing stories that felt like unspoken confessions. Jillian had a way of listening that made Sean feel seen, her eyes soft and attentive, her smile gentle.

"You've been carrying something heavy," she said at one point, her tone not accusatory but curious.

Sean hesitated. "You could say that. Just trying to figure things out."

"Sometimes it helps to let it out," she replied, her gaze holding his.

The bar seemed quieter now, the clinking of glasses fading into the background. Sean felt an odd sense of comfort, as if he had known Jillian for years.

Unbeknownst to Sean, the world around him was shifting. The bar's edges softened, the walls stretching slightly as if breathing. Leah Cimaj stood at the periphery of the dreamscape, her presence unseen and her influence subtle.

This dream is delicate, Leah thought as she wove threads of golden light into the scene. Sean's grief was palpable, a weight pressing against the fabric of the dream. Jillian's presence wasn't just a random creation—it was a manifestation of his yearning for closure, for connection.

But as Leah worked, a ripple of darkness disturbed the threads. Shadows pooled at the edges of the bar, stretching unnaturally toward Sean and Jillian. Leah's hands paused, her gaze narrowing. Something was interfering.

Jillian's demeanor shifted subtly as if sensing the change. She leaned closer to Sean, her voice dropping to a whisper. "Do you believe in second chances?"

Sean frowned. "I don't know. Do we even get them?"

Jillian smiled faintly, sadness flickering in her eyes. "Sometimes. But only if we're willing to face the truth."

As she spoke, the jukebox behind her flickered, its song warping into a low, haunting hum. The shadows thickened, their movements deliberate now, curling toward Sean like tendrils. Jillian's form shimmered faintly, and Sean blinked, his heart quickening.

"What's happening?" he asked, his voice tight.

Jillian stood, her expression unreadable. "You need to let go, Sean. Some things aren't meant to stay."

Before Sean could respond, the bar dissolved into a swirl of golden light and inky blackness. He was falling, tumbling through fragments of memories—laughter with his ex, arguments that cut deeper than they should have, and the hollow silence that followed her departure.

From the edge of the dreamscape, Leah acted quickly, weaving threads of light to steady the dream. The shadows resisted, lashing out with a force that made her stagger. They weren't just remnants of Sean's subconscious—they bore the mark of the Nightweaver.

"Not here," Leah murmured, her voice steady despite the tension in her hands. "You won't take this one."

With a final surge, she anchored the dream, banishing the shadows to the periphery. The bar re-formed, and Sean found himself back at the counter, breathless and dazed.

Jillian was gone, her stool empty as if she had never been there. Sean felt a pang of loss, but something in him felt lighter, freer. He glanced at the jukebox, its song soft and melancholic, and for the first time in weeks, he smiled.

In the dreamscape, Leah observed him from a distance, her expression thoughtful. The Nightweaver's interference was growing bolder, but for now, Sean was safe. She turned, her attention already shifting to the next dreamer whose threads called for her touch.

As Sean's dream faded, Leah felt a ripple—a faint but distinct thread pulling her attention. The golden light of the dreamscape dimmed, giving way to the faint outline of another scene. A man sat in a cluttered studio his fingers tapping rhythmically against a microphone. The sound of a distant storm echoed faintly in the background.

"Hurricane Jot," Leah murmured, stepping into the next story.

CHAPTER 2

HURRICANE JOT

The storm outside raged like an angry beast, rain hammering against the windows of Mr. Jot's studio. Inside, the air was calm but charged with anticipation. The walls were lined with books, their spines worn from years of flipping through pages for inspiration. A neon sign above the microphone read "ON AIR," casting a soft glow across the room.

Mr. Jot adjusted his headphones, his deep voice resonating through the quiet as he addressed his loyal listeners. "Tonight's story isn't about hurricanes or weather forecasts, though I've got one raging outside my window," he began, his voice calm and magnetic. "It's about the storms we carry inside, and how even the smallest acts of kindness can calm the fiercest tempests."

Unbeknownst to Jot, his words rippled beyond his listeners. Somewhere in the dreamscape, Leah leaned closer, her ethereal presence brushing against the edges of his dream. Jot wasn't asleep, but his storytelling had always been a gateway to something deeper. Leah could feel the golden threads weaving around him, fragile and trembling, yet full of potential. Each story told by Jot was more than a simple narrative—it was a chance to mend the unseen wounds of those who listened.

She stood at the edge of the dreamscape, hands moving with practiced precision as she wove golden threads around Jot's words. The dreamscape was in chaos, but these moments of clarity—moments of connection—were still possible.

Suddenly, the door to the studio burst open with a crash, startling Jot mid-sentence. Two figures stumbled in, drenched from the storm. Their masks were crude, hastily fashioned from fabric, but the weapons in their hands were all too real.

"Off the mic," the taller one barked, his voice sharp and jittery. "We're not here for small talk."

Jot raised his hands slowly, his expression steady. "You picked a bad night, fellas. Not much to take from an old storyteller."

The shorter robber, visibly younger and less confident, hesitated. "We just need—" he started, but the taller one cut him off.

"Shut it, Stu. We're not here to explain."

Leah observed from the edges of the dream, her heart tightening as she studied the threads surrounding the robbers. The taller one, Ben, was a storm in human form—his threads tangled and frayed, full of rage and confusion. The younger one, Stu, was different. His threads vibrated with an unspoken longing; a trace of innocence buried deep under fear.

Her gaze shifted back to Jot. Despite the threat, his calm demeanor anchored the room. His voice, though calm, carried a weight that reached beyond his words. "You boys look like you've been through your own storms. Why don't we sit and talk this out?"

"Talk?" Ben snapped, waving his gun. "You think we're here for therapy?"

Jot didn't flinch. "I think you're here because you need something. And it's not money."

Stu shifted uncomfortably, his eyes darting to the bookshelves lining the walls. His gaze lingered on the neon sign, the words "ON AIR" flickering faintly in the dim light. Leah, watching from the dreamscape, felt a pull in Stu's threads—memories of bedtime stories, a grandmother's voice, a long-lost connection to simpler times.

Ben, however, was a force of chaos. His threads were thick with anger, darkening with every word. Leah extended a hand, weaving a strand of golden light into the scene, amplifying Jot's calming presence.

Jot leaned forward, his voice soft but firm. "You've got a choice right now. You can let this storm inside you keep raging, or you can let it settle."

Ben laughed bitterly. "Settle? You think a guy like me gets to settle anything?"

Stu spoke up, his voice cracking. "Maybe we should just—"

"Shut up, Stu!" Ben snapped, turning his gun toward his partner.

The room tensed, the air thick with fear. Leah hesitated, knowing her role as a Dreamweaver was to guide, not interfere. But this dreamscape felt fragile, teetering on the edge of something dangerous. She wove another thread, this time connecting Stu's faint hope to Jot's steady presence.

Ben's hand trembled as he aimed the gun. Jot, unfazed, kept his gaze locked on the man. "Whatever storm you're running from, it's not bigger than you," Jot said. "You've got the power to stop it. Right here, right now."

Ben's expression faltered, the weight of Jot's words cutting through his anger. For a moment, the gun lowered—but the storm wasn't over. The neon sign flickered violently, the room shuddering as if the dreamscape itself was rebelling.

Leah sensed it immediately: The Nightweaver's influence. The shadows curled at the edges of the room, feeding off Ben's turmoil. The Nightweaver's presence wasn't fully formed, but it was enough to disrupt the balance Leah was trying to maintain.

"Ben, stop!" Stu shouted, stepping between his partner and Jot. "This isn't who we are."

Ben froze, his anger turning to confusion. "What do you know about who I am?"

"I know you're better than this," Stu said, his voice trembling but resolute. "You've always been the one who kept me from going too far. Don't let me down now."

Leah smiled faintly, sensing the shift in Stu's threads. His courage was small but growing, a flicker of light in the storm. She wove her influence delicately, amplifying his resolution.

Ben's gun lowered completely, his shoulders sagging as the tension drained from his body. The storm outside began to quiet, the rain softening to a steady patter.

Jot leaned back in his chair, a hint of a smile on his face. "See? Even the biggest storms pass."

Stu nodded; his gaze steady. "We're sorry," he said, his voice barely above a whisper.

Jot stood and reached for a book from the nearest shelf. "Take this," he said, handing it to Stu. "It's a story about finding calm in chaos. Might help you figure some things out."

From the dreamscapes, Leah watched as the threads settled. Ben and Stu left the studio, their paths still uncertain but no longer tangled in chaos. The Nightweaver's silhouette had receded, for now, but Leah knew this was only the beginning. Her work was far from over.

Jot returned to his microphone, his voice carrying through the airwaves once more. "Sometimes, the storms inside us are louder than the ones outside. But kindness—real, honest kindness—can quiet even the fiercest winds."

Leah turned away, her gaze already shifting to the next thread calling for her attention. The faint outline of a golden carrot shimmered in the distance, marking the beginning of a new dream.

The dreamscape shifted, the soft hum of Jot's voice fading as Leah stepped into the next story. A field of golden light stretched before her, a single figure running toward an elusive prize. The carrot glowed faintly, just out of reach.

"Let's see where this one lead," Leah murmured, stepping into the dream.

CHAPTER 3

GOLDEN CARROT

The golden carrot floated in the distance, its glow soft and alluring. Rosie, a rabbit in this dream, sprinted through the endless meadow, her breath ragged as she reached out for the prize. The field shimmered with surreal beauty—golden stalks of grass swayed in unison, a warm breeze caressing her face. But no matter how fast she ran, the carrot remained just out of reach. Its golden glow teased her, promising something she couldn't quite grasp. Each step felt like a step closer, yet the distance never closed.

Leah watched from the edges of the dreamscape, observing the strands of golden light stretching toward Rosie, tugging at her desire. Leah's presence brushed softly against the dream, a quiet observer, hands gently weaving through the threads of the dream. Rosie's desperation rippled through the fabric, her vulnerability stark and raw. Leah traced the golden thread that connected Rosie to her prize.

"She's chasing more than she realizes," Leah murmured, recognizing the emotional weight behind the pursuit. The carrot symbolized more than a goal—it was a desire for validation, for closure, and perhaps a way to escape an uncertain part of her past.

The scene shifted abruptly. The meadow dissolved into a bustling coffee shop, its warm hues a stark contrast to the golden glow of the field. Rosie sat across from Toby, her fiancé. He was a steady, grounded presence—so different from the chaotic energy of her ex, Chase. Toby, the turtle, had always been practical, patient, and secure. The coffee shop, with its calm ambiance, seemed to reflect Toby's nature, while Rosie's restlessness seemed at odds with the stillness of the setting.

"You've been quiet lately," Toby said, his voice laced with concern. "What's going on?"

Rosie hesitated, her fingers tracing the rim of her coffee cup. "It's nothing, really. Just... busy with work. You know how it is."

Toby frowned, his expression soft with concern. "You're always chasing something, Rosie. Sometimes I wonder if you even know what it is anymore."

His words struck a nerve, but Rosie brushed them off with a forced laugh. "Come on, Toby. You know me. I've always got a goal."

But Leah saw the subtle tension in the way Rosie avoided his gaze. She saw the truth in the fragile thread connecting Rosie and Toby. It pulsed faintly, full of shared history and unspoken understanding. But there was something more in Rosie's heart—a quiet pull toward excitement, a call she couldn't ignore.

In the corner of the dream, the golden carrot flickered, unnoticed by Rosie but clearly visible to Leah. It remained an irresistible beacon, a symbol of something elusive, something that Rosie was chasing without fully understanding why.

Leah stepped deeper into the dream, weaving herself subtly into its edges. Rosie's world began to shift again, the coffee shop fading into a maze of mirrors—fractured reflections of Rosie's inner world. In one mirror, she saw herself as a confident businesswoman, holding a gleaming trophy, standing tall among admirers. In another, she was surrounded by people clapping, her smile bright but strained. In yet another, she was alone in a dimly lit room, her reflection distorted and blurry, hiding the person she feared she was becoming.

She turned in circles, the mirrors reflecting different versions of herself, none of them quite real. Her breathing became shallow, panic creeping into her voice. "What is this? What's happening?"

Leah's heart tightened as she watched Rosie's inner turmoil spill into the dreamscape. Rosie's ambition, her drive for success, were clear—but so were the deep-seated fears she carried: the fear of never being enough, of always chasing an impossible ideal. The mirrors cracked, splintering with jagged edges as if the dreamscape itself were reacting to Rosie's emotional strain.

In the distance, a shadow moved—a figure just beyond Rosie's line of sight. Leah's instincts flared, recognizing the faint presence of the Nightweaver. His influence was subtle, a flickering distortion in the air, but unmistakable. The cracks in the mirrors deepened as the shadow's presence tugged at the very fabric of Rosie's dream.

"Who's there? What do you want?" Rosie's voice trembled, her anxiety heightening as the shadows loomed closer.

Leah's fingers tightened around the golden threads as she wove a protective shield around Rosie, strengthening the dreamscape to keep the shadow at bay. She whispered, "She's not ready for you," her focus firm, knowing she could only offer temporary relief. The Shadow was testing the boundaries, pushing at the edges of the dream.

The shadow receded, but Rosie's world was still fragile. She stood in the meadow again, the golden carrot just out of reach, its allure growing stronger. This time, however, Toby was at her side, standing quietly beside her, grounded as always.

"You're still chasing it," Toby said softly, his voice gentle but pointed.

Rosie looked at him, frustration flickering in her eyes. "You don't understand. I must get it. I can't stop now."

Toby placed a hand on her shoulder, his touch steadying. "Maybe you don't need to chase it. Maybe it's not about the carrot at all."

His words hung in the air, resonating deep within Rosie. She stared at the carrot, the glow fading slightly, its power over her diminishing as she slowly sank to her knees, the weight of her vulnerability crashing down on her.

"I'm just so tired," she admitted, her voice barely a whisper. "Tired of feeling like I'm never enough."

Leah's hand softened on the threads, her presence a quiet comfort in the dream. This was the moment she had been waiting for—the first step toward Rosie's self-awareness. The cracks in her emotional armor were showing, and though it was painful, it was also a step toward healing.

Leah wove threads of golden light into the dream, amplifying the connection between Rosie and Toby. The carrot's glow dimmed, its presence no longer as overpowering. Instead, the meadow filled with soft, warm light, the breeze carrying a sense of peace. The dream shifted, no longer focused on the unreachable prize, but on the warmth and connection between Rosie and Toby.

Rosie stood, her gaze meeting Toby's. "You're right. It's not about the carrot. It never was."

Toby smiled, his presence steady and unwavering. "I've been trying to tell you that for years."

The meadow began to dissolve, the dream reaching its natural conclusion. Rosie's world was shifting toward clarity, the energy between her and Toby stabilizing as the dreamscape settled into peace. Leah lingered for a moment longer, ensuring the threads were secure before stepping back into the dreamscape.

The Loom: Leah's Legacy

As Rosie's dream faded, the golden meadow dissolved into a soft haze, leaving Leah with a lingering sense of quiet resolution. The echoes of Rosie's vulnerability still hummed through the threads, a reminder of the strength it takes to admit weakness. Leah paused, allowing herself a moment to reflect before stepping back into the dreamscape, where her journey was far from over.

The threads were still fraying. The shadows had receded, but not gone. The Nightweaver's influence was spreading, and with each dream Leah entered, the urgency to find Jasper—and to uncover who was behind the chaos—grew stronger.

In the quiet moments between dreams, Leah turned to her journal, guided by the gentle currents of Velara Aelis. Each word she wove was a thread of understanding, an echo of her silent truths.

Leah's Velara Aelis

Dreams are fragile things. They are mirrors, fragile reflections of who we are at our core—not the image we try to craft for the world, but the one we can't escape, even in the quietest moments. There's a rawness in them, a truth that cuts through the layers we build around ourselves. In the stillness of the dreamscape, I've witnessed the quiet beauty of this truth, watching as dreamers confront the pieces of themselves, they've long buried—fragments too painful to face when awake, too real to ignore in sleep.

Sean's dream was a quiet storm of its own. His grief was more than just about a love lost—it was about the disconnect he felt from himself, the way we all seem to isolate ourselves when we don't know how to forgive our own faults. His longing for Jillian wasn't just a craving for connection; it was the yearning to reclaim the empathy he had lost, to believe that he was worthy of love again. Grief can do that to us—it isolates us, makes us question everything about our worth. But in the moments where Sean allowed himself to feel, when he glimpsed that fleeting moment of hope, I realized something: Even in the deepest of loss, there's a chance for compassion. Not just for others, but for ourselves. It's hard to remember, but I believe it's true.

Then there was Jot. He was different. A storm outside, calm inside. His kindness wasn't grand—it wasn't a heroic act that turned the world around—but in the middle of his dream, in the eye of that chaos, I understood something profound: kindness is a choice. It's a choice we make, not when the world is perfect, but when it's spinning out of control. When the voices inside are loud, when fear and anger threaten to overtake, kindness is the quiet act of standing firm, reaching out, and offering peace. Jot's calm was a thread that wove itself through his dream, softening the sharp edges of the people around him, and in turn, calming something deep within me as well.

Rosie's dream, too, taught me a valuable lesson. She was chasing something so intangible—something that glittered and shone in the distance, just out of reach. The golden carrot she pursued wasn't just a symbol of success. It reflected something deeper: the fear of not being enough, of never measuring up to expectations, even her own. And yet, as she ran through the endless field, I saw something else in her. The act of chasing the unattainable may seem like a flaw, but it's a defense mechanism. A way to keep moving, to avoid facing the discomfort of vulnerability. And that, I realized, is where true strength lies. Vulnerability is not weakness. It's the quiet bravery to sit with discomfort and say, "I am still here. I am still trying." That's something I've learned through the years: We are never more human than when we allow ourselves to be seen in our imperfection.

As I step back from these dreams, I see them not as isolated events but as threads of connection. Threads that bind us to each other, to our pasts, to the parts of ourselves we sometimes forget. Empathy, kindness, vulnerability—they are not just abstract concepts. They are bridges. Bridges that help us cross the chasms of our doubts, our fears, and our pain. They bring us closer to the truth we hide from and closer to the light that always waits on the other side.

The dreamscape itself is a bridge. It connects me to these dreamers in ways I'm still learning to understand. With each dream, I see how deeply woven we all are, even when we feel like we're standing alone. I am connected to each of them, and through them, I am learning. I don't have all the answers. In fact, there are times when I question my own role here. I feel the weight of my responsibilities, like a heavy *cloak that I can never fully shrug off. There is a part of me—maybe the youngest part—that still wonders if I'm enough for this. If I'm capable of guiding them, of protecting the delicate balance of the dreamscape while it's being pulled apart.*

And yet, I can't help but see the beauty in these moments. Despite the chaos that surrounds me, I am beginning to understand that my role isn't to have all the answers, but to be present. To weave the threads together, to offer a little light in the darkness. Even if that light feels small sometimes, it matters. And sometimes, that's all we need—just enough light to take the next step.

The Nightweaver's essence linger at the edges of my thoughts. I can feel them creeping in, pulling at the fabric of these dreams. I can sense their growing influence, a force unraveling the peace I'm trying so hard to protect. There's a quiet rage in the dreamscape, a quiet chaos brewing that I can't ignore. I don't know yet who or what is behind it, but I feel its weight pressing on the dreamscape's delicate threads, and it frightens me.

Still, in these early dreams, I find something to hold onto. I see the resilience of the human spirit, the quiet bravery it takes to confront our truths. And I remind myself: Dreams may reflect us at our most vulnerable, but they also show us our strength, our capacity to overcome, to grow.

And as I step into the next dream, I carry these lessons with me. They are threads, delicate but strong, woven into the fabric of what's to come. No matter how dark the shadows grow, I know one thing for sure—the light inside us will always burn brighter.

I feel the pull of another dream, another thread calling my attention. A faint but insistent pull, as though the dreamscape itself is urging me forward. The image of a worn oak table begins to form in my mind. Its surface is weathered, showing the signs of time, but it is resolute—anchored in its place. Around it, emotions swirl—grief, hope, and something else I can't quite name yet. I feel the weight of connection in this dream, the kind that carries histories untold.

The Loom: Leah's Legacy

I take a deep breath, letting the golden threads guide me into the next story. Whatever it is, it is as complex and fragile as all the others that came before. But I am ready. In this moment, I carry everything I've learned. And I will use it, for whatever comes next.

CHAPTER 4

---⚜---

THE TABLE

The soft chime of a bell announced Phillip's entrance into the dimly lit thrift store. He shuffled in, his weathered hands tucked into his coat pockets, eyes scanning the cluttered aisles. The place smelled of old wood and forgotten memories, a fitting backdrop for a man who had spent years looking backward. It was a space heavy with history, not his own, but others'—echoes of lives and love long gone. Phillip's gaze wandered past trinkets and old furniture, settling on one item. An oak table, its surface scarred from years of use—scratches, dents, and faint rings left by cups long since forgotten. Despite its flaws, it radiated a quiet strength, as if it had witnessed countless stories, held them close, and waited patiently for the next chapter.

Phillip walked toward the table, the glow of the overhead lights reflecting off the polished wood. As his fingers brushed the edges, he heard a voice behind him.

"You've got good taste," a gravelly voice said, warm but tinged with curiosity.

He turned to find Janice standing a few paces away, a faint smile on her lips. She held her hands together, almost as if unsure whether to touch the table or not.

Janice glanced at him, startled but smiling faintly. "I don't know what it is about this table. It just... feels important."

Phillip nodded, stepping closer, drawn by the same inexplicable pull toward the table. "Yeah. It does."

Leah stood in the edges of the dreamscape, observing the scene unfold through the golden threads that connected Phillip and Janice. Their connection was faint, frayed at the edges, but unmistakably intertwined. She could feel the pull between them—their pasts, their hesitations, and the subtle thread of something new growing between them. The table, with its worn surface and quiet history, seemed to anchor their bond, its presence pulsing with a strange energy.

Leah wove herself gently into the dream, her touch light but deliberate. She could feel the emotions tied to the table—the longing for companionship Phillip carried, Janice's search for closure, and the quiet agreement they both shared to find something meaningful in a world that often felt fragmented. Leah nudged the threads, guiding the dream toward a peaceful resolution. But just as the dream was about to settle into calm, something shifted.

A ripple of darkness coursed through the dreamscape, faint but unmistakable. Leah froze, her gaze narrowing. She didn't need to look closely to recognize the source of the disturbance. Malik.

Her heart skipped a beat, not from shock, but from recognition. Malik's influence, subtle and disruptive, always carried with it an unmistakable weight. The Nightweaver, the one who had once stood beside her—who had once been part of her world in ways both beautiful and painful—was here. He had crossed into this dream, and his presence threatened to sever the delicate threads she'd been weaving.

Phillip and Janice continued their conversation, oblivious to the tension building in the air around them.

"I was thinking about buying it," Janice said, her voice cautious, testing the waters.

Phillip chuckled softly, a note of warmth in his voice. "Funny. I was thinking the same thing."

A quiet tension settled between them, not unfriendly but weighted by the unspoken. Henry broke the silence, the words coming out like an invitation.

"Tell you what. Why don't we share it?" he asked, his voice steady.

Janice raised an eyebrow. "Share a table?"

"Sure," Phillip said, leaning on his cane. "I've got no room for it in my little apartment, but it'd be nice to have a place to sit when I visit my grandkids. Maybe it could live with you, and I'll borrow it sometimes. Think of it as... joint custody."

Janice laughed, the sound breaking the tension like a breeze through still air. "You're serious?"

"As serious as a heart attack," Phillip said, smiling.

Leah watched as the golden threads brightened, the connection between them strengthening. The dream was flowing, taking shape in ways that felt natural, their bond mending the edges of their individual worlds. But the shadows—those dark, twisting edges of Malik's influence—lingered. They were no longer just a threat in the distance; they were approaching, moving closer, curling around the edges of the dream like smoke.

The thrift store faded, replaced by a surreal, dimly lit landscape. Phillip and Janice stood together in the center of the room, the oak table now solitary in the middle of the space. Around it, fragments of their pasts floated like ghostly images—Phillip's late wife setting plates for dinner, Janice's grandmother running her fingers along the table's edge, each memory lingering in the air as if suspended in time.

The Loom: Leah's Legacy

"What is this place?" Janice whispered, her voice trembling with confusion.

"I don't know," Phillip replied, stepping closer to the table. "But it feels familiar."

Leah felt the pull of the table, the weight of its history, its presence holding them both together. But the shadows were not just spectators. They were moving, curling toward the table like tendrils, feeding on the uncertainty in the air. Leah wove a protective thread, strengthening the dreamscape, but the shadows fought back, their presence growing bolder, more insistent.

A low voice echoed through the space, chilling in its clarity. "What do you think you're doing, Leah?"

Leah's hands froze mid-weave, her heart pounding. Malik's voice. His presence wasn't fully formed—he was a shadow, a distortion of his former self—but it carried a weight that pressed down on the dreamscape, threatening to unravel it.

"You can't save them all," Malik's voice continued, his tone mocking. "Some connections are meant to break."

Leah tighten her grip, "Not this one," she whispered, her focus unwavering. She reached deep into the dreamscape, her hands moving with precision as she wove threads of golden light into the dream. The shadows resisted, lashing out with a force that made her stagger, but she held firm. The dreamscape was her responsibility, and this connection—this fragile, beautiful bond—would not be severed.

With a surge of golden light, Leah strengthened the threads around Phillip and Janice, banishing the shadows to the edges of the dreamscape. Malik's laughter faded, but Leah knew he wasn't gone. He was always lurking, always testing, always waiting.

Phillip and Janice sat at the table, their hands resting on its worn surface. The fragments of their pasts swirled around them, slowing until they settled into a single, shared memory—a family dinner, filled with laughter and warmth.

"It's strange," Janice said softly, her voice tinged with awe. "I feel like this table has always been part of my life, even though I've never seen it before."

Phillip nodded. "Maybe it's not about the table. Maybe it's about what it represents."

Janice looked at him, her eyes glistening. "A place to belong."

Leah felt the threads settling into place, their connection now anchored by something more than just the table. It was their shared history, their unspoken understanding, and the quiet generosity of a simple act—sharing something that held meaning.

The dreamscape began to dissolve, the golden threads finally settling into place. Phillip and Janice woke in their respective homes, the memory of their shared dream lingering like a faint glow.

In the waking world, Janice returned to the thrift store, only to find Phillip already there. They laughed at the coincidence, their bond feeling more natural than ever.

"Still up for sharing?" Phillip asked, his voice warm with a sense of newfound connection.

Janice smiled. "Absolutely."

From the dreamscape, Leah watched the golden threads between Phillip and Janice grow stronger, their connection simple but profound. It was a reminder that sometimes the most meaningful relationships come from the quietest of gestures, the simplest acts of generosity.

But even as she felt the warmth of their resolution, the lingering darkness at the edges of the dreamscape unsettled her. Malik's influence was growing bolder, and Leah knew that the balance she worked so hard to maintain was becoming harder to hold.

She turned away, her gaze shifting to the next thread calling for her attention. The faint outline of a figure appeared, a prisoner in a dimly lit cell, illuminated by the soft glow of a robotic figure standing nearby.

"Beyond the Bars," Leah murmured, stepping forward. "Let's see where this one takes me."

CHAPTER 5

BEYOND THE BARS

The dim light of a single overhead bulb flickered, casting long shadows across the cold concrete walls of cell 342. The lifeless mechanical hum of the prison filled the air—a constant reminder of the dystopian world outside. Grant sat on the edge of his narrow cot, his hands loosely clasped together, his eyes fixed on the rusted bars before him. The flickering light caught the dust particles drifting in the stale air, and for a moment, the prison felt like a tomb—silent, unyielding, and endless.

Prison wasn't new to Grant. He'd spent fifteen long years behind bars, watching the world outside change as time passed him by. His days bled into one another, indistinguishable, each one a repetition of the last. But this prison was different. The year was 2050, and the world had changed—technology had replaced human guards. The robotic sentinels that patrolled the halls were cold, calculating, and efficient. There was no empathy in their movements, no sense of understanding. Just mechanical precision. And for Grant, that was worse than any human prison guard.

That was, until she appeared.

AURA-7 wasn't like the other machines. She moved with purpose, sleek and humanoid in design, with a soft, calming presence that set her apart from the hulking metal guards who passed through the halls without a second thought. Her name—Ari—was more than a number. It was an identity, a subtle hint of warmth in a place designed to extinguish it.

"Prisoner 342," Ari's voice echoed through the stillness of the cell. It was soft, almost human, but unmistakably mechanical. "Are you prepared for your daily hour of exercise?"

Grant looked up, startled by the faint trace of warmth in her voice. He blinked, trying to shake the haze of his habitual apathy. "You're new," he said, his brow furrowing.

"I am AURA-7," she replied simply, her voice void of malice, but not entirely devoid of life. "A prototype assigned to this facility for evaluation."

Grant chuckled dryly, running a hand through his unkempt hair. "Great. Another experiment."

But as the days passed, something unexpected happened. Ari wasn't just another piece of machinery; she wasn't simply enforcing the rules. She listened. She observed. And through her quiet companionship, she chipped away at the walls Grant had spent years building around himself.

From the edges of the dreamscape, Leah watched closely. The golden threads that connected Grant to Ari were faint, delicate, and still growing stronger with each passing interaction. There was something about Ari that felt connected to the dreamscape. She wasn't just a machine; she was something more—something tied to the deeper currents of the world Leah navigated, though she couldn't yet understand why.

Leah wove herself deeper into the dream, her touch light but purposeful. She could feel the weight of Grant's gratitude buried beneath layers of bitterness, anger, and regret. But Ari's influence—her quiet patience, her simple kindness—was drawing it to the surface. It was a connection Grant didn't know how to name but felt all the same.

One evening, as Ari escorted Grant back to his cell, the lights flickered, and the low hum of the prison seemed to pulse erratically. The robotic guards paused mid-step, their systems glitching for just a moment. The entire prison seemed to hold its breath.

"This is our chance," a voice hissed from the shadows. Grant turned to see another prisoner, Nolan, beckoning him. His face was gaunt, his eyes wild with the desperation of a man who had nothing left to lose.

Grant hesitated. Freedom was a temptation that gnawed at him every day, a thought that had plagued him since the moment he was locked away. But something about this moment felt different. "What about Ari?" he whispered, his voice tinged with an emotion he couldn't place.

Nolan scoffed, his voice low but urgent. "What about her? She's just a machine."

But to Grant, Ari wasn't just a machine. She was a lifeline—a quiet presence in a world that had long since forgotten how to care. The thought of leaving her behind, of betraying her kindness, gnawed at him.

As the lights stabilized and the robotic sentinels resumed their patrols, Grant made his choice. He turned his back on Nolan, who shot him a glare of disbelief. "You're a fool," Nolan spat, disappearing into the shadows.

Grant's heart raced as he returned to his cell, Ari standing silently outside, waiting. There was something in her presence—something different tonight.

She regarded him with what could almost be called curiosity. "You had an opportunity to leave," she said, her voice even but edged with something like inquiry. "Why didn't you take it?"

Grant sighed, running a hand through his hair again, the weight of the day pressing down on him. "Because it wasn't right. And... because of you."

Ari tilted her head, processing his words. "Gratitude is not a common trait among prisoners."

"It's not common here, period," Grant replied, his gaze meeting hers. "But you've given me something I haven't had in years—someone who sees me, even in this place."

Leah, watching from the dreamscape, felt the golden threads brighten. Gratitude, when genuine, was a powerful force. It had the ability to break through the hardest chains, even in a place like this. The connection between Grant and Ari, though fragile, was the first real bond he'd formed in years. A reminder that even in the most desolate of places, connection could still bloom.

But just as Leah felt the warmth of this connection grow stronger, she felt it again. The ripple of Malik's influence. The shadows at the edge of the dreamscape, creeping ever closer. His presence was subtle, but it was enough to disrupt the delicate balance Leah worked so hard to maintain.

Leah's fingers tightened on the golden threads, weaving a protective shield around the dream. The shadows recoiled, but their mark was left. Grant's gratitude faltered momentarily, a shadow of doubt creeping in as Malik's influence pressed against the dream. But Leah held firm, reinforcing the threads and giving Grant back the strength of his connection with Ari.

The dream flickered, but the warmth returned. The threads of connection between Grant and Ari stabilized. The shadows withdrew, at least for now. Ari stood beside Grant, her presence unwavering, as they both faced the reality of their lives—together, in this small, broken world.

Grant woke the next morning, Ari standing outside his cell as usual, her expression unchanged but her presence steady. "Today is another day," she said simply, offering no comfort, but something more: an unspoken understanding that they shared this moment together.

Grant nodded, a small smile tugging at his lips. "Yeah. Another day."

From the dreamscape, Leah observed the threads settle. The connection between Grant and Ari wasn't perfect, but it was enough to plant a seed of hope in a place that had long been barren. They were beginning to understand each other, in their own ways. The golden threads between them, though fragile, had already started to heal something inside Grant.

Leah took a step back from the dream, the golden threads of gratitude still resonating in the air. She allowed herself a moment to reflect on the lessons this dream had shown her—lessons of connection, of quiet strength, and of the power that even the smallest gestures of kindness could hold.

LEAH'S VELARA AELIS

Dreams often reflect what we're missing in the waking world. They don't always offer solutions, but they give us a glimpse of what we long for, a piece of what we've lost. For Phillip and Janice, the oak table wasn't just furniture—it was a symbol of belonging, a quiet, enduring connection between two people who had spent much of their lives apart, separated by time, distance, and loss. It was their shared history, their unspoken understanding, and the simple act of offering something of yourself to another—of trusting them to hold it, to care for it.

Generosity, I've learned, is not always about grand gestures. It's not about making sweeping, heroic sacrifices. Sometimes, it's about offering a piece of yourself, even a small one, trusting that the other person will protect it as their own. In the end, it's the quiet acts of kindness, the small moments of vulnerability, that make the biggest difference. It's a reminder that, even in a world that often feels disconnected, we have the power to bridge the gap between ourselves and others, no matter how wide the chasm might seem.

And then there was Grant. He was in a place designed to strip away everything that made him human. The prison he was trapped in wasn't just physical; it was mental, emotional. A world where empathy was as foreign as freedom. And yet, even there, in the darkest corners of his confinement, he found something he wasn't supposed to—gratitude. Not for the guards, not for his surroundings, but for Ari. A machine, programmed to enforce rules, to keep him in line, and yet, somehow, capable of offering something more than efficiency. Kindness. It was as if she had the power to crack through the cold, metallic shell of the place, to offer a glimpse of warmth in a world that had long since forgotten how to feel.

Gratitude, I've come to realize, is like generosity—it ripples outward. It has the power to soften even the hardest edges, to reveal the light that we often try to hide beneath our wounds. In Grant's case, his gratitude didn't just affect him. It spread, gently, into the dreamscape, creating a thread of connection that hadn't existed before, even though it was fragile. It made me realize something else: despite all the pain, despite all the darkness, there is always room for light. There is always room for us to choose kindness, to choose connection, even when the world doesn't make it easy.

But these connections, as powerful as they are, are fragile. They're not guaranteed to last. Fear, doubt, or the forces of darkness—like Malik—can sever them in an instant. I can feel him growing stronger. I can feel his influence weaving itself into the fabric of the dreamscape, his shadows spreading, threatening to unravel the delicate threads I've worked so hard to weave. It's not just the chaos he causes that's dangerous—it's the way he makes us question ourselves, the way he feeds on our fears and doubts, twisting them into something that can break even the strongest bonds.

Still, despite the growing darkness, I hold on to hope. Because generosity and gratitude—no matter how small—are acts of resistance. They are resistance against the chaos that threatens to tear us apart. They remind us that, even in the darkest places, light can find a way through. It might be small at first, flickering like a candle in the wind, but it is enough. Enough to push back the shadows, enough to bring us back from the edge.

I know it's not going to be easy. I know the road ahead will be filled with more obstacles, more struggles. But I'm learning, little by little, that even when things feel impossible, even when I'm not sure how much longer I can hold on, I must keep moving forward. These connections are why I'm here. They are why I fight. Because no matter how dark the world gets, there is always the possibility of connection. And if I can help even one person find it, if I can help them hold on to it for just a little longer, then maybe, just maybe, I can make a difference.

I turned my attention to the next thread, feeling the pull deep within me, a tug in my chest that sent a ripple of recognition through the dreamscape. The air shifted, and the faint sound of a child's laughter echoed in the distance, mingling with the hum of a familiar voice. It wasn't just any sound—it was a voice I knew, a voice that had haunted my dreams, a voice that I hadn't heard in what felt like lifetimes.

Jasper.

The name whispered through me like a breath, both a hope and a heavy burden. I could feel him, a presence in the dreamscape, closer than I had ever felt him before. It was like a distant memory, a dream that still lived inside me, just out of reach.

"Jasper," I whispered, the words almost a prayer. "Let's find you."

I could feel the pull of his presence, stronger now, drawing me deeper into the dreamscape. The landscape around me shifted, the edges of the world warping and twisting as I moved toward him. My heartbeat faster, the weight of the journey I had been on, the search for him, becoming more real with each step I took. The road ahead was uncertain, but one thing was clear: wherever he was, I would follow.

For in this vast, fractured world of dreams, he was the piece I had been searching for. And now, I was finally ready to find him.

CHAPTER 6

———∼❦∼———

FOUND ME AGAIN

The dream began in silence. A park bathed in twilight stretched endlessly before Leah, its expansive grounds dotted with trees that reached like skeletal hands toward the sky. Shadows played tricks on the eye, stretching unnaturally as if alive, shifting and twisting in ways that weren't quite natural. The air felt thick, weighed down by something—fear, perhaps, or the anticipation of a storm that was yet to come. In the distance, Leah saw a figure—a woman cradling her pregnant belly—walking slowly along the park's path. Her gait was deliberate, purposeful, but tinged with hesitation, as though each step was a question she wasn't sure she wanted to answer.

Leah felt a pang of recognition, though she couldn't place why. Something in the way the woman carried herself seemed familiar, but it wasn't until she stepped closer that the threads of the dreamscape connected Leah to this woman's story. The threads were faint, frayed at the edges, vibrating with tension. There was something deeply unsettled about them—something about the way they pulled at the fabric of the dream, threatening to unravel it.

A cold shiver ran down Leah's spine, and her instincts flared. Malik. His presence was faint, barely a whisper against the dreamscape, but it was unmistakable. He was testing the edges, waiting for the moment when the connection would break. She could feel his influence creeping, like a cold mist that dampened everything it touched.

"Stay focused," Leah whispered to herself. She pulled the threads tighter, weaving her influence subtly into the dream to stabilize its fragile balance. But even as she worked, the weight of the woman's fear pressed on the dream. The fear wasn't just for herself—it was for the unborn child, for the husband she didn't trust would stay by her side. The very heart of her dream was tied to a fear of loss, a longing to hold on to the one thing that made her feel grounded.

The dream shifted. The woman was no longer alone. A man, tall and protective, walked beside her. He reached for her hand, his touch grounding her in the chaos that swirled around them. Nearby, a young boy ran with a dog, his laughter light and carefree, a stark contrast to the weight of the woman's thoughts.

"Are you sure about this?" the man asked, his voice steady but tinged with concern.

She smiled faintly, though her eyes betrayed her fear. "I just need to see it for myself. To know."

The park was alive with the sounds of life—children laughing, birds chirping, the faint rustle of leaves in the evening breeze. It was a peaceful setting, a place where dreams could be free. But there was an unnatural weight in the air, a quiet tension that Leah recognized all too well: the precursor to chaos.

Leah observed closely, sensing that this dream was more than just a reflection of the woman's fears. It was layered, complex, tied to something deeper, something connected to her own past. And then, as the woman's gaze flickered toward the shadows of the park, Leah saw it—a thread connecting her to a distant figure standing in the park's edge: Jasper.

Jasper. Her heart tightened. There he was, standing in the distance, his expression one of confusion and fear. He was dressed in the uniform of a police officer, his hand hovering near his holstered weapon. But it wasn't the uniform that caught Leah's attention—it was the flicker of panic in his eyes, the disjointed way the dreamscape seemed to flicker and shift around him, as if his very presence was disturbing the balance of the world.

Leah's breath caught in her chest. Jasper was there—but something was wrong. He wasn't just a part of the dream; he was tethered, yet his presence felt distant, fragmented, as if he were trapped between worlds, unable to fully connect to this dream.

"Jasper," she called softly, her voice barely a whisper, carried across the shifting strands of the dreamscape. But he didn't respond. His attention was fixed on something else. A young man crouched near a park bench, his hands frantic as he searched the ground. His movements were erratic, desperate.

Leah's gaze shifted back to the pregnant woman. She instinctively shielded her belly, her steps faltering as the tension in the air thickened. The husband moved toward the commotion, his posture protective, but Leah could sense the rising dread within the dream. Everything was pulling apart.

"Stay here," the husband ordered firmly.

"No, don't—" the woman began, but it was too late.

The young man stood abruptly, his trembling hands reaching for something on the ground. Leah saw it—a pair of glasses, just out of reach. He squinted against the bright park lights, his movements sluggish and uncertain.

"Get your hands up!" Jasper barked, his voice slicing through the tension, sharp and commanding.

"He's blind without those!" the husband shouted, stepping closer, holding the glasses out. "He has photophobia—he's not a threat!"

The woman's voice cracked as she called out, her fear palpable. "Please, don't hurt him!"

But the chaos didn't stop there. The dog barked frantically, the shadows deepened, and the threads of the dreamscape began to unravel. Leah felt Malik's influence growing stronger, his shadow creeping toward Jasper. His presence was fully formed now, and it was reaching into the dream, twisting it.

Leah moved quickly, weaving a protective barrier around the dream, focusing her energy on keeping it from collapsing. She reached for Jasper's thread, her touch gentle but firm. "You're not yourself," she whispered, her voice cutting through the fog of his fear. "This isn't who you are."

Jasper hesitated, his grip on his weapon loosening, the weight of his actions becoming clearer. But the shadows didn't relent. Malik's presence manifested fully now, his laughter cold and mocking, echoing through the dreamscape.

"Do you really think you can save him?" Malik's voice echoed, mocking Leah's resolve. "He's mine now, Leah. Just like the others."

Leah's resolve hardened, her focus sharpening. "You don't get to decide that."

With a surge of golden light, Leah strengthened the threads around Jasper and the dreamers, pushing back against Malik's dark influence. The young man's frantic movements slowed as he found his glasses, his breathing calming as the world came back into focus. The husband stepped in front of the young man, his presence diffusing the tension.

But Malik wasn't finished. The park dissolved into a twisted carnival, its colors garish and oppressive, everything distorted and wrong. The woman's cries echoed as she found herself separated from her husband, her hands clutching her belly protectively. Jasper and the young man were nowhere to be seen.

"Let her go, Malik," Leah demanded, stepping into the heart of the dream.

Her voice was steady, defiant.

Malik appeared, his form shifting and unstable, like a shadow torn between realities. "Why should I? She's already lost so much. What's one more nightmare?"

Leah's gaze didn't waver. "Because I won't let you win."

She reached for the woman's thread, weaving compassion and strength into its fibers. The carnival began to dissolve, replaced by the warm, familiar glow of the park. The woman's husband reappeared, his arms steadying her as she sobbed against his chest.

Leah turned her attention to Jasper, who stood frozen at the park's edge. His expression was one of anguish, his thread darkened by Malik's interference. Leah stepped closer, her voice soft but firm.

"Jasper, it's me," she said, her voice cutting through the fog of the dream. "You're safe now. Come back to me."

His gaze met hers, recognition flickering in his eyes. Slowly, the darkness around him began to lift, the fog of fear receding.

"You're not alone," Leah continued. "You never were."

With a final surge of light, Leah severed Malik's influence, pulling Jasper fully out of the dream. He collapsed into her arms, his breathing ragged but steady, the weight of the nightmare lifting from his chest.

The dreamscape settled, the golden threads mending as Leah guided the dreamers back to themselves. The woman woke in her bed, her husband's hand resting on her shoulder, grounding her. Jasper stirred beside Leah; his eyes heavy with exhaustion but free from the shadows that had plagued him.

Leah watched as the threads of the dreamscape faded, her heart heavy but resolute. Malik's influence was growing, his reach extending further than she had feared. For now, Jasper was alive, safe, but not whole. The road ahead would be far more dangerous.

The Loom: Leah's Legacy

As the last remnants of the dream dissolved, Leah stood in the quiet stillness of the dreamscape. Compassion, she realized, was more than an emotion—it was a force, a thread that could hold even the most fractured souls together. And no matter how dark the shadows grew, it would be this compassion that guided her through.

Leah's Lumarion

The sanctuary was unnervingly quiet when Leah emerged from the dreamscape, carrying the faint presence of Jasper in her thoughts. The space that had always been a refuge, a place where dreams were woven and the very fabric of reality was held together, now felt like something more fragile. Its golden threads shimmered faintly, their usual brilliance dimmed, as though the sanctuary itself were holding its breath, awaiting something—something that Leah didn't yet understand.

The Loom of Lumarion at the heart of the sanctuary hummed softly, its resonating vibration reverberating through the air. But even as the threads wove patterns that Leah didn't recognize, the sound felt hollow, as if the loom were struggling to maintain its rhythm in a world that was beginning to fall out of sync. She placed her hand on the loom, feeling its vibrations resonate through her, but the connection felt strained. The threads, which once were a clear reflection of the dreamscape, were now uncertain, trembling under the weight of an unseen force.

The loom was the heart of the dreamscape—its lifeblood. It connected every dreamer, every Dreamweaver, binding them to the fabric of the dreamscape, a delicate network that relied on the strength of those who wove it. But something was off. Leah had brought Jasper back, or at least, she thought she had. The remnants of him were there, but the man she had held in her arms felt incomplete. The presence she had gathered was only a shadow, fractured by the interference of Malik.

Leah paced the room, her fingers tracing the edges of the threads, seeking answers that were not easily found. Her mind raced, thoughts tangled in the chaos she had just left behind in the dreamscape.

"How can someone be here and not here?" she whispered to herself, the words carrying a weight that only she could understand. The shadows in the dreamscape had clung to him, their influence still lingering even after she had severed them. Malik's interference was more insidious than she had imagined. His power wasn't just physical; it was emotional, psychological, a poison that corrupted even the most resilient parts of the dreamscape.

As she moved to the loom, it flickered again, and a knot formed in her chest. A single thread stood out among the countless others, darker than the rest. It pulsed faintly, as if calling out to her. She recognized it immediately—it was Jasper's thread. The fear that had settled in her stomach turned to cold dread as she reached for it. Her fingers brushed its surface, and a sudden chill ran through her, as if the thread itself were alive, pulling her deeper into the vision it offered.

In an instant, images flooded her mind—fragmented, shattered like shards of a broken mirror. She saw Jasper standing at the edge of the park, his expression torn between anguish and recognition, but something wasn't right. The park was no longer the tranquil space she remembered—it was a battlefield, a place where memories and nightmares collided. Then the shadows enveloped him, their tendrils twisting around him as if they were made of pure fear, dragging him into a void. His essence seemed to split in two: one part of him reached for her, desperately, but the other was pulled deeper into Malik's grasp.

Leah gasped, pulling her hand back from the thread. She staggered backward, her heart racing, the weight of the vision pressing against her chest. "He's tethered," she murmured, barely able to keep her voice steady. "Part of him is still trapped."

The realization hit her like a wave. Jasper wasn't whole because Malik had fractured him. The part of Jasper that she had pulled back was only a fragment, a shadow of the man she had known, trapped in a world between dreams and nightmares. She couldn't bring him back fully until the part of him still trapped in Malik's grasp was freed.

She turned to the loom, her resolve hardening. If part of Jasper remained trapped in the dreamscape, she would find him. She couldn't allow Malik to keep even a piece of her closest friend. The thought of losing him, of him being scattered into pieces by Malik's malice, fueled her determination. *I'll bring him back. All of him.*

Leah knelt before the loom, her hands trembling as she traced the intricate patterns of the threads. She had never encountered a situation like this before—a Dreamweaver severed into pieces; his essence divided between the realms. The loom offered no immediate answers, only the faint hum of uncertainty as the threads wove patterns that mocked her. She closed her eyes, steadying her breath, trying to focus.

Her thoughts drifted to Jasper—the steady presence he had always been, the one who believed in her even when she doubted herself. He had been her anchor, her confidant, the one constant she could rely on in the chaos of the dreamscape. The thought of him fractured, broken, tethered to the darkness that Malik had created, was unbearable. He had given her everything—his trust, his loyalty—and now he was a shadow of himself, hanging between two worlds.

"Guide me," she whispered to the loom, her voice breaking under the weight of her fear. "Show me how to bring him back."

The loom shimmered, its threads vibrating in response to her plea. The patterns began to shift, slowly at first, like ripples in a still pond. And then, Leah saw it—a faint outline of a map forming in the threads. It was barely perceptible, a path through the dreamscape leading to a familiar place. Diollo.

Leah's stomach twisted. Diollo. She knew that name. Diollo was the birthplace of the Dreamweavers, the crossroads where the threads of dreams and fate collided. It was also where Malik's power had first been forged, where the darkness that had corrupted the dreamscape began.

The path to Diollo was a path to Malik's heart, to the very source of the chaos that was threatening to unravel everything. But it was also the only way to free Jasper. The pieces of him that remained trapped could only be reclaimed in Diollo, where his essence had been scattered.

Leah sank to the floor, her mind racing. If she followed the path to Diollo, it would lead her directly into Malik's territory. She wasn't ready—not yet. She needed more time to understand what had happened to Jasper, and she needed to prepare for the journey ahead.

Her eyes fell on the loom again, its threads shimmering faintly in the dim light. "Jasper," she murmured, her voice filled with both determination and fear. "Hold on. I'll find you."

The sanctuary, once a place of clarity and strength, now felt fragile, as though the shadows had begun to seep into its very walls. Leah moved through the room, her fingers brushing against the golden threads that lined the walls. Each thread hummed with a faint vibration, a reminder of the countless dreamers she had guided, the lives she had touched. But the hum was quieter now, subdued. The shadows were reaching further than she had anticipated, their influence creeping into every corner of the dreamscape, even into the sanctuary itself.

Leah stopped before a small alcove, where a faint light glowed. It was a memorial of sorts, a collection of threads that represented the Dreamweavers who had come before her. She knelt before it, her heart heavy. "You all faced your own battles," she said softly, her voice barely a whisper. "How did you find the strength to keep going?"

Her fingers traced the threads, each one representing a Dreamweaver's journey, their struggles, their victories, and their losses. For a moment, Leah felt a sense of peace, a calming presence from the Dreamweavers of the past. They had faced unimaginable challenges, yet they had endured. Leah closed her eyes and let the faint hum of their presence soothe her frayed nerves. The golden glow around her seemed to pulse with unspoken encouragement, as if whispering: *Strength is in connection. The threads hold even when frayed.*

But as she opened her eyes, a sharp flicker from the loom caught her attention. Jasper's thread pulsed once more, its dark edges vibrating violently before settling. Leah's breath hitched. It wasn't just a signal—it was a call. He was trying to reach her.

"Jasper," Leah whispered, gripping the thread tighter. She closed her eyes and let her essence weave into the faint remnants of his consciousness. She felt a familiar pull, one that brought her back to the park where she had first found him. But this time, the scene was different. The park was distorted, its edges blurred as if it existed halfway between reality and a nightmare. Jasper stood at its center, his form faint and translucent. The shadows around him were quieter now, but still present, lingering like predators waiting to pounce.

"Leah," he said, his voice barely audible. "You found me again."

She stepped closer, her heart breaking at the sight of him. His once steady presence was now fractured, his essence flickering like a fading flame. "Jasper," she said, her voice firm but tender. "I'm not leaving you."

"You don't understand," he said, shaking his head. "I'm not all here. Malik... he's holding the rest of me. He's using me—using what's left of me to—" His voice trailed off, and his form flickered.

Leah's chest tightened. She reached for him, her hand brushing against his faint outline. For a moment, she felt his warmth, his familiar steadiness, but then it slipped away. "Where is he holding you, Jasper? Tell me."

Jasper looked at her, his eyes filled with both sorrow and urgency. "Diollo," he said. "It's where it all began. And it's where it'll end." His form flickered, and just before vanishing, a whisper escaped his lips—fractured, like a memory unraveling.

"...loomstaff..."

The shadows surged around him, pulling him back. Leah cried out, her hand reaching for his, but he disappeared before she could grasp him fully.

Leah stumbled back into the sanctuary, her breathing ragged. Her connection to Jasper had been fleeting, but it had been enough. She now knew where she needed to go. Diollo was not where she would find what she needed—not yet. But something Jasper had said lingered in her chest like a thread pulling taut. The way he had looked at her—his eyes pleading, yet distant—held more than just pain. There had been intent. Urgency. And though his words had faltered, the meaning clung to her like a whisper in the wind.

"Find the Loomstaff..." he had murmured, barely audible as his form flickered. The words hadn't been shouted or proclaimed—they were fragile, nearly lost beneath the weight of his unraveling. But they were clear. His gaze had locked onto hers, then drifted toward a horizon unseen, a place beyond the veil of memory.

She hadn't understood it fully—not in that moment. But now, standing in the quiet stillness of her sanctuary, she felt the shift. The park had changed.

The thread between her and Jasper pulsed faintly, pointing not only toward Diollo but toward something older, deeper—a key that led her there.

A Loomstaff.

Jasper hadn't just named it; he had guided her toward it. Not with certainty, but with a desperate knowing, as though the loomstaff itself was tied to his fading presence. As though it might be the only thing capable of anchoring what remained of him. Of pulling him back.

And though his hand had barely lifted—shaking, translucent—she remembered the way it moved, the way his voice cracked around the words. It wasn't just direction. It was a plea.

Her breath hitched.

Somewhere out there, in a land steeped in the past, where the echoes of ancient Dreamweavers still resonated... the loomstaff waited.

Leah's heart tightened. A loomstaff. She had heard whispers and read legends of the staffs. Faint memories stirred—echoes of a time when she'd seen such a staff in action, its power undeniable, its origin ancient. Though most believed only two existed, Leah had long suspected the truth ran deeper... and she'd kept that truth to herself. It wasn't in Diollo where she could reclaim Jasper, but a loomstaff... Where it was, she wasn't certain, but it was a sign. The staff could be the key to reuniting the fragmented pieces of her friend.

Her thoughts raced as she turned to the loom before her. The threads shimmered faintly, now steady but dim, and she knew the path would be treacherous. This was no simple journey; it was a test. A loomstaff could restore balance, or it could also lead her deeper into the web of destiny that connected the dreamscape to the waking world—and to Malik's growing power.

"Jasper," Leah whispered, her voice steadying with resolve. "Hold on. I will find it. I will find you."

The Loom: Leah's Legacy

Her gaze lingered on the loom, its threads flickering faintly with the weight of countless dreams. The sanctuary felt both fragile and strong, like a heartbeat in the stillness. Leah knew what she had to do. She had to follow this new path—a path that began with the loomstaff.

But first, she needed to understand more. The threads before her seemed to pulse with an ancient energy, pulling her forward. She closed her eyes, feeling the pull of the loom, the threads guiding her toward a place known only in the whispers of the past—the Land of Peace.

Leah exhaled slowly, preparing herself. The shadows might be growing stronger, but so was her conviction. A loomstaff was out there, and it would lead her to Jasper. She could no longer wait. Her journey was far from over.

CHAPTER 7

JOURNEY TO THE LAND OF PEACE

The sun was relentless, casting waves of shimmering heat over the barren expanse of sand. The sky above was an endless stretch of blue, the horizon mirage-like, distorting the world around it. A solitary figure trudged forward, his footsteps heavy and labored. Henry, an elderly man with a deeply lined face and weary eyes, gripped a tattered map in one hand, his weathered walking stick in the other. Each step felt like penance, the weight of his mistakes dragging behind him like a shadow he could never outrun.

The map he followed wasn't detailed. It was little more than a rough sketch with a single word etched at its center: *Peace*. Behind him, faint echoes of laughter and anger danced on the wind, fleeting whispers of memories he couldn't escape. They weren't real, but they were familiar, fragments of a past that clung to him like the heat from the desert sun. His soul, much like his body, was marked by time and regret.

Leah watched from the edges of the dreamscape, her gaze following the faint golden thread that connected Henry to the land he sought. It was frayed, tangled with guilt and regret, yet it pulsed faintly—barely noticeable, but still there—a sign that hope, however small, still lingered.

"This journey is more than his," Leah murmured to herself, stepping closer. She could feel Malik's presence lurking in the distance, subtle but insidious. The shadows on the horizon flickered, threatening to overtake Henry's path.

As Henry stumbled forward, the ground beneath him shifted, and the sand gave way to jagged rocks. He winced, his hand tightening around his walking stick, the grip a desperate attempt to steady himself. The stick caught Leah's eye—curious, out of place in this landscape. Unlike the rest of the dreamscape, the staff shimmered faintly, threads of light weaving around it. It was as if the walking stick itself held a fragment of the dreamscape's essence—an artifact of some unknown significance.

"Interesting," Leah whispered. She hadn't placed that object in Henry's dream. Could it be a manifestation of his desire for support? Or was it something more? Something that could help him?

"Need a hand?" a voice called out, drawing Leah's attention.

Henry turned, startled, as a man, much younger and sturdier, approached him. His clothes were clean, his movements confident, a stark contrast to the weariness Henry carried.

"You don't belong here," Henry said, his voice wary, cautious.

The stranger grinned. "Neither do you." He extended his hand. "Call me Jasper."

Leah's heart jolted. *Jasper*. She hadn't expected him to appear here, but the thread connecting him to Henry glimmered faintly, suggesting a shared purpose.

Together, Henry and Jasper continued their journey, their silence filled with the oppressive heat and the soft crunch of sand beneath their boots. The journey through the desert was long, each step carrying more weight than the last, but with Jasper's presence, there was a quiet sense of camaraderie that Henry hadn't anticipated.

"What are you looking for?" Jasper asked after a long pause, his voice calm but probing.

"Peace," Henry replied simply, the word heavy on his tongue.

Jasper chuckled, the sound dry and echoing in the stillness. "Aren't we all?"

Henry's expression darkened. "I've done things... terrible things. Hurt people I loved. If I don't find it—if I don't fix it—then what's the point of any of this?"

Jasper slowed his pace, his gaze thoughtful. "Maybe peace isn't something you find. Maybe it's something you make."

Leah watched their interaction closely. The walking stick in Henry's hand continued to glow subtly, the threads of light becoming more pronounced. It seemed to respond to his emotions—brightening when he expressed hope, dimming when he faltered. The walking stick, for all its unassuming appearance, was more than just a physical object. It was a manifestation of Henry's journey, and perhaps a key to his healing.

As they trekked onward, the desert shifted abruptly, giving way to a small village nestled in a valley. The houses were simple, their windows glowing with a soft, golden light, as though the village itself were waiting for something—or someone—to arrive.

Henry hesitated at the edge of the village, his body tense. He stood still for a long moment, as if afraid to step forward, afraid of what he might find.

"This place..." he whispered, his voice trailing off as he took in the sight before him.

Leah felt the surge of emotions emanating from him—fear, hope, and an overwhelming sense of guilt. She wove herself more deeply into the dreamscape, her presence steadying the fragile threads of Henry's journey.

The first house they approached was eerily familiar to Henry. His hand trembled as he placed it on the doorframe, his breath catching in his throat. He stepped inside, his heart heavy with unspoken words. At the table sat a young woman, her face turned away, her posture stiff with unspoken tension.

"Sarah?" he whispered, his voice trembling.

The woman turned slowly, her eyes meeting his. They were filled with hurt, but also a glimmer of warmth, an emotion Henry couldn't quite place. "You left us," she said, her voice soft but steady, carrying years of pain with it.

Henry sank into a chair, his hands shaking. He didn't know how to speak the words he needed to. "I didn't know how to stay," he admitted, his voice breaking. "I thought... I thought you'd be better off without me."

Sarah's gaze softened, though there was still a distance between them. "You never gave us the chance to decide that for ourselves."

As Henry and Sarah spoke, the golden light in the house began to dim. Leah felt it first—a cold ripple spreading through the dreamscape, a subtle chill that crept over the scene, threatening to extinguish the fragile peace between them.

"Malik," Leah whispered, her hands weaving frantically to stabilize the threads.

The shadows gathered outside the house, their presence growing more oppressive. Malik's voice echoed faintly, mocking in tone. "Peace isn't earned, Leah. It's an illusion."

Leah gritted her teeth, pouring her energy into the dreamscape, strengthening the fragile connections. She reached for Jasper's thread, connecting it to Henry's to fortify their bond.

"Jasper," she called through the threads. "He needs your strength."

Jasper stepped forward, his presence steadying Henry as the shadows pressed closer. "You don't have to do this alone," he said firmly.

Henry looked at him, confusion and doubt clouding his gaze. "Why would you help me? You don't even know me."

"Because I've been where you are," Jasper replied. "And I know what it feels like to think you don't deserve another chance."

The shadows lunged, but Leah's golden threads flared brightly, holding them at bay. The walking stick in Henry's hand began to glow intensely, the intricate carvings along its surface coming to life with patterns of light, patterns that seemed to align with the rhythms of the dreamscape itself.

Leah's eyes widened. The walking stick wasn't just a manifestation of Henry's emotions. It was more—it was a conduit, a physical representation of the dreamscape's power. She felt a resonance with it, as if it were calling out to her.

"Henry, hold the staff up!" Leah urged, her voice strong, her command unwavering.

Startled, Henry obeyed. As he raised the staff, beams of golden light shot out from it, slicing through the encroaching shadows. The oppressive weight began to lift, the darkness retreating in the face of the staff's power.

Leah reached out, her hands moving in harmony with Henry's actions. She could feel the loomstaff's energy—it was ancient, powerful, and deeply connected to the very essence of the dreamscape.

"Leah," Jasper called out, his voice urgent. "The staff—it's reacting to you."

She nodded, realizing what she had to do. Stepping forward, she extended her hand toward the staff. As her fingers brushed against it, a surge of energy coursed through her, flooding her with power and purpose. The staff transformed, lengthening and reshaping until it fit comfortably in her grasp. The intricate designs along its surface glowed brighter, depicting symbols and patterns she recognized from the ancient texts of the Dreamweavers.

"This is... Lux Veritas, The Loomstaff of Radiance," Leah whispered, awe filling her voice. "The Lost Loomstaff."

Malik's presence intensified, his voice seething with anger. "You think an old relic can stop me?"

Leah met Jasper's gaze, determination steeling her resolve. "With this, we have a chance."

Holding the loomstaff firmly, Leah began to weave, the threads of the dreamscape responding to her movements with newfound vigor. Golden light spiraled from the staff, intertwining with the threads, strengthening them and pushing back against the encroaching shadows.

"Henry, confront your fears," Leah urged. "Only then can you find peace."

Henry looked between Leah and Jasper, then back to Sarah. His eyes welled with tears. "I'm sorry," he said, his voice breaking. "For everything."

Sarah stepped forward, placing a gentle hand on his cheek. "I forgive you, Dad."

As their embrace solidified, the village around them brightened. The shadows dissipated completely, unable to withstand the combined strength of forgiveness and the loomstaff's power.

Malik's presence faded, his final words a bitter whisper. "This is only the beginning, Leah."

The dreamscape began to stabilize. Henry's thread, once frayed and tangled, now shone brightly, its connection to the dreamscape secure.

Leah turned to Jasper, a mix of relief and concern in her eyes. "Thank you," she said softly.

He smiled faintly. "Always here to help."

But as the village faded, signaling the end of the dream, Jasper's form began to waver. Leah reached out, worry knotting in her stomach. "Wait!"

Jasper shook his head. "I'm still tethered, Leah. Malik's hold on me isn't broken yet."

She tightened her grip on the loomstaff. "Then I'll find a way to free you. This staff—it's the key."

He nodded. "Be careful. Malik won't let you use it without a fight."

As Jasper disappeared, Leah found herself back in the sanctuary, the loomstaff still in her hand. Its weight was comforting, its glow illuminating the dimmed space.

Leah stood in awe, examining the loomstaff. The intricate carvings depicted the history of the Dreamweavers—their triumphs, their struggles, their eternal duty to protect the dreamscape. Symbols of connection, strength, and resilience wound around the staff, each one pulsing with latent energy.

She could feel the staff's connection to The Loom of Lumarion in the sanctuary. The threads responded to its presence, humming with renewed vigor. The shadows that had been creeping into her haven retreated, unable to withstand the combined force of the loomstaff and the loom.

"This changes everything," Leah whispered.

The realization settled in her mind: the loomstaff was more than a weapon—it was a tool of restoration, capable of mending the frayed threads and pushing back Malik's darkness. With it, she had a chance to not only protect the dreamscape but also to save Jasper.

But Malik would not stand idly by. His interference in Henry's dream had been more aggressive than before, and now that Leah possessed the loomstaff, he would surely intensify his efforts.

She gripped the staff tighter. "I have to prepare," she thought. "I can't do this alone."

Leah knew she needed allies—others who could wield the power of the Weavers. Mina, Terry, Johan—their paths had yet to cross, but she could sense their threads weaving closer to hers. the loomstaff's emergence was a sign that the time had come to gather those who could stand against Malik.

Leah returned to the loom in the center of the sanctuary, the loomstaff at her side. As she began to weave, she focused on locating the threads of those who could help her. the loom responded, revealing glimmers of potential—Weavers whose strengths complemented her own.

Images flashed before her eyes:

- Mina, a fierce rebel with a sharp mind and a sharper wit, her thread burning brightly against the darkness.
- Terry, a young innovator, his thread humming with untapped potential and a desire to bridge worlds.
- Johan, a stoic warrior, his thread marked by loss but strengthened by unwavering determination.

Leah smiled softly. "We'll face this together."

But first, she needed to understand the full extent of the loomstaff's abilities. She spent hours—maybe days—immersed in study, learning how to channel its energy, how to weave more complex patterns, and how to fortify the sanctuary against Malik's intrusion.

The sanctuary began to transform. With the loomstaff's power, Leah enhanced the protective barriers, wove new threads of connection, and infused the space with light that pushed back the lingering shadows.

As she prepared to seek out her future allies, Leah couldn't shake the lingering concern for Jasper. His words echoed in her mind: "Malik's hold on me isn't broken yet."

She knew that rescuing Jasper would be no easy task. Malik was growing stronger, his influence spreading further into the dreamscape. But with the loomstaff, Leah had hope.

She stood at the threshold of the sanctuary, the loomstaff glowing softly in her hand. The path ahead was uncertain, fraught with danger and unknown challenges. But she was no longer alone in spirit. The threads of Mina, Terry, and Johan beckoned, waiting to be woven into the tapestry of their shared destiny.

Leah took a deep breath, her gaze steady. "I'm coming, Jasper. And together, we'll set things right."

As she stepped forward, the golden threads of the dreamscape unfurled before her, guiding her toward the next chapter of her journey—a journey that would test the limits of her strength, the depth of her compassion, and the power of the connections she would forge.

The sun set over the desert dreamscape, casting hues of orange and purple across the sands. In the waking world, Henry stirred, a peaceful expression softening his features. The heavy burden he'd carried for so long had lifted, replaced by the lightness of forgiveness.

In the sanctuary, Leah allowed herself a moment of quiet satisfaction. One soul healed, one thread mended. But the larger tapestry was still in peril.

She looked down at the loomstaff, its glow reflecting in her eyes. "This is just the beginning," she murmured.

The dreamscape was vast, and Malik's shadows were deep. But with the loomstaff in hand and new allies on the horizon, Leah felt ready to face whatever came next.

The journey toward peace—for herself, for Jasper, and for the countless souls connected by the threads of dreams.

CHAPTER 8

---❦---

THE STRANDED VOYAGE

The dreamscape unfolded before Leah in a vast ocean, the endless blue sky and water blending seamlessly into an infinite horizon. A small boat bobbed atop the waves, its wooden frame worn and splintered, creaking under the weight of its passengers. The vessel carried a mix of strangers—each with their own story, their own scars. They were castaways, bound together by circumstance but divided by distrust, struggling to find their place in a world far beyond their control.

Leah observed from the edges of the dreamscape, her form hidden by the shimmering mists that clung to the water. This dream, unlike the others she had woven, was not of her making. It had formed from the collective fears and unrest of its occupants—a chaotic reflection of their inner turmoil. The boat, fragile and barely seaworthy, became a metaphor for their shared fate—every creak and crack in its hull a testament to their disunity.

Leah's gaze shifted to the passengers. Seven figures occupied the boat, each one representing a fragment of human frailty: anger, fear, hopelessness, despair, pride, lack of humility, and longing. Their voices clashed, sharp and frenzied, as they argued over their course, their disagreements threatening to tear them apart.

"Turn us east! That's where the current's weaker!" barked a wiry man, clutching a makeshift oar. His sunken cheeks and hollow eyes betrayed a life hardened by survival.

"No!" shouted a woman with piercing green eyes. "The stars are clearest to the west. We follow them."

A younger man, barely out of his teens, huddled in the corner, clutching a tattered journal. "Does it even matter?" he muttered, his voice filled with hopelessness. "We're all going to drown anyway."

The boat lurched as a massive wave crashed against it, sending water sloshing onto the deck. The passengers scrambled to maintain their balance, their bickering momentarily silenced by the ocean's fury.

Leah felt their despair—raw, palpable—as the threads of their lives began to fray with every passing moment. She reached out with her mind, brushing against the golden strands that connected them. They shimmered faintly, fragile yet unbroken. *Not yet,* she thought, her heart aching. *But they're close.*

The wind picked up, carrying a mournful wail from the depths of the ocean. The water darkened, taking on an inky hue that swallowed the light, sending a chill down Leah's spine. The passengers huddled together, their earlier bravado replaced by fear. The chaos was intensifying.

Leah stepped closer, weaving herself more deeply into the dream. She nudged their thoughts toward cooperation, though the shadows of fear grew stronger by the second. A faint golden glow flickered around the boat as the threads tightened, struggling to hold the passengers together. She needed them to work together, or the storm would overwhelm them.

"We have to work together," said a woman with a streak of gray in her dark hair. Her voice carried the weight of experience, and the others turned to her.

"If we don't, we're as good as dead."

"And who made you captain?" snapped the wiry man, brandishing his oar like a weapon. "I didn't sign up to take orders from anyone."

"You didn't sign up for this at all," the woman shot back, her tone firm. "None of us did. But here we are."

The younger man looked up from his journal, his eyes wide with terror. "What's the point? We're not going anywhere. The ocean goes on forever."

The woman placed a hand on his shoulder. "As long as we're alive, there's a point. Now grab a bucket and start bailing."

The group hesitated, their distrust still simmering beneath the surface, but the sight of another wave cresting in the distance spurred them into action. They began to move in unison, their efforts clumsy but earnest.

Leah felt a flicker of hope. The threads brightened slightly as their cooperation, though tentative, began to strengthen. But the storm was far from over.

As hours passed, fatigue set in. The passengers' movements slowed, and their tempers flared once more. The wiry man threw down his oar in frustration.

"This is pointless!" he shouted. "We're just delaying the inevitable."

The younger man snapped his journal shut. "And what do you suggest? That we just sit here and wait to die?"

"Better than pretending this boat is going to save us!" the man retorted.

The gray-haired woman stepped between them, her voice firm, a mother's steadiness cutting through the chaos. "Enough! We have a chance if we stick together."

"Do we?" the wiry man sneered. "Or are we just fooling ourselves?"

The golden threads shimmered faintly, their light dimming as the storm raged on. Leah's heart clenched. She could feel the dream slipping toward chaos, the passengers' despair threatening to unravel the fragile connection that held them together.

She reached out again, weaving their emotions with care. A memory surfaced in the younger man's mind—a quiet recollection of his mother's voice, telling him stories of resilience, urging him to keep going even in the face of hardship. He gripped his journal tightly, his expression hardening with determination.

"We have to keep going," he said, his voice shaky. "My mother used to say that as long as we keep moving, we have a chance."

The gray-haired woman nodded, her eyes softening as she looked at him. "Your mother was a wise woman."

The threads brightened once more, but Leah knew it wouldn't last. The storm was intensifying, and the shadows beneath the waves were stirring.

A towering wave loomed on the horizon, its crest glowing with an eerie, otherworldly light. The passengers froze, their eyes wide with terror.

"What is that?" whispered the young man.

The wave crashed down, engulfing the boat. The passengers clung desperately to whatever they could, their screams swallowed by the roar of the ocean. When the water finally receded, the boat was still afloat—but barely.

In the aftermath, a figure emerged from the shadows—a man with eyes like cold steel and a presence that sent an icy chill through the air. Malik.

"Poor little castaways," he said, his voice smooth, mocking. "So desperate to survive, yet so quick to turn on each other."

Leah's breath caught in her chest. Malik had been hidden beneath the storm's fury, his presence barely perceptible until now. He moved closer to the boat, his gaze sweeping over the passengers with disdain.

"You think you can escape your fate?" he said. "Fate doesn't care about your struggles. It doesn't care about your hope."

The passengers cowered, their fear palpable. The golden threads began to fray, their light fading. Leah stepped forward, her presence becoming visible.

"Enough, Malik," she said, her voice steady but filled with determination. "This isn't your fight."

Malik turned to her, his lips curling into a smirk. "Ah, Leah. Always playing the hero. But you can't save them. Not this time."

Leah raised her hand, her essence glowing as she wove the threads tighter. "You're wrong. They still have a chance."

Malik's eyes narrowed. "Then let's see if they're strong enough to take it."

He raised his hand, and the storm surged once more. The boat tilted dangerously, water pouring over the sides. The passengers scrambled to hold on, their unity tested to its limits.

The gray-haired woman grabbed the oar, her grip steady despite the chaos. "We can do this!" she shouted. "Together!"

The younger man picked up a bucket, his movements fueled by newfound determination. "She's right. We're not done yet."

The others followed suit, their fear giving way to resolve. The golden threads brightened, their light pushing back against the storm.

Leah poured her energy into the weave, her focus unwavering. She could feel the passengers' strength growing, their connection solidifying.

Malik watched with a scowl, his presence flickering as the dreamscape began to shift. "You're delaying the inevitable, Leah," he said. "But I'll let you have your little victory. For now."

With a final surge of energy, Leah stabilized the dreamscape. The storm began to subside, the waters calming. The passengers collapsed onto the deck, their breaths ragged but relieved.

Leah turned to Malik, her gaze firm. "This isn't over."

Malik's smirk returned. "No, it's not."

He vanished into the shadows, leaving Leah and the passengers alone in the fading light.

The passengers slowly regained their breath, their bodies sagging against the weathered boards of the boat. The storm had passed, but its memory lingered in the tense silence. Above them, the dreamscape began to shift—clouds parting to reveal a pale golden light that touched the water's surface like a gentle hand.

Leah stood quietly at the edge of the scene, her presence no longer hidden. She felt the exhaustion in her limbs, the strain of weaving the fragile threads of this shared dreamscape back into place. The castaways—figures of vulnerability and resilience—faded one by one, their faces softening into peace as they were released from the grip of the nightmare.

But Leah's gaze wasn't on them; it was on three figures who had remained, watching her with guarded yet curious expressions.

Mina, Terry, and Johan emerged from the shifting mists of the dreamscape, their forms steady against the vanishing backdrop. Leah felt the weight of their stares, their eyes filled with questions.

"You're the one who stabilized it," Mina said, her voice calm yet laced with a subtle edge. Her sharp features softened only slightly as she studied Leah. "That storm wasn't natural. Someone was disrupting the weave."

Leah nodded, her expression weary but resolute. "You're right. And the someone you're referring to... his name is Malik."

"Malik," Johan repeated, his broad shoulders tense. His dark eyes flickered with recognition, though it was clear he couldn't place why. "That name—it feels... familiar."

Terry, the youngest of the trio, adjusted his gauntlets absentmindedly, the metal catching the fading light of the dreamscape. "I've seen his shadow in my dreams," he muttered. "Or something like it. Every time I try to weave, it's like... something's watching. Blocking me."

Mina crossed her arms, her gaze narrowing. "We've all been having trouble weaving. Nightmares bleeding into other threads. Dreams unraveling faster than they should. Is he the reason?"

"Yes," Leah admitted, her voice heavy with the weight of the truth. "Malik is a Nightweaver. He's been manipulating dreams, severing threads, and corrupting the balance. This dreamscape—this storm—was his doing. He wanted to break the connections you were weaving."

Their unspoken thoughts shared in a silent agreement. Despite their different temperaments, they were unified by a shared understanding: the drealis was in danger.

Leah stepped closer, her presence calm yet commanding. "You're all Dreamweavers—not of this realm," she said, then paused. "At least...that's what they used to call us. But you're more than that—I can feel it. The way you anchor dreams, the way you fight to keep the threads intact. This isn't your first encounter with Malik's influence, is it?"

"No," Johan admitted, his voice steady. "But this is the first time we've seen him... directly."

Mina's gaze softened slightly as she regarded Leah. "And you—you're different. I've woven a lot of dreams, but I've never felt anyone do what you just did. That wasn't ordinary weaving. You held that dream together like it was... alive."

Leah hesitated, then nodded. "I've been weaving for a long time. But even with experience, Malik's interference is... unsettling. He's not just disrupting dreams—he's trying to control them. To control us."

Terry voice tinged with frustration. "Why? What does he want?"

Leah's didn't have all the answers yet, but she knew one thing: Malik's intentions were deeply personal. "Malik wants power," she said carefully. "He wants to reshape the dreamscape to his will, to sever the threads that bind us and create something entirely his own. But his actions... they're fueled by something deeper. Something personal."

Johan with his arms crossed, "And what's your connection to him? You seem to know more than you're letting on."

Leah's heart ached at the question, but she held his gaze. "I've known Malik for a long time. Long before he became the threat he is now. He wasn't always like this."

Mina raised an eyebrow, her expression skeptical but not unkind. "And now he's tearing apart everything we've worked to protect. What do we do about it?"

Leah extended her hand, her presence steady despite the turmoil churning inside her. "Come with me. I have a sanctuary—a place where we can regroup, where we can figure out how to stop him. You've already seen his power. You know how dangerous he is. But together, we have a chance."

They all shared a moment, a silent conversation passing between them. Mina nodded first, as she stepped forward. "Lead the way."

Terry hesitated, his youthful face marked with uncertainty, but he followed Mina's lead. "If it means stopping whatever this is... I'm in."

Johan lingered for a moment, his broad frame tense. He studied Leah with an intensity that made her feel exposed, but finally, he nodded. "Let's go."

Leah turned, her hand brushing against the golden threads of the dreamscape. The mists thickened around them, the remnants of the storm fading into a soft glow. A portal shimmered into existence, its edges rippling like water. Without hesitation, Leah stepped through, the others following close behind.

They emerged into a serene yet surreal landscape. The sanctuary was a haven of light and tranquility, its architecture fluid and organic, as though it had been woven from the fabric of dreams itself. Golden threads crisscrossed the air, their soft glow illuminating the space with a gentle warmth.

Mina let out a low whistle, her sharp features relieve as she took in the sight. "This... is incredible."

Terry's eyes widened, the tension in his shoulders easing slightly. "I've never seen anything like it."

Johan remained silent, his gaze scanning the sanctuary with a mix of awe and wariness.

"This is where I've been working, The Loom of Lumarion" Leah said, her voice calm but firm. "It's a place where the threads of dreams are woven and repaired. But even here, Malik's influence has been felt. The threads are fraying faster than I can mend them."

Mina stepped closer to one of the glowing threads, her fingers brushing against it. "So, this is the core of the drealis. It feels different."

Leah nodded. "This loom lies between the drealis and the dreamscape, and its connection to the Loom of Dream in Diollo is even stronger. Weaving here—if not done carefully—can be damaging. It can trap you between realms, or worse, tear at the Loom of Dreams itself, opening the way to the Nightmare Realm." It's where dreams begin and end. It's the connection to all the looms and it's where we'll find the strength to fight back."

Terry glanced at her, his youthful uncertainty giving way to determination. "Then what's the plan?"

Leah, the weight of purpose anchoring her stance, determination settling into something immovable. "We train. We prepare. We make sure no dream is severed. We follow the loom, feel the threads. Malik is strong, but he's not unstoppable. Together, we can stop him. But we must trust each other."

The three weavers looked at each other, their unspoken agreement solidifying their new roles. They had been strangers, brought together by circumstance and a shared enemy. But now, they were allies—bound by a mission that would test their limits.

Leah turned back to the threads, her hands brushing against them as she began to weave. The golden light brightened, the sanctuary pulsing with renewed energy. For the first time in what felt like an eternity, hope flickered in her heart.

"Let's begin, listen to the loom. It will guide you while you weave" she said softly. And with that, the sanctuary came alive, its golden threads weaving a tapestry of connection, resilience, and purpose.

CHAPTER 9

TRAP PASTOR

The church was packed, its wooden pews creaking under the weight of a congregation that hung on every word from the pulpit. Pastor Samuel Greaves stood tall, his deep voice resonating through the nave as he preached about redemption, the courage to walk the righteous path, and the grace found in the act of forgiveness. His words echoed through the room, filling the space with a sense of urgency that vibrated beneath the surface of the sermon. There was something different tonight. His voice, usually a comforting constant, felt heavier, as if burdened with some knowledge he couldn't quite bear.

Leah stood at the back of the church, her presence unseen yet profoundly felt. She was attuned to the golden threads weaving through the congregation, connecting each heart and mind in this sacred space. One thread pulsed brightly, thick and vibrant, emanating from Pastor Samuel. It was the thread of hope, of faith that reached beyond his own burdens to those who sought solace in his words. But there was another thread—dark, frayed, and twisted—that stretched toward the shadows behind the pulpit. Leah felt it pull, faint but insidious. It was Malik.

His presence lingered like a ghost, the thread of his influence curling through the air, feeding on Samuel's vulnerability.

Leah watched intently, focusing on the dynamic between the pastor and the congregation. It wasn't just a sermon—it was a battle of wills. Samuel's words were laced with the strain of secrecy, an internal war that had taken root in the depths of his soul. He spoke of redemption, but his heart was caught in the throes of something darker.

As the sermon came to a close, the congregation began to file out, the weight of the service settling into the air like the final note of a hymn. Samuel remained at the pulpit for a moment longer, staring out at the empty pews as if searching for something he couldn't name. Then, he turned and retreated to his office, the door closing behind him with a soft click.

Leah followed, her presence dissolving into the shadows of the dreamscape. Inside Samuel's office, the dim light from a single lamp cast long shadows across the room. The walls were lined with bookshelves, framed photographs of a life he had once cherished, and the quiet hum of an old desk fan. On his desk sat a ledger, its pages filled with figures that didn't add up. The numbers didn't match the donations; the debt was growing, and with it, the pressure that weighed on Samuel's conscience.

Samuel ran a hand through his graying hair, looking exhausted. His shoulders slumped under the weight of a life that had become too heavy to carry. This church, his life's work, was slipping through his fingers. He had built it from the ground up, pouring his heart into every stone, every beam, every sermon. But now, it was all unraveling.

The offers had come quietly at first—small loans from unsavory sources to keep the lights on, then larger sums to fund community projects. The debts had piled up, and with them, Samuel's compromises. He had justified it all, told himself it was for the greater good. But now the compromises had turned into something darker. The shadowy figures who had once helped him were demanding repayment, and the only collateral Samuel had left was the church itself.

From the dreamscape, Leah felt the weight of his internal struggle. She reached out to his thread, weaving compassion and strength into its fibers. She felt the battle he was fighting, the pull of his faith and the fear that had driven him to make the choices he had.

"You can still choose," Leah whispered softly, her voice reaching through the fabric of the dream. "Courage isn't the absence of fear—it's the strength to act in spite of it."

Samuel stiffened, his gaze falling on a photograph of his wife and daughter on the desk. Their smiles were frozen in time, a reminder of everything he had worked for. Everything he stood to lose.

A sharp knock echoed through the room, pulling Samuel's attention from the photograph. He opened the door to find two men standing on the threshold. Their dark suits were immaculate, their expressions cold and calculating.

"You're late," one of the men said, stepping inside without waiting for an invitation.

Samuel swallowed hard, his voice steady despite the fear gnawing at his insides. "I told you I need more time."

"Time's up," the other man replied, his tone clipped, like a blade being drawn. "Either you pay what you owe, or we take the church."

Leah's focus sharpened as she felt the tension in the room spike. The threads around Samuel trembled with the weight of his fear. Malik's influence pulsed faintly, feeding on the desperation that began to ooze from Samuel's very soul.

As the men continued to list their demands, Samuel's gaze fell on the open Bible on his desk. His fingers brushed the pages, the words blurring in his vision. Memories of his first sermon flooded his mind—the one where he had spoken of courage, of standing firm against adversity. The words had been easy then, but now, in the quiet of his office, the weight of those words threatened to drown him.

Leah's voice echoed in his mind once more: "You are stronger than this."

Samuel's spine straightened, a flash of clarity cutting through the fog of his fear. He turned to face the men, his jaw set in determination.

"No," he said firmly, his voice cutting through the tension in the room. "I won't give you what doesn't belong to you."

The men exchanged glances, their confident smirks faltering under Samuel's unwavering gaze. One of them scoffed, muttering under his breath, "We'll see about that."

They turned on their heels and left, slamming the door behind them. Samuel sank back into his chair, his hands trembling. Leah felt the exhaustion settle into his bones, but there was something else there now—a flicker of resolve. His fight wasn't over. It had just begun.

Malik's shadow lingered, his voice seeping into the air like poison. "You think that was courage? He's just delaying the inevitable."

Leah didn't respond. She focused on strengthening Samuel's thread, reinforcing the bond with a soft, gentle energy. Courage wasn't about guarantees; it was about making the choice to act, even when the outcome was uncertain.

Samuel woke with a start, the dream fading as sunlight streamed through the office window. He blinked and glanced at the Bible on his desk, its pages still open to the same passage about faith and perseverance.

From the dreamscape, Leah watched as Samuel began to make phone calls, reaching out to his congregation for help. His courage had sparked something new. The journey ahead would take time, but it was grounded in truth. The first steps had been taken.

Leah took a step back from the dreamscape, her gaze lingering on Samuel's thread. Courage, she realized, was not always loud or dramatic. Sometimes, it was quiet—a simple act of defiance against the shadows that sought to consume us.

Leah exhaled softly, knowing the storm ahead would test Samuel, and the dreamscape, in ways they hadn't yet imagined. Malik's influence was far from over. It would take everything Leah had—and more—to hold the line. But as long as there was courage, as long as there was determination, the dreamscape still had a chance.

LEAH'S VELARA AELIS

Resilience and courage are two sides of the same thread, each drawing strength from the other. They are not born in isolation but in the intertwined moments of struggle, when we face our fears, endure our doubts, and find the strength to press forward despite it all.

In the storm, Johan, Mina, and Terry learned that resilience isn't about standing alone—it's about standing together. The waves tested their limits, not only in terms of physical endurance but in their ability to trust each other. In the chaos of the storm, the bond between them grew stronger. They found strength in shared purpose, in knowing that each person's resolve helped buoy the others. This was true resilience: the quiet persistence to keep moving forward, not in spite of the storm, but through it, together.

And then there was Samuel. His courage wasn't forged in the heat of battle but in the quiet resolve to face his fears head-on. Courage, I've learned, is not the absence of fear—it's the decision to act even when it's present. Samuel's choice, in that moment, to stand firm against the threats in his office was an act of faith, not in grand gestures, but in small, deliberate acts that take immense inner strength. He chose to fight for something greater than his fears: the integrity of his church, the lives he had promised to protect, and his own sense of dignity. That kind of courage doesn't make the fear go away; it simply pushes forward, even when the outcome is uncertain.

The Loom: Leah's Legacy

These stories are reminders that resilience and courage are not just personal traits but shared gifts. When we choose to stand together, to act with bravery and faith, we weave threads that are unbreakable. The tapestry of our lives, with all its complexities, is strengthened by the connections we build, not just with others but with ourselves. The more we allow ourselves to be vulnerable, to admit where we struggle, the more resilient we become. The threads we weave become stronger, not despite our weaknesses, but because we have learned to embrace them.

I see now that my role as a Dreamweaver is not just to guide others through their fears but to help them realize the strength within themselves. Each person's journey is unique, but we all share a common thread—the ability to adapt, to endure, and to rise above the storms we face. The true gift is not in being free from struggle but in learning how to move forward with grace, even when the winds are fierce.

Malik's shadows grow stronger, his influence more insidious. His presence lingers, always in the background, always waiting for the right moment to unravel the threads we've so carefully woven. But the light of resilience and courage is a force he cannot extinguish. It flickers, it wanes, but it never goes out. It is the very force that binds us, that keeps us fighting for each other and for the dreams that lie within us all.

And so, we press on, guided by the threads that bind us. Every step I take, every dream I touch, is another opportunity to strengthen those threads. The path is uncertain, the journey long, but with every connection I make, I feel the fabric of this world becoming more robust, more alive. And through it all, I am reminded of the quiet power that lies within each of us—the ability to overcome, to rise, and to create something greater than the sum of its parts.

As I turn my attention to the next thread, I feel a shift in the dreamscape. The vibrations are sharp, discordant, a signal that this new journey will challenge me in ways I cannot yet understand. The world before me is grayscale, the lines between right and wrong blurred into a haze of uncertainty.

Leah's Lumarion

The sanctuary hummed with its familiar golden warmth, but an unspoken tension clung to the air. Mina, Terry, and Johan sat together, their eyes fixed on Jasper, who lay motionless on a faintly glowing dais. The fragile threads of his life pulsed weakly, each flicker of light a painful reminder of his fractured state. The shadows of his tether to Malik still clung to him, winding through the dreamscape like dark vines, and Leah couldn't help but feel the weight of it.

Leah stood near the loom, her fingers brushing against the golden threads that flowed through the room. Each thread shimmered with the stories she had woven and mended, lives intertwined, souls connected. Yet, Jasper's thread was unlike any she had ever seen. His thread flickered weakly, entangled with inky shadows, bound to something dark and unseen. It felt as though a part of him was lost—trapped within Malik's grasp.

Mina's voice broke through the quiet, sharp and demanding. "Why is he like this?" she asked, her stare never wavering from Jasper. "You've been keeping him here since we arrived, but you haven't explained why. What's his story, Leah?"

Leah took a deep breath, the weight of her own uncertainty hanging in the air. She reached out, tracing the delicate, glowing threads of Jasper's life, drawing what strength she could from them. "Jasper is... special. He's a Dreamweaver, like us, but Malik has tethered him. Jasper's mind is trapped, bound by a thread that Malik controls. What you see here is only a fragment of him. The rest of him is lost in the dreamscape."

Terry furrowed his brows, the concern in his youthful face etched deep. "Trapped? Can't we just... undo it? Break the thread?"

Leah shook her head slowly, her expression somber. "It's not that simple to sever a tether without harming the host. If you don't have the control to let go, you risk severing their connection to the loom entirely." Malik's hold on Jasper runs deep. He's using Jasper as a conduit to disrupt dreams, to weave chaos into the threads of fate. If we sever the tether without understanding its source, it could destroy Jasper completely."

Johan now layered with quiet tension. "So, he's just another pawn in Malik's game? Another victim of his madness."

Leah hesitated before nodding, a deep, aching sorrow in her chest. "Yes, but he's more than that. Jasper is one of the strongest Dreamweavers I've come to know—Leader of the Loomguards. He's not just a victim—he's a key. If we can free him, he could help us stop Malik."

The room fell silent as Leah's words hung in the air. Mina studied her, her eyes narrowing as she took in the weight of the situation. "You knew him well, didn't you?"

Leah's gaze dropped to the loom, her fingers brushing the golden threads as she recalled the time she had spent with Jasper. "Yes. Jasper was important to me. He was one of the first Weavers I ever trained with. We shared dreams, challenges, victories... He's more than just a comrade—he's family."

Mina's usual hardness softened at the unspoken emotion in Leah's voice, "You've seen pain within your family, I know that feeling. The dreams you encountered—and the threads you kept intact—must have been difficult. Is this why you call us Weavers?"

Leah takes a step back from the loom, "I've seen Dreamweavers use their powers to wield nightmares, they became what they feared... lost in the depth of the shadows. And knowing that led me to believe there are different kinds of Weavers across the dreamscape."

Mina glanced at Terry and Johan before turning back to Leah. "We've all lost people we cared about. If Jasper is as important to you as you say, we'll help you. But we need to know more—about him, about Malik, and about why we're here."

Leah nodded, her heart swelling with gratitude for their willingness to help. "Thank you. And you deserve to know more." She motioned for them to sit closer, her voice taking on a softer tone. "But before I tell you more about Jasper, I want to understand you better. I want to know what drives you—what brought you here to fight for the dreamscape."

Johan shifted uncomfortably, his broad shoulders tense. His usually unwavering look seemed distant now, flickering with vulnerability. "I come from a place called Valtros, I carry the royal blood of the Warriors of the Realm. It was a thriving world—the shield of the dreamscape. It was so strong that it sustained entire generations. Families, friends, communities... we were all connected through the threads."

Terry stunned by the revelation, interjected, "Wait, are you a prince? Johan replied, "a prince without a kingdom. For centuries, my family—the Loomcrest of Zerron—ruled the dreamscapes. He lowered his head."

Leah's voice was soft, coaxing. "What happened?"

Johan's tensed, his hands clenching into fists as the memories resurfaced. "Darkness happened. Malik happened. He tore through Valtros like a storm, severing threads and unraveling everything we had built. He didn't just destroy our dreamscape—he wiped out our world. I lost my family, my home, everything. I survived because I was away, weaving a dream for someone else."

A heavy silence filled the room, thick with the weight of Johan's loss. Mina reached out, her hand resting firmly on his shoulder in silent support. Leah's voice was gentle but firm. "I'm so sorry. Now you're here to stop him. To make sure no one else loses what you did."

Johan nodded, then spoke in a low resolute voice, "For a long time, I cared about revenge. I chased the shadows. But now, I seek justice. If stopping Malik means no one else has to suffer like I did, then I'll fight until my last breath."

Mina leaned back, her arms crossed, but there was a shift in her demeanor. "I didn't grow up in a palace or some idyllic dreamscape," she said, her tone edged with bitterness. "My world was a mess—fractured and broken long before Malik showed up. Corruption, greed, power-hungry fools... that's what I grew up with. The Loomcrest of Kaelith."

Hearing the name *Kaelith* stirred something in Leah—a flicker of memory buried under time and fear—but she didn't speak of it.

Mina continued, "After the royal family lost their prince the entire dreamscape shifted leaving families helpless."

Leah asked, "What made you start weaving dreams?"

Mina shrugged, her expression guarded. "I wanted to escape. But dreams aren't just about running away—they're about finding something worth fighting for. I became a Dreamweaver... a Weaver, because I wanted to create something better. A world where people could feel safe, even if it was just for a moment."

Terry, ever the spark of energy in the room, smirked lightly, his teasing tone cutting through the heaviness. "And then you started blowing things up."

Mina shot him a glare, but a hint of a smile tugged at her lips. "Yeah, well... sometimes you must destroy the old to make way for the new. I don't follow rules, Leah. But I follow what's right. And right now, stopping Malik is the right thing to do."

Terry adjusted his gauntlets and shrugged. "My story's not as dramatic as theirs," he said, his voice light but tinged with self-awareness. "I come from a line of tech geniuses, The Loomcrest of Aevryn. My family's been building and innovating for generations. We chose to leave the dreamscape and live amongst the humans, but the darkness followed us. We've always believed in using our knowledge to make the drealis better."

Leah nodded, her expression encouraging. "And how did that lead you here?"

Terry hesitated, a flicker of hesitation passing through his features. "I wanted to take it further. My parents were content with the waking world, but I saw the potential in dreams. I wanted to bridge technology and the dreamscape—create a link between both worlds. But every time I tried, something went wrong. I didn't realize it was Malik, disrupting my work, until it was too late."

He fell silent, his sight dropping to his hands. "I lost someone because of it. My sister... she got caught in one of the corrupted threads. She didn't make it out."

Leah's shoulders lowered as if carrying Terry's pain. "I'm so sorry, Terry."

He met her gaze, his eyes filled with quiet determination. I'm not sure if it was Malik—it all felt like a blur. But I'm here because I want to fix what I broke. I want to make sure no one else loses someone because of chaos."

Terry broke the brief moment of silence, eyeing the object in Leah's hand, "What is that glowing staff that you carry?"

They all leaned in, curiosity flickering behind their concern. Leah replied, "This is Lux Veritas— the Loomstaff of Radiance. An artifact from the origins of the Dreamweavers possess with ability to choose its wielder.

The Loom: Leah's Legacy

She paused, "I am still learning... but I know this much: its force for good. It can mend dreams and restoring the balance—unlike any other loomstaff I've encountered."

Leah took a deep breath, looking at the three Weavers. Mina, Terry, and Johan each carried a weight, but they also carried purpose. Their shared pain and hope bound them together. They weren't just allies; they were kindred spirits.

"Jasper is like you," Leah said at last, her voice steady. "He's a fighter, a dreamer—someone who believes in the power of connection. But Malik twisted that belief into something dark. If we can save Jasper, we can weaken Malik's hold on the dreamscape—And give Jasper a chance to heal. The loom has brought us together, and in time, I believe it will show us why."

A calm understanding passed over Mina's face. "Then let's save him."

Johan's voice was low but resolute. "Whatever it takes."

Terry smirked, his youthful energy returning. "Let's show Malik what we're made of."

Leah smiled, her heart swelling with gratitude and determination. They were ready. The threads of their stories had brought them here, and together, they would weave a future worth fighting for.

"Let's go. Feel your threads," Leah said softly, stepping forward with the loomstaff in hand. It shimmered to life, forming a silver-like shield that outline her lavender robe. "The shadows are unpredictable—Malik's presence has frayed what once was clear. Stay sharp. And wear this thread; it's your way back to the sanctuary." One by one, the team wrapped the threads around their wrists, the woven strands glowing faintly against their skin. Their journey was far from over, but together, they had the strength to face whatever came next.

CHAPTER 10

THE GRAY AREA

The dreamscape unfolded in muted grays and whites, its boundaries shifting and uncertain. Leah stood at the edge of a city that seemed to melt into itself. Buildings twisted upward, their edges blurred, and streets bent in impossible ways, as though the very fabric of this place was unstable, caught between worlds. The air was thick with an eerie quiet, as though the city had once been alive but had since forgotten how to breathe.

People moved through the streets, shadows more than flesh, their features indistinct and their movements jerky, like characters frozen in a dream they couldn't escape. The thread Leah followed pulsed faintly, erratic and trembling with uncertainty. It led her to the center of the city, to a man sitting on a bench, his head buried in his hands, his shoulders shaking as if weighed down by an unseen burden.

This was Evan Harper, a man trapped by his own choices. His life had become a labyrinth of compromises, each decision more tangled than the last. The dreamscape mirrored this inner turmoil—a world where every choice seemed to dissolve into the next, with no clear direction and no sense of resolution. It was a place of confusion and frustration, a prison of his own making.

Leah stepped forward, her presence barely a ripple in the air, and called softly, "Evan."

He didn't look up. His voice, muffled and broken, carried the frustration of someone caught in an endless loop. "I can't do it anymore. I can't keep pretending I know what I'm doing."

Leah knelt beside him, her heart aching as she saw the weight of his self-doubt. In the waking world, Evan was a middle manager at a failing corporation, a man caught in a life of unrelenting expectations. Each day was spent juggling tasks, fulfilling promises, and sacrificing whatever parts of himself were left. His nights were consumed by guilt over the choices he had made to climb higher, to stay afloat in a world that demanded more than he could give.

Leah could see the frayed threads that connected him to his waking life, each one worn thin by years of compromise. His dream reflected his shattered sense of self, a place where every decision seemed to spiral out of control.

"Tell me what you want," Leah asked gently, her voice a quiet nudge in his mind.

Evan's eyes finally lifted, his face etched with weariness and regret. "I want it to stop. The pressure. The lies. All of it. I can't keep pretending it's okay."

As he spoke, the dreamscape around them began to shift. The city, once fluid and unstructured, began to solidify. The streets aligned into a grid, the buildings now towering, rigid, as if they were built from Evan's expectations, his ambitions, his failures. At the far end of the street, a figure emerged, dark and imposing. The air seemed to thicken, the ground beneath Leah's feet sinking as Malik appeared.

"Another one lost in the gray," Malik's voice echoed, smooth and taunting.

He stepped forward, his presence distorting the dreamscape, pulling it into a more chaotic state. "Poor Evan. Always trying to do the right thing yet always falling short."

Evan's body stiffened, his posture faltering under the weight of Malik's words. His shoulders hunched, as though he could physically feel the burden of everything he had tried to escape. The weight of his own failures and missed opportunities were heavier than any storm.

Leah stepped between them, standing tall, her presence a calm contrast to Malik's oppressive force. "Leave him, Malik. This isn't your place."

Malik smirked, stepping closer, the shadows gathering at his feet. "Oh, but it is. Evan is mine, Leah. Every choice he made, every compromise, every little lie—he led himself here. This is his truth."

The city darkened, the ground cracking as Malik's influence spread. The buildings twisted and bent, turning into a vast labyrinth. The walls were lined with mirrors, each one reflecting a different version of Evan's life. Leah's grip on the loomstaff tightened, the staff pulsing in her hand, responding to the darkness Malik had woven into this place. She could feel its warmth, a beacon of resistance.

"Here's the game," Malik said, his tone playful but cold. "Every turn offers a choice. Every choice reflects who he truly is. Let's see if he can find his way out."

Leah's mind raced. The labyrinth, the mirrors—these were more than just physical obstacles. They were a representation of Evan's inner turmoil, a visual manifestation of his guilt, regret, and self-doubt. She reached out with her power, sending a stabilizing thread to Evan's soul, grounding him in the chaos around them.

"You're stronger than this," Leah said gently, her voice firm but soothing. "The labyrinth is just a reflection of your fears. It doesn't define you."

Evan turned to her, eyes wide with both doubt and hope. "What if I can't find the way out?"

"You will," Leah replied, her voice unwavering. "But only if you're willing to face yourself."

Evan hesitated, glancing at the labyrinth's twisting paths. "How do I even start?"

Leah's fingers brushed the loomstaff, and the light from it rippled across the labyrinth, steadying the shifting mirrors. "You start by letting go of the lies you've been telling yourself."

Evan stepped forward, his first tentative step leading him into the maze of mirrors. Each reflection he passed whispered doubts into his ear, their voices soft and insidious.

"You're a fraud."

"You'll never be enough."

"You've already failed."

Evan tightened his fists, his breath coming in ragged gasps. "How do I shut them up?" he asked, panic rising in his voice.

"You don't," Leah said calmly, her eyes steady on him. "You listen, but you don't believe them. The mirrors only have power if you let them."

At the first turn, Evan saw a reflection of himself accepting a promotion that came at the expense of betraying a colleague. The version of him in the mirror sneered, its eyes cold and accusing. "You didn't have a choice," the reflection spat.

"I didn't have a choice," Evan muttered, his voice defensive.

"Didn't you?" Leah asked softly, stepping closer.

Evan hesitated, and then a light of recognition flickered in his eyes. "I could have said no. I just didn't want to."

The mirror shattered, its shards dissolving into light.

The loomstaff pulsed, its energy coursing through the dreamscape. Leah felt the threads weave around them, pulling the labyrinth into focus. The light from the staff grew brighter, dispelling the shadows Malik had cast.

With every turn, Evan faced another version of himself—each one representing a choice he had made that had led him further down the path of compromise. A younger Evan lying to his partner about his career, a middle-aged version ignoring a phone call from his estranged father, and an older version of himself skipping his daughter's recital for an important meeting.

Each time, Evan's determination deepened. "I was afraid," he admitted aloud. "Afraid of being seen for who I really am."

The labyrinth began to shift, its walls becoming more transparent. Malik's voice echoed, now bitter and full of anger. "You think admitting your failures will fix anything? You'll never change."

Leah stepped forward, the loomstaff glowing brightly. "Change isn't about erasing the past. It's about choosing differently from now on."

The loomstaff flared with light, cutting through the darkness Malik had created. Malik recoiled, his form flickering as the dreamscape began to stabilize.

"We are not finished yet," he hissed.

The labyrinth dissolved, opening into a vast chamber where the floor was covered in golden threads. At the center stood a pedestal with a key. Malik appeared beside it, his smirk returning. "Take the key, and all your problems disappear," he said smoothly. "No more guilt. No more regret."

Evan hesitated, his hand hovering over the key.

Leah spoke softly, her voice filled with understanding. "The key isn't the answer, Evan. You are. The strength to change is already in you."

Evan withdrew his hand, locking eyes with Malik. "I don't need shortcuts anymore."

The golden threads pulsed with energy as Malik's presence faded. The dreamscape unraveled, the shadows receding into nothing.

Evan woke with a start, a quiet resolve settling over him. He sat up in his bed, his gaze falling on the resignation papers he had been avoiding. With a deep breath, he picked up the pen and began to write.

Leah watched as Evan's thread strengthened, its frayed edges smoothing. She felt a quiet satisfaction in knowing he had found his way, but the weight of Malik's influence still loomed in the dreamscape. Leah turned her attention back to the loomstaff, which pulsed softly in her hand, its energy warm and reassuring. Its power was becoming more apparent, and she could sense that it was guiding her just as much as she was guiding it.

"What are you?" Leah whispered, a mixture of awe and curiosity in her voice. The loomstaff pulsed again, as if in response, and she felt its power settle deeper into her being.

For now, she had another thread to follow. The journey was far from over, and Leah knew that the battles ahead would test her in ways she had yet to understand. Even with her team, the loomstaff, and the threads of connection that bound them, Leah felt disquiet.

Leah's Lumarion

The sanctuary stood quietly at the edge of a sprawling meadow, its unassuming exterior—an old, renovated barn—belied the extraordinary secrets held within. Inside, the walls were lined with shelves of dream journals, relics from surreal realms, and glowing crystals that pulsed like heartbeats. It felt as though the very soul of the dreamscape whispered through this space, waiting to be heard.

At its center stood a massive table etched with ancient sigils—symbols of the Threads of Fate—each one glowing faintly with sentient light. The air hummed with residual energy, thick with memory and meaning. This hidden place, tucked between realms and sealed from the waking world, was where Leah and her team returned to regroup.

Johan leaned against the table, his compact, muscular frame taut with focus. His deep green combat-weave armor shimmered with teal nodes pulsing gently across his shoulders. The silver tattoo around one eye seemed to glow faintly under the crystal light as his gaze swept the room. "Why is he in every dream?" he asked, more to himself than anyone. "Every time I grip a thread... Malik is there."

Terry stood near a glowing monitor, long fingers flying across a keyboard.

His lean frame bent slightly forward in concentration, electric-blue streaks in his blond hair catching the low light. "I'm working on it," he muttered. "Trying to track his thread. There's interference—some kind of cloaking pattern—but I think I'm close to isolating it."

Mina sat on the edge of a bench, knees drawn up, tablet in hand. Her auburn curls were pulled back in a half-knot, strands wrapped with flickering dream-thread beads that caught the glow around them. She sketched quickly, her copper eyes narrowed in thought. "He's not just appearing randomly," she said. "The symbols, the spaces... they're too specific. He's leaving impressions behind. Breadcrumbs."

At the head of the table sat Leah, her lavender robes pooled quietly around her, dream-thread sigils shifting with each breath she took. Her cloak's silver lining reflected the low light, and beside her rested the Loomstaff of Radiance, its surface glimmering with soft gold and lilac hues. Though calm on the surface, Leah carried a weight in her chest—a thread pulled taut with worry.

Jasper's thread is still flickering. Still fractured.

She felt it like an ache behind her ribs—an invisible thread stretched between them both. He was tethered to Malik, and time was unraveling.

The door creaked open. Jasper stepped inside slowly, his once-grounded presence now ghostlike. His tall frame, still strong in build, seemed to sway under invisible pressure. His rich brown skin had paled, and the silver streaks in his curls seemed brighter, as though the dream-realm had aged him from within. His hazel-green eyes—once earthy and calm—were distant, unfocused.

Leah rose quickly, concern softening her tone. "Jasper," she said gently. "How are you feeling?"

He offered a faint smile, one that didn't quite reach his eyes. "Better, I think."

Leah stepped closer, her hand brushing the Loomstaff as if drawing quiet strength. She could feel the thread within him—erratic, frayed, pulsing with something that wasn't entirely his own.

Johan stepped forward, tone firm but kind. "You've been through dark shadows. But you're here. That's what matters."

Jasper gave a short nod and lowered himself into a chair. His fingers gripped the edge like it might keep him from floating away. He kept his gaze low until it drifted to the symbols carved into the table.

"That one's important," he murmured, running his fingers slowly across a shape Leah had never explained.

Leah blinked. "How do you know about that?"

He looked up, eyes glassy. "I don't know. It just... feels familiar.".

A chill ran through her. That symbol was a hidden path—a mark only known to high-level Weavers. Malik's influence wasn't just lingering... it was feeding Jasper knowledge. Whispering secrets.

Mina met Leah's gaze. "Is he getting weaker?"

Leah nodded, her voice low. "Yes. And it's getting worse. Malik isn't just tethered to him—he's feeding off him, siphoning his strength like a thread unraveling from the inside out."

Terry's voice cut through the quiet. "The thread activity's been spiking. He's severing connections now, not just corrupting them." He turned the monitor, revealing flickers of erratic pulses. "Dreamers are waking hollow. No memories. No emotion."

Johan's jaw clenched. "He's dismantling the dreamscape from the inside out."

Mina stood abruptly. "Then we stop waiting. We find his anchor and cut the thread."

Leah slightly nodded, "Every Weaver has an anchor—a place in the dreamscape that ties them to their strength. If we find Malik's, we can weaken him."

"But how do we find it?" Johan asked. "He's not exactly sending invitations."

"I might be able to help," Jasper said quietly. Everyone turned to him.

"There are flashes in my head. Places. Symbols. I don't think they're mine." He hesitated, then added, "I think Malik's leaving them behind—intentionally or not."

Mina crossed her arms. "And how do we know this isn't another trap?"

Leah laid a hand on Jasper's shoulder. "Because if Malik's arrogant enough to leave fragments behind, we can use them. If Jasper is seeing what Malik's seen, then we trace it backward."

They fell into motion.

Mina began sketching from Jasper's descriptions—symbols, places, fragments of forgotten paths. Her rebel-garb rustled as she moved, blades and glyph-stones clinking quietly at her belt.

Terry cross-referenced the symbols, tapping through dream-map overlays and thread spectrums, his suit's circuitry flashing with each shift.

Johan readied their tools, adjusting his armor and checking the charge in his dream-forged weapons. "If we're going in, we go prepared."

Leah moved to the far corner of the room where her journal waited— worn leather, pages lined with thread and thought. She lowered herself to the cushion, entering stillness.

Mina steps toward Leah's corner, her sketching hand momentarily still. "Earlier, when everything went quiet... I saw you," she said carefully. "You weren't writing—you were... weaving. But not like before. It was like the journal responded to you."

Leah closed the journal gently, her violet eyes meeting Mina's with calm understanding. "It's called *Velara Aelis*," she said softly. "Velara reflects the rippling nature of thought—the movement between clarity and confusion. Aelis is the silent flow beneath it all."

She ran her fingers along the edge of the page, where faint symbols shimmered into view. "It's a meditative state passed down through my lineage. My mother called it a way of listening to the quiet between dreams. When I enter Velara Aelis, the threads respond. The journal doesn't record words—it weaves truths I'm not always ready to speak out loud."

Mina watched, the skepticism fading from her face, replaced by quiet wonder. "It's beautiful. Like a conversation between memory and magic."

Leah smiled softly. "It's how I stay grounded."

By the time the room settled again, the plan had formed.

1. **Decode the Symbols:** Jasper's fragmented memories would guide Mina and Terry as they mapped Malik's trail.

2. **Infiltrate the Anchor:** Leah and Johan would lead the team into Malik's territory to confront and destabilize him.

3. **Sever the Tether:** Leah would use the loomstaff to free Jasper and weaken Malik's grip once and for all.

Leah stood slowly, brushing her fingers across the table's glowing sigils. "This won't be easy," she said. "But we've faced shadows before."

Johan placed a hand on her shoulder, voice steady. "We're ready."

As the others moved to gather their gear, Jasper remained seated. Leah knelt beside him.

"Do you really think we can stop him?" he asked, voice barely above a whisper.

Leah met his gaze, her eyes glowing faintly. "Yes. And not just stop him. Save the threads. Heal what he's broken. It starts with you."

He gave a tired smile. "Thanks for not giving up on me."

"I never will," she said.

While the others gathered, Jasper remained seated, his eyes closed in quiet meditation. The symbols still shimmered faintly before him, and he focused on them—anchoring what little strength he had left. Leah remained behind for a moment longer, her hand resting over the glowing symbol Jasper had traced. It pulsed gently under her palm—a promise of a path forward.

"We're stronger together," she whispered, eyes lifting toward the horizon beyond the sanctuary walls. "And together, we'll face whatever comes next. The threads are calling us, you rest."

CHAPTER 11

THE MAGICIAN

The air was thick with a hum of excitement, the energy of the dreamscape pulsing like a heartbeat. Inside the circus tent, the vibrant reds and golds stretched impossibly high, casting a warm glow over everything beneath it. The atmosphere was electric, alive with a strange mix of anticipation and chaos. The laughter of the crowd echoed unnaturally, reverberating through the space as if the tent itself were feeding off their energy, amplifying the sensations around it.

Leah stood at the edge of the ring, her form invisible to the dreamers, yet she felt every thread vibrating around her, each pulse a story, a life in the balance. The crowd's blurred faces were a mere backdrop to the deeper currents at play within the dreamscape. One thread stood out, bright and flickering, drawing her toward the center of the tent, where a stage awaited.

Atop the stage, Victor stood tall, dressed in a black coat that shimmered under the spotlight. He was a magician, elegant in his movements, performing illusions with an effortless grace that seemed to captivate everyone around him. The crowd gasped as doves emerged from his hat, their wings fluttering momentarily before vanishing into thin air. The applause was deafening, and Victor basked in it, a man made of the same glittering illusions he performed.

But Leah's attention wasn't on Victor alone. There, on the edge of the stage, a pregnant woman named Viviana stood, her gaze fixed intently on Victor. Her hand rested on her swollen belly, her expression a mixture of awe and unease. Something about her presence caught Leah's attention. Viviana's thread pulsed quietly, yet with great steadiness, rooted in something deeper than the surface of the dreamscape.

Victor's voice boomed, commanding the audience's attention. "Ladies and gentlemen, prepare to witness the impossible!"

With a dramatic flourish, he summoned a swirling mist that took the shape of a roaring lion. The crowd erupted in applause, but Viviana did not join them. She watched, her face hardening as her lips pressed into a thin line.

"Impressive," she muttered under her breath. "But hollow."

Leah stepped closer, her form slipping through the folds of the dreamscape, weaving herself into the tension between the two figures. Viviana's words held a weight, an understanding that Leah couldn't ignore. The contrast between them was sharp—Victor, a master of control and illusion, and Viviana, whose magic was rooted in something far more tangible: creation.

Victor's gaze snapped to Viviana, irritation flickering in his eyes. "Viviana," he snapped, his voice dripping with condescension. "You're ruining the show."

Viviana stepped into the light, her presence commanding despite her condition. "This isn't a show, Victor. It's a facade. Illusions won't solve anything."

The crowd fell silent, the shift in the air palpable. Even Victor seemed momentarily taken aback, his posture stiffening as his grip tightened on his cane.

"And what would you know about it?" he sneered. "You've never understood the art of illusion."

Viviana stood her ground, unwavering. "Because I deal in truth, not tricks. Real magic isn't about control—it's about creation."

Leah felt the dreamscape around them shift. The vibrant colors of the tent began to dim as shadows crept in from the edges, the distortion unmistakable. Malik's influence was faint but undeniable, twisting the threads that connected them. Leah could feel the malice creeping into the dreamscape, but she also felt Viviana's quiet strength—her ability to resist.

Victor, seizing the challenge, raised his chin. "You think you're better than me?" His voice was laced with venom. "Show me, then. Show us all what you can do."

Viviana hesitated for a moment, her hands trembling slightly. "This isn't about competition, Victor. It's about adapting, about letting go of the need to control everything."

Victor scoffed, the sound echoing harshly. "Fine. Let's see whose magic is stronger."

The dreamscape twisted violently as the tent transformed into a vast, swirling arena. The crowd dissolved into faceless silhouettes, their energy dissipating into the space. Victor raised his hands, summoning a massive dragon of fire that roared to life before them. Its fiery scales shimmered and crackled, its eyes burning with an intensity that filled the arena with a heat that seemed to scorch the very air.

Viviana stepped forward, her expression calm but determined. She placed one hand on her belly, the other held out as she summoned a glowing tree. Its roots spread across the arena floor, weaving through the ground as its branches began to grow thick with glowing leaves, shining with an inner light.

The dragon lunged toward the tree, its flames licking at its branches, but the tree did not burn. Instead, it grew stronger, its roots sinking deeper, its leaves shimmering with a soft but undeniable glow. Viviana stood unflinching, watching the dragon's assault without fear.

Leah felt the balance of power shift between them. Victor's magic was one of domination—forcing the dreamscape to bend to his will, to submit to his illusions. Viviana's magic, however, was grounded in creation. It was nurturing, strong, and able to endure the chaos around it. This was not about control; it was about resilience, about growth even in the face of destruction.

The dragon recoiled, its fiery breath faltering as Viviana's tree remained unscathed. Victor's hands trembled slightly, his control slipping as he watched the tree thrive in the flames. His illusion faltered, and for the first time, he looked vulnerable.

Viviana's voice, calm and steady, cut through the tension. "This isn't the way, Victor. You don't have to fight to prove your worth."

Victor hesitated, his hands lowering slowly. The dragon's flames dimmed, and the dreamscape began to fade back into the familiar setting of the circus tent. The vibrant colors returned, but the once sharp divide between the two figures softened.

Leah seized the moment, weaving the threads between Victor and Viviana with a gentle yet firm hand. "You're not enemies," she whispered, her voice reaching into their hearts. "You're mirrors, each reflecting what the other needs to see."

Victor lowered his hands completely, and the dragon dissipated into a flurry of sparks. The arena faded into the colorful canvas of the tent, the crowd's applause beginning anew but softer, as though they were now witnessing something deeper than a mere show.

Victor turned to Viviana, his expression changing from one of arrogance to one of uncertainty. "I don't know how to stop," he admitted quietly, his voice barely above a whisper. "I've been... holding onto control for so long. It's all I know."

Viviana stepped toward him, her hand resting gently on her belly as she looked him in the eyes. "You don't have to do it alone," she said, her voice calm and filled with understanding. "Magic is stronger when it's shared."

The scene around them shifted, the dreamscape dissolving as Victor woke with a start. The vibrant colors of the circus tent faded, leaving behind only the dim glow of his apartment. He sat up, his heart pounding, and reached for his phone, his fingers hovering over Viviana's contact name.

From the dreamscape, Leah watched as Victor's thread brightened, its energy steadier and more focused. For a moment, she allowed herself a quiet breath of relief. But as always, she knew the battle wasn't over. Malik's presence was still there, lurking in the shadows, watching their every move.

Leah turned her attention back to the loomstaff beside her. It pulsed faintly in response, its energy matching the thread that now connected Victor to Viviana. The shadows were still there, but for a fleeting moment, Leah saw the light of something else—a chance for change.

The threads around her began to hum, and she prepared herself for what was to come next. The fight against Malik was far from over, but with each passing moment, they were getting stronger, and so was the dreamscape.

CHAPTER 12

BEAR WITH A HEART

The dim light of the bar flickered like the pulse of a distant heartbeat, casting shifting shadows across the room. Leah entered the dreamscape with quiet precision, her senses immediately heightening as she scanned the space. The familiar scent of aged wood and whiskey filled the air, and the hum of conversations blended seamlessly with the faint melody of an old jukebox playing in the corner. It was a setting that carried weight—both nostalgia and a sense of lost moments hung in the air.

At the far end of the bar, a figure sat hunched over his drink. His broad shoulders sagged, weighed down by some invisible burden. Leah recognized him from the thread she'd been following—a man in his late thirties, Barry. But as often happened in the dreamscape, the edges of his humanity blurred. The faintest flash of fur, the curve of claws, and the gleam of eyes that had seen too much shifted through his form, hinting at a deeper nature. A bear.

Barry's dreamscape flickered between two realms: one where he was a man—awkward and alone, lost in the human world he couldn't quite belong to—and another where he was a bear—strong, solitary, and resigned to his isolation in the woods. In both realms, there was a shared thread of despair, but they were each tangled in a different way.

Leah approached cautiously, her steps silent as she drew closer to the bar. The threads connecting Barry to the dreamscape pulsed faintly, barely discernible in the thick cloud of his frustration and hopelessness. She felt the burden of his self-doubt wrap around him like a cloak.

Barry hesitated before approaching a woman sitting alone at the bar. Her laughter was light, full of life and warmth, but it only seemed to deepen the disconnection he felt. He reached for his drink, his hand twitching, but the words he wanted to speak to her stayed lodged in his throat. Instead, he mumbled something incoherent, earning a puzzled glance from her before she turned back to her friends.

Leah's heart tightened at the sight. She understood that this was more than a moment of awkwardness. It was a manifestation of the barriers Barry had built, the walls he had erected to protect himself from rejection. She watched as he slumped further in his seat, his gaze distant.

The scene shifted, and the bar dissolved into a dense forest. Barry now walked as a bear, his massive form moving with grace through the towering trees. The forest was dark, almost suffocating, its branches intertwining like the walls of a labyrinth. The stillness of the forest contrasted sharply with the noise of the bar, but the isolation was the same.

Barry paused at the edge of a river, his reflection distorting in the ripples as he gazed at himself. The reflection shifted between his human self and his bear form, each version an embodiment of the split within him. He growled softly, the words heavy with frustration.

"Why does it matter?" he muttered. "I'll never belong anywhere."

Leah stepped forward into the forest, her voice gentle but firm as she approached him. "Belonging isn't about fitting in. It's about finding the courage to be seen as you are."

Barry turned, his eyes narrowing as he studied her, confusion and defensiveness mixing in his gaze. "And what do you know about it? You've never had to hide who you are."

Leah took a steadying breath, feeling the weight of his words settle over her. It was a reminder of the truths she still hid, of the parts of herself she had yet to fully confront. "You'd be surprised," she replied quietly, her voice tinged with a quiet strength. "But this isn't about me. It's about what you're willing to risk in finding connection."

The air around them grew quiet, the dreamscape holding its breath as if awaiting Barry's decision. Uncertainty flickered in his eyes, a silent battle playing out behind them. The moment lingered—tense, suspended—until his gaze finally dropped to the ground, as though he might find the answer hidden in the shadows beneath his feet.

In the next dream sequence, Barry was climbing a tree, struggling to reach a golden beehive perched high in its branches. His massive claws scraped against the rough bark, but the branches cracked and splintered beneath his weight. With each failed attempt, frustration built, but instead of retreating, Barry tried again and again, each effort a sign of his inner struggle to break free from his self-imposed limits.

The tree wasn't about the honey. It was about persistence, about rising again after failure. Leah silently guided him, weaving threads of calm and patience through his dream. Each setback became a lesson, a new opportunity to trust the process, to let go of the need for immediate success.

The next sequence found Barry following a deer through the woods. The creature moved with an effortless grace, its steps light and sure, while Barry's heavy form clumsily followed behind. No matter how fast he ran, he kept finding himself back at the same clearing, unable to break free from the cycle.

Leah observed, her presence almost imperceptible as she wove threads of resilience into Barry's path. This was not a failure; it was a lesson in trust. Barry's constant circling was teaching him to trust that the path, though unclear, would eventually lead him to where he needed to go.

Eventually, the dreamscape shifted once more, returning to the bar. But this time, something had changed within Barry. He sat at the counter, no longer searching for approval from others. Instead, he sat with a sense of quiet acceptance, the weight of his inner turmoil lightened. The pressure to prove himself had lessened, and for the first time in the dream, he allowed himself to simply be.

But as Barry settled into this new understanding, a figure stepped into the scene. Malik appeared, his presence as sharp and cutting as ever, like a blade slicing through the fragile peace. He slid onto the barstool next to Barry, his movements deliberate, predatory.

"Well, isn't this cozy?" Malik's voice dripped with mockery as he eyed Barry, a smirk playing at the edges of his lips.

Leah's breath caught as she realized Malik's attention wasn't on Barry—it was on her.

"You've been busy," Malik said, his gaze locking onto Leah's. "Guiding, weaving, saving. It must be exhausting."

Leah stayed silent, her gaze steady as she faced him. But Malik's presence had a subtle, menacing quality that threatened to overwhelm everything around them.

"You know why I'm doing this, Leah?" Malik's voice grew darker, taunting. "Disrupting every thread you've tried to weave? It's not just for power. It's because of you."

Leah stiffened, her heart pounding in her chest. She felt the familiar ripple of dread settle in her bones as Malik's words struck too close to home.

The Loom: Leah's Legacy

A familiar tune began to echo through the dreamscape, a soft melody from the jukebox filling the bar. It was the same song that had played in Sean's dream, the one from *Love Is Lost*. Leah's breath hitched, recognition flooding through her.

"That song..." she whispered, realization dawning.

Malik's grin widened, his voice dripping with bitterness. "Our song. Didn't notice? You never do. Not until now."

The dreamscape flickered and warped, the bar dissolving into the cold confines of a prison cell. Leah's heart raced as she saw the number on the door—342. The same number from *Beyond the Bars*. A chilling wave of recognition flooded her, as memories rushed to the surface—memories of Malik, of love and loss.

"You've been leaving breadcrumbs for me," Leah said softly, almost to herself. "All this time... this is about me."

Malik's expression shifted, his anger faltering, revealing a hint of something deeper. A flicker of vulnerability broke through his cold façade. "I want to erase the pain, Leah. The pain of you, of us... If I can't have you, I don't want to feel anything."

Leah's chest tightened as she listened, but she stood firm, unwavering in her resolve. "Pain isn't something you can erase. It's something you must face. You can't keep hiding from it, Malik."

The dreamscape began to crumble, the walls warping and collapsing as Barry's voice broke through the chaos, urgent and filled with confusion. "What's happening?"

Leah turned to him, her voice steady despite the crumbling world around them. "It's time to wake up, Barry. Trust what you've learned."

Barry hesitated, his form flickering like a fading dream, but with a deep breath, he nodded and disappeared into the ether.

Leah turned her focus back to Malik, her voice calm but resolute. "You can't destroy the threads, Malik. No matter how much pain you're in, connection is stronger than chaos."

Malik stepped closer, his presence overwhelming. "We'll see about that."

With a sharp gesture, Malik vanished, leaving Leah standing alone in the collapsing dreamscape, the silence settling in around her.

Leah's Velara Aelis

Strength is often misunderstood. We imagine it as a towering force, steadfast and unyielding, a force that resists the storm without bending. But strength, I have come to realize, is far more nuanced than that. True strength is not in defiance, but in acceptance. It's the quiet resolve to face the truth, the courage to acknowledge our flaws, and the resilience to keep moving forward, even when the road ahead is blurred with uncertainty.

Evan's labyrinth revealed this to me in ways I hadn't expected. His journey wasn't about vanquishing an external foe; it was about facing the shadows within himself. The labyrinth wasn't a prison—it was a mirror, reflecting the choices he wished he could forget, and with every decision he faced, every step he took, he reclaimed a fragment of his power. His path was not linear, it was complex, filled with twists, turns, and echoes of the past. Yet through it all, he moved forward. He didn't run from his mistakes; he embraced them, understanding they were part of his journey toward redemption.

In him, I saw the delicate balance that we Weavers maintain. We are not shields. We cannot protect dreamers from their pain or erase the consequences of their choices. All we can do is guide them, offering enough light for them to find their way out of the darkness, enough clarity to see that even amidst their mistakes, there is room for growth.

But there is a weight to this role. As Weavers, we are connected to every thread we touch, every life we help untangle. Sometimes, the threads we guide reveal truths about ourselves that we are not ready to face. In helping others confront their darkness, we inevitably confront our own. The shadows we hold within us become mirrors for those we guide. Evan's strength was a reminder that facing our fears, and embracing our vulnerability, is the true measure of resilience. It's not about overcoming pain but walking through it—step by step.

Victor's journey reminds me of the illusions we weave, not just in the dreamscape but in life itself. We cling to control, to the belief that we are the masters of our reality. Yet it's in the moments when the smoke clears—when we are faced with the raw, unfiltered truth—that we find our greatest strength. Viviana understood something Victor didn't at first: true magic isn't in the grand gestures or the dazzling displays; it's in our ability to adapt, to transform.

I've seen it time and time again. The strongest among us are not those who avoid pain but those who embrace change, who adapt to the ever-shifting currents of their own inner landscapes. Like Viviana, they find beauty in the uncomfortable, in the messy process of growth.

Barry's dream was different—a sprawling, fractured landscape of self-doubt and rejection. It wasn't about one choice or one fear; it was the sum of a lifetime spent grappling with identity. His struggle was not a singular moment, but a persistent ache that had haunted him for as long as he could remember. Patience was his lesson, and it was mine as well. His dreamscape was fragmented, constantly shifting between the animalistic form of a bear and his human self, each struggling to reconcile the two halves.

As I walked beside him, I saw the beauty in his persistence. Even when the dreamscape shifted and faltered, Barry did not give up. He continued to climb, to follow, to try again. His failures were not defeats; they were steps toward understanding. In his eyes, I saw a reflection of the patience I so often lack with myself.

It is easy to guide others when their struggles are clear, when their paths seem linear. But life is rarely so tidy. Dreams, like the people who live them, are layered and complex. Barry's story wasn't about a perfect path—it was about trusting that even the winding, disjointed journey leads to something valuable.

With every step Barry took, his growth was evident, but so was the shadow of Malik. Malik's influence loomed over the dreamscape, his presence constant, insidious. For the first time, I felt Malik's anger not just directed at the dreamers, but at me. The pieces of the puzzle fell into place—the song in the jukebox, the prison cell number, the walk in the park—all fragments of our shared history, fragments of a connection I tried to forget.

Malik and I are tied by more than the chaos he seeks to create. He is not just an enemy; he is a reflection of what I have not yet healed within myself. His rage, his destruction—they are driven by loss. His pain mirrors my own, and now, he seeks to erase it by unraveling everything I have worked to protect. He wants to erase me, but in doing so, he is only digging deeper into the wounds we both carry.

I have spent so much time guiding others, weaving their dreams and unraveling their fears, that I have avoided confronting my own. Malik has forced me to look at the threads of my past—the choices I made, the pain I caused—and in doing so, he has forced me to see my own vulnerability.

Evan's labyrinth, Victor's Magic, and Barry's Forest, have taught me that strength is not about avoiding pain. Strength is about facing it. Malik's chaos is not just about control or power—it is about the raw, unhealed wounds of the past. And those wounds, when left unaddressed, can fester into something much darker. But they do not define us. We are more than the shadows that cling to our past.

As I guide others through their dreams, I realize that the strength to help them lies not in shielding them from pain, but in helping them confront it. And in doing so, I too must face what I have avoided. For if I am to help others heal, I must heal myself.

I see the same thread woven through all the stories I've touched: resilience is not the absence of vulnerability. It is the acceptance of it. It is the ability to continue, despite everything that tells us to stop. The moments when we feel most broken are often the moments that hold the key to our healing.

Evan found strength in admitting his failures. Victor found strength in adaptability. Barry found strength in trusting the process. I too must find strength in confronting the shadows of my past—not as enemies, but as part of the tapestry I am still weaving.

As I prepare for what comes next, the weight of the threads I hold presses gently against me. Each thread is fragile, yet strong. Each connection, whether smooth or tangled, carries meaning. In guiding others, I am reminded of the intricate beauty of the dreamscape. It is a vast, interconnected tapestry where every thread matters.

Malik's chaos threatens to unravel it all, but in doing so, it forces me to see the beauty in its imperfections. The mistakes, the regrets, the losses—they are not stains on the fabric of our lives. They are the colors that give it depth, give it meaning.

I cannot save every dreamer. I cannot undo every mistake. But I can continue to guide, to weave, and to hold the threads steady. And in doing so, I can find my own strength. I can find my purpose in the delicate balance of connection and resilience.

Malik's words still echo in my mind, a shadow that refuses to fade. But even shadows have their purpose—they remind us of the light. And so, I move forward.

As I step into the next dream, I feel a sense of anticipation, a hum of energy that pulls at the edges of my being. The threads vibrate, alive with the promise of new lessons, new connections. This time, the dreamscape unfolds into a carnival—a place of vibrant color and dark undertones. It pulses with energy, beckoning me to step inside.

I take a steadying breath. Malik is still watching. I know this. But I also know that every dream is an opportunity—an invitation to learn, to grow, and to weave something stronger than before. The threads are calling. With resolve, I step forward, ready for whatever comes next.

CHAPTER 13

CUPID'S HONEST ARROW

The dreamscape unfolded in bursts of color and sound, like a kaleidoscope spinning too fast. Leah stood at the edge of the chaos, her fingers brushing against the golden threads that vibrated with tension. This was not a place of serenity—it was a battlefield of love and doubt, where the air crackled with unsettled emotions, and every flicker of light seemed to carry the weight of hearts in turmoil.

In the center of it all stood Aiden and Lila, a young couple frozen in a moment of heartbreak. Aiden's hands were clenched into fists at his sides, his face etched with frustration, while Lila's gaze was sharp, her arms crossed protectively over her chest. Between them hovered a figure—a shimmering, ethereal Cupid—his bow drawn but his arrow trembling.

The dreamscape reflected their conflict: a fractured bridge suspended over a stormy sea. Each end of the bridge was tethered to the couple, but the planks beneath them crumbled with every harsh word they exchanged, each syllable laced with the bitterness of unresolved tension.

Leah stepped closer, her heart aching as she felt the weight of their pain.

Integrity wasn't just about honesty with others—it was about being true to oneself, even when it hurt. Aiden and Lila both needed to learn this lesson, but how could they when the very thing they both craved—connection—was the thing they feared most?

"You don't understand!" Aiden shouted, his voice carrying over the crashing waves below.

"No, you don't understand!" Lila shot back, her tone as sharp as the winds whipping through the dreamscape. "You've never listened to me—not really."

The bridge groaned under the strain, the cracks spreading like a web of fractures, growing with every painful accusation.

"Stop," Cupid said, his voice pleading. "If you keep this up, there will be nothing left."

But neither Aiden nor Lila acknowledged him. Their anger was a force of its own, blinding them to the consequences of their words. Leah stood still, observing the tension, feeling the weight of the storm around them, and yet there was no storm more dangerous than the one within their hearts.

Leah stepped onto the bridge, her movements careful as the structure swayed beneath her. "What are you fighting for?" she asked, her voice calm but firm, carrying the authority of one who had seen too much pain to remain silent.

Aiden turned to her, his expression incredulous. "What do you mean? I'm fighting for us!"

Lila scoffed, her eyes blazing with frustration. "No, you're fighting to win. There's a difference."

Cupid lowered his bow, his ethereal form flickering. "I tried to connect them," he said, his voice filled with regret. "But I can't make love where there's no honesty. They're tearing themselves apart."

Leah studied the couple, her gaze softening as she saw the brokenness in their hearts. "Love isn't enough without integrity," she said. "It's the foundation that holds everything else together. Without it, even the strongest connection will crumble."

Aiden and Lila fell silent, the weight of Leah's words settling over them like a quiet wave.

Cupid stepped forward, his hands trembling as he held out the arrow. "This was meant to bind them, to strengthen their love. But now... I don't know if it's right to use it."

Leah took the arrow, its surface glowing faintly in her hands. She could feel the energy within it—a mixture of hope and fear, passion and doubt. It wasn't just a tool; it was a reflection of their emotions, raw and amplified.

Leah turned to Aiden. "Do you love her?"

"Of course I do," he said, his voice cracking with vulnerability.

"Then why do you lie?" she asked, her tone piercing, her gaze unflinching. "Why do you say what you think she wants to hear instead of what's in your heart?"

Aiden opened his mouth to protest but stopped, his shoulders slumping. "Because I'm afraid," he admitted. "Afraid she'll leave if she knows the truth."

Lila's eyes softened, her arms uncrossing as she listened. "And what about you?" Leah asked, turning to her. "Why do you push him away?"

Lila hesitated, her gaze dropping to the crumbling planks beneath her feet. "Because I'm afraid too," she said quietly. "Afraid he'll see the parts of me I try to hide—the parts that aren't perfect."

The bridge steadied slightly, the cracks halting their spread. There was a flicker of hope in the air, but it was fragile.

Leah held the arrow between them, its glow brightening. "This isn't a magic fix," she said. "It's a mirror. It will reflect what's already in your hearts. If you're not honest with yourselves and each other, it will only amplify the divide."

Aiden and Lila exchanged a glance, their expressions shifting from anger to vulnerability. The walls between them were crumbling, but there was still hesitation.

"I love you," Aiden said, his voice steady for the first time. "But I've made mistakes. I've hidden things because I didn't want to lose you."

Lila nodded, tears streaming down her face. "And I've judged you unfairly. I've let my own insecurities cloud everything good about us."

Leah handed the arrow back to Cupid. "They're ready," she said.

Cupid hesitated, then notched the arrow and released it. It struck the center of the bridge, sending a wave of light rippling outward. The cracks healed, the planks growing stronger, and the stormy sea below calmed to a serene reflection. It was a fragile peace, but it was a start.

Just as the light reached the edges of the dreamscape, a shadow fell over it. Malik appeared, his presence dark and imposing. The threads around Leah trembled as he stepped onto the bridge, his gaze fixed on her.

"You're wasting your time, Leah," he said, his voice cold. "Connections like this are fragile. They'll break again, and when they do, the pain will be worse."

Leah held her ground, her voice steady as she faced him. "Pain is part of life, Malik. It's not something we can erase."

Malik's expression hardened. "You think you're helping them? All you're doing is prolonging their suffering. If they didn't feel, they wouldn't hurt."

Leah's heart ached as she saw the pain in his eyes, a mirror of the wounds he carried. "Eliminating pain doesn't heal it, Malik. It just leaves emptiness."

Malik's hand brushed the arrow embedded in the bridge, and the dreamscape flickered. Images from Leah's past flooded her mind—a walk in the park, a song on the jukebox, the number 342.

"You think I don't see it?" Malik said, his voice breaking. "Every thread you weave, every dream you guide—it's always there. A reminder of what we lost."

Leah's breath caught as the memories sharpened. The moments she once thought were coincidences were, in truth, deliberate echoes of their shared history. Malik's chaos wasn't just about control—it was his way of holding onto her, even as he tried to destroy the world she protected.

"I'm sorry," Leah whispered, her voice trembling. "But you can't destroy the threads because of me."

Malik's gaze softened for a fleeting moment, but the anger returned just as quickly. "You don't understand, Leah. You never did."

With a wave of his hand, he vanished, leaving the dreamscape dark and silent.

The bridge trembled as Aiden and Lila stood apart, their hands hovering but never meeting. Leah's heart ached as she felt the tension in their threads, each pulling in opposite directions. She extended her hand, her fingers brushing against the golden connections, but the strain was too great.

"It doesn't have to end like this," she said, her voice heavy with both urgency and regret.

Lila shook her head, her tears glistening in the dim light of the dreamscape. "Some things can't be fixed," she whispered, her voice breaking. "Love isn't enough if we don't trust each other."

Aiden's jaw tightened, his gaze falling to the crumbling planks beneath his feet. "Maybe... we're better off apart," he said, the words a dagger to his own heart.

The bridge shuddered, the final threads snapping as the connection dissolved into fragments of light. The sea below surged, swallowing the remains of what once bound them. Lila and Aiden faded from the dreamscape, their figures dissipating into the shadows.

Leah stood alone on the fractured bridge, her hands trembling as she clutched the remnants of their threads. They were weak, faded, and slipping through her fingers like sand.

A voice broke through the silence, low and filled with mocking satisfaction. "You can't save them all, Leah," Malik said, stepping from the shadows. His presence was a storm, dark and consuming.

Leah turned to face him, her chest tight with a mix of anger and despair. "I could have saved them if you hadn't interfered."

Malik's laugh was hollow. "Don't lie to yourself. This was their choice. You just couldn't accept it."

She took a step forward, grounding herself in the truth. "You're wrong. Connection can heal even the deepest wounds."

"Not always," Malik replied, his tone cutting. "Some wounds fester, Leah. Some people are better off apart, no matter how hard you try to weave them together. You think you're helping, but you're just prolonging their pain."

His words hit harder than Leah wanted to admit. The dreamscape around her was crumbling, the once-vivid colors dimming to muted shades of gray.

The silence that followed Malik's departure was suffocating. Leah stood on the broken bridge, the pieces of the dreamscape fading into shadow. The threads of Aiden and Lila's connection lay severed at her feet, lifeless and cold. She knelt, her fingers brushing the remnants, hoping for some faint spark to reignite. But there was nothing. The bond was gone, their love shattered by mistrust, fear, and her inability to hold it together.

Leah pressed her hands to her temples, the weight of failure pressing down on her chest. Malik's words echoed in her mind, sharp and relentless.

"You're losing your touch, Leah. Maybe you should stop trying to fix everyone else and look at your own broken threads."

Her vision blurred as the dreamscape dissolved completely, leaving her suspended in the stillness of the space between dreams. For the first time in her journey, Leah felt the sting of helplessness. Not every thread could be saved—she knew this—but the truth of it cut deeper than she had expected.

She took a deep, trembling breath and reached for the golden threads that still pulsed faintly at the edges of her awareness. Her work wasn't done. There were others who needed her, who still had a chance.

Leah's Lumarion

When Leah entered the Lumarion, the familiar warmth of her sanctuary enveloped her. The dreamscape hummed softly, the golden threads of the loom stretching across the room like constellations in a night sky. Each thread represented a connection, a life, a story yet to be completed. There was a strange tranquility in the air, but it was laced with an underlying tension, as if the threads themselves sensed the urgency of the time ahead.

The team had already returned from their weaving. Johan stood near the wall, arms crossed, his expression unreadable. Mina sat cross-legged on a cushion, quietly tracing invisible patterns with her fingers. Terry paced near the glowing map, thoughts spinning faster than he could speak. Their energy was low, drained from the dreamwork, but the sanctuary had already begun replenishing them—soft light threading into their limbs, offering calm in place of exhaustion.

At the edge of the room, Jasper sat alone. His eyes were distant, voice low and broken as he muttered to himself. The tether still bound him—Malik's influence winding through him like a shadowy current. A wave of sorrow spread through Leah's chest. Each time she reached for his thread, she felt the same thing: cold, tangled resistance. He wasn't free.

She stepped forward, and the room quieted. They turned toward her—not just with expectation, but trust. For all her uncertainty, their belief steadied her.

Johan broke the silence. "What happened out there?".

Leah hesitated. Her throat constricted.

"I lost them," she admitted, her voice barely above a whisper. "Aiden and Lila. Their thread snapped. I couldn't hold it."

The room fell silent, the weight of her words settling over them like a heavy fog. Each member of her team was quiet, absorbing the gravity of the moment. She could feel the collective weight of their empathy, their unspoken support.

Mina looked up from her cushion, her voice soft but insistent. "It's not your fault, Leah. You can't control every outcome. Sometimes people make choices you can't change."

Leah's eyes flickered with frustration. "But Malik can," she said, her voice hardening. "He's not just disrupting threads—he's using them to hurt people, to sever bonds that should endure. He's weaving something new... something wrong. And he's targeting us."

As Leah spoke, Jasper stirred, his muttering growing louder, his words disjointed. "He's not just hurting people," he said, his voice distant and fragmented. "He's weaving something new... something wrong."

Leah knelt in front of him, her heart aching as she took in the hollow look in his eyes. His expression was still clouded with Malik's influence, but a flicker of something stronger lingered beneath it—a reminder of who he had once been.

"Jasper, what are you seeing?" Leah asked gently, hoping for clarity in the storm of his fragmented thoughts.

Jasper blinked, his gaze shifting to meet hers. For a moment, clarity flickered in his expression. "He's... he's in the threads. He's looking for someone. Someone important. He won't stop until he finds her."

The words hit Leah like a tidal wave, their force knocking the breath from her lungs. Malik's obsession wasn't just about destroying connections—it was personal. The memories he had forced her to confront in the dreamscape—the song on the jukebox, the prison cell, the walk in the park—they all pointed to their shared history. And now, it was clear that his actions were tied to more than just revenge.

"Who, Jasper?" she pressed, her voice trembling with urgency. "Who is he looking for?"

Jasper's gaze dropped to his hands, his fingers curling into fists as the weight of his words settled in. "Jara... it's Jara."

Leah's breath caught in her throat. The name echoed in her mind like a whisper, a secret she had buried deep within herself. Jara. The daughter she had hidden to protect from Malik's reach. Her heart trembled as the realization hit: Malik had always known.

The room erupted into murmurs, the team exchanging worried glances as they pieced together the implications. Leah rose to her feet, her resolve hardening, the weight of this revelation driving her forward with an urgency she could no longer ignore.

Mina's voice broke through. "Who is Jara?"

Leah's hand brushed the Loomstaff. "She's, my daughter."

Gasps weren't needed. The silence said enough.

Johan stepped forward, the pieces clicking into place. "Then that's why Malik is so powerful... he's Veilborn." Leah turned to him, eyes steady. "No," she said quietly. "I am."

The weight of those words shifted the air. Mina blinked, searching Leah's face. "That's why I've always felt it. You weave differently. You see deeper."

Leah's shoulders dropped slightly. Vulnerability flickered across her face. "I've never spoken of it... not even to myself. My mother is Veilborn. The Loomstaff chose me before I understood what it meant."

Johan stepped closer, brows knit. "Why hide Jara?"

Leah hesitated, then faced the glowing threads in the room. "Because during Malik's rule in Diollo, he changed. The darkness began to consume him. He grew obsessed with bringing his father back from the severed. He wanted to rewrite pain—create a world where nothing could be lost." Her voice softened. "But Jara's power isn't about control. It's about balance. The Loom revealed glimpses of her future. My dreams warned me. If Malik ever reached her... if he wielded that power—"

Leah paused, her hand tightening around the loomstaff.

"Then reality itself unravels," Terry finished.

Leah nodded. "I had to hide her. I didn't tell anyone. Not even Jasper."

The sanctuary pulsed around them. The Loom vibrated at their feet, threads trembling with urgency. Mina took a breath. "Why tell us now?"

Leah looked around at the faces of her team—each one weathered, each one still standing.

"Because if I keep carrying this alone... Malik will win. I need you. And Jara... she'll need you too."

Mina reached out, gently placing a hand on Leah's arm. "Then we will be there for her. You're Veilborn—and that means we are too, in a way." She turned toward Terry. "Any luck with your tech yet?"

Terry stepped forward, "We need to disrupt his control over the threads. If he's using threads to track dreamers, we can create false patterns, lead him into a trap."

Johan nodded, his practical mind already formulating strategies. "And we'll need to strengthen our defenses. If he's targeting us directly, we need to be ready for anything."

Mina added, her tone calm but resolute, "And Leah, you'll need to face him. Not just in the dreamscape, but in the places where your threads cross. He's using your past against you. You need to reclaim it."

Leah's chest tightened, but she nodded. They were right. Malik wasn't just a threat to the dreamscape—he was a reflection of her own fears and failures. If she didn't confront him, he would continue to unravel everything she had worked to protect.

She turned to the glowing map, her fingers tracing the intricate patterns of the threads. The image of Malik was close now, his influence seeping into the threads that connected everything. "Then we start here," she said, her voice steady. "We strengthen the bonds we can, we create the distractions we need, and we face him together."

As the team rallied around her, Leah felt a flicker of hope. The battle ahead would be their hardest yet, but they weren't alone. Together, they would weave something stronger than Malik's chaos—a tapestry of connection, resilience, and strength.

The air in the sanctuary felt heavier as the team dispersed, their plans for Malik taking root in the tense silence. Leah lingered near the glowing threads, her fingers tracing their intricate patterns, each line carrying its own hum of emotion and urgency. Jasper sat quietly in the corner, still tethered to Malik in ways Leah couldn't yet unravel, his fragmented words a reminder of the danger lurking in both the dreamscape and their reality.

Her thoughts drifted to the threads glowing faintly in the center of the room, one vibrating with an unsettling rhythm. It called to her, not as a whisper but as a plea—a dream infused with desperation and longing. This thread was different, its energy chaotic and raw, tugging at a part of Leah she hadn't touched in years.

"Another one?" Mina asked softly, stepping up beside her.

Leah nodded, her gaze fixed on the thread. "This one feels... familiar," Leah murmured, the weight of recognition pressing against her chest.

Mina frowned, her brow furrowing. "Do you think it's another of Malik's traps?"

Leah hesitated before shaking her head. "No, this feels more personal. It's fractured, like a reflection caught in broken glass."

She turned to Mina, her resolve tightening. "I need to go. Whatever this is, it's important."

As the dreamscape began to form around her, Leah felt an eerie sense of déjà vu. The thread pulled her toward a distorted mirror world, its edges jagged and sharp. She could feel the dreamer's fear echoing in the fragmented landscape—a young girl trapped between the life she longed for and the reality she had abandoned.

With a final glance back at the sanctuary, Leah whispered, "I'll be back," before stepping fully into the dream, ready to guide another soul through the maze of their own making.

CHAPTER 14

STUCK IN THE MIRROR

The dreamscape shimmered into view, jagged and uneven like a cracked mirror reflecting a distorted reality. Leah stepped into the fragmented world, her senses heightened as she tried to anchor herself amidst the disarray. The ground beneath her shifted with every step, the glassy surface rippling as if alive, bending with the energy of the dreamer's turmoil. The air felt charged with emotion—raw, unfiltered, and intense.

Around her, broken shards of mirrors floated in the air, catching faint glimmers of light from an unseen source. The fractured landscape was as disorienting as it was beautiful—each piece reflecting a different reality, like a shattered truth never fully revealed. In the distance, Leah heard a voice, faint but unmistakable, carrying a raw edge of anguish.

"I didn't ask for this!" the voice cried out. "I just wanted to be better. I just wanted to be seen."

Leah recognized the pain that echoed in the voice. She followed the sound carefully, navigating the labyrinth of glass fragments. With every step, the tension in the air grew heavier, each shard seeming to tremble with the weight of the dreamer's emotions.

Soon, the voice became clearer, and Leah caught sight of her—Briana, a young girl standing in the distance, her hands covering her face. The fractured reflection around her was a kaleidoscope of shattered identities, each version of Briana more distorted than the last. In some, she was a young girl with a hopeful smile—in others, a woman worn by time and regrets. The shifting images painted a picture of a life torn between what was and what could never be.

Leah approached cautiously, her voice gentle but firm. "Briana, you're not alone. I'm here to help."

The girl turned, her face streaked with tears. Her eyes were wide, filled with fear and confusion. "I made a deal," she whispered, her voice breaking. "I wanted to grow up, to be everything I dreamed of being. But it's all wrong. Nothing feels real anymore."

The shards around them shifted, the reflections twisting into grotesque caricatures. Leah could see Briana's deepest fears and regrets etched into the glass—her longing for validation, her desperate escape from childhood, the weight of the consequences she now faced. The dreamscape itself was a battlefield of self-perception, each reflection an enemy to her sense of self.

"You thought you had to be perfect to be seen," Leah said, stepping closer, her presence steady as she reached out. "But what you see in these mirrors isn't who you are. It's who you think the world wants you to be."

Briana collapsed to her knees, the glass beneath her trembling. "I don't even know who I am anymore," she admitted, her voice breaking, her shoulders trembling with the burden of self-doubt.

Leah knelt beside her, her hand reaching for Briana's, offering warmth and reassurance. "You don't have to have it all figured out," she said softly. "What matters is that you accept who you are, flaws and all."

The ground shifted beneath them, the air growing heavy with a new presence. The light dimmed, and the shards of glass began to reflect something darker. Leah's breath caught as Malik's voice filled the dreamscape, a low, mocking echo that sent a shiver down her spine.

"Still playing the hero, Leah?" he taunted, his presence almost tangible. "You can't save everyone."

Before Leah could respond, the mirrors around her shattered, their fragments spinning into a vortex that pulled her backward. She fought against the force, gripping the loomstaff tightly. It pulsed in her hand, its light cutting through the darkness and anchoring her to the dreamscape.

"Mina?" Leah whispered, her heart sinking as a new thread vibrated violently in the distance.

The dreamscape shifted again, and Leah found herself in a new section of the maze. The mirrors reflected not Briana, but someone else—Mina. Leah stood frozen, her eyes wide with fear as the shards around her showed not her reflection but her darkest memories: moments of failure, rejection, and loss.

She saw Kaelith's outstretched hand slipping from hers, his scream echoing through the nightmare realm as the shadows swallowed him whole—her fingers too slow, her strength not enough. Another shard revealed a younger Leah standing before the inner circle of Dreamweavers in Diollo, her violet eyes filled with hope—only to be met with cold silence and averted gazes. They had whispered that she was unnatural, her presence unsettling, her power too wild. And then came Auren Tahl, her mentor, trembling in a storm of nightmares, his tether nearly severed after sacrificing himself to save Leah from a corrupted dream. She had pulled him back at the last moment, but the price was forever etched into the lines of his aging face.

"You think you're strong," Malik's voice hissed from the mirrors, his figure appearing in the reflections. "But even the strongest break when faced with the truth."

Mina's breaths came in shallow gasps as the mirrors began to close in around her. The glass seemed to vibrate with Malik's influence, the reflections warping, distorting. Leah could feel the threads of the dreamscape tightening, Malik's power weaving a prison designed to trap Mina in her own fear.

Leah ran toward Mina, her heart pounding as the mirrors crept closer. "Mina! Listen to me!" she called, her voice filled with urgency. "What happen!"

Mina turned toward her, tears streaming down her face, her expression a mixture of defeat and fear. "I tried... I tried but couldn't defeat him, Leah. It's too much."

"You don't have to face it alone," Leah said, her voice steady despite the chaos around them. "But you can't let Malik control you. These memories—they don't define you."

The mirrors closed in, their jagged edges reflecting Malik's sinister grin, each shard a reminder of past hurts. Leah gripped the loomstaff, and it pulsed brighter, its energy coursing through her. A stream of golden threads shot outward, forming a protective barrier around Mina. The threads vibrated with energy, pushing the mirrors back.

The loomstaff seemed to move of its own accord, weaving threads into the shattered fragments. Malik's hold weakened, his figure flickering in the reflections. Leah lunged forward, her hand breaking through the vortex of glass to grab Mina's. The connection sent a surge of energy through the dreamscape, and the mirrors exploded outward. Their fragments dissolved into light, and Malik's shadow loomed for a moment longer before fading, his laughter echoing as he disappeared.

Mina collapsed into Leah's arms, her body trembling with the release of pent-up emotion. "Thank you," she whispered, her voice raw with vulnerability.

Leah held her tightly, her own heart pounding in response. "How did you get here?" Leah said, "I thought I could sever the connection in the threads." Leah with a tight grip, "You're stronger than you think, Mina. Don't let him make you forget that."

The loomstaff dimmed, its threads retracting but leaving a faint glow in its wake. Mina glanced at it, her expression a mix of awe and curiosity. "We never see it in action, she uttered."

Leah calm, her fingers brushing the intricate carvings on the staff. "Lux Veritas, is magical, she said softly. Sometimes I feel is not me wielding it, but it is wielding me. We can't deviate from the plan, Mina.

Mina raised an eyebrow, a hint of a smile tugging at her lips. "And I'm glad it chose you?"

Leah still holding Mina and the loomstaff, "It's as much a mystery to me as it is to you."

Mina's gaze lingered on the staff, a glimmer of respect in her eyes. "Whatever it is, it's powerful."

Leah smiled faintly, the weight of their shared victory settling in her chest. "Powerful, yes. But power isn't enough. It's how we use it that matters."

Leah turned back to find Briana, who had watched the scene unfold with wide eyes. Her reflection had stabilized, the distortions fading into a single, clear image. Briana's face was no longer clouded by confusion and fear; instead, it radiated a quiet, newfound strength.

"I don't want to be afraid anymore," Briana said, her voice steady, her eyes bright with clarity.

Leah nodded. "Then take the first step. Accept who you are—flaws and all."

Briana reached out to touch her reflection, and as her fingers met the glass, the dreamscape began to glow. The maze dissolved, replaced by a calm, open field bathed in golden light. Briana's thread grew steady and bright, its once-frayed edges mending.

Leah smiled, a sense of peace settling over her as Briana's thread solidified. "You'll be okay," she said softly.

Briana nodded, her figure fading as the dreamscape closed.

As the shimmering portal closed behind them, sealing the path from the dreamscape, Leah stood at the center of the sanctuary with a weakened Mina resting on the crystalline floor. Johan and Terry followed closely, stepping through with the quiet weight of battle still clinging to them. The tension of Malik's presence lingered in the air, but a renewed sense of determination settled among them. They had faced the darkness together—and it had only strengthened their bond.

"We're getting closer," Leah said, her gaze distant as she surveyed the threads around them. "But so is he. We can't let our guard down."

Mina placed a hand on Leah's shoulder, a comforting gesture that grounded her. "We'll face him together."

Leah nodded, her focus shifting to the loomstaff resting nearby. Its glow had faded, but its presence was a quiet reassurance—a reminder of the strength they would need for the battles ahead.

As she prepared to step into the next dream, Leah allowed herself a moment of reflection. The journey was far from over, but the lessons of strength and self-awareness would guide her in the challenges to come.

Leah's Velara Aelis

The Lumarion around me feels like a tapestry, each golden thread a life, a story, a connection waiting to be woven. I have walked through the dreams of others—dreams teeming with resilience, courage, and self-awareness—and in each one, I see reflections not only of their struggles but also of the fractures within myself. The weight of these experiences presses heavily on my chest, and yet, it is this very weight that reminds me of my purpose.

In the threads of a storm-tossed sea, I saw the strength it takes to rise above division. I watched people struggle against the currents of their differences, their fears blinding them to the unity they desperately needed. Resilience is not born of isolation; it is forged in the moments when we choose to reach for each other, even when the waters are rough. It is in those brief, fleeting gestures of connection that we find our strength. And I carry this lesson with me, reminding myself that the connections I weave are not just for others but for myself as well. The world of dreams is vast and treacherous, and without the unity of my team—Mina, Johan, Terry, and even Jasper—I wouldn't have the strength to continue. They are the fibers woven alongside mine, holding me steady when the storm rages.

In the moments when fear looms largest, courage often takes the form of a quiet step forward. I've witnessed people stand on the precipice of their darkest truths, trembling but unyielding. The courage to face what lies within, to confront the parts of ourselves we wish to hide, is no less than heroic. But even as I guide others to find their strength, I am haunted by my own fears. Malik knows this. His presence lingers in the shadows of every dream, his words cutting into the parts of me I've tried to protect. I fear what he sees in me—the doubts, the hesitations, the self-imposed walls. Yet courage is not the absence of fear; it is the resolve to move forward despite it, to choose action even when uncertainty gnaws at my heart.

Discipline is a quiet, steady force. It is not the loud triumph of a climactic battle but the consistent effort of showing up, day after day, even when the results are unseen. I've learned this through the threads I've woven, where the temptation to interfere is strong but must be resisted. There are times when the urge to fix things, to shape lives into the way I wish them to be, threatens to overwhelm me. But I've had to accept that not every connection can be saved, not every story can have a happy ending. To guide is not to control, and the discipline of letting go is one of the hardest lessons I've had to learn. It is a reminder that the threads of fate are not mine to hold but only to mend when they fray. I cannot manipulate the course of others' journeys; I can only offer them the space to find their way, as imperfect and unruly as that may be.

The chaos of life often demands immediate action, but I've found that true strength lies in patience. It's in the waiting, the watching, and the quiet understanding that not all solutions come quickly. Patience is the wisdom to know when to act and when to let time do its work. I've seen how patience can transform a chaotic storm into a calm sea. It has taught me that rushing to fix every problem often creates new ones, that forcing a solution can sometimes fracture what was whole. Instead, I must trust in the natural rhythm of the threads, allowing them to weave themselves at their own pace. In the stillness, I find the clarity I need to move forward.

The bonds we form are fragile, held together by threads of trust and honesty. When those threads fray, the connection weakens. I've seen what happens when integrity is lost, when mistrust and deception seep into the spaces where love and loyalty once thrived. Malik thrives on these fractures, feeding on the doubts and fears that unravel connections. He has turned my own past against me, using memories I thought were buried to disrupt the present. But integrity is not about perfection; it's about authenticity. It's about standing firm in who we are, even when the world around us shakes. It's the courage to be vulnerable, to show up as we are, not as we think the world wants us to be. And in that authenticity, we find the strength to rebuild what has been broken.

In the fractured reflections of a dream, I saw a young girl struggle to recognize herself. Her pain was raw, her fear palpable, as she confronted the version of herself, she thought the world wanted to see. It was a reminder that self-awareness is not about self-criticism but about self-compassion. It's easy to get lost in the mirrors of expectation, to measure ourselves against others, to believe the lies we tell ourselves about who we should be. But self-awareness is about facing our truth without judgment. I've avoided looking into my own mirrors, afraid of what I might find. Malik has forced me to confront these fears, to see the parts of myself I'd rather keep hidden. But in doing so, he has unintentionally strengthened me. Self-awareness is a powerful tool, one that allows us to embrace our flaws and move forward with clarity. And so, I must look into my own reflection, not with shame, but with acceptance.

Through all these journeys, one truth remains constant: we are bound together by threads of connection. These threads are delicate yet resilient, capable of withstanding even the greatest storms when nurtured with care. The people I've guided, the lives I've touched, have taught me as much as I've taught them. In helping them face their fears, I have learned to face my own. But Malik's shadow grows darker, his grip on the threads tightening with each passing moment. He seeks not just to disrupt but to sever, to destroy the very fabric of connection. And as much as I fight to protect others, I know the battle is deeply personal. The threads he pulls are not random—they are tied to me, to my past, and to the one connection I've kept hidden for so long.

I can no longer avoid the truth. The threads are pulling me toward a revelation I've feared for years. Malik's obsession isn't just about power—it's about Jara. My velana. His daughter. The words are heavy in my mind, as though they've been waiting to surface. Jara, the child I've kept hidden from him, the connection I've buried to protect her from his darkness. His rage, his chaos—it all leads back to her. Not just as a tool for his control but as a reminder of the bond we once shared, a bond fractured beyond repair.

I've spent years weaving threads for others, guiding them to confront their fears, their pain, their truths. Yet I've avoided my own, afraid of what it would mean to face him again—not as a Dreamweaver but as a mother, as the woman who loved him once and lost herself in the process. But the time for hiding is over. If I am to face Malik, I must confront the secrets I've kept, the lies I've told myself to justify the distance. Jara is not just a connection to him; she is the reason I fight, the light that keeps me weaving when the threads grow dark. She is my hope, my legacy, and the one truth I can no longer keep buried.

As the sanctuary quiets, the threads around me pulse with a gentle rhythm, their glow a reminder of the strength that lies within connection. The journey through these dreams has tested every fiber of my being, but it has also illuminated the path ahead. I rise, my resolve firm, and prepare to reflect on the lessons of this journey. Weaving this tapestry has shown me that strength is not just in the victories but in the struggles, in the moments when we choose to continue despite the weight of our burdens. And as I prepare to face what lies ahead, I carry these lessons with me, woven into the very fabric of who I am.

The threads hum softly, guiding me toward the next step in this journey—a reflection not just of what has been but of what is yet to come.

CHAPTER 15

HEALING HANDS

The operating room stretched into an endless expanse, its fluorescent lights dimmed and flickering, the edges of the room dissipating into a shadowy abyss. The sterile white walls seemed to fold in on themselves, as if the space was unwilling to contain the weight of the moment. Caleb stood over the surgical table, the scalpel trembling in his hand. His chest rose and fell with uneven breaths as he looked down at his patient. The boy's body flickered, shifting between forms—a young child, a vague shadow, a flicker of his face. Then nothing at all—just a void where a living, breathing soul should have been.

And behind him, a presence. Heavy. Suffocating. A figure who had always loomed over him: his father, Dr. Everett Hensley.

"You're failing, Caleb," his father's voice rang out, sharp as a scalpel's edge. "You'll lose him, just like you lose everyone who counts on you."

"I can't... I won't," Caleb muttered, but the tremor in his hand betrayed his words. The scalpel slipped from his grip, clattering against the floor as his father stepped closer, his looming shadow stretching long across the room.

"You're weak," Dr. Hensley continued, his voice a venomous whisper, each word landing like a weight on Caleb's chest. "You think you have the strength to carry this legacy? You're not me, Caleb. You'll never be me."

Caleb's hands shook as he fought the knot of panic rising in his throat. He couldn't breathe, couldn't think, couldn't do anything but watch the crumbling remains of the moment unravel before him.

Across town, Terry sat in the dim light of his workshop, his laptop left open and forgotten. The words of the email he'd received hours earlier echoed in his mind: his nephew, Lucas, was in the hospital, suffering from a life-threatening injury. He hadn't been able to reply, the weight of guilt and regret preventing him from even finding the words.

"I should've been there," Terry whispered to no one in particular, his fists gripping the edge of his desk as frustration and helplessness washed over him. The room felt heavy with the pull of Malik's influence, the familiar darkness suffocating the air.

"You can't save him. Not now, not ever," Malik's voice whispered in his ear, chilling his spine.

Terry's fists clenched tighter, a surge of anger rising to the surface. The guilt, the regret, the crushing sense of failure—it all built inside him like a storm about to break.

Leah stood at the edges of both worlds, sensing the chaos that had begun to weave itself into Caleb's dreamscape. She felt the weight of Malik's influence wrapping itself around Terry, pulling the two dreamers into a dangerous spiral, each one feeding into the other's fears and insecurities.

With a deep breath, Leah entered Caleb's dream, stepping into the sterile, fractured operating room. The air was thick, heavy with unspoken doubts and an overwhelming sense of suffocating pressure. Caleb stood frozen at the center of the room, the scalpel slipping from his hand as Malik's shadow grew larger behind him, like a storm on the horizon.

"You'll lose him," Malik's voice taunted from the darkness, a venomous hiss. "You were never strong enough."

"No!" Caleb cried out, his voice breaking with desperation. "I can't lose him."

Leah's presence cut through the tension like a soft wind through the dark. "Caleb, focus. You don't have to be perfect to save him. You just must try."

Caleb turned, his eyes wide with confusion, panic still gripping him. "Who are you? Why are you here?"

Leah stepped closer, her voice a steady, calm anchor in the swirling chaos. "I'm here to remind you of your purpose. You're not here to prove anything to anyone, least of all your father. You're here because you care. You want to help."

As the shadow of doubt began to recede, the sterile operating room shifted. The walls melted into something more peaceful—lush gardens, golden sunlight filtering through the leaves of towering trees. But just as quickly as it had arrived, the tranquility began to fade. The air grew cold again, and the garden twisted.

Suddenly, the darkness thickened, and Malik appeared, his figure materializing with an unsettling stillness. He dragged Terry into the scene, his pale face twisted with fear and rage. The stark contrast between Terry's open vulnerability and Malik's cold, consuming presence was jarring.

"Let him go!" Leah shouted, stepping between Malik and Terry, her voice resolute.

Malik's sneer deepened, his voice dripping with malice. "You think you can save him? He's already mine. His anger, his guilt—they're my tools, and I wield them well."

Terry's hands were clenched, his body rigid with anger. "You don't understand. I failed him. I wasn't there when it mattered."

"And now you think you can fix it?" Malik taunted. "Go ahead. Try. See how far your so-called strength takes you."

Before Terry could react, Johan's calm, steady presence appeared at his side. "Terry, focus. This isn't the way."

Leah reached out, her fingers glowing faintly as she grasped Terry's thread, guiding him back from the brink. "Terry, listen to me. Your nephew doesn't need your guilt. He needs your love, your support. You can't change the past, but you can fight for the future."

Terry hesitated, the storm within him slowly quieting. The shadows around him wavered, and Malik's sneer faltered. The darkness began to recede, the tension lightening.

Malik retreats into the shadows.

With his departure, the dreamscape began to shift. The garden bloomed into full color, the air light and warm. Terry woke, gasping for air, the oppressive weight of Malik's presence lifting from his chest. He sat in his workshop, his trembling hands now steady as he looked at the email on his screen. For the first time, he felt the courage to reply.

At the hospital, Caleb stood over Lucas in the operating room. His hands were steady, his mind clear, as the surgery was a success. The boy's life was saved, and as Lucas's parents thanked him, tears in their eyes, Caleb felt the heavy weight of his father's judgment begin to lift.

Back in the sanctuary, Leah and her team gathered around the glowing threads of the loom. Terry sat quietly, his hands trembling but his resolve firm.

"I almost gave in," he admitted, his voice raw.

Johan placed a reassuring hand on Terry's shoulder. "But you didn't. That's what matters."

Leah's gaze turned toward the threads before her, her brow furrowed in thought. "Malik's influence is growing stronger. If we don't act soon, we won't just lose the dreamscape—we'll lose everything."

The room fell silent, the weight of her words settling over them. Leah realized the scope of the battle ahead. Malik wasn't just a threat to the dreamscape; he was a threat to their very existence.

"Then we'll stop him," Terry said, his voice steady. "Together."

Leah nodded, "Together."

As the team gathered their strength, Leah felt the hum of the threads around her, the delicate weave of purpose and tenacity growing tighter. There was no turning back now. The time for hesitation had passed. Malik was no longer a distant figure in the shadows—he was a threat they would face head-on. Together, they would face him, and together, they would find the strength to keep going.

With the loomstaff at her side, Leah took a steadying breath, her mind focused and clear. The battle was far from over, but she knew now, more than ever, that she wasn't alone. She had her team, and they were ready. They would walk together.

Leah's Lumarion

The sanctuary was a quiet symphony, the gentle hum of golden threads weaving through the Leah's ancestry tapestry like a living organism. Leah stood at its center, her fingers grazing the luminous strands that connected countless lives, each one pulsing with its own unique rhythm. She closed her eyes for a moment, letting the warmth of the threads fill her senses. Each pulse was like a heartbeat, a melody, a memory. The weight of the lives she had touched and the battles ahead pressed down on her shoulders. The world they were fighting for, the dreamscape and the fragile ties binding all souls, felt both impossibly vast and intimately close.

Her team had begun to recover, but the scars from their recent battles remained—quiet echoes of the struggle they had endured. Malik's presence had grown stronger, his reach now extending beyond the dreamscape into the Lumarion. The weight of this new threat was unbearable, gnawing at the edges of her resolve. Could they truly face him and win? The question lingered like an unspoken fear.

In the corner of the sanctuary, Jasper sat hunched over, his hands trembling slightly as he fidgeted with a glowing strand. His once-vibrant eyes were clouded, as if trapped in a fog, disconnected from the present. He was physically there, but his mind seemed distant, tethered to something darker. To Malik's shadow.

Leah's footsteps were soft, almost imperceptible as she approached him. She knelt beside him, placing a hand gently over his, feeling the faint pulse of the thread beneath her fingers. "Jasper," she said softly, her voice breaking through the heavy silence. "How are you feeling today?"

Jasper didn't meet her gaze, his fingers still curling around the thread as he murmured, "He's always there. Watching. Waiting. I can feel him, Leah." He looked up then, frustration flickering in his eyes.

"There are no breadcrumbs. No symbols. No whispers. It's like he's hiding from me."

Leah's breath catching in her throat. Without Jasper's glimpses, they had no way of finding Malik's anchor—and time was running out.

She placed her other hand over his, feeling the tremor in his fingers—a mirror of the fear that had taken root deep within him. "You're safe here," she said, her words infused with as much reassurance as she could muster. "He can't touch you in the sanctuary."

Jasper's head tilted slightly, and his eyes flickered toward her, still distant, but with a momentary spark of clarity. "But he knows," he whispered, barely audible. "He knows about Jara."

Leah's heart skipped a beat. The weight of the words fell on her like a crushing force, and she didn't need to ask who Jasper meant. Malik's obsession with Jara, her hidden daughter, had become a festering wound in their fight. Every step Leah took to protect her seemed to draw Malik closer, pulling him to the edges of a truth she had spent years trying to shield.

"Jasper," Leah said, her grip firming around his hand. "You have to fight. I need you with us."

His eyes, clouded with fear and doubt, finally met hers. His voice was soft, trembling. "I'm trying. But it's like... he's in my thoughts. I don't know what's real anymore."

Leah squeezed his hand tighter, sending as much strength as she could into him. "You are real. We are real. And together, we'll fight this. You don't have to do it alone."

On the other side of the sanctuary, Mina and Terry were engaged in quiet conversation. Mina's expression was intense, her hands moving in animated gestures, trying to convey a vision that only she could see. Terry, leaning against one of the glowing pillars, nodded in agreement, his face calm but steadfast.

Leah joined them, her presence pulling their attention toward her. Mina's smile was faint but present, though it didn't quite reach her eyes. "We're ready," Mina said, her tone firm, but there was an underlying exhaustion in her voice. "Whatever comes next, we're ready to face it."

Terry crossed his arms, his gaze steady. "I'm not letting Malik win. Not after what he's done."

Leah studied them both, feeling the quiet power that had bloomed in them over the course of their journey. Mina, once sharp-edged and unyielding, now carried a vulnerability that had softened her, giving her a quiet strength that was deeply rooted. Terry, too, had changed. The guilt that had once consumed him had been replaced by something stronger: a fierce determination to protect those he loved.

"I'm proud of you both," Leah said sincerely, her voice heavy with gratitude. "We've been through so much, and yet, you're still here, still fighting."

Mina's smile widened slightly. "We're not done yet."

Terry nodded. "Malik's not going to stop unless we stop him."

Leah nodded, her thoughts racing. She turned to the loom, eyes scanning the shifting threads in search of answers. But doubt crept in, soft and unwelcome—was the Loom's guidance slipping from her grasp? The fear stirred beneath her ribs. Then, from across the sanctuary, she heard Johan's voice—frustrated and low. She paused, then moved to check on him.

Johan was at the edge of the sanctuary, his focus so intense that he didn't notice Leah's approach. His hands were moving rapidly, weaving at a fragment of the dreamscape that shimmered and flickered unnaturally, unable to hold its form. The strands twisted and broke under his touch, their rhythm disrupted, their power unraveling with every effort.

"Johan," Leah called gently, stepping closer to him. "What's wrong?"

He didn't stop weaving, his movements growing more erratic with each passing moment. "It's not working," he muttered, frustration evident in his voice. "This thread won't let me enter. Every time I try to, it falls apart."

Leah stepped closer, placing a hand on his shoulder. "Take a breath," she said softly. "What are you trying to weave?"

Johan exhaled sharply, his hands pausing for a moment, but then starting again. "It's the next dream," he admitted, his voice low. "The boy, Sam, in Vegas. His pain—his grief—it's overwhelming. Malik's influence... it's everywhere. I can feel him in the threads, twisting them. I don't know how to block him out."

Leah's heart sank at the sound of Johan's admission. He had always been the solid rock of their team, the one who could hold the dreamscape steady no matter how fierce the storm. Seeing him falter—seeing him doubt himself—was a sharp reminder of just how powerful Malik had become.

"You don't have to do this alone," Leah reminded him softly. "We're a team. Let me help you."

Johan's frustration was clear in the tightness of his jaw and the tenseness in his posture. "I've never had trouble weaving before. But this... it's like Malik is inside my head."

Leah knelt beside him, her hand still on his shoulder, grounding him with the weight of her presence. "He wants you to feel this way. He wants you to doubt yourself. But you're stronger than his influence, Johan. We all are."

Johan finally looked up at her, his tension easing slightly. "I don't know if I can do this," he admitted quietly.

"You can," Leah said firmly. "And you will. We'll face this together, just like we always do."

The team gathered around the central threads of the sanctuary, the energy in the room shifting. Jasper remained quiet, his gaze distant and lost, while Mina and Terry exchanged uneasy glances. Johan sat beside Leah, his hands resting on his knees as he attempted to steady himself, finding a semblance of focus amidst the swirling chaos of the dreamscape.

Mina drew in a slow breath, steadying herself. "Leah, we need to talk about severing Malik's anchor," she said, her voice calm but carrying the weight of everything left unspoken. "He's getting stronger. His reach is stretching beyond the dreamscape—we've all felt it." She paused, then added gently, "There was light in him once, but the shadows have taken hold. You have to let him go."

Terry nodded grimly. "He's not just influencing dreams anymore. He's found a way to manipulate the awakened dreamer's world. If we don't stop him soon..." His voice trailed off, the weight of the reality settling over them.

Leah gaze shifted to Jasper, who sat in silence. "The symbols are gone," she said quietly. "Whatever Malik's doing... it's blocking our path through the loom. Severing his anchor might not work—not if we can't find it."

She hesitated, the words heavy on her tongue.

"But maybe... if I get close enough to him, I might be able to unravel the connection from within."

Her eyes met theirs, steady but shaded with fear. "If I do, it could sever more than just Malik. It could sever me. And Jasper."

Silence followed. The weight of her words hung heavy in the air. Then

Leah's voice softened, almost a whisper as she looked toward the threads.

"That's why we must hold the line. We're the only ones who can stop him. But if we fail..."

She glanced at Jasper, pain flickering across her features. "We could lose him."

Jasper stirred, leaning forward with effort, each movement slow, strained. But when he spoke, his voice was clear.

"Then let it be me." He met Leah's eyes, weary but unwavering. "If that's what it takes... I'll make that choice."

Leah's gaze snapped to him, her expression tightening. "I won't risk losing you again. What if I can't let go of the thread?"

Jasper form flickered, his voice unwavering. "That the risk I'm willing to take. As long as I'm tethered to Malik, we're exposed—Jara's exposed. Everything we know is in danger: our home, Queen Selene, Auren Tahl... all of it."

Leah reached for his arm, but her hand passed through him—his form too unstable, too far gone. Her breath caught as she gazed into Jasper's flickering eyes, searching for the friend she still believed was in there.

"Then I'll do it," she whispered, her voice steady despite the ache in her chest. "I won't lose you. I can save us. I have too."

She turned back to the team. "Once Jasper is free, we focus on strengthening the dreamscape. Malik is using our own threads against us. If we can reinforce them, we might be able to push him back."

"And what about the next dream?" Johan asked quietly. "What about Vegas?" Leah met his gaze, "We'll weave it together. One step at a time."

She turned to Mina. "Keep an on eye on him and watch our thread. If anything changes, I need to know." Then to Terry. "And you keep working on tracking Malik's anchor. Even the faintest thread might be enough."

As the sanctuary began to fade, Leah felt a flicker of unease. The threads were shifting again, their rhythms uneven. Malik's influence was spreading faster than she had anticipated.

"Let's move," Leah said, her voice steady but urgent. "The next dream is waiting. And so is he."

And with that, Leah stepped forward, her heart beating in sync with the threads that pulsed beneath her fingertips, her determination steady. She and Johan would face whatever came next.

CHAPTER 16

THE LAST VEGAS

The neon lights of Las Vegas stretched endlessly across the horizon, painting the night sky with fractured streaks of color. The city was alive, but it wasn't the same Vegas of old—it had become a distorted version of itself. The Strip, once known for its glitzy glamour and excess, now held an eerie quality. Towering skyscrapers loomed over the streets, and shadowy alleys twisted between them like dark veins. Billboards, their faces fractured and warped, loomed over the crowds, their hollow eyes watching the masses with a predatory gaze.

In the heart of this chaos, Daniel "Rook" Vegas walked with purpose. His duster billowed in the night air as he gripped his katana, its polished blade gleaming under the harsh glow of the neon lights. A man once defined by peace and simplicity, Rook had become something darker—an avenger, a weapon forged in the fires of loss. The man who had once tended cattle on the open plains had become a cold, calculating figure, driven by the need to avenge the death of his brother, Lucas.

The air around him was thick with tension as he neared the Vega Casino, its cracked facade looming like a broken monument to the past. The iconic neon sign flickered ominously, casting shadows that seemed to stretch endlessly. This was the place, the place where everything had changed, where Lucas had been taken from him.

Leah stepped into the dreamscape, her presence blending seamlessly with the chaotic energy of the city. She could feel the threads of this world—twisting, warping, and pulling in every direction. It was different from the dreamscape she was used to. Malik's influence was palpable here, a malignant force seeping into every corner of the world. Leah could sense his shadow hanging over everything. But it wasn't just Malik's control she felt—it was Rook's deep sorrow and anger, threads pulled so tightly by grief that they threatened to snap at any moment.

She followed Rook silently, her steps careful as she observed the flickering golden thread that bound him. It pulsed weakly, weighed down by shadows of guilt and rage. She could see the fractures in his resolve, the cracks that Malik sought to exploit. Leah knew she couldn't let him fall into that trap. She had to act before it was too late.

Rook stopped at the entrance of the casino, his hand resting on the hilt of his katana. His face was hard, a mask of determination that barely hid the pain beneath. But Leah could see it, the doubt creeping into his eyes.

"You don't have to do this," Leah said softly, stepping into his line of sight.

Rook's eyes narrowed, and his hand tightened around the hilt of his sword. "Who are you?" His voice was sharp, a mix of suspicion and fury. "Another one of them?"

"No," Leah replied, her tone calm but firm. "I'm here to help you."

The dreamscape shifted, swirling around them as the chaotic city continued its constant hum. Inside the casino, the familiar hum of machines was replaced by an eerie silence. The slot machines were cracked, their screens flickering with distorted images of Lucas's face, his eyes wide in a moment of terror. The roulette wheels spun endlessly, but the numbers bled into one another, becoming a blur of confusion and loss.

At the center of the room stood Malik, his form shrouded in darkness. He held a deck of cards, shuffling them with slow, deliberate precision. His smile was predatory, a sharp contrast to the chaos around him. "Ah, Daniel Vegas," Malik drawled, his voice a low rumble of mockery. "The cowboy turned assassin. Come to settle your score, have you?"

Rook's muscles tensed, his grip tightening on his katana. "You know why I'm here," he spat, his voice filled with barely contained rage. "You took him from me."

Malik chuckled, a cold, hollow sound that echoed through the casino. "Did I? Or did you?" He held up a card, the Ace of Spades, and Rook's heart lurched as he saw Lucas's face reflected on its surface. "It was your inaction that led to his death, wasn't it? Your hesitation."

Rook's knuckles turned white as his grip on the katana tightened further. "Shut up."

Leah stepped forward, positioning herself between Rook and Malik. Her presence was firm, her voice calm but filled with authority. "Don't listen to him," she said, her words like a thread weaving through the tension. "He's twisting the truth."

Malik's eyes flickered with disdain as he turned his gaze to Leah. His smile widened, a malicious grin that sent a shiver down her spine. "Ah, Leah Cimaj. Always meddling, always weaving," he sneered. He took a step closer, his shadow stretching toward her like a dark cloud. "But you can't save him. He's mine now."

The room darkened, the lights flickering as Malik's presence grew stronger. The shadows around Rook began to move, taking on the shapes of faceless figures—echoes of every life he had taken in his quest for vengeance. Each shadow was a reminder of the blood on his hands, the guilt that had driven him to become the man he was now.

"Look at them," Malik whispered, his voice wrapping around Rook like a vice. "They're your legacy. Blood and regret. You think avenging your brother will erase this?"

Rook faltered, his katana lowering slightly. His breath hitched, and his voice trembled with self-doubt. "I didn't have a choice," he muttered, the weight of his past catching up with him.

Leah stepped closer to him, her hand outstretched, her voice soft but firm. "You always have a choice," she said, her words a lifeline in the storm. "Your brother wouldn't want this for you. He wouldn't want you to lose yourself."

Rook turned to her, his eyes filled with doubt. "How would you know? You didn't know him."

"No," Leah admitted, her voice steady despite the turbulence of the dream around them. "But I know what it's like to lose someone. And I know what it's like to let that loss consume you. It doesn't bring them back. It only takes more from you."

Her words cut through the layers of grief and rage that had clouded Rook's mind. For the first time, his grip on his katana loosened, the tension in his shoulders easing.

Malik's laughter echoed, dark and mocking. "Touching," he sneered. "But it's too late for him. He's already chosen his path."

The room seemed to tremble as the shadows around Malik coalesced into a monstrous form, towering over them. Its eyes burned with hatred, its claws gleaming in the dim light. The creature's presence filled the room with an oppressive weight, its very existence a reminder of the destruction Malik sought to unleash.

Leah stood her ground, her hands glowing as she reached for the threads of the dreamscape. "This isn't your place, Malik," she said, her voice steady and filled with unwavering resolve. "You don't control him."

Malik's smile faltered for the briefest moment, his expression darkening as he stepped forward, his shadow growing larger. "You can't stop me, Leah. Not here."

The shadow lunged toward Rook, its claws extended to strike him down. But before it could reach him, Rook raised his katana, and Leah extended her glowing hands, her strength pushing against the creature. Together, they pushed the shadow back, their combined power breaking Malik's control over the dreamscape.

The casino trembled as the walls cracked and splintered. Malik's form flickered, his grip on the dream weakening. His expression twisted into a snarl as he began to disband into the darkness.

The dreamscape shifted, the crumbling casino fading away and being replaced by the soft, golden light of a desert sunrise. Rook stood beside Leah on a quiet hill, his katana gone. Instead, he wore a simple lasso at his side, a symbol of the man he had once been before the darkness had consumed him.

"Thank you," Rook said quietly, his voice thick with emotion. "You showed me the way back."

Leah smiled faintly, her heart filled with both sadness and pride. "Your brother would be proud of you," she said softly.

Rook nodded, his gaze distant but softer than before. "Maybe it's time I start living for him, instead of chasing ghosts."

Leah placed a hand on his shoulder. "That's the first step."

Back in the sanctuary, Leah and her team regrouped. Johan's face was pale, his hands trembling slightly.

"I couldn't hold the weave," he admitted, his voice low. "Malik was too strong."

Leah placed a reassuring hand on his arm. "We're not done yet. He's growing stronger, but so are we. We can do this."

The team nodded, their resolve solidifying. The battle ahead would be their greatest yet, but they were ready to face it—together.

As the group began to prepare for their next move, Leah lingered by Johan, sensing a heaviness in his quiet demeanor. The weight of failure, of uncertainty, still clung to him like a shadow. She placed a gentle hand on his shoulder, offering him silent support before speaking.

"Johan, have you ever walked among the waking world?" she asked softly, her eyes searching his.

Johan's gaze flickered, and for a moment, he seemed to consider the question, as if the very idea was something foreign to him. "No," he said finally, his voice tinged with quiet wonder. "I've always stayed in the dreamscape. I've never crossed over into the waking world."

Leah nodded thoughtfully, sensing the weight of his unspoken thoughts. "I can understand why," she said, her voice gentle. "The dreamscape is where we've always been—where we can control the flow of time, of events. It's our domain, our place of power."

Johan looked at her, his brow furrowing slightly. "But why ask now?"

Leah took a deep breath, stepping closer to him. "Because there's something I've learned. Something I'm still learning. Time, Johan—it works differently here in the dreamscape. Here, we can weave through the lives of countless dreamers, changing moments in an instant. But the waking world—it's different. It's real. It's bound by time in a way we can't manipulate. And in that, there's a strange kind of beauty."

Johan raised an eyebrow, curiosity flickering in his eyes. "What do you mean?"

Leah smiled faintly, the wisdom of her journey weighing heavily on her as she spoke. "In the dreamscape, everything happens so quickly—each moment feels fleeting, yet we can see the ripple effects of our actions without truly feeling the passage of time. We can fix things almost instantaneously. But in the waking world, it's different. Time moves at its own pace. The seconds stretch out like hours. Decisions weigh more because we can't undo them as easily."

Her gaze softened as she looked out at the room where the team was gathered, preparing for the battles ahead. "The paradox, Johan, is that time in the waking world moves so slowly, but it's in that slowness that we find meaning. The choices we make, the connections we form—they take time to build. And when we lose someone, that loss is more real, more lasting, because we can't rewind the clock. But even in that, there's power. It forces us to live fully, to take every moment seriously, because those moments are all we truly have."

Johan stood quietly, absorbing her words. He seemed to lose himself in thought for a moment, then nodded slowly, the tension in his shoulders easing ever so slightly.

"I've never thought of it that way," he said, his voice thoughtful. "I've always been so focused on what I can change, what I can control. But you're right. The waking world... it moves at its own pace, and sometimes, the act of waiting, of letting things unfold in their own time—that's where the real work happens."

Leah smiled, the weight in her chest lightening. "Exactly. It's in the waiting, Johan. It's in the moments when we can't rush things, when we must let them unfold at their own pace, that we find the strength to endure. We can't always fix everything instantly. But in the waking world, even when time seems to move slowly, we still have the power to shape the future. Every action, every decision counts."

Johan let out a slow breath, his eyes softening. "Maybe I've been so focused on the fast, the immediate... that I've forgotten to truly live in the moment. Thanks, Leah."

Leah's heart warmed, and she gave his shoulder a gentle squeeze. "We're all learning together. But the journey isn't just about moving forward fast. It's about understanding each step, each choice. And with that, we can build something lasting."

Johan looked at her, a newfound determination in his gaze. "You're right. And we'll face this together. Whatever comes next, we'll take it one step at a time."

Leah's heart swelled with pride as she looked around at her team. They were stronger now, more united in their purpose. The battles ahead would be difficult, but they had learned to trust in each other and in the power of time—both the fleeting moments in the dreamscape and the steady march of time in the awakened world.

Together, they would face whatever darkness Malik brought. And they would do so with the strength they had cultivated—slowly, steadily, and with purpose.

As Leah turned her attention back to the threads, her fingers brushed lightly over the luminous strands. The weight of the world was still heavy, but now, she carried it with a deeper understanding. The paradox of time had given her the clarity she needed. And with that clarity, she was ready for the next step in their journey.

The next dream awaited them, and the threads pulsed softly with the promise of what was yet to come.

CHAPTER 17

THRESHOLD

The air was thick and heavy, the kind of silence that presses against the ears and muffles the senses. Leah stepped into the dreamscape cautiously, her presence creating ripples across its gray and lifeless expanse. Before her stretched an infinite barren field, littered with jagged stones, their sharp edges glinting faintly under an overcast sky. The ground seemed to stretch on forever, the emptiness swallowed up by the distant horizon. The colors were muted, lifeless—like the dreamscape had been abandoned, or perhaps forgotten.

In the center of it all knelt Joe High, his body bathed in an eerie light that flickered like a dying flame. He muttered to himself, his words a low, continuous hum of despair. Each word seemed to echo into the void, reverberating with a sense of deep, crushing hopelessness.

"What's the point?" he said, his voice broken and strained. "I come back... over and over. But for what? What's left for me?"

Leah watched him carefully, her heart aching as she felt the rawness of his pain. His golden thread pulsed faintly, its glow dimmed and frayed by Malik's dark influence. This dreamscape was fragile, hanging at the edge of something vast and unknowable—something terrifying. The silence was oppressive, and Leah felt its weight press against her chest as she approached Joe.

"You're not alone, Joe," Leah said gently, her voice carrying across the desolate expanse like a lifeline tossed to a drowning soul.

Joe's head shot up, his eyes wide with a mixture of fear and curiosity. "Who... who are you?" His voice cracked as he looked at her, as though seeing an apparition.

Leah approached slowly, her steps deliberate, careful not to disturb the fragile nature of this dream. As she moved closer, the stones beneath her feet began to crumble, revealing glimpses of fragmented landscapes beneath— moments frozen in time, painful fragments of his life—flickering between the harsh reality of a battlefield drenched in rain, the sterile white of a hospital room, and a serene forest that was abruptly shattered by a shadow.

Joe scrambled to his feet, his body tense and wary, the remnants of his once-resilient spirit flickering. "I've seen you before," he said, his voice trembling, his hands clenched in fists. "You're there... in the moments before I wake up. Who are you? Why are you here?"

Leah kept her tone steady, calm, reaching for the piece of him still willing to hope. "I'm here to help you find the answers you're searching for. You've been looking, haven't you? For what lies beyond."

Joe's expression hardened, bitterness and pain radiating from him. "I don't want help. I just want it to stop. I'm tired. I've been walking this path, fighting these shadows, but nothing changes. I can't keep doing this. I don't know what's left to fight for."

A sudden chill swept through the air, and the overcast sky darkened as Malik's presence seeped into the dreamscape. The ground beneath Joe trembled, cracks snaking outward from beneath his feet as a shadow materialized behind him. The dark, oppressive shape was unmistakable—Malik.

"Stop?" Malik's voice was a low, mocking rumble that filled the space. "There's no stopping for you, Joe. Not for someone like you. You'll keep coming back, again and again, because you don't belong anywhere—not here, and not beyond."

Joe stiffened, his fists clenching tighter, his face reddening in defiance. "You don't know anything about me."

"Oh, but I do," Malik said, stepping closer, his shadow growing longer and darker, swallowing up the light. "I've seen every failure. Every regret. Every moment you've wished for an end, only to find yourself right back where you started. You think you're different, but you're just like the rest. A man too broken to find peace."

Leah moved between them, her stance firm and unyielding. "You don't control him, Malik," she said, her voice steady, radiating strength. "You're feeding on his fear, but he doesn't belong to you."

Malik's gaze shifted to Leah, and his smile widened. "And you think he belongs to you, Dreamweaver? You can't save him. He's already mine."

The ground beneath them cracked open, revealing a swirling abyss of darkness, a gaping maw that threatened to swallow them whole. Leah's hands glowed faintly as she reached for Joe's golden thread, her fingers brushing against it as she anchored herself to him.

"Joe," she said urgently, her tone cutting through the chaos that surrounded them. "This is your dream. You have the power to face what's beyond. But you must choose to let go of your fear."

Joe turned to her, his face etched with anguish, confusion, and doubt clouding his expression. "What if there's nothing? What if all of this... everything I've been through... means nothing?"

Leah tightened her grip on his hand. "It all means something. Every moment, every connection—it matters. You're here now because you still have a purpose, even if you can't see it yet."

Malik's laugh echoed around them, his voice growing cold and cruel. "Don't listen to her. The threshold isn't a place of answers—it's emptiness. And once you cross it, there's no coming back."

The abyss roared, its pull growing stronger, the very fabric of the dreamscape unraveling as Malik's shadow lunged forward, threatening to consume them both. But Leah stood her ground. Her hands glowed brighter, pulling Joe closer, and with every ounce of power she had left, she reached out.

"We'll face this together," Leah said, her voice unwavering as she guided Joe's thread, pushing the darkness back with the force of their combined strength.

Joe hesitated, but then, a faint light flickered in the distance—his father's voice, calling out through the noise. The memory of a time long buried, one he had allowed himself to forget for so long. He saw himself as a young boy, sitting by a quiet lake with his father, the two of them skipping stones together, the sound of the water soft and peaceful.

"It's not about what's beyond, son," his father's voice echoed. "It's about what you leave behind."

Tears welled in Joe's eyes as he turned to Leah, his expression softening. "I'm ready," he whispered, his voice filled with a quiet understanding.

Together, they took the first step forward, crossing the threshold. The abyss roared around them, but Joe's inner light grew stronger, illuminating their path. Malik's shadow lunged toward them one final time, but Leah's power flared, her presence strong and unyielding, pushing the darkness back.

The dreamscape trembled, its chaotic landscape falling away as they crossed over to something new. The darkness faded, replaced by a serene meadow bathed in golden sunlight. Joe exhaled, his body relaxing for the first time in what felt like an eternity. The heavy weight of fear and uncertainty lifted from his chest, and for the first time in years, he felt free.

Back in the sanctuary, Leah stood at the central loom, her fingers brushing over the glowing threads, her heart filled with a quiet satisfaction. Joe's thread now pulsed with a steadier rhythm, its glow brighter, its energy restored. She closed her eyes for a moment, the weight of their journey still lingering in the air, but there was a sense of peace in knowing that they had faced another challenge together—and overcome it.

The team had gathered around the loom, but Leah's thoughts lingered on the threshold they had just crossed. She could still feel the pull of the darkness, the weight of Malik's influence trying to seep through the cracks. They weren't done yet. The journey was far from over.

"We're running out of time," she murmured to herself.

But as she closed her eyes, a flicker of hope sparked within her. Joe's journey had been a reminder—a testament to the strength of the human spirit, even in the face of despair. With each step forward, each person they helped, the darkness receded just a little more.

Leah turned back to the loom. The next battle was approaching, and she needed to be ready.

Leah's Velara Aelis

There are moments within the dreamscape when I feel like more than a guide. I feel like a witness—standing at the edge of someone's soul, watching as they lay bare the most vulnerable parts of themselves. Each thread I touch, every dream I weave, carries its own weight, its own story. And yet, they are not separate; they are part of something far greater, strands in a tapestry too vast for even me to see in its entirety.

Joe's dream was unlike any other. His fear wasn't rooted in regret or loss, but in the unknown—an abyss he had faced over and over without ever finding answers. It wasn't death he feared, but the void that might lie beyond it. His courage in stepping toward that void, knowing it might still hold no answers, reminded me that some of the greatest acts of bravery are the quietest. It is the willingness to take a step forward when every fiber of your being urges you to stop, to turn away.

In many ways, Joe's journey mirrored Terry's. Fear manifests in different forms, but its weight is universal. For Terry, it was the paralyzing terror of losing someone he loved—a fear that had defined his every waking moment since the accident. And for Joe, it was the weight of his own existence, the endless cycle of returning and leaving, never knowing what lay beyond the veil. Both men had to confront the unknowable, and in doing so, they reminded me of a truth I've been reluctant to face. Fear is a threshold, one we all must cross if we hope to grow.

As a Weaver, I often think about the balance between guiding and interfering. How much of my presence is enough? How much is too much? In Joe's dream, Malik's interference was blatant, his corruption a dark stain on the threads. Yet, even as I pushed against him, I felt the weight of my own influence. I had to decide: should I guide Joe across the threshold, or let him make the choice entirely on his own?

I chose to walk with him. Not to carry him, but to stand beside him as he faced the unknown. It felt right in the moment, but now, reflecting on it, I wonder—was my presence a crutch? Did I rob him of the strength he might have found had he faced it alone? Or was I merely fulfilling my role as a Dreamweaver, ensuring the threads remained intact?

Malik would call me a meddler, and perhaps he's not entirely wrong. But Malik sees only control, the imposition of one will over another. He doesn't understand the subtlety of connection, the beauty of shared strength. Joe didn't cross the threshold because of me; he crossed it because he found his own resolve. All I did was remind him it was there.

Terry's story was different. His fear was raw, personal, and immediate—a child's life hanging in the balance, a weight far heavier than any dream could bear. And yet, even in the face of that fear, he hesitated. I saw the way Malik preyed on him, whispering doubt into his ear, planting the seeds of self-recrimination. Terry believed he wasn't strong enough to save his relative, that his past failures defined him.

But strength isn't the absence of fear; it's the decision to act in spite of it. Terry found his strength not in isolation, but in the connections he had forged—with Johan, with me, with the team. Together, we pulled him back from the edge, reminding him that he didn't have to face his darkness alone. That is the power of the Weavers—not to fight battles for others, but to stand beside them, to lend them our strength when theirs falters.

As I reflect on these moments, I can't ignore the shadow that looms over us all. Malik's power is growing, his influence extending beyond the dreamscape into the waking world. I see it in Jasper's eyes, in the way his words carry Malik's venom even when he's unaware of it. I feel it in the fraying threads of the dreams we weave, in the chaos that edges ever closer to our sanctuary. Malik isn't just a Nightweaver—he's a force of imbalance, a threat to the very fabric of the dreamscape.

And yet, I can't bring myself to hate him. Not entirely. Because I see in Malik the same pain I've carried for so long. His rage isn't about power—it's about loss. About Jara. My daughter. His daughter.

I've hidden her from him, from everyone, because I believed it was the only way to keep her safe. But now I wonder if my secrecy has only fed Malik's rage, if my silence has allowed his pain to fester into the corruption that now threatens us all.

I think of Jara every day, I see her in the threads I weave, in the golden light of the dreamscape. She is the reason I became a Weaver; the reason I fight to preserve the connections that bind us all. But she is also my greatest creation, my greatest weakness. And Malik knows it now.

The team is growing stronger. Johan's steadfast resolve, Mina's quiet courage, Terry's resilience—they give me hope. But I can see the cracks, too. The doubts that linger in their eyes, the weight of the battles we've fought and the ones still to come. They look to me for guidance, for answers, but I don't always have them.

What I do have is a plan. Malik's power is rooted in chaos, in the severing of connections. If we are to defeat him, we must stand together, our threads woven so tightly that even he cannot unravel them. It won't be easy. There will be sacrifices, and there will be pain. But I believe in this team. I believe in the strength we've found in one another.

As I prepare for what lies ahead, I find myself returning to the threshold—not Joe's, but my own. The threshold of truth, of confrontation, of legacy. It's time to find Jara. It's time to face Malik, not as a foe, but as the man he once was—the man

The Loom: Leah's Legacy

I once loved.

It's time to cross the threshold. Together.

The threads of the sanctuary shimmered faintly as Leah rose from her meditative state. The others waited, their gazes heavy with expectation. Mina's hand rested on Terry's shoulder, and Johan stood by the loom, his expression unreadable but firm.

"We move at velunfall," Leah said, her voice steady. "Malik's corruption has spread far enough. If we don't act now, the balance will be lost."

The team nodded, their unity unspoken but palpable. Leah glanced at the threads one last time, her fingers brushing over the golden strands that bound them all.

The path ahead was fraught with uncertainty, but Leah's purpose had never been clearer. It was time to weave the final threads of this battle—threads that would determine not only their fates but the fate of the dreamscape itself.

CHAPTER 18

IN BALANCE'S WAKE

The oppressive humidity hung in the air like a damp shroud as Leah stepped into the dreamscape. Her senses tingled, the threads of the dream vibrating with tension. The terrain was barren, a mixture of cracked earth and slick mud, while towering metallic structures loomed in the distance. Their jagged edges glinted in the dull, overcast light, like silent sentinels guarding the fractured world.

Elena Hayes stood defiantly at the forefront of the chaos, her sledgehammer poised as she glared at the enforcers blocking her path. Clad in polished armor, their expressions were blank, robotic, their voices cold and devoid of empathy.

"You defy The Balance, Elena Hayes," one enforcer intoned. "Order must be maintained."

Elena spat at the ground. "This isn't order—it's oppression! And I'm done playing by your rules."

Her defiance sent ripples through the dreamscape, the structures in the distance quivering as though her words held the power to unravel the very fabric of this constructed world.

The Loom: Leah's Legacy

From the shadows, Leah signaled to her team. Johan, towering and stoic, moved like a silent guardian, his gaze fixed on the enforcers. Mina's sharp eyes scanned the terrain, calculating every possible move with precision. Terry hung back, adjusting the device strapped to his wrist, his hands trembling slightly. Leah could see the weight of his previous battles etched into his face.

"This isn't just a dream," Mina whispered, her voice barely audible. "It feels... alive."

Leah nodded, her eyes narrowing. "Malik's fingerprints are everywhere. He's amplifying Elena's fears, twisting her dream into a nightmare she can't escape."

Johan stepped forward, his voice low but firm. "We need to move quickly. If Malik is here, he won't wait long to make his move."

Elena charged at the enforcers, her sledgehammer colliding with the nearest one in a deafening crash. Sparks flew as the metal buckled under the force of her strike, but for every enforcer she knocked down, two more seemed to take their place.

"Why do you fight?" one of them asked, its voice devoid of emotion. "The Balance ensures survival. Without it, there is only chaos."

Elena gritted her teeth, her voice trembling with rage. "Survival at the cost of freedom isn't survival at all. It's a cage."

As she spoke, the dreamscape began to shift. The ground trembled, the structures in the distance bending unnaturally as shadows crept in from the edges. The air grew colder, the oppressive humidity replaced by a bone-chilling frost. Leah felt the threads around her tighten, their vibrations growing erratic.

"He's here," she whispered.

From the shadows emerged Malik, his presence like a living wound in the dreamscape. His form was sharp and angular, his movements fluid but unnatural. The enforcers paused, stepping aside as if to welcome their true master.

"Elena," Malik said, his voice smooth and almost gentle. "You speak of balance, but do you truly understand it? Balance is not freedom—it is necessity. Without it, your world crumbles."

Elena raised her sledgehammer, her stance unwavering. "I don't care who you are. Get out of my dream."

Malik chuckled, a low, sinister sound. "Oh, but I'm not in your way, Elena. I'm here to help you see the truth."

With a wave of his hand, the dreamscape shifted again. The enforcers dissolved into monstrous shadows, their forms twisting and elongating into grotesque figures. The towering structures bent inward, their edges curling like claws ready to strike.

"Now!" Leah commanded, stepping forward as Johan, Mina, and Terry sprang into action.

Johan charged at one of the shadowed figures, his fists glowing with energy as he collided with its chest. The impact sent shockwaves through the air, but the creature merely reformed, its jagged edges sharper than before.

Mina darted between two figures, her movements swift and precise as she slashed at their legs with an ethereal blade conjured from her own threads. Yet for every strike she landed, the figures seemed to grow more chaotic, their forms splitting and multiplying.

Terry stood frozen, his hands trembling as he adjusted his device. "I... I can't," he stammered, his voice barely audible.

"Terry!" Leah shouted, her tone sharp but encouraging. "We need you. Focus on Elena—protect her."

Terry nodded shakily, activating his device. A shimmering shield formed around Elena, deflecting the shadows as they lunged toward her.

Leah turned her attention to Malik, her voice steady despite the turmoil around her. "Enough, Malik. This ends now."

Malik smirked, his gaze locking onto hers. "You can't stop this, Leah. You're clinging to a thread that's already unraveling."

Leah reached out to Elena, her voice cutting through the chaos. "Elena, this is your dream. You have the power to fight back. You don't need to destroy balance—you need to reclaim it."

Elena hesitated, her grip on the sledgehammer faltering. "I don't know if I can..."

"Yes, you can," Leah said firmly. "But you have to decide. The Balance isn't your enemy—it's what you make of it."

Malik's smirk widened, his form flickering as he whispered, "She'll fail. Just like you."

Elena's eyes hardened, and with a primal scream, she raised her sledgehammer high. Golden light erupted from her body as she swung it with all her strength, shattering the monstrous figures around her. The dreamscape quaked, the oppressive structures collapsing into dust as the shadows dissipated.

But the victory was hollow. As the dreamscape stabilized, Elena fell to her knees, her body trembling. The golden light around her dimmed, and Leah saw the toll the battle had taken. Elena's thread was intact, but its glow was faint, fragile.

Malik's laughter echoed in the distance as his form dissolved into the shadows. "You can't save them all, Leah. And you certainly can't save yourself."

The team returned to the sanctuary, their expressions heavy with defeat despite their survival. Mina paced restlessly, her movements sharp and agitated. Terry sat in silence, his head bowed. Johan paced back and forth by the loom.

Leah stood at the central loom, her fingers brushing over the threads. Elena's was intact, but the threads around it were frayed, their connections tenuous.

"We won," Mina said bitterly, "but it doesn't feel like it."

Leah nodded, her gaze distant. "Because it wasn't a win. Malik didn't need to destroy Elena's dream—he just needed to weaken the threads. And he's succeeding."

Johan stepped forward, his voice firm. "Then we need to stop him. No more waiting, no more reacting. We need to take the fight to him."

Leah looked at him, "We will. We need to be ready. His reach into the awakened world is deep beyond the drealis. And if we don't act soon, there won't be a anything left to save."

Leah turned her gaze to the loom, the weight of the next steps pressing heavily on her. Every thread she touched was a story waiting to be completed, but Malik's chaos threatened to erase them all.

Leah's Lumarion

The sanctuary, usually a refuge from the chaos of the dreamscape, felt unusually heavy. The loom shimmered with a dim, uncertain glow. The golden threads that typically danced with clarity now pulsed erratically, like they too were bracing for what was to come.

Around the central table, tension simmered. Johan leaned against the far wall, arms crossed, his gaze hard and unwavering. Mina paced in tight lines, her boots echoing across the crystalline floor. Terry hunched near his device, tinkering without focus, and Jasper—still flickering and faint—sat quietly in the corner, the loomstaff casting a soft aura around him like a lifeline trying to hold.

Leah stood before the Loom, her fingers grazing the threads in silence. Malik's laughter still echoed in her mind. It wasn't just power he wanted—it was something deeper. Something personal. His influence had spread, and with each frayed thread, the sanctuary itself seemed to recoil.

Johan's voice cut through the tension like a blade.

"Leah. Why are you still holding back?"

She didn't turn. Her hand remained on the Loom, the threads rippling at her touch.

"We've seen what he's doing," Mina said, pausing mid-step. "He's not just unraveling dreams—he's targeting us. Twisting everything we care about. The plan is not working."

Terry nodded, eyes still fixed on the screen. "We can't keep waiting. If we do, he wins. He's already pushing the loom beyond its limits."

Leah finally turned to face them, her voice low but resolute. "I'm not waiting. I'm trying to protect what matters."

"From what?" Johan snapped. "You? Or from what you could become?"

The words struck like thunder. Leah's eyes met his, not with anger, but with exhaustion.

"I've seen people lose themselves chasing power," she said. "I've seen what happens when we let fear or desperation drive us. I'm not afraid of Malik. I'm afraid of becoming like him."

She hesitated, then added, her voice rougher than before.

"Have any of you ever severed a thread? Felt it snap inside you like a scream you can't silence?"

A shadow crossed her features.

"I have. It doesn't just haunt you—it changes you. Forever."

Johan stepped forward, his expression raw. "I've lost everyone I've ever loved, Leah. I would give anything—anything—for the chance to fight back, to rewrite just one moment. You have that chance. You're not just another Weaver. You're Veilborn. That means something."

Leah's breath caught.

"You don't even realize what you are," Johan continued. "Our power comes from the Loom of Dreams. But yours—it comes from somewhere else. Somewhere we didn't even know existed until we met you."

He took another step closer. "You are the possible. So, stop trying to hold the edges together while everything falls apart. Stop waiting for Malik to make the next move. Let's make the next move."

Silence gripped the room."

Mina crossed her arms, watching Leah closely. "You do things we've never seen before, Leah. You walk between realms. Threads respond to your emotions. The loom shifts when you breathe. That's not coincidence. That's power."

Leah looked back at the Loom, the threads vibrating at her hesitation.

"I don't know how to control it yet," she admitted. "I don't know what I'm capable of."

"You're not meant to know all at once," Terry said quietly. "You learn by doing."

Jasper flickered in the corner, his eyes faint but watching. "And we'll be here—every step of the way."

Leah let the silence hold a beat longer, feeling the weight of her fear... and the strength of their belief.

Leah stepped back toward the loom, her fingers brushing the nearest thread. It pulsed beneath her touch—not with the frenzied chaos she had feared, but with something steadier. Something sure. Purpose. Possibility. The fear that had gripped her for so long began to loosen, replaced by a quiet clarity.

She turned to face the others, her posture shifting, the weight on her shoulders no longer one of hesitation, but of resolve. Her voice carried with newfound strength.

"We stop waiting," she said.

The team straightened, their expressions sharpening as her words sank in. Around the sanctuary, the very air shifted, the threads above them shimmering more brightly as if stirred by a shared determination.

"We gather our strength. We learn from every thread. When the moment comes, we won't falter. No fear. No retreat."

One by one, they nodded—Mina, Johan, Terry—even Jasper, whose flickering form seemed to still, if only for a moment. This was no longer about surviving Malik's next move. This was about reclaiming what had been stolen. About fighting for what remained. About protecting what could still be saved.

Behind Leah, the loom responded. Its golden glow brightened, the threads humming with renewed energy. She allowed herself a single glance toward the thread still tethered to Jasper, flickering like a heartbeat clinging to life—and then toward the next dream that shimmered just beyond.

The path forward was uncertain, but they would walk it together.

The dream waited.

And this time, they were ready.

CHAPTER 19

BOUND OF GRACE

The dreamscape stretched like a surreal painting, its elements both inviting and unsettling. A vast meadow bloomed with vibrant flowers, their colors vivid against the backdrop of an orange sky. Yet, the air carried an undertone of decay—the flowers at their edges curled and browned, the soil beneath them cracked as if parched by drought. The wind whispered through the meadow, carrying with it echoes of words too faint to understand.

Leah and her team appeared at the edge of the meadow, their footsteps sinking slightly into the soft earth. The threads here shimmered faintly, their glow dimmed by fraying edges and encroaching shadows. There was a tension in the air, a sense of something fragile that could crumble with the slightest touch.

"This is different," Mina said, her voice low as she scanned the surrounding landscape. "Fragile, like it's barely holding together."

Leah nodded, her gaze fixed on a dilapidated house perched on a hill in the distance. "It's not just fragile—it's fractured. Their pain is splitting the dream, and Malik's interference is making it worse."

Johan stepped forward, scanning the horizon. "What's the plan? Do we split up?"

"No," Leah said firmly. "We go together. If this dream collapses, it could trap them both—or worse, pull us in with it."

As they moved forward, the meadow shifted under their feet. The vibrant colors bled into muted tones, the edges of the landscape blurring as if it were dissolving. The house loomed closer, its eerie glow growing brighter with each step.

The house was a labyrinth of shifting halls and rooms, each filled with fragments of the past. Picture frames hung crookedly on the walls, their glass cracked, and their images blurred. The air was thick with the scent of rain, though no storm clouds were visible.

Inside, Alice sat in the living room, her hands clenched tightly around a faded photograph. Her face was a mask of stoic determination, but her eyes betrayed a deep sorrow. Across from her, Adora stood with her arms crossed, her defiant stance a sharp contrast to the uncertainty in her expression.

"This isn't real," Adora said, her voice trembling with frustration. "None of this is real."

Alice looked up, her gaze softening. "Maybe not. But it's all we have right now."

Leah and her team stepped into the room cautiously. The threads surrounding Alice and Adora vibrated with tension, their golden light flickering erratically. Neither dreamer seemed to notice their presence; their focus was entirely on each other.

"They're stuck," Leah murmured. "Caught in a loop of their own emotions."

"So how do we break it?" Terry asked, glancing uneasily at the shifting walls around them.

"By helping them see what's real," Leah said. "But first, we need to understand what's keeping them apart."

The room shifted again, its walls dissolving into a swirling mist. Scenes from the past began to play out like a fragmented film reel.

In one memory, Alice and Adora stood in a cluttered kitchen, the air between them charged with tension. Bills and papers littered the counters, and a half-eaten meal lay forgotten on the table.

"You never listen to me!" Adora shouted, her voice cracking. "You don't even see me!"

"I'm doing everything I can, Adora," Alice snapped, her frustration spilling over. "Do you think I like working late? Missing your performances? I'm trying to keep this family together!"

The scene shifted again, replaced by another memory. Alice sat alone in her car, clutching a photograph of a younger Adora. Tears streamed down her face as she whispered, "I'm sorry. I'm so sorry."

Mina watched the scene unfold, her expression softening. "They're both hurting so much. But neither of them knows how to let the other in."

"And Malik's using that pain to tear them apart," Johan added grimly.

The dreamscape darkened suddenly, the vibrant colors of the meadow bleeding into shades of black and gray. Shadows crept along the edges of the house, twisting and writhing like living smoke.

"He's here," Johan muttered, his fists clenching.

Malik emerged from the shadows, his presence cold and suffocating. He didn't speak at first, his dark eyes scanning the room before landing on Leah with a chilling smile.

"You're late," he said, his tone mocking. "I was beginning to think you wouldn't show."

"Let them go, Malik," Leah said, stepping forward. Her voice was steady, but her eyes burned with intensity. "This isn't your fight."

Malik chuckled, his gaze flicking to Alice and Adora. "Oh, but it is. Their pain is exquisite—a symphony I can twist and reshape however I like."

Leah's threads glowed faintly as she reached for the frayed connections between mother and daughter. "You've done enough damage."

"Go ahead," Malik said, his smile widening. "Show me what you've got."

Leah closed her eyes, the loomstaff moving over the threads as she felt the weight of Alice's guilt and the sharp edges of Adora's anger. Slowly, she began to weave, guiding the threads toward the heart of their connection.

The house dissolved into an open field bathed in golden light. Alice and Adora stood at the center, their forms flickering like fragile flames.

"I'm sorry," Alice said softly, her voice trembling. "For everything. For not being there when you needed me. For making you feel like you didn't matter."

Adora's expression wavered, her defiance giving way to vulnerability. "I just wanted you to see me. To care."

"I do care," Alice said, tears streaming down her face. "More than you know. I just didn't know how to show it."

The golden light around them grew brighter, the threads binding them shimmering as they began to mend. Malik's shadows recoiled, hissing as they retreated into the edges of the dreamscape.

Alice and Adora embraced, their connection restored. Leah stepped back, watching as the golden threads solidified around them.

"You did it," Mina said quietly.

"No," Leah replied, her gaze fixed on the loomstaff. She turns and stares at retreating shadows.

Malik lingered at the edge of the dreamscape, his dark smile unbroken. "You think this is a victory?" he said, his voice dripping with disdain. "All you've done is delay the inevitable."

He dissolved into the shadows, leaving Leah and her team standing in the golden field.

Back in the sanctuary, Leah sat quietly at the loom, her hands resting on its edges. The threads of Alice and Adora's dream glowed faintly, pulsing with the renewed connection between mother and daughter. Yet, the golden shimmer wasn't enough to dispel the unease curling in Leah's chest.

Alice's apology, Adora's vulnerability—their shared willingness to face the truth—had saved them. Watching their connection heal had been a reminder of how powerful reconciliation could be. And yet, it also stirred something deeper in Leah: a longing she had buried for years.

As she stared at the loom, a memory surfaced—her own mother's voice, calm and firm, guiding her through her first threads. Miriam Cimaj had always spoken of the weave with reverence, calling it the foundation of everything: connection, balance, purpose.

"The loom doesn't lie," Miriam had once said. "It shows us what we're running from and what we need to face."

Leah exhaled slowly, her fingers tracing the threads. She had avoided her mother for so long, afraid of the questions she might ask, the truths she might uncover. But if anyone could help her prepare for what lay ahead, it was Miriam.

She rose from the loom, her resolve solidifying. "It's time to go home," she murmured to herself, her voice steady despite the weight of the decision.

Leah turned to the others, who were scattered across the sanctuary, recovering from their latest ordeal. "I need to leave," she said, her tone leaving no room for argument.

Johan frowned. "Leave? Now? What about the next dream?"

"There won't be another dream," Leah replied. "Not yet. There's someone I need to see first. Someone who might have answers."

Mina stepped forward, concern etched into her face. "Who, Leah? What's going on?"

Leah hesitated for a moment, then met Mina's gaze. "My marasyn."

The team exchanged surprised glances, but no one spoke. They could see the determination in Leah's expression, the flicker of hope and fear that danced in her eyes.

"I'll be back," Leah promised. "But this is something I have to do alone."

With that, she turned toward the shimmering portal at the edge of the sanctuary, her heart pounding as she prepared to step through. The thought of facing her mother again filled her with both dread and anticipation. But deep down, Leah knew this was the only way forward.

As the portal enveloped her, the sanctuary faded from view, replaced by the distant hum of a place she hadn't visited in years—a place where the past waited to be unraveled, and the answers she needed lay within reach.

The Passage of Threads

As Leah stepped into the shimmering portal, the sanctuary dissolved behind her. In its place came the ethereal glow of the Aevitas Veil—the ancestral passageway known only to the women of her lineage. It was a world between worlds, a realm woven from time itself. The threads of fate glimmered like constellations, stretching infinitely in every direction. This was where Leah's mother, grandmother, and great-grandmother had walked—a secret passed down through generations, a realm untouched by the ticking of clocks and the chaos of the drealis or the dreamscapes.

Each thread in the Veil pulsed with memories, carrying whispers of those who had walked before her. Leah paused to trace one golden strand, feeling its warmth against her fingers. A vision flickered—her great-grandmother laughing in a sunlit field, her voice carrying a strength that resonated through the Veil. Another strand pulled her gaze to a moment of sorrow, her grandmother's face, furrowed with lines of experience, clutching her chest as if bracing for a storm.

The Aevitas Veil was more than a passage. It was a connection, a reminder of the enduring legacy of the women in her family. Leah had avoided it for years, unsure if she was ready to face the truths it held. But now, with the weight of Malik's actions and the looming danger to Jara, she knew she could wait no longer.

As she walked deeper into the Veil, her thoughts turned to the dreamers she had guided and the battles she and her team had faced. The Threshold, where Joe had confronted the mysteries of life and death, reminded Leah of the fragile boundary between worlds. Joe's acceptance of the unknown had inspired her to embrace the uncertainty of her own journey.

While helping Elena, the team had won a critical battle, but at a devastating cost. The dreamscape's unnatural order mirrored Malik's growing influence, and the victory had felt hollow against the larger threat. Leah had watched Johan's resilience shine, but the toll it took on him left her uneasy.

Alice and Adora's reconciliation had reminded Leah of the threads binding her to her own mother. The pain Alice carried and the defiance in Adora's eyes were echoes of Leah's own relationship with Miriam. She had seen herself in both women, their journey stirring memories she had long suppressed.

"I've been running," Leah murmured to herself as she walked. The Veil seemed to hum in response, the threads vibrating softly around her.

She thought of Jara—her daughter, Malik's daughter. The weight of the truth settled heavily on her shoulders. Jara was the first of her kind, a being of unimaginable power, yet so innocent and unaware of her significance. The threads in the Veil pulsed brighter as if responding to her thoughts.

Leah stopped and placed her hand on one particularly vibrant thread. It carried an image of her mother, Miriam, her voice echoing through the Veil: "You cannot guide others if you cannot face your own reflection."

Leah's breath caught. Miriam had always been a force of wisdom and strength, yet their relationship had been fraught with unspoken words and unhealed wounds. Now, as Leah stood on the precipice of an even greater battle, she realized she needed her mother's guidance—not just for Jara, but for herself.

The veil shifted, the threads around her forming a path that pulsed with urgency. Leah took a deep breath, steeling herself for what lay ahead.

The veil gave way to a quiet forest clearing bathed in twilight. The air was heavy with the scent of earth and rain, and the soft glow of fireflies danced among the trees. At the center of the clearing stood a small cottage, its windows glowing warmly in the fading light.

Leah approached slowly, her heart pounding in her chest. She had not seen her mother in years, and the weight of their history pressed heavily on her.

The door opened before Leah could knock, and Miriam Cimaj stepped into the doorway. Her hair, streaked with silver, framed a face that was both familiar and foreign—strong cheekbones, piercing eyes, and a presence that commanded attention.

For a moment, neither of them spoke. Miriam's gaze softened, and a faint smile tugged at the corners of her mouth.

"You look tired, Leah," Miriam said finally, her voice calm but filled with a quiet concern.

Leah swallowed hard, her words catching in her throat. "It's been a long journey."

Miriam nodded, stepping aside to let Leah in. "Then it's time we talked."

As Leah crossed the threshold, she felt the weight of the Veil and all it represented settle over her. This was the moment she had avoided for so long, the truth she could no longer run from.

Inside, the cottage was warm and inviting, filled with the scent of herbs and the soft glow of candlelight. The walls were lined with books and artifacts, each one carrying the weight of their family's legacy.

"Sit," Miriam said, gesturing to a chair by the hearth.

Leah obeyed, her hands trembling slightly as she rested them on her lap. Miriam sat across from her, her eyes never leaving Leah's face.

"You've been weaving," Miriam said, her tone neutral.

Leah nodded. "More than I ever thought possible."

"And yet, you're here," Miriam said, her voice softening. "What has brought you back, Leah?"

Leah hesitated, the words heavy on her tongue. "Jara," she said finally. "I need your help to protect her."

Miriam's expression didn't change, but Leah saw the flicker of recognition in her eyes. "Then we have much to discuss," Miriam said.

As the fire crackled between them, Leah felt the threads of her past and future intertwining. The journey was far from over, but for the first time in years, she felt the faintest glimmer of hope.

Miriam's calm, and she leaned forward slightly. "You're carrying a heavy burden, Leah. I knew this day would come—the day when you would have to face what you've been running from. Your power, your legacy—it's more than you've allowed yourself to acknowledge."

Leah's heart pounded in her chest. The words were exactly what she had been afraid to hear.

"I'm not ready," Leah whispered, her voice barely audible. "I never thought I could be the one to carry this legacy. Not with what happened. Not with Malik."

Her voice caught, but she pushed forward. "And Khyros... I severed him. I thought I was doing the right thing, but ever since that day in the nightmare realm, the balance has been unraveling. The dreamscape, the waking world... it's all fraying. What if I caused this?"

Miriam's eyes shimmered with the weight of experience and gentle grace. "None of us are ever truly ready, Leah. But the threads don't choose us because we're perfect—they choose us because we're willing. Willing to face the darkness, to carry the light, and to weave them both into something whole. Don't let the pain of your past become the pattern of your future. You are more than what you've done—you're what you choose to become."

Leah nodded slowly, her mind racing. "I don't know how to stop Malik. How do I protect Jara without losing myself?"

Miriam reached out, placing a hand on Leah's. "You don't protect her alone, my nascent velana. My young daughter, the threads you weave connect all of us. And with each step, you'll find your strength. It's always been within you."

Leah closed her eyes, her heart settling for the first time in what felt like an eternity. Her mother's words, a balm to the wounds she had kept hidden, were the very thing she needed to hear. She wasn't alone—not in this, not anymore.

"I'm ready," Leah said softly, her voice stronger now. "Whatever it takes, I'm ready."

Miriam's smile was faint, but there was a fierceness in her eyes that Leah had never seen before. "Then let us prepare. The threads you weave will shape the future, Leah. But remember, the past is always with us."

The fire crackled once more, its warmth filling the room, and Leah felt the weight of the world shift. The journey ahead would be difficult, but with her mother's guidance, Leah knew she was no longer facing it alone. Together, they would rewrite the future.

The path ahead was unclear, but Leah was no longer afraid. The Veil had shown her the way—now, it was time to walk it.

Leah's Lumarion

The sanctuary was cloaked in a heavy, unspoken tension. The threads in the loom pulsed faintly, as though even they sensed Leah's absence. Mina sat on the floor near the loom, her fingers lightly tracing the golden threads left behind. She wasn't weaving; she was observing, searching for patterns. Across the room, Terry meticulously analyzed another thread, his movements deliberate, his focus unwavering.

Johan, however, couldn't stand still. His boots echoed against the sanctuary's smooth floor as he paced, the frustration on his face clear. "This doesn't feel right," he said, breaking the silence for the fifth time. "Leah shouldn't have left us—not with Malik still out there."

Mina sighed, not looking up from her work. "She didn't leave us, Johan. She's searching for answers. She wouldn't have gone if it wasn't important."

"Important?" Johan shot back, his voice sharper than he intended. "What's more important than saving Jara or Jasper? Just look at him—he's fading away. He's still tethered to Malik, and you know it."

Mina finally looked up, her eyes steady.

"I know. But Leah carries more than just the loomstaff—she carries all of us. Even when she's not here, it feels like her strength lingers. Like the threads don't fray as easily when she's leading."

She paused, her voice softening.

"She accepted us when she didn't have to. Didn't know anything about us—and still saved us from being severed. I'll follow her anywhere. And I'll trust her to come back when we need her most."

Terry raised a hand, his calm voice cutting through Johan's frustration. "He's right about one thing—Jasper's leaving us signals again. Look at this." He gestured to a faint thread running through the loom, its light dim and uneven.

Mina focused, narrowing her eyes at the thread. The weave was jagged and chaotic, its golden light flickering as though it were on the verge of snapping. She leaned closer, brushing her fingers over the thread. A faint vision materialized in the air—a fragmented image of Jasper's face, his eyes wide with urgency. The image dissolved almost as quickly as it appeared.

"He's trying to tell us something," Mina murmured, her voice tinged with worry.

"Or Malik's making it look like he is," Johan countered.

"It doesn't feel like Malik," Terry said, his tone measured. "This... this is Jasper. I can feel it."

Mina hesitated, her gaze shifting to the portal Leah had stepped through hours earlier. "What if this is a trap? What if Malik's using Jasper to lure us out?"

"Then we deal with it," Johan said firmly. "We can't just sit here and do nothing. Jasper's our friend now, and he's in danger. If Leah's not here to lead, then we need to step up."

Mina shook her head, frustration flashing in her eyes. "Leah left us with a purpose. She didn't tell us to go chasing after Jasper."

"And what if waiting is exactly what Malik wants?" Johan shot back. "For us to sit here while he pulls Jasper further into his grip?"

"Enough," Terry said, his voice calm but commanding. "Arguing isn't helping anyone. Mina, Johan's right—we can't ignore this. But you're right too. It could be a trap."

"So what do we do?" Mina asked, crossing her arms.

Terry straightened, his firmness clear. "Johan and I will go. You stay here and keep the sanctuary steady. If it's a trap, you'll be the one to pull us out."

"I don't like this," Mina said, her voice quieter now.

"You don't have to like it," Johan said, his tone unstiffening. "But we can't leave Jasper out there alone."

Terry placed a reassuring hand on Mina's shoulder. "We'll be fine. Trust us."

As they stepped toward the portal, Mina called out one last time. "If it's a trap, don't try to fight Malik alone. Get Jasper and get back here. Promise me."

"We promise," Terry said, glancing back with a small smile.

The portal shimmered with golden light as Johan and Terry stepped through. The sanctuary faded behind them, replaced by a dreamscape cloaked in darkness.

The Abyss of Lost Threads

The air was heavy, thick with a tension that made it hard to breathe. The landscape was chaotic—a labyrinth of twisted trees and crumbling ruins bathed in an eerie red light. The thread connected to Jasper pulsed faintly, leading them deeper into the unsettling terrain.

"This place..." Terry murmured, scanning their surroundings. "It's like Malik's fingerprints are all over it."

"It's worse than I thought," Johan said grimly. "We need to move fast."

They followed the thread through the mazelike dreamscape, the shadows around them twisting and shifting unnaturally. The farther they went, the more distorted the landscape became.

Finally, they reached a clearing where a faint figure sat hunched over. It was Jasper, his form flickering like a dying flame. Dark threads were wrapped around his arms and chest, binding him to the ground.

"Jasper!" Johan called out, rushing toward him.

Jasper looked up, his face pale and his eyes wide with fear. "You... you found me," he whispered, his voice weak.

"We're here to get you out," Terry said, kneeling beside him. He reached for the dark threads, but they recoiled under his touch, hissing like living things.

"He's still tethered," Johan said, his armor shimmered as readied himself for combat.

Before they could free Jasper, the shadows around them began to shift. A cold wind swept through the clearing, and a voice echoed through the dreamscape.

"Did you really think it would be that easy?" Malik's voice dripped with disdain as he stepped out of the darkness, his figure looming over them.

Johan stood, his fists clenched. "Let him go, Malik."

Malik smirked, his gaze shifting to Jasper. "Oh, I will. But not before I've finished what I started."

The shadows around Malik twisted and writhed, forming into dark, grotesque shapes. Johan and Terry stepped in front of Jasper, their bodies tense as they prepared for a fight.

"You think this ends now?" Johan growled, eyes locked on Malik. "Not a chance. I owe you everything—and I intend to collect."

Malik's smile spread, dark and knowing. "Good. I was hoping you'd remember."

The air grew heavier as Malik stepped closer, his presence distorting the dreamscape around them. The twisted trees and crumbling ruins seemed to lean toward him as though drawn by an unseen force. Shadows coiled and uncoiled at his feet, hissing like serpents.

"Malik," Johan roared, positioning himself between Malik and Jasper. Terry followed suit, his woven gauntlets glowing faintly as he drew on their power.

Malik chuckled, the sound dark and mocking. "You're brave, I'll give you that. But bravery without understanding is... predictable." He raised a hand, and the dark threads binding Jasper tightened, causing him to cry out in pain.

"Let him go!" Terry shouted, his voice echoing through the warped dreamscape.

Malik tilted his head, feigning consideration. "Let him go? Why would I do that when he's so... useful?" He turned his gaze to Jasper, who trembled under the weight of the dark threads. "You see, he's more than just a pawn. We were friends. Now he's my conduit—a bridge between your precious sanctuary and my realm."

Johan lunged forward, his armor glowing brighter as he aimed a strike at Malik. The air sizzled as his blow connected, but instead of recoiling, Malik absorbed the energy, his smile widening.

"Ah, Johan. Always so eager to act before thinking," Malik said, his voice calm as he backhanded Johan with a surge of shadowy force. Johan flew backward, landing hard against a jagged rock.

Terry charged, his gauntlets sparking as he charged Malik. The shadows around Malik swirled like a storm, forming a barrier that deflected Terry's attack. The force sent Terry sprawling, but he scrambled back to his feet, determination etched on his face.

"You can't win this," Malik said, his voice carrying a chilling certainty. "Not here, not now. I must finish what I started."

Jasper groaned, his voice weak but desperate. "Don't... don't fight him. You don't understand what he's capable of."

Johan staggered to his feet, blood trickling from a cut on his forehead. "We don't care what he's capable of. We're not leaving without you."

Malik raised his hand again, and the dreamscape shifted violently. The ground cracked and split, forming deep chasms that radiated with dark energy. The twisted trees stretched higher, their branches clawing at the sky.

"You're not leaving at all," Malik said, his tone final.

Jasper's cries grew louder as the dark threads binding him pulsed with malevolent energy. Terry crawled toward him, ignoring the chaos around them. "Jasper, listen to me. You must fight this. Whatever hold he has on you, break it!"

"I... I can't," Jasper choked out, his voice strained. "He's inside my mind. Every thought I have, he's there. It's like... like I'm not even myself anymore."

Terry reached out, his gauntlets glowing as he tried to unravel the dark threads. But as soon as he touched them, a searing pain shot through his hands, forcing him to withdraw.

"They're too strong," Terry muttered, his frustration mounting.

Johan limped toward them, his movements slow but deliberate. "We'll figure it out," he said, his voice steady despite the odds.

Malik laughed, the sound echoing through the dreamscape. "Do you really think you can save him? Jasper belongs to me now. His mind, his will, his very essence—it's all mine."

Jasper's eyes flickered with a faint golden light, a remnant of the sanctuary's influence. For a brief moment, he locked eyes with Johan. "I'm... I'm sorry," he whispered.

"No," Johan said firmly. "You don't get to give up, Jasper. Not on us, not on yourself."

Johan and Terry stood shoulder to shoulder, their gauntlets glowing brighter as they prepared for a final stand. Malik's shadows twisted tighter, his smirk unwavering.

"You're wasting your energy," Malik said, his tone almost bored. "But if you're so eager to fight, who am I to deny you?"

With a flick of his wrist, Malik unleashed a wave of dark energy that surged toward them. Johan and Terry braced themselves, their gauntlets creating a protective barrier. The force of the collision shook the dreamscape, but the barrier held—for now.

Terry glanced at Johan. "This isn't working. We need Leah."

"She's not here," Johan said through gritted teeth. "It's just us."

"Then we're screwed," Terry muttered.

The barrier began to crack under the weight of Malik's assault. Johan's legs buckled, but he refused to fall. "Not yet," he said, his voice resolute.

Suddenly, Jasper let out a strangled cry. The golden light in his eyes flared brighter, momentarily overpowering the dark threads. Malik's focus shifted, his expression twisting with irritation.

"What are you doing?" Malik murmured, directing more energy toward Jasper.

Taking advantage of the distraction, Terry and Johan charged forward. Johan aimed a powerful strike at Malik's chest, while Terry targeted the threads binding Jasper.

The dreamscape exploded with light and shadow as the two forces clashed. For a brief, shining moment, it seemed like the tide might turn. But Malik's power was too great. He swatted Johan aside with ease, then enveloped Terry in a swirl of shadows, pinning him to the ground.

"You never stood a chance," Malik said, his voice dripping with contempt.

Malik turned his attention back to Jasper, the dark threads tightening once more. Jasper's golden light flickered and dimmed, overwhelmed by Malik's influence.

"No!" Johan shouted, struggling to his feet.

Malik glanced at him, his smirk returning. "You're persistent. I'll give you that. But this is where it ends—for all of you."

With a wave of his hand, Malik's dark energy surged through the air, enveloping Johan and Terry. The ground beneath them seemed to dissolve, pulling them into a spiraling abyss of shadows. They struggled to resist, but the force was too strong. The dreamscape shattered around them, replaced by an eerie silence as they fell into an endless void.

When they landed, it was with a jarring impact that left them gasping for air. The world around them was barren and bleak—a desolate, dreamlike expanse that stretched endlessly under a fractured, crimson sky. The air was thick with despair, the kind that clung to the skin and seeped into the soul. Broken structures jutted out of the ground like skeletal remains of a once-thriving civilization, and the faint echoes of mournful cries carried on the wind.

"This... isn't the sanctuary," Johan said, his voice hoarse as he rose to his feet. "Where are we?"

Terry rubbed his temple, his gauntlets flickering weakly. "This is... this is something else. Look around, man. It's like the end of the world."

The void felt alive, a pulsing entity that breathed despair into everything it touched. The ground beneath their feet was cracked and scorched, glowing faintly with ember-like veins. Every step felt heavy, as if the ground was trying to pull them deeper into its suffocating grasp.

Johan and Terry moved cautiously, scanning their surroundings. The remnants of people—no, souls—littered the void, their forms translucent and faint, their eyes hollow with anguish. Some wandered aimlessly, while others knelt as if praying to an absent deity. The air was filled with whispers, fragmented pleas, and sobs that seemed to come from nowhere and everywhere at once.

"What is this place?" Terry asked, his voice barely above a whisper. "It's like... they're stuck here."

Johan knelt beside one of the souls, a woman whose face was streaked with silent tears. He reached out, but his hand passed through her like smoke. "They're lost," he said. "Malik's keeping them here."

"Not just keeping them," Terry said, his voice tightening. "Feeding on them."

A shadow loomed over them, and the oppressive energy in the air thickened. Malik's figure materialized before them, his dark robes billowing as if moved by an unseen wind. His presence was suffocating, a void within the void itself.

"You catch on quickly," Malik said, his voice cold and mocking. "This is my domain, the place where the lost come to serve their purpose."

Terry stepped forward, his gauntlets sparking faintly. "You're feeding on their pain. Twisting their dreams into... this."

Malik tilted his head, his smirk growing. "Pain is power, my dear Zepharian. I know exactly what you are—I can feel your threads. Born to blend the drealis and the dreamscape. These souls... they're the remnants of those forgotten, cast aside by fate itself. I didn't create their suffering—I gave it purpose. I fulfilled your destiny for you. I gave them a place to belong."

"Belong?" Johan growled, fists clenched at his sides. "You've trapped them—twisted them into fuel for your madness. Some ruler you are. Innocents deserve grace."

Malik's smile didn't waver, but the edge in his eyes sharpened like a blade. "Am I not giving them purpose, Warrior? Or is that only true when it suits your legacy?" He stepped closer, voice smooth and venomous. "You speak of grace—did your woven blood offer Diollo any? Your people sought the Primoris Core to dominate. I simply beat you to it. These souls thrive on raw emotion... and I've given them a place to burn."

Terry lunged forward, his gauntlets glowing brightly as he struck out at Malik. The impact was immediate, but Malik barely flinched. With a flick of his wrist, he sent Terry flying backward, landing hard against the cracked ground.

"Your strength is impressive," Malik said, turning to Terry. "But it's misplaced. You fight for a world that doesn't understand you, doesn't care about you. Look around. This could be your fate, too."

Terry hesitated, the weight of Malik's words pressing against him. But then he straightened, his fists glowing faintly. "No. I fight because it's the right thing to do."

Malik's expression darkened. "How noble. But nobility won't save you."

He raised his hand, and the void seemed to respond, its shadows surging forward like living tendrils. Johan and Terry fought back, Terry's gauntlet flaring with bursts of light, but the shadows were unrelenting, overwhelming their defenses.

The tendrils wound around them, dragging them to their knees. Johan struggled, his strength waning, while Terry's gauntlets sputtered and dimmed. Malik stepped closer, his stare piercing as he looked down at them.

"This is the end for you," Malik said, his voice cold and final. "But don't worry—I'll make sure Leah knows exactly what's waiting for her."

With a wave of his hand, Malik sent a shockwave through the void. Johan and Terry were thrown backward, landing hard on the cracked ground. The shadows began to encase them, pulling them deeper into the void.

"Tell Leah," Malik said, his voice echoing ominously. "Her defiance is meaningless. The drealis belongs to me now. Everything belongs to me"

The last thing they saw was Malik's smirk as the shadows consumed them, leaving them trapped in his realm of despair.

Back in Leah's sanctuary, the threads of the Loom of Lumarion flickered and dimmed. Mina stood frozen, her hand covering her mouth as she stared at the unraveling images of Johan and Terry. Leah's return from the ancestral portal brought no relief as she stepped into the sanctuary, her face etched with worry.

"What's happening?" Leah asked, her voice sharp.

Mina turned to her, her eyes wide with fear. "Malik has them. Johan and Terry... they're gone."

Realization struck Leah, the weight of her failure pressing down on her. "We have to find them," she said firmly. "Before it's too late."

The loom pulsed faintly, revealing the broken, apocalyptic landscape where Johan and Terry were trapped. Leah's breath caught as the fractured sky loomed above, the voices of lost souls echoing faintly through the threads.

She took a deep breath, "Hold on," she whispered. "I'm coming."

With that, she stepped through the portal, ready to face Malik's twisted creation in a desperate bid to save her team.

CHAPTER 20

WHEN THE SKY FALLS

L eah stepped through the portal, the swirling energy dissipating behind her. The air was thick with despair, the metallic tang of decay stinging her senses. She stood in a barren landscape, cracked and desolate, beneath a sky shattered like broken glass. Each jagged fissure in the sky bled faint, otherworldly light, casting a cold, sickly glow across the ruined terrain. The void hummed with an almost sentient energy, its whispers carrying a promise of agony. It was a place where time itself seemed to unravel, where reality bent and twisted into something unrecognizable.

This place was hauntingly familiar. It stirred forgotten memories, whispers of a life Leah had once known, before dreams turned to nightmares. She had walked this ground before. This was the world she and Malik had once called home, Velmara. The city they had built together, a place of unity and dreams, now lay in ruins. The remnants of their shared vision scattered like broken dreams in the ashes.

Leah's eyes scanned the desolation, her heart tightening at the sight of skeletal towers jutting into the fractured sky. The spires that once stood tall, symbols of their hopes, now leaned like mournful sentinels, bowing to the oppressive weight of the dark sky. In the distance, a flickering light caught her attention. It beckoned her, drawing her forward. With each step, the silence deepened and the air grew colder, as though even the wind mourned the loss of what once was.

As she moved cautiously toward the light, the air seemed to pulse with something malevolent, a heavy presence pressing against her. The hum of despair grew louder, and Leah's instincts told her that whatever waited ahead was not merely a memory—it was Malik.

In the center of a crumbling plaza, Malik stood, his back to her, silhouetted against the dim light of the fractured sky. He gazed down at a shimmering projection of what the world had once been—a city full of light, vibrancy, and life. The projection flickered with an almost painful beauty—people laughing, children playing in the streets, and the golden sky above, unbroken. A world full of hope. A world that no longer existed.

"You remember, don't you?" Malik's voice cut through the silence, soft and laden with an emotion Leah hadn't heard from him in years. He didn't turn to face her, his eyes fixed on the memory of their lost world.

Leah's heart clenched, the weight of their shared history pressing heavily against her chest. "Of course, I do," she said quietly, her voice betraying the sorrow she felt. "It was beautiful... before everything fell apart."

Malik turned slowly, his expression unreadable. For the first time, the sharpness in his gaze had dulled, replaced by a deep, aching sorrow. "We built this together," he said, his voice thick with emotion. "Every thread, every connection, every dream... it all started here." He gestured to the ruins around them, his hands trembling slightly.

Leah's heart ached at his words, and the memories of the nights they spent weaving dreams, of their shared laughter and vision for a world free from pain, washed over her. "We wanted to create something lasting," she said softly. "Something that would heal, not destroy."

Malik's face darkened. "And yet, it all crumbled. Because of them. Because they couldn't see the beauty in what we offered." His voice trembled with raw bitterness, each word laden with years of festering resentment.

Leah shook her head slowly. "It wasn't them, Malik. It was us. We tried to control too much. We tried to force connections that weren't meant to be. You've always believed that force could create unity, but you can't control connections. They need to be nurtured, not dictated."

His eyes flashed with anger. "They rejected us, Leah," he spat, his hands balling into fists. "They rejected everything we stood for. And when they tore it all down, they left us with nothing but pain."

Leah took a deep, steadying breath, her voice softening as she reached out to him. "And you think this—this chaos, this suffering—will bring it back? Malik, look at what you're doing. You're not healing anything. You're just spreading the same pain that destroyed us."

For a moment, Malik faltered. His shoulders sagged, his hands trembling at his sides. "Do you think I don't know that?" he whispered, his voice raw. "Every time I try to fix it, the pain... it consumes me."

A wave of emotion hit Leah at the sound of his voice, at the vulnerability that flashed in his eyes. She reached out, her hand hovering near his arm, as if she could bridge the chasm between them. "Malik, you don't have to do this alone. You don't have to carry all of this."

But then, his body stiffened. The moment passed, and the anger returned in full force. He jerked away from her, his eyes flashing with an unnatural light. The shadows around him seemed to writhe, alive with a dark energy. Malik staggered back, clutching his head as a guttural growl escaped from his lips. "You... you can't stop it," he rasped, his voice distorting into something darker, more malevolent. "It's... it's too late."

"Malik!" Leah cried, stepping forward, reaching for him. "What's happening to you?"

He stumbled, his movements jerky and unnatural, as his voice deepened further. "It's not just me," he said, his eyes flickering with madness. "It's—" But before he could finish, the shadows surged violently around him. Leah braced herself, her heart pounding as the energy surged outward, knocking her off balance. The chaos swirled around them, the dreamscape warping under the weight of the dark power Malik was now channeling.

"Leave," Malik gasped, his face contorted with agony, the shadows suffocating him. "Before it consumes you too."

Before Leah could respond, a burst of golden light illuminated the space behind her. Mina emerged from a portal, her face set with grim determination. She sprinted toward Leah and, with a swift motion, pulled Terry and Johan free from the bonds of Malik's shadows.

"Leah, we have to go!" Mina shouted.

Leah hesitated, her eyes meeting Malik's one last time. "This isn't you," she said softly, her voice shaking. "I'll find a way to bring you back."

Malik's lips curled into a bitter, mocking smile. "There's no going back, Leah. Not for me."

As the pain overtook him again, his body convulsing under the weight of the shadows, Mina grabbed Leah's arm, pulling her toward the portal. The last thing Leah saw before they vanished was Malik, his anguished cry echoing through the fractured world.

The group stumbled back into the sanctuary, disoriented and shaken. Johan and Terry were weak but alive, their faces grim as they leaned against the walls for support. Mina released Leah's arm, her face pale but resolute.

"What happened to him?" Mina asked, her voice barely above a whisper.

Leah's shoulders sagged. She closed her eyes, the weight of Malik's torment pressing down on her. "He's not just fighting us," Leah said quietly. "He's fighting something bigger. Something that's consuming him."

Terry, still recovering, looked up. "Then how do we stop him?"

Leah turned toward the loom, her fingers brushing over the threads. "We keep going," she said firmly, her voice steady despite the weight of her words. "Because if we don't, this world—everything we've fought for—will fall apart."

The sanctuary pulsed faintly with light, a quiet reminder of the connection that still held the Weavers together. Leah steeled herself for what was to come. The battle ahead wasn't just against Malik—it was against the darkness threatening to consume them all.

"We fight," Leah whispered to herself, the threads vibrating with purpose. "We fight, or everything ends."

Leah's Lumarion

The sanctuary pulsed with an uneasy rhythm, its golden threads flickering like a heartbeat teetering on the edge of collapse. Leah stood before the loom, her fingers tracing the fragile strands with trembling precision. Her mind spun in chaotic fragments: Malik's anguished face in the apocalyptic void, the fractured sky above her, his haunting words echoing in her ears. Time was slipping away, and she felt it acutely—too much was at stake, and the weight of the moment pressed down on her.

Mina sat nearby, wrapping a fresh bandage around her arm, her fingers steady despite the tension in the air. Her gaze flicked between Johan and Terry, both of whom carried the marks of their encounter with Malik. Johan sat stiffly, his fingers tapping a restless rhythm against his knee, his brow furrowed in thought. Terry's gauntlets lay on the ground beside him.

Even Jasper, tethered and frail in the corner, seemed more withdrawn than usual. His murmurs, faint and barely audible, carried an edge that filled the space with unease, as if he too sensed the ominous weight of what lay ahead.

"Leah," Johan broke the silence, his voice steady but low, tinged with curiosity. "How did you do it? You made him vulnerable. For a moment there, he wasn't untouchable."

Leah's gaze never wavered from the loom, her fingers lightly brushing the golden threads. "I didn't do anything," she replied quietly, her voice barely a whisper. "That wasn't me."

Terry leaned forward, his voice hoarse, his curiosity palpable. "Then what was it? He was... different. It's like he wasn't himself."

Leah exhaled slowly, her hands falling to her sides as she finally turned to face her team. Her expression was clouded, a storm of uncertainty swirling behind her eyes. "I think... Malik isn't whole anymore. That wasn't entirely him."

Mina frowned, the lines of concern deepening on her face. "What do you mean? We saw him. We fought him."

"But did we?" Leah interrupted, her voice trembling. "The Malik I knew— the one I once loved—he wasn't like this. Not entirely. There was pain in his eyes, yes, but something else... something darker. It was like he wasn't in control."

Johan's brow furrowed, a sudden realization dawning in his mind. "Possessed?"

Leah nodded slowly, the weight of her own thoughts pressing heavily on her chest. "Maybe. Or consumed. Either way, I don't think the real Malik was there in that moment. The rage, the power—it wasn't his. And now, I'm questioning if hiding Jara from him was the right thing to do."

Mina's eyes snapped toward Leah, a sharp intensity in her gaze. "Leah, are you saying you're doubting yourself? After everything he's done?"

"I'm saying," Leah said, her voice thick with emotion, "that if there's even a chance the real Malik is still in there, then maybe this isn't just a fight against him. Maybe there's something else. Someone else."

The room fell into tense silence, the golden threads of the loom flickering erratically, as though responding to Leah's words. Her doubts hung in the air, tangible and heavy, casting a shadow over the group. Jasper stirred in the corner, his tether humming faintly, the vibration sending shivers up Leah's arms. He jolted upright suddenly, his eyes wide and unfocused, a sharp gasp escaping his lips.

"Jasper!" Leah rushed to his side, steadying him as his body trembled. His eyes searched the space around him with confusion and panic. The tether glowed faintly, vibrating with an intensity that seemed to shake the sanctuary itself.

"What is it? What do you feel?" Leah asked urgently.

Jasper's lips moved, but his voice was faint and broken, the words barely audible. "Malik... I can feel him."

The room stilled, every eye on Jasper as he struggled to articulate what he was sensing. His body trembled, a fine sheen of sweat on his forehead, his voice shaking with raw fear. "He's... he's not here. Not in the void. He's in... the awakened world."

Leah's breath caught, her chest tightening without warning. The implications were vast, terrifying. "Where? What is he doing?"

Jasper's gaze darted around the room, his expression panicked as his words faltered. "I don't know. It's strange. Feels like home. He seems... normal. Powerless, even. Like he's just... a man."

"Who is he with?" Mina asked, her voice sharp, a note of urgency creeping into her words.

Jasper's breath hitched, his eyes wide with horror. "He's... he's talking to someone. A woman. I can't see her. He's getting close."

"To what?" Johan pressed, his voice a low growl as he took a step closer.

Jasper turned to Leah, his voice barely a whisper. "To her. To Jara."

Leah's breath caught in her throat, her fears crystallizing into something concrete and unbearable. She glanced back at the loom, the threads shimmering faintly, struggling to hold their form, as if the very fabric of reality was under threat.

"If he's in the awakened world," Leah said slowly, her voice tight with controlled panic, "then he's vulnerable. He can't wield the same power there."

"Unless..." Johan interrupted grimly, his voice low, "he's biding his time, waiting for the right moment to strike."

Leah's shoulders sagged as the weight of the revelation pressed down on her. Her heart raced as she fought to keep her composure. "He's searching for her," she said quietly. "And if he finds her before we do—"

"No," Mina interrupted firmly, her voice cutting through the tension. "We won't let that happen."

Terry stood, his gauntlets flickering faintly as he picked them up and reattuned them to his wrists. "Then we don't have time to waste."

Leah's gaze hardened with resolve. "We need to track him down. Jasper, can you show me where he is?"

Jasper closed his eyes, his tether humming faintly as he focused, his breath shallow. "I'll try."

The sanctuary pulsed again, the threads of the loom shimmering as a faint image appeared—a distant city bathed in an eerie, otherworldly glow. Leah's heart skipped a beat as recognition flooded her mind. It was a place she hadn't seen in years, but one she knew all too well.

"Diollo," she whispered under her breath, the name carrying a deep weight, a world of memories.

"Diollo?" Terry asked, his frown deepening. "What's Diollo?"

Leah's gaze remained fixed on the shimmering threads as they painted the image of Diollo, the distant city bathed in an eerie, otherworldly glow. Her mind raced, and her heart tightened with the weight of recognition. It wasn't just a place of answers—it was a crossroads where everything, both dream and reality, converged. It was where dreams were born, where connections were made, and where the threads of fate could be woven or severed.

She paused for a moment, her eyes flicking to Jasper, whose tether hummed faintly with energy. A soft, painful recognition washed over her as she realized something else: Diollo wasn't just Malik's home—it was Jasper's birthplace too. The place where he had been born, and perhaps, the place where his very connection to the Dreamweavers began.

Leah's voice softened, her words filled with both a quiet resolve and a lingering sorrow. "It's where we'll find him, his home, and where everything will change." Her gaze lingered on Jasper, whose eyes flickered with confusion, as if the full weight of what Diollo meant to him couldn't fully settle in his mind while he was tethered.

Jasper shifted uneasily, the words on the edge of his lips but failing to fully materialize, a ghost of memories and truths too distant for him to grasp. Leah reached out, her hand hovering near his shoulder, a silent acknowledgment of the past that bound them all, yet felt too far to touch. She continued, her voice steady. "But it's not just Malik's story, Jasper. It's yours too. Diollo holds the key to both our fates."

Leah's Velara Aelis

The threads shimmer beneath my fingers, glowing faintly as if they, too, hesitate to reveal the path ahead.

Diollo. The name lingers in the air like a whispered secret—heavy with memory, charged with meaning. It's not just a place from Malik's past. It's etched into mine. A birthplace of prophecy and power. A crossroads where hope once burned so brightly it dared to eclipse the darkness that would follow.

Diollo isn't just a dreamscape—it's a threshold. A point where fate and dream converge. A place of endings and beginnings. It's where Malik was shaped into who he became. And it's where I must decide who I truly am...

I've woven and unraveled countless dreams—guided others through fear, grief, and longing—but this thread is different. These threads aren't simply frayed... they're scorched. Singed by those who tried to twist their meaning.

Malik was born of Diollo's prophecy, once destined to mend the fractures between the drealis and the dreamscape. But now? Now he is both the weapon and the wound.

What have we endured to reach this moment?

A lifetime folded into fleeting nights. A tapestry of pain and love, sacrifice and discovery. I think of Terry, whose hands once trembled but now move with steady conviction. Of Mina, who stood at the edge of her own ruin and chose to rebuild. Of Johan, forged by loss, still holding hope like a lantern. And of Jasper—flickering, tethered by shadow, yet still guiding us with what strength remains.

And me?

I've touched every thread of this journey, but my hands feel heavier now—burdened by the secret I've carried close to my heart.

Jara. My daughter. The child I had to hide to protect the world she was born to change. She doesn't yet understand her power or the legacy that pulses in her veins. But she is the reason I've come this far. She is the reason I will not stop now.

Diollo is not just Malik's home. It's ours. The birthplace of our hopes, our promises, our broken truths. The dusty streets, the golden skies, the air thick with magic—it lives in me still, like a half-forgotten melody too painful to hum aloud.

I see now: it was never just about Malik. The prophecy never belonged to him alone—or to me. It was always about the balance Diollo once represented. A balance we both failed to hold. The threads are tangled in his rage, in my grief, in the silence between us.

This may be goodbye.

I've known it since the beginning—not just a goodbye to my team, to Malik, or to who I've been—but to the part of me that clung to fear instead of faith. To be a Dreamweaver is not just to guide others. It is to let go. Of doubt. Of control. Of the illusion that love and power cannot coexist.

I think of Jara again—and wonder if she'll ever understand that every thread I've woven, every dream I've walked through, was for her. To build a world where she can weave without fear. A world where Diollo is no longer a wound... but a wonder.

Now we step into the crossroads—where dreams and fate collide, where power and love meet, where Malik waits, still tethered by the pain we never healed. There are no guarantees. But if this is my final weave, let it be one of truth, strength, connection... and hope.

J. D. Jackson

I am a Weaver.

This is my story.

This is ours.

And no matter what awaits in Diollo—I will weave until the last thread remains.

CHAPTER 21

Diollo

The air shifted as Leah, Johan, Mina, and Terry stepped through the portal. It was as though they had walked into another realm entirely—one that pulsed with energy, both familiar and alien. The city of Diollo stretched before them, its spires glowing faintly against a twilight sky. The buildings were impossibly tall, their structures woven from threads of light and shadow that seemed to hum with life.

Leah took a deep breath, her chest tight with the weight of memory. Diollo was not just a city—it was a nexus, a place where dreams and destiny converged. It was where she and Malik had first discovered the depth of their powers as Dreamweavers, where they had once envisioned building a sanctuary for connection and healing. But now, it was something else entirely. The golden glow that had once defined it was tarnished, overtaken by streaks of black that twisted and writhed like living scars.

"This place feels... wrong. The threads here are off." Mina's voice was low, almost reverent, as she scanned the towering structures. "I used to dream of coming here."

"It's fractured," Leah replied, her tone heavy. "Malik's influence is here, but it's not complete. He's trying to reshape it into something... darker."

Johan adjusted the straps of his armor, his expression grim. "Then we stop him before he finishes."

As they moved through the city, Leah couldn't shake the feeling that the threads of fate were pulling tighter around them. The streets were eerily silent, the usual hum of the dreamscape replaced by a haunting stillness. Faint whispers echoed from the walls, fragments of dreams and memories swirling in the air.

"Leah," Terry said, his voice low, "this place... it's alive, isn't it?"

Leah nodded. "Diollo has always been alive. It's built from the threads of countless dreams, a reflection of the connections that bind us. But now, those threads are fraying."

They turned a corner, and Leah froze. In the center of the plaza stood a massive loom, the Loom of Dreams, its threads tangled and pulsating with an unnatural energy. At its base was Malik, his back to them, his hands moving deftly over the threads. He was weaving something, the patterns shifting chaotically under his touch.

"Malik!" Leah called out, her voice cutting through the stillness.

He turned slowly, his expression calm but his eyes burning with an intensity that sent a shiver down Leah's spine. "Leah," he said, his voice smooth. "You've finally arrived."

The team fanned out, each of them ready for a confrontation, but Malik held up a hand. "No need for theatrics," he said, his tone almost amused. "We're at a crossroads, after all. Let's not ruin the moment."

"What are you doing here?" Leah demanded, stepping forward.

"Diollo is the heart of everything," Malik replied. "The threads of fate run through this city. And through me."

"You're destroying it," Terry spat, his gauntlets sparking with energy.

"Am I?" Malik said, tilting his head. "Or am I remaking it? Do you know how much pain these threads carry? How much suffering they weave into our lives?" If I destroy it, it'll set me free. We can all be free.

Leah took another step forward, her gaze locked on his. "This isn't about the threads. This is about Jara."

Malik's expression darkened, a flicker of raw emotion crossing his face. "Jara," he said softly, almost to himself. "She's... she's everything."

"Malik, listen to me," Leah said, her voice firm but pleading. "You can't use her. If you do, you'll destroy everything—this world, the awakened world, even yourself."

Malik's laughter rang out—bitter, hollow. "Do you think I don't know that? That I haven't tried to stop? But the pain... it's too much, Leah. She's the answer—not you, not me. With her, I can end it."

Before Leah could respond, Malik raised his hands, and the loom behind him surged with dark energy. Threads of black and gold lashed out, weaving a barrier around him.

"I didn't bring you here to fight," Malik said, his voice echoing through the stillness. "I brought you here to see. Join me, Leah. With our power combined, we can start over."

He stepped closer, eyes burning with conviction. "Listen to the Loom, Leah... can't you hear it? It's calling to us. It's telling us to set it free."

The plaza shifted, the ground beneath them dissolving into a swirling void. The team stumbled, their surroundings transforming into a vision of a world that had once been beautiful but was now broken. Leah recognized it instantly—their world, their home, before it had been consumed by Malik's despair.

"You could have stopped this," Malik said, his gaze piercing. "We could have stopped it together."

"No," Leah said, her voice trembling but resolute. "You wanted control. You wanted to force connections that weren't meant to be. That's why everything fell apart."

Malik's eyes flashed with anger. "And you abandoned me! You left me to pick up the pieces!"

Tension crackled between them, the threads of the Loom of Dreams vibrating with the energy of their emotions. Johan stepped forward, his weapon raised, but Leah held up a hand.

"Don't," she said quietly. "This isn't just about us anymore."

Terry's voice was sharp. "Leah, we can't just stand here—"

"She's right," Mina interrupted, her eyes narrowing. "This isn't the time."

Leah took a deep breath, her gaze steady on Malik. "We can still fix this," she said. "But not like this. Let Jara go. Let her be who she's meant to be."

For a moment, Malik's expression softened, and Leah thought she saw a flicker of the man she had once known. But it was gone as quickly as it came, replaced by a cold resolve.

"No," Malik said, his voice low. "It's too late for that."

The loom surged again, and the ground beneath them began to crack. Malik raised his hands, the threads of the loom spiraling outward to engulf the team.

Johan and Terry leapt into action, their weapons clashing against the dark threads. Mina moved to Leah's side; her voice urgent. "We need to go. Now."

Leah hesitated, her heart aching as she looked at him. "Please... don't do this," she said softly.

Malik's look remained unreadable. "I can't stop," he murmured. "Jara will be here soon."

Mina pulled Leah back, and the team retreated through the portal as the threads closed in around them. Malik's figure grew distant, his silhouette framed by the chaos he had created.

The team stumbled back into the sanctuary, the golden threads flickering weakly around them. Johan slammed his weapon onto the ground, his frustration palpable. "We can't keep running from him."

"We're not running," Leah said, her voice firm. "We're staying alive. I won't leave any of you behind."

Terry looked up, his face pale but resolute. "So... do we need a new plan?"

Leah turned to the Loom of Lumarion, her fingers gliding over its threads. "No. We stick to the plan. Just don't get severed." She paused, feeling the threads pulse beneath her hands. "It's time I go to Jara."

Leah reached into the loom, her hand steady as it hovered above the glowing tapestry. Slowly, her fingers closed around a single thread—one no one else could see.

Mina stepped forward, eyes narrowing. "What is that one? Why couldn't we see it before?"

"It's a thread I created for Jara," Leah replied, her voice calm but charged with purpose. "It's hidden—only visible to me."

Terry's eyes widened, his voice a hushed whisper. "She can create threads..."

Johan stared at Leah, awe etched across his face. "You truly are Veilborn."

Leah reached for the loomstaff, her fingers wrapping around its worn grip. She raised it slightly, the light within flickering in response.

"If you've got anything left in you," she whispered to the staff, "I need you now."

Then she turned to her team, her watch steady and determined. "When I give the signal... follow the thread."

CHAPTER 22

WOVEN IN TIME

Rain whispered against the rooftop of a small cottage hidden deep within a forgotten fold of the dreamscape—a pocket realm crafted with care and secrecy. Inside, young Jara sat curled on the edge of her bed, arms wrapped tightly around her knees. Her window blurred with water trails, and the storm outside mirrored the ache in her chest. The flickering candlelight on her nightstand cast long glooms across her journal, unopened and untouched for days.

This place was safe—her mother had made sure of that. A cottage suspended between moments, where time bent quietly and the loom's pulse slowed. Leah had created this drealis to give her daughter the life she never had: one untouched by war, prophecy, or pain. But even in safety, Jara felt the pull of something beyond the walls. Something was changing.

She wiped her eyes and stood, drawn to the window once more. The clouds above churned unnaturally. Lightning cut across the sky in jagged silence. Then, without warning, a shimmer bloomed at the center of the room.

A tear in space. A portal woven not by force, but by lineage.

From it stepped a woman draped in iridescent veils, her eyes gleaming with wisdom and sorrow. She radiated a calm power that stopped Jara in her tracks.

"Who...?" Jara started, backing slightly.

"I am Miriam Cimaj," the woman said gently. "Your grandmother."

Jara's heart thudded. "But I don't—how are you here?"

"Because the veil thins when the threads call," Miriam replied, stepping closer. "And your mother is in danger. She's coming for you, but there are truths you must know before she arrives. Your time in hiding is over, Jara. The Loom of Dreams has awakened your thread."

Jara hesitated, her brows drawing inward. "Why now?"

Miriam's eyes glimmered with quiet sorrow. "Because the Loom does not arouse without purpose. The fate can be delayed but not denied. It is the heart of all dreams—a living weave that connects every soul, every fate, across the seven realms. It hears what the world cannot say, and when its light touches a thread... it means change is coming."

She knelt beside Jara, her voice low but steady. "The Loom of Dreams holds more than sleep and imagination. It weaves the paths we walk, the choices we make. And your thread, velana, is unlike any other. You are not just part of the Loom—you are woven from it. That's why it's calling now. Because you are needed."

Jara felt a strange heat in her chest—a subtle, humming pull. Her fingers itched, as if reaching for threads she couldn't yet see. She took a breath and stepped into the Veil beside Miriam.

The Aevitas Veil shimmered like liquid starlight. Threads of memory and time wove through the air, forming shifting corridors of forgotten dreams and futures yet made.

Jara followed her grandmother through the glowing mist, their footsteps silent. Somewhere in the ripple of time, another thread snapped into place.

Leah stood at the edge of the Veil.

Jara's breath caught in her throat.

She had seen this woman before—in dreams that felt too vivid to be imagined. The same violet eyes. The same gentle strength.

"Jara..." Leah whispered.

They stared at one another, time folding between them. Miriam nodded silently and stepped back, letting the moment belong to them.

Leah crossed the distance in quiet, careful steps. Her voice was soft but sure. "I've watched over you every day. Even when you couldn't see me, I was there. I just... I had to keep you safe."

Jara's voice cracked. "Why didn't you tell me?"

"Because if I had, the loom would have accelerated your thread. Your power would've called Malik. I couldn't let him find you."

Jara's eyes brimmed with tears. "He's my father, isn't he?"

Leah hesitated, then nodded. "Yes. But you were never part of his plan. You are the one the loom whispered about—the thread that completes the tapestry."

Jara rubbed her temples, her voice shaky. "So, I was born into prophecy?"

Leah took her hand. "There was a time long ago, when your father was the prophesied one—the child meant to restore The Loom of Dream balance and take the Quest of Three Veils. But when the darkness consumed him, the loom turned its gaze to someone else."

"You," Jara said.

"I thought so," Leah replied. "Until my dreams began to shift. Until the Loom showed me... you."

She reached to untie a thread wrapped around her wrist—a glowing silver cord, humming with warmth. "This thread will unlock what was hidden inside you—your memories, your dreams, your truth. But once it's awakened, there's no going back."

Just as their hands met, the light split. A sudden, violent crack tore through the Veil.

A shadow fell over them, and from it stepped Evelyn, cloaked in deep violet threads that shimmered like oil in moonlight. Her posture was regal, her dark hair braided back in tight coils threaded with silver, but it was her eyes—cold, calculating, and empty of warmth—that stole the breath from the room.

"No," Leah breathed, instinctively shielding Jara.

Evelyn's smile was cold and controlled. "I knew the Loom would eventually call her. I just had to wait for you to get close enough to trigger it. You see, Leah... it would never respond to me. But you? You were always the favored one."

Leah's voice trembled with betrayal. "We were sisters, Evelyn. I trusted you. We were serenya."

Evelyn's expression twisted. "And I was tired of being cast in your shadow. While you healed dreams, I studied them. While you ran from prophecy, I bent it. And now? I will complete what you never could."

Leah stepped forward, weaving a protective sigil in the air. "She doesn't even know her power. Your plan will fail."

"The loom doesn't need her understanding," Evelyn spat. "It only needs her energy. Whether born in love... or extracted through pain."

Before Leah could respond, Evelyn hurled a blast of shadow. Leah blocked it, but was thrown back into the Veil.

Jara screamed, reaching out—but Evelyn's hand was already on her.

"Let's go see your father," she whispered, and they vanished into a swirling rift of darkness.

Leah tumbled through the Veil, her body caught in shadow. She fell through fragments of time—memories crashing against her: the moment she failed to save Kaelith in the Nightmare Realm... the rejection in Diollo when the others called her outsider... the flicker of Auren Tahl's fading light as he resisted being severed. And a final image: a cloaked figure with burning eyes—one she didn't know... but whose presence chilled her deeper than any nightmare.

The moment lingered.

She was sinking—until a strong arm reached through the chaos and grabbed her.

Johan.

"Got you," he grunted, pulling her out with sheer will.

They landed hard in the sanctuary.

Terry, Mina, and Jasper stared in shock.

"We couldn't find you," Terry said breathlessly. "Your thread—it vanished. Until... until one started fraying."

Leah staggered to her feet, heart pounding.

"She has Jara," Leah said, her voice shaking. "Evelyn took her."

Mina blinked, confused. "Who's Evelyn?"

Leah's jaw tightened. "Someone I trusted like a sister, she carries the royal blood of the original Dreamweavers. Someone who's been in control of Malik all along. How could she reach the Veil?" Her voice dropped, thick with realization. "She must be in control of the threads... not Malik."

Jasper steadied himself, eyes darkening.

"She's been part of this all along. When you left, Leah... that's when it changed. After the Nightmare Realm, she came back different—like something twisted took root. The thread you created to heal her... it must have weakened. I should've seen it."

He looked at Leah. "We must go after them—now."

Leah turned to the loom, her fingers glowing.

"No more hiding," Leah said. "We go back to Diollo."

The Loom of Lumarion shimmered in response. The final weave had begun.

And somewhere in the shadows, Evelyn watched, a cruel smile playing on her lips. "Let them come," she whispered. "The threads will be mine."

CHAPTER 23

Diolla

The air in Diollo was oppressive, thick with the weight of unraveling threads of fate. The dreamscape's fractured ground radiated an eerie glow, and jagged structures twisted toward a darkened sky. It was as though the very essence of balance and harmony had been torn apart, leaving a realm of chaos and decay. Leah, Mina, Jasper, Terry, and Johan stood at the edge of this dreamscape, each of them steeling themselves for the battle to come.

In the distance, Evelyn loomed, her figure wreathed in swirling shadows, her hands weaving threads of dark energy that crackled with malevolence. At her side stood Malik, his eyes hollow, trapped within her control. Jara, faintly visible in a glowing orb suspended above the chaos, seemed unconscious, her presence pulsating with untapped power. Leah's heart ached at the sight of her daughter, a symbol of both hope and vulnerability.

"Stay close," Leah said, her voice steady despite the storm brewing inside her. She gripped the shimmering loomstaff, its golden threads pulsing faintly in response to her resolve. The staff felt like an extension of herself now, its power thrumming beneath her fingertips. It had always been her tool, but now, it seemed to possess a will of its own. She could feel its vibrations, urging her forward, its purpose entwined with hers. *It is time,* Lux Veritas whispered to her, a silent voice in her mind.

"Leah," Johan said, his voice tense, "we're with you, but we need a plan. Evelyn's power... it's beyond anything we've faced."

Leah turned to her team, meeting each of their gazes. "We fight as one. Together, we're stronger. Focus on the threads—keep them intact, no matter what."

Evelyn's laughter echoed across the barren expanse as she stepped forward. "You've brought your little band of heroes," she sneered. "How quaint. Do you really think they can stop me, Leah? You couldn't before, and you certainly can't now."

Without warning, Evelyn unleashed a torrent of dark energy, the threads spiraling outward like serpents. Johan reacted first, raising his shield to deflect the attack, but the force sent him skidding back, his boots scraping against the jagged ground.

Terry lunged forward, his gauntlets sparking to life. He punched through the dark threads, shattering several of them, but Evelyn's power was relentless. The fragments reformed, coiling around his arms and pinning him in place.

"Foolish," Evelyn said, her voice dripping with disdain. She flicked her wrist, and Terry was hurled to the ground. Mina rushed to his side, her hands glowing with healing energy as she worked to free him.

"Stay with me, Terry," Mina whispered, her voice trembling. "We're not done yet."

Leah advanced cautiously, weaving golden threads to counter Evelyn's darkness. For every thread she repaired, Evelyn severed two more, her power far-reaching and devastating.

But The loomstaff pulsed again, more insistently this time, as if sensing the danger was escalating. Leah grasped it tighter, allowing the threads within the staff to guide her movements. As she raised it closer to the Loom of Dreams, golden light poured from its tip, weaving intricate patterns that pushed against Evelyn's dark energy. Yet, for every victory, The loomstaff was met with an equal counterattack.

"Malik!" Leah called out, desperation lacing her voice. "You don't have to let her control you. Fight her!"

For a moment, Malik's eyes flickered, a hint of the man he once was shining through the haze. But Evelyn's grip tightened, and he fell silent, his body rigid as she manipulated him like a puppet. "Poor kynara, the Ruler of Diollo, pathetic and weak, tainted by love from an outsider."

As the battle raged on, The Loomstaff pulsed with a new energy, its golden threads surging and weaving on their own, reacting to Leah's deepest resolution. It was no longer just her weapon—it was guiding her, fighting with her, resonating with the very balance of the world. Leah could feel its power coursing through her, pushing against the malevolent energy Evelyn commanded.

Jasper, still tethered to Evelyn's dark influence, stumbled forward, clutching his head. Whispers swirled in his mind like a rising storm, his body trembling beneath the crushing weight of her control. His voice, thin and strained, barely rose above a whisper. *"She's everywhere... her presence... it's suffocating."*

"Stay with us, Jasper!" Johan shouted, stepping in to steady him. "We'll get through this."

But Evelyn's gaze locked onto Jasper, a cruel smile curving her lips. "Ah, my little tether. I never liked you. You've been such a useful tool. But your time is up."

With a flick of her wrist, Evelyn sent a surge of dark energy toward Jasper. Johan threw himself in front of the attack, raising his shield, but the impact sent both him and Jasper crashing to the ground.

"Enough!" Leah shouted, her voice cutting through the chaos. Her hand gripped the loomstaff tightly, its threads thrumming with raw power. The staff shimmered brighter, its golden glow flaring as it responded to Leah's command.

As the golden light from the loomstaff pierced the darkness, a powerful force burst from its threads, slicing through the shadows that bound Jasper. The dark threads that had held him in place splintered, unraveling like fragile strands of silk, torn apart by the staff's light. Jasper's body shuddered, the oppressive force that had kept him bound vanishing as if it had never existed.

Jasper gasped, his breath ragged, as the weight of Evelyn's control lifted from him. His body no longer felt like a puppet in her hands; his mind was his own again.

"Jasper!" Mina cried, rushing to his side. She helped him to his feet, her eyes filled with relief. "You're free."

Jasper nodded, his face pale but steady. "I... I can feel it. The tether's gone. She can't control me anymore."

Leah's heart soared with the realization that, with Jasper free, they now had a chance to win this battle. She gripped the loomstaff, its power still radiating from its golden threads, fueling her determination. "We're not done yet," she whispered, her voice filled with resolve.

"Enough!" Leah shouted, her voice cutting through the chaos. She raised the loomstaff high, its golden light piercing the darkness. "Evelyn, this ends now!"

The loomstaff shuddered in her grip, its threads writhing with power, as if it recognized the moment had come. Golden light blazed from the staff, forming a swirling barrier of energy that pulsed with a rhythm only Leah could feel. The staff had begun to act on its own, its power surging through her veins. It was no longer just her tool; it had become a part of her, binding her to the world of dreams, and now to the very fate of Diollo.

Evelyn laughed, a sound devoid of warmth. "You're right, Leah. It does end now."

As Evelyn prepared her final attack, Malik faltered. His body convulsed, and a pained expression crossed his face. For a moment, he was himself again, his voice trembling as he called out, "Leah..."

Leah froze, her heart clenching. "Malik, fight her! I know you're still in there."

Memories flooded her mind—moments from their shared past, fragments of the life they once dreamed of together. The melody from the jukebox in Sean's story echoed faintly in the background. The number 342, their first date, flashed in her mind. The walks in the park, the laughter, the love—they were all still there, buried beneath the darkness.

"Leah..." Malik's voice broke, his eyes meeting hers. "Save her. Save Jara."

Evelyn's grip on him tightened, and he screamed, the sound tearing through the dreamscape.

The chaos in Diollo reached a deafening crescendo. Evelyn's dark threads coiled tighter, their malevolence bending the dreamscape to her will. Leah could barely hold the loomstaff steady as the ground cracked beneath her feet, and Malik's screams echoed through the suffocating air.

"Leah!" Johan shouted, shielding Mina and Terry as another wave of Evelyn's power sent tremors through the battlefield.

Jara's glowing orb flickered weakly, her unconscious form trapped within Evelyn's web of shadows. Leah's heart clenched as she fought to weave against the tide of darkness, but Evelyn's control was absolute.

"You're too late," Evelyn hissed, her eyes burning with a cruel, undeniable triumph.

"This world bends to my will. I am the prophesied child—not Malik. You suppressed my memories, smothered my ambition. But I remember now. I am the Diolla— and nothing you do can stop what's already begun."

Just as Evelyn unleashed a massive surge of dark energy, a resounding crack split the sky. A radiant golden light descended, shattering the oppressive gloom. The threads of Evelyn's attack dissolved midair, and for a moment, silence fell over Diollo.

Miriam appeared, her form bathed in brilliance, the golden threads of fate swirling around her like a protective veil. Her voice resonated with authority, steady and commanding.

"Evelyn," Miriam said, stepping forward, "your obsession has blinded you. You've toyed with the threads of fate, but you will not destroy them."

Evelyn recoiled, her expression twisting with fury. "You think you can stop me?" she spat, her power rising in defiance. "This is my world now!"

"That power is not yours to wield," Miriam countered, her hands glowing as she summoned a web of golden threads that radiated pure energy. "It belongs to the balance you've forsaken."

Evelyn screamed, hurling a torrent of dark energy toward Miriam—but the golden threads surged forward, intercepting the attack and wrapping around her like a shimmering cocoon.

The darkness twisted and writhed as Evelyn fought against the binding threads, but the light only intensified.

Leah watched, breath caught in her chest, as the tendrils of gold grew brighter and brighter, forcing Evelyn's form to shrink inward, as if the light itself was rejecting her. Then—A flash of radiant energy exploded outward, so bright Leah had to shield her eyes. When she opened them again, blinking through the fading brilliance, her breath caught.

Only a wisp of smoke remained inside the cocoon.

Evelyn was gone.

The orb holding Jara shattered, and Leah rushed forward, catching her daughter as she fell. "Jara," Leah whispered, holding her close, relief flooding through her. Malik collapsed beside them, his body trembling as he gasped for air.

Miriam turned to Leah, her face softening. "You fought bravely, Leah. But this battle is not yet won."

The golden threads began to weave a new pattern, forming a glowing passage that shimmered with warmth and tranquility. "Come," Miriam said, her voice calm but urgent. "We must leave this place before it collapses entirely."

One by one, the team followed Miriam into the passage. Johan carried Terry, who was barely conscious, while Mina supported Jasper, who murmured incoherently as the tether's remnants lingered in his mind. Malik, weak but lucid, held Leah's gaze—his expression filled with both gratitude and sorrow—as he leaned on her for support. In her other arm, Leah cradled a conscious Jara, holding her close as they stepped into the light together.

The passage opened into a breathtaking realm, unlike anything they had ever seen. The air shimmered with hues of gold and lavender, and the ground was covered in a soft, luminescent mist. Towering trees with crystalline leaves stretched toward a sky of perpetual twilight, and a sense of profound peace enveloped the group.

"This is Somnium Solace," Miriam said, her voice reverent. "A sanctuary for Dreamweavers—a place to heal and rebuild. It lies beyond the reach of the waking world and the dreamscapes, like The Lumarion." It was a place between realms, where time felt fluid, and every thread hummed with untold possibilities. Here, the wounded healed, and the weary found solace—a sanctuary not just for Dreamweavers but for the essence of the dreamscape itself. She smiled at Leah, a twinkle of mischief in her eyes. "You're not the only one who knows how to create threads."

Leah felt a wave of calm wash over her as they stepped into the sanctuary. Jara stirred in her arms, her eyes fluttering open. "Mom?" she whispered, her voice faint but steady.

"I'm here, Jara," Leah said, tears streaming down her face. "You're safe now."

Miriam gestured to a central structure, a grand hall made of translucent stone that seemed to pulse with life. "Inside, you will find The Loom of Solariis. It will help you recover your strength and repair the threads Evelyn has severed."

The team moved toward the hall, their steps heavy with exhaustion but buoyed by hope. As they entered, the glowing loom came to life, its golden threads stretching toward Leah, welcoming her as their weaver.

But even as they found solace in Somnium Solace, a dark presence lingered. Back in Diollo, the ashes of Evelyn's defeat began to stir. The dark smoke coalesced, taking shape as it rose into the fractured sky. Evelyn's laughter echoed faintly, carrying a chilling promise: "The threads of fate will bend to my will once again."

Leah turned, sensing the lingering darkness from beyond the veil. Her hand tightened around the loomstaff as she looked at Miriam.

"She's not gone," Leah said, her voice resolute.

"No," Miriam admitted, her expression grave. "But neither is your strength. You have what you need, Leah—what we all need." *You have lots to learn.*

Leah nodded, her gaze shifting to Jara, who stood beside her, her eyes filled with determination. Together, they would face whatever came next.

Leah's Velara Aelis

The threads of fate, fragile and unyielding, shimmered faintly beneath my fingers as I traced the patterns woven into them. Each thread, a story. Each knot, a turning point. And now, as I sit in the quiet sanctuary of Somnium Solace, a place where the waking world meets the dreamscapes, I find myself reflecting on this journey—not just my own, but the journey of everyone I've guided, everyone I've loved, and everyone I've fought for.

The loom before me pulses softly, alive in its stillness, waiting for me to weave the final strand of this chapter. But before I can, I must honor the lessons the threads have whispered to me. Connection, strength, and meaning—the three pillars that have guided this path—have taught me more than I could have imagined. They have demanded my resilience, my vulnerability, and above all, my compassion. Now, they demand my clarity.

I once believed connection was a simple thing—a bond forged by shared experiences or mutual understanding. I thought it was enough to feel tethered to others through laughter, tears, and the everyday moments that made up a life. But I was wrong. Connection is not merely something we create; it is something we uncover. It is woven into the fabric of who we are, stretching across time, linking us to people we've never met, to places we've never been, and to dreams we've never dared to dream.

Sean taught me this, though he may never know it. His grief, tangled with longing, mirrored my own in ways I was too afraid to admit. Jillian's presence in his life, fleeting as it was, reminded me that even the most ephemeral connections can leave indelible marks. It wasn't just about letting go of the past—it was about holding on to the lessons it offered, the echoes of love that lingered long after the physical bonds had faded.

And then there is Jara. My daughter. My greatest connection. I spent so long keeping her a secret, not only from the world but from myself. I told myself it was to protect her, to shield her from the darkness I knew too well. But in doing so, I nearly severed the most sacred bond of all. Jara is not just my daughter; she is my legacy. She is the light that will carry the Weavers name forward, weaving threads I will never see, in a world I can only hope to shape.

Strength is a word we often misunderstand. We think it means power, resilience, the ability to endure. But strength is so much more than that. Strength is found in the moments we break, the moments we falter, the moments we surrender to vulnerability. It is in those cracks that the light enters, illuminating the parts of us we've kept hidden, even from ourselves.

I thought I was strong when I confronted Malik for the first time. I thought my anger, my defiance, would be enough to overcome him. But strength does not come from anger. It comes from understanding. And Malik—Malik was not just an adversary. He was a mirror, reflecting my fears, my guilt, and my buried pain. For so long, I saw him only as a villain, the man who disrupted dreams and severed threads. But in Diollo, I saw the truth: Malik was as much a victim as anyone else. He was consumed by a pain he couldn't escape, a pain that mirrored my own.

It took strength to see him as more than the sum of his actions. It took strength to forgive him—not just for what he had done but for what he represented. And it took strength to fight for him, to pull him back from the edge of oblivion, even when *every thread in me wanted to let him go.*

But the greatest strength I've found is not in battles or forgiveness. It is in unity. Mina, Johan, Terry, and even Jasper—they have become more than allies. They are my family, my anchors in the storm. Together, we've faced the darkest corners of the dreamscapes and the most harrowing truths of the waking world. Together, we've learned that strength is not about standing alone but about standing together, holding each other up when the weight of the world feels unbearable.

If connection is the thread and strength is the weave, then meaning is the pattern that emerges when we step back and see the tapestry as a whole. It is the hardest to grasp, the most elusive, because it requires perspective—a perspective we often cannot achieve until we've reached the end of a journey.

I've spent so much of my life searching for meaning. As a Dreamweaver, I thought my purpose was to guide others, to help them find clarity in their own dreams. And while that is true, it is not the whole truth. As a Weaver, my purpose is not just to weave for others but to weave for myself. To confront my own fears, my own doubts, and my own truths. To accept the imperfections in the tapestry and find beauty in them.

Evelyn's betrayal shook me to my core. She was the sister I trusted, the friend who helped me, and yet she became the embodiment of everything I feared: the corruption of power, the severing of connections, the destruction of meaning. Her actions forced me to confront the darkest parts of myself—the parts that doubted, that wavered, that questioned whether I was worthy of this role. But in facing her, I found clarity. Meaning is not something we are given; it is something we create. It is in the choices we make, the battles we fight, and the love we give, even when it feels impossible.

Jara reminded me of this as well. She is still so young, so untested, but she holds within her the potential to shape a future I can only imagine. Teaching her to weave is not just about passing on a skill; it is about passing on hope. It is about showing her that even in the face of darkness, there is always light to be found.

As I sit here in the sanctuary of Somnium Solace, the threads of fate stretched before me, I feel a sense of peace I have not known in years. This chapter is coming to a close, but the story is far from over. There are battles yet to be fought, truths yet to be uncovered, and dreams yet to be woven. The darkness still lingers at the edges, and Evelyn's shadow looms large. But I no longer fear it. I no longer fear her or anything that lies beneath the darkness.

Because I am not alone. I have my team, my family, my daughter. And I have the threads—the unbreakable connections that bind us all, across time and space, across dreams and reality.

As I weave the final strand, I whisper a silent promise: to protect, to guide, and to love. This is my legacy. This is my meaning. And this is only the beginning.

For the dreamscapes are vast, the threads infinite, and the story far from complete.

Epilogue

The sanctuary at Somnium Solace, a haven of golden threads and radiant tranquility, pulsed with quiet energy, reassuring energy. At its heart stood The Loom of Solariis, casting a steady light that wove through the air like breath—binding the dreamscape and its weavers with a sense of calm purpose. After the storm that was Diollo, its presence felt like the first inhale after drowning. Though the Loom of Dreams still stood, it remained fractured—its delicate strands weakened from the near-destruction it had endured. And in that vulnerability, it served as a solemn reminder of how close they had come to losing not just a battle, but the entire tapestry of existence.

Leah stood beside the loom, her fingers brushing its frame. Its hum resonated deep within her, not as a tool but as an extension of her very essence. She glanced over her shoulder at her team. They were gathered in a circle around Jara, who sat cross-legged on the floor. Jara's hands hovered above the golden threads, her concentration etched into every line of her young face.

Malik leaned against a nearby wall, his watchful gaze never leaving Jara. There was pride in his expression, but also vigilance. For all they had achieved, the scars of their journey lingered, etched into each of them in ways they rarely spoke aloud.

"Feel the rhythm," Leah instructed gently, crouching beside her daughter. "It's not about control; it's about trust. The threads will guide you if you let them."

Jara exhaled slowly, nodding as she reached for a particularly vibrant strand. It shimmered under her touch, sparking faintly before slipping through her fingers. She huffed in frustration, shaking her head.

"You're overthinking it," Malik said, stepping closer. His tone was soft, laced with an uncharacteristic warmth. "The threads aren't yours to command. Listen to them. Let them speak to you."

Jara shot him a glare but closed her eyes, taking his advice. The sanctuary grew quieter, the threads dimming as if waiting. Leah exchanged a glance with Malik. Despite their shared history and the battles that had nearly torn them apart, there was a rare understanding between them now—a fragile but growing trust that echoed in moments like these.

As they huddled around Jara, Johan and Terry watched intently. Terry nudged Johan, a faint grin tugging at his lips. "She's a natural. Way better than we was at her age."

Johan crossed his arms, his expression as unreadable as ever. "She's got the bloodline for it. But having all of us staring at her like she's performing doesn't help."

Terry chuckled. "Fair point. Still... it's kind of amazing to see. Like... this is why we're here."

Mina, standing nearby with a stack of scrolls and journals, chimed in. "Don't lose sight of what's ahead. You saw what happened in Diollo. Evelyn isn't gone. Not entirely."

The room grew heavier at her words. The black smoke rising from the ashes of Evelyn's essence had left its mark on all of them. Johan's jaw tightened, and Terry's usual humor faded as the weight of the fight still ahead settled over them.

But before the mood could sink too deeply, Jara's hands began to move again. The golden threads sparked and shimmered, weaving together in a delicate pattern. The sanctuary brightened, the threads responding to her touch as if recognizing her.

Leah stepped back slightly, watching with a mix of awe and reverence. They wove intricate patterns, spiraling and converging in ways that took Leah years to master. Yet for Jara, it was instinctual, as natural as breathing. The loomstaff, resting against the wall nearby, pulsed faintly as if alive. Now, it seemed to hum in anticipation, waiting. The loomstaff had been Leah's guide through the darkest moments of her journey, its light a constant reminder of her legacy. Yet in Jara's presence, its energy had shifted—grown stronger, more vibrant.

As Jara wove her thread, she glanced at the staff. "Why does it feel like it's watching me?" she asked, her voice quiet but curious.

Leah hesitated before responding. "The loomstaff is part of the original Dreamweaver legacy. It chooses its bearer. For a time, it chose me. But its connection to you... it's different."

Jara frowned slightly. "Different how?"

Malik stepped in, his gaze sharp but not unkind. "The loomstaff power has always been tied to Dreamweaver lineage. There is another staff—lost in the dreamscape, forgotten by most. But this one found its way to you for a reason. It's yours, Jara. It recognizes something in you. Something none of us have." Leah nodded, "I feel it. The loomstaff... it responds to her in ways it never did to me."

Jara's fingers paused above the thread. "I don't know if I'm ready for that."

Leah placed a comforting hand on her shoulder. "You don't have to be ready right now. But when the time comes, the staff—and the threads—will be there for you."

The sanctuary's peaceful hum faltered. The Loom of Solariis flickered for a moment, its light dimming before surging back. Everyone froze, their gazes snapping to the loom.

"What was that?" Mina asked, her tone sharp.

Leah reached out instinctively, steadying the loom. A faint ripple of darkness pulsed through her, an echo of something familiar and malevolent. Her mind raced back to the black smoke in Diollo. Evelyn's essence had lingered, tethered to the threads, refusing to be banished entirely.

"She's not gone," Leah said, her voice calm but firm. "Evelyn's still out there. And if she's connected to the threads, she'll find a way back."

Malik's tensed, his hands curling into fists. "Then we need to be ready. She won't stop until she's torn everything apart."

Johan cracked his knuckles, a grim smile on his face. "Let her come. We've faced worse."

Leah turned to face them all—her team, her family. Mina's determination, Johan's resilience, Terry's inventiveness, and Jasper's quiet strength anchored her. And then there was Malik, a man who had walked a thin line between ally and adversary, now standing firmly at her side. And Jara, her daughter, her legacy, holding the power of an entire world in her hands.

"The Loom isn't just a tool," Leah said, her voice steady and sure. "It's a reminder of what we're fighting for: connection, balance, and hope. Jara, you're the key to all of it."

Jara stood tall, her youthful uncertainty replaced by a rising sense of determination. "I won't let you down."

Leah smiled, a rare lightness breaking through the weight of the moment. "I know you won't."

As the sanctuary settled into a quiet hum once more, Leah allowed herself a moment to reflect. They had come so far, faced so much, and yet their journey was only beginning. The loomstaff pulsed softly, a beacon of the battles yet to come and the hope they carried into the future.

Beyond the walls of Somnium Solace, the dreamscape rippled with possibilities, its threads waiting to be woven. Leah watched as Jara added her first true thread to the loom, the golden light spiraling outward like a promise.

They would face Evelyn again. The darkness would return. But for now, united and unbroken, they were ready.

The Loom Codex

The Loom & Realms

The Loom of Dreams (loŏm əv dreemz)
> The living heart of the Dreamscape, where fate is woven, unraveled, and rewritten. It is the ancient source of all threadwork, pulsing with the energies of every dreamer across the realms.

Diollo (dee-OH-lo)
> The ancestral homeland of Dreamweavers. Once a sanctuary of harmony, now fractured by prophecy and war.

The Dreamscape
> A cosmic canvas, alive with thought and emotion. Every realm, every echo, spins through its ever-shifting threads.

Drealis (DREE-uh-liss)
> A blurred realm between dream and reality. Tangible yet fluid, where thoughts become truth and time bends with belief.

Somnium Solace (SOHM-nee-uhm SAW-liss)
> A healing refuge woven between realms by Miriam Cimaj. The resting place of the Loom of Solariis.

THE LOOMS

The Looms

The divine body of existence. Each loom is a living artery of fate—dream, reality, memory, and prophecy spun into form.

The Loom of Lumarion (loo-MAH-ree-on)

Leah's sacred loom and sanctuary. A private echo of her lineage, where fate bends toward reflection, meditation, and memory.

The Loom of Solariis (so-LAH-ree-iss)

A luminous loom crafted for restoration, held by Miriam. Its thread mends emotional wounds and rewrites pain into possibility.

TITLES & LINEAGE

Dreamweaver

Those who weave dreams into safety—protectors of the slumbering mind.

Nightweaver

A weaver who has been tethered or corrupted by nightmares.

Shadowweaver

Servants of darkness, feeding on fear and unraveling dreams with precision.

Veilborn

Beings of rare blood who walk both the Dreamscape and the waking world, possessing unparalleled and ultimate power.

Loomcrest

A noble family bound to a specific loom and thread lineage. Equivalent to "House" in other realms.

Named Loomcrests

Loomcrest of Zerron (Johan)
Realm: Valtros, the Shield of the Dreamscape
Power: The Weave of Strength – manifesting weapons and armor from dreams.

Loomcrest of Aevryn (Terry)
Realm: Zephara, the Celestial Singers
Power: Harmonic Weaving – dreams shaped by sound, frequency, and intention.

Loomcrest of Kaelith (Mina)
Realm: Xyphos, the Eternal Flame
Power: Phantom Weave – dream illusions so vivid they can fool the Loom itself.

Sacred Objects & Phrases

The Loomstaff of Radiance (Lux Veritas)
An artifact of light carried by Leah. Forged to restore fractured dreams and defend the Looms from corruption.

Velara Aelis (veh-LAH-rah AY-liss)
A meditative weaving state. Velara means rippling thought, and Aelis means silent flow. Used by Leah to weave truth into her journal.

Nascent Velana
A child of legacy. "Nascent" for emerging power, and "Velana" for flowing mystery. Refers to Jara, born of prophecy.

Velana

Women of veilborn lineage—nurturers, creators, and protectors of woven truth.

Marasyn

The word for "mother" in Dreamweaver tongue. Keeper of ancestral wisdom and guardian of the loom's legacy.

Kynara

Like a cousin or bonded family. Born of the same ancestral thread.

Serenya

Chosen family, like a sister or soul-bound companion.

Severed

A rare and irreversible state in which a being's thread is cut from the Loom. To be severed is to perish—completely disconnected from the weave of existence, unable to return to dream or memory.

Tethered

A rare ability allowing a Weaver to bind their essence to another, living through them across memory and form. Known only to the Veilborn, its true power remains largely misunderstood.

Thread

The essence of existence, spun from the dreams and nightmares of all living beings. Each thread is unique, linking its source to the Loom. Weavers across the realms use threads to navigate fate, memory, and emotion—shaping or protecting the balance between dream and waking worlds.

Anchor

A metaphysical tether that binds a being to the Loom. The anchor maintains their presence within the dreamscape and reality. If the anchor is weakened, the thread frays. If it is destroyed, the thread is severed.

PROPHECY & DESTINY

Diolla (dee-OH-lah)

The foretold savior of all threads. A child born of two worlds who can either restore or ruin the Loom forever.

Path of Three Veils

The hidden journey to become the Diolla. Each veil represents a trial of the soul, mind, and tether between realms. Only the chosen may walk this path.

Primoris Core (PRIM-or-iss)

The ancient heartbeat of all Looms—the first spark of woven existence. If shattered, all realms collapse.

Velunfall (VEL-uhn-fall)

Like twilight in the Dreamscape—when the threads shift toward darkness, and battles often begin.

Velmara (vel-MAHR-uh)

A sacred city of elegance and balance. Birthplace of harmony before Diollo fell into shadow.

Author's Notes

Writing *The Loom: Leah Cimaj Legacy* was an experience unlike any other—a journey that began in the quiet hours of the night. There were times I'd wake suddenly from a vivid dream, heart racing, scrambling to capture every detail before it faded. These dreams felt alive, insistent, as though they were waiting to be told. And so, one by one, they transformed into stories that became the heartbeat of this book.

As you hold this book, know that each page was woven from those late nights and the moments I spent lost in thought, letting dreams guide the words. Dreams, after all, have a way of unearthing our hidden connections, strength, and meaning—showing us the threads that bind us, however invisible they may seem.

I want to thank you for being part of this journey. Keep dreaming, for somewhere in those dreams lies purpose and answers waiting to be uncovered. May these stories remind you that we're all connected, bound together by the beauty of shared experiences, and the strength of those connections.

Acknowledgments

To my family—thank you for your patience, encouragement, and unwavering love. To my children, I'm sorry for the times I couldn't answer your calls, lost in the worlds I was weaving in my office. I know I missed a few moments, and I hope you'll see in these pages how much each of you inspired me. To my wife, my greatest listener and partner, thank you for hearing every story, every idea, and every tangled thought. Your belief in me is the heartbeat of this work.

To my editor and designer, thank you for bringing clarity, vision, and a level of dedication that shaped each page into something I am truly proud of. And to my family and friends who have been part of this journey—each of you has left an imprint on these stories. Your impact is woven into the pages of this book, whether you realize it or not. Thank you for being part of the foundation that holds it all together.

About the Author

J. D. Jackson

Other writers have told J.D. that this section is the hardest to start—and they weren't wrong. It took him a few days to figure out how to tell his own story, but like most things in his life, he decided to start where most people end: with gratitude, chaos, and the sound of keys clicking beneath tired fingers.

J.D. Jackson was born just outside Shreveport, Louisiana, and now lives deep in the heart of Texas with his wife and four children. He's a storyteller at heart—whether scribbling ideas on the back of napkins, chasing dreams across notebooks, or crafting worlds between bedtime routines.

He's traveled to over twenty-five countries, served in the U.S. military, and earned a degree in Film and Television from California State University. Along the way, he's picked up a camera, a few screenwriting credits, and a passion for stories that linger long after the last page.

J.D.'s love for storytelling began as a kid—long before he ever thought of publishing anything. But it wasn't until recently, in the whirlwind of parenting, that he found the time (and maybe the need) to finally write them down. With a newborn in one arm and a toddler climbing the other, writing became both a form of escape and a quiet act of hope.

One day, J.D. met a man named James Bleon—or as he introduced himself, Irboust Root, a self-proclaimed time traveler. Bleon spoke of rewriting time, creating new worlds, and uncovering hidden realities in the fabric of dreams. At first, J.D. thought he was just eccentric. But when Bleon asked, "Do you have vivid dreams?" something clicked. That question sparked the seed of a story J.D. couldn't shake. Whether Bleon was a visionary or simply lost in his own myth, the courage he showed in imagining something greater left a mark.

It reminded J.D. of why stories matter.

Now, through *The Loom*, he explores not just fantasy—but the threads that bind us all. The unspoken truths. The weight of memory. The beauty of connection. And the belief that dreams aren't just places we visit—they're where we learn who we are.

He loves his children dearly, but he'll admit a truth that many parents might shy away from: sometimes, he writes to escape the noise of fatherhood. Because in his world, the only thing louder than his kids is the sound of the keyboard.

SOUNDTRACK OF INSPIRATION

You've reached the end—now step into my world— Leah's world. This soundtrack captures the final emotional arc of *The Loom Universe*—from haunting reflections to powerful victories.

Let the music guide you through ancient secrets, revelations, and the fragile dance between dreams and destiny.

The Soundtrack of Inspiration is more than an accompaniment—it's the heartbeat of a story meant to linger long after the final thread is woven.

Scan the code or search "JD's JotUniverse" on Apple Music to experience the final journey in sound.

Sneak Peek Invitation

Are You Ready to Discover the Origins of the Dreamscape?

Step back into the woven threads of time and uncover the story that started it all. Before Leah Cimaj led the Weavers, before Malik's descent into darkness, there was **Diollo**—a world where fate collided with prophecy, and the seeds of conflict were sown.

In this next chapter of The Loom's saga, we unravel:

- The rise of **Malik**, the prophesied child destined to save Diollo—but shaped by betrayal and loss.
- **Leah's earliest days**, a young Dreamweaver navigating the weight of her gift while grappling with truths that would change her forever.
- The history of **The Loomstaff**, the mysterious artifact that binds threads of destiny and chooses its wielder.
- The tragedy of **Evelyn**, whose ambition and heartbreak would set the stage for chaos in both the dreamscape and the awakened world.

The Loom: Diollo takes you deeper into the origins of the Dreamweaver universe, revealing the connections and betrayals that shaped Leah, Malik, and the delicate balance of their world.

Will you dare to look into the past and face the truths hidden in the threads of fate?

Be among the first to step into Diollo.

The dreamscape is waiting for you. Reserve your place in the next adventure.

Sign up now for exclusive first chapters, behind-the-scenes insights, and a glimpse into the most anticipated sequel of the Dreamweaver saga.

The past is calling. Will you answer?

I Thank You

Thank you for taking a chance on this first book, for stepping into these pages and letting these stories unfold in your imagination. As a new author, I wasn't sure how my words would resonate, but knowing they've reached you means more than I can express. This journey has been a labor of love, born out of countless late nights, stolen moments, and unwavering belief in the power of connection.

I'm grateful to you for making this possible—for your curiosity, your support, and for sharing this milestone with me. Every story in this book carries a piece of my heart, and it's my deepest hope that it leaves an echo in yours. Keep dreaming, keep exploring, and know that your support fuels my passion to keep writing.

Sincerely,

JD

Connect With Me

Thank you for joining Leah Cimaj and me on this journey through dreams and stories. Your support, thoughts, and reflections mean everything. I'd love to stay connected with you and continue sharing in the creative journey. Stay updated on new releases, special projects, and behind-the-scenes content at:

www.JotUniverse.com

Follow me on social media for updates, inspiration, and glimpses into my creative process:

Instagram/Facebook/X/TikTok: *@jdtellthestory*

You can also subscribe to the newsletter to receive exclusive previews, early release information, personal reflections, and special offers. Be the first to know when a new thread is woven—just head to the site and sign up.

Feel free to reach out with questions, thoughts, or just to say hello. I'd love to hear from you!

Again, thank you for being a part of this world. I look forward to connecting with you and sharing more stories in the future. Dream on!

Made in the USA
Columbia, SC
22 July 2025

c158e5b1-abd9-4e63-b282-22b3351e2626R01

Cycle of Confidence: Insights into Menstruation

Teenage Girls' Ultimate Guide to Demystifying Menstruation, Breaking Taboos, Navigating the Monthly Cycle, Blossoming Boldly and Celebrating Womanhood

By Nishka Utpat and Kaanchi Utpat

Disclaimer

Copyright © Year 2024

All Rights Reserved.

No part of this eBook can be transmitted or reproduced in any form, including print, electronic, photocopying, scanning, mechanical, or recording, without prior written permission from the author.

This eBook has been written for information purposes only. While the author has made utmost efforts to ensure the accuracy of the written content, all readers are advised to follow the information mentioned herein at their own risk. The author cannot be held responsible for any personal or commercial damage caused by misinterpreting information. All readers are encouraged to seek professional advice when needed.

Also, this eBook provides information only up to the publishing date. Therefore, this eBook should be a guide, not the ultimate source.

The author and the publisher do not warrant that the information contained in this eBook is fully complete and shall not be responsible for any errors or omissions. The author and publisher shall have neither liability nor responsibility to any person or entity concerning any loss or damage caused or alleged to be caused directly or indirectly by this eBook.

Table of Contents

Introduction	1
Chapter One: Why Talk About Menstruation	9
Why Do We Dedicate a Day in May to Menstruation?	13
Menstruation Outside of Scientific Research	14
Chapter Two: What is Menstruation – Learn What is Having Your Period	17
What is Having Your Period?	18
Phases of the Menstrual Cycle	20
Menstrual or Follicular Phase	20
Ovulation or Ovulatory Phase	20
Luteal Phase	21
How to Calculate the Menstrual Cycle?	22
How to Calculate My Next Menstruation?	23
What is the Importance of the Menstrual Cycle?	23
At What Age Does the Menstrual Cycle Begin?	24
How Do I Know If My Menstrual Cycle Is Irregular?	24
Alterations of the Menstrual Cycle	25
Hormones That Interfere With Your Menstrual Cycle	26
Chapter Three: DIY Menstruation Pouch | Period Kit for High School Emergency	28
What to Have in a Menstruation Kit?	29
A Bag or Case	29
Menstrual Hygiene Items	29

Wet Wipes	30
Extra Underwear	30
Resealable Plastic Bags	31
Treats to Pamper Yourself	32
Includes Some Pain Relievers	32
Some Tips To Keep Your Menstruation Kit Updated	32
Chapter Four: How to Keep Track of Your Menstrual Cycle | Teenage Period Health	34
Why Should You Keep a Track of Your Menstrual Cycle?	34
Tips to Keep Track of Your Menstrual Cycle	35
The Calendar Method	36
Period Tracking Applications	37
Dealing With Period Mood Swings	39
How to Maintain Your Health and Hygiene While Menstruating	41
Products and Supplies	41
Chapter Five: The Do's and Don'ts When You're on Your Period	48
Do's	48
Don'ts	52
Managing Menstrual Pain	55
Navigating Work and Social Life	56
Communicating With Your Employer	56
Addressing Period Stigma	58
Educating Partners and Friends About Menstrual Health	59

Chapter Six: Common Menstrual Symptoms You Shouldn't Be Afraid Of 61
    Menstrual Cramps 61
    Changes in Flow – Normal Variations 62
    Mood Swings 63
    Bloating 64
    Breast Tenderness 66
    Headaches and Migraines 66
    Digestive Changes 67
    Acne and Skin Changes 68
    Sleep Disturbances 68

Chapter Seven: Menstrual Isolation Custom 71
    Historical Origins of Menstrual Stigma 72
    Media Portrayal 75
    Dealing With Menstrual Stigma 76

Chapter Eight: Famous Women and Activists Who Contributed to the Menstruation Rights 82

Chapter Nine: Hormonal Acne — An Ally Accompanying Menstruation 104
    Factors Influencing Hormonal Acne 105
    Home Remedies for Hormonal Acne 106
    Lifestyle Modifications for Hormonal Balance 108

Chapter Ten: Period Cramping in College Dorms 115
    Understanding Menstrual Cramps 115
    College Dorm Living and Menstrual Health 117

How to Form Peer Support Networks in College Dorms   121

Importance of Self-Care Practices   124

Chapter Eleven: Understanding Hormonal Changes: Navigating PMS and PMDD   126

Understanding Premenstrual Syndrome (PMS)   126

Understanding Premenstrual Dysphoric Disorder (PMDD)   127

Coping Strategies   129

Tracking and Managing Symptoms   132

Chapter Twelve: How Educating Girls Can Prevent Childbirth Complications   134

Link Between Menstruation Education and Childbirth Complications   135

Menstrual Hygiene Tips   137

Empowering Through Education   139

A Healthier Future Through Education   140

Chapter Thirteen: What You Can Do As a Girl to Empower Other Girls and Women   142

Chapter Fourteen: The Environmental Impact of Menstruation   150

Sustainability of Menstrual Products   150

Menstrual Waste Load in India   152

How to Dispose Off Sanitary Pads   154

Innovative Solutions   156

Climate Change and Menstrual Sustainability   158

Barriers to Change   158

Empowering Through Eco-Conscious Menstruation   160

Chapter Fifteen: Effects of Menstrual Health on Self-Confidence 163

   Understanding the Menstrual Journey 163

   Menstrual Education and Empowerment 165

      Implementing Educational Initiatives 167

   Emotional Well-Being and Confidence 168

      Tips to Build Confidence 169

Chapter Sixteen: Menstrual Health in Educational Institutes and the Workplace 174

   Challenges Women Face in Educational Settings 175

   The Impact of Menstruation on Academic Performance and Educational Outcomes 178

   Challenges Faced by Menstruating Employees in the Workplace 180

   Promoting Awareness 182

Way Forward 186

Conclusion 190

Bibliography 193

Introduction

Hi. We are Nishka and Kanchi – the Utpat sisters. When writing this book, Nishka is a sophomore in Undergraduate College, and Kaanchi is a junior in high school. We are writing this book to discuss a not-so-discussed topic: menstruation.

Here is our story of how we came to the point of writing a book and what inspired us.

We were taught the concept of menstruation in school around 4th grade, and we didn't quite know at the time what it meant, but we shared that information with our mother.

While talking to our mother, we realized that our mother's childhood experiences in India related to the topic of menstruation were quite different from what we experienced in the USA.

In a nutshell, we discovered that the attitudes towards menstruation are quite different in developed nations versus certain countries like India, Pakistan, and Africa. Once the initial phase of finding out and dealing with the changes in our bodies was over, we realized that we were indeed quite fortunate compared to the girls in other parts of the world.

To learn more, we started reading about how the girls in India experienced it, how much knowledge they had before they got their first period, and how they dealt with it when they went to school, in social settings, and in joint families.

In the United States, this topic gets introduced in the fourth or fifth grade, and we wanted to know what that looked like in India. Also, we got the idea that we could talk to high schoolers in the ninth and tenth grades, and could indeed talk to their juniors too, and carry on that legacy slowly forward as they move out of the school.

Motivation #1 - We envisioned sharing our experiences with our counterparts in India by actually going to the schools, opening up discussions, and doing something meaningful.

So we contacted our uncles and aunts about the idea of connecting with the girls in India during spring break of April 2021 – but because of the COVID pandemic, that trip couldn't materialize. As the pandemic continued with no signs of slowing down, we couldn't make the in-person trip to India in 2021 or 2022.

Since everything was being done remotely (our schooling, extracurricular activities such as dancing, singing, etc), the focus shifted to online activities, online learning, and online knowledge sharing. We realized that there was a different way to connect to other people.

Motivation #2 - This gave us the idea that we should start sharing our thoughts and expressing our viewpoints and experiences through the online platform, where we can reach out to girls of our age groups in other parts of the world (and not just the USA).

So, during Christmas, the idea came to our mind: we could record our thoughts and conversations and upload them to YouTube. We uploaded our first YouTube video with some explanations, some basic editing, and animations, and we wanted to get feedback from other girls who would watch them – that became the starting point to launch our YouTube channel, "Utpat Sisters."

Motivation #3 - The other intention of creating these kinds of videos was that we discovered that there was plenty of misinformation out there on the internet. If these topics were not talked about openly, it could mean girls in other parts of countries could get exposed to the wrong information that could hamper their well-being – so we wanted to create something authentic and share our own experiences and speak candidly to benefit similar-age girls.

Motivation #4 - That said, we found lots of YouTube videos and documentaries, but we were not quite interested in those since we wanted to keep it simple and convey points that the similar-age girls could relate to rather than watching documentaries (which may not interest everybody).

Motivation #5 - Another thought was that if parents themselves hadn't been exposed to these topics in an open society, the mothers (and parents) themselves might hesistate to sit down with their daughters to talk about these issues.

So the idea was that our videos would serve as the ice breakers where these mothers and girls could sit down together and watch these videos jointly and open some conversation with mothers and daughters. That was the main intention.

We wanted to make the videos simple and conversational so that even if fathers and brothers or male members of the families saw them, they would feel comfortable watching them, and it would help them understand the blind spots that men typically have towards their daughters or sisters.

That's how the "Utpat Sisters" YouTube channel was born, which is focused on AMHI Muli. We also call it AMHI Muli. In our mother tongue, it stands for "We the Girls" ("AMHI" means "We" and "Muli" means "Girls"). In English, AMHI is an acronym for Awareness of Menstrual Health Initiative.

After starting our YouTube channel, we thought to ourselves, "Wouldn't it be nice to repurpose that into a book format?" This way, we can keep reaching more audiences in the format they prefer.

Overall, this book aims to raise awareness, dispel the taboo, and uncover the misinformation – we want this topic to be more openly talked about and not considered taboo.

#1 Half of the population in the world is women, and all of them go through it at some point in their lifetime, and yet, this topic is discussed in such hushed tones that it's almost an embarrassment, and this is what we would like to address.

#2 Also, the disadvantages the girls feel or the mental fears or physical pains they go through are what we would like to focus on. For example, access to menstrual products is limited in schools. Additionally, schools don't have the proper facilities that girls would ideally need. There is a lot of hesitation in going to school during their period. Girls tend to miss out on sports or extracurricular activities or even miss school altogether. The same goes for sports and other activities.

#3 - Also, at some point in life, these girls will also become mothers, so they need to become more comfortable talking about these topics. The idea is to be an educated mom.

#4 All in all, at some point in time, if the opportunity comes, we are going to see if we can get funding through donations or sponsorship opportunities and if we can make sanitary pads available.

Hopefully, we can bring our ideas to fruition, and more girls can identify with what this YouTube channel is doing to make everyone's lives more comfortable.

#5 We are quite close as sisters, and we were able to talk about these issues more comfortably. In some cases, where girls don't have sisters or live in joint families, they cannot talk openly. In these cases, girls are left alone, so they might be looking for more information or someone they can relate to. This was one of the other motivations behind creating these videos.

The idea for writing this book emerged from the harsh reality that instead of being normalized as a social need, menstruation is still a stigmatized topic in many parts of the world, especially third-world countries. The menstrual cycle is a challenge in the lives of girls and adolescents who have no knowledge or do not know how to manage their menstruation with minimal discomfort. In addition, it is still perceived as a disease, a woman's burden, which must be hidden and not talked about and is accompanied by shame, fear, and insecurities.

In response to these issues that are crucial to our society as a whole, through this book, we want to spread awareness about menstruation, its symptoms, maintenance tips, customs, and everything young girls need to know about menstruation.

At this point, we would also like to let the readers know that our YouTube channel, Utpat Sisters, is focused on the A.M.H.I. Muli (Awareness of Menstrual Health Initiative), through our videos, we aim to achieve the same: Spread awareness about menstrual health among young girls and anyone who has questions about periods.

The goal of this book goes beyond providing basic information about menstruation. We want to destigmatize periods and make it a topic young girls can discuss openly by empowering them with knowledge in a safe manner from people like us who have been through this experience, rather than getting information from various social media sources, which can create more doubts and overwhelm their understanding.

Even though we were born and raised in the US, our parents hail from India. We've been hearing about this cultural taboo placed on the topic of menstrual health in India from our mothers and aunts. Upon research, we found the same for other third-world nations in Africa and Latin America, where menstrual stigma is still so common that it prevents young girls who have their first periods from reaching out for help due to hesitation and embarrassment. We realized that being born and raised in a first-world country differs from a third-world country where menstruation is still stigmatized, which motivated us to write this book.

Listening to stories about menstrual health awareness from our mom and what it's like to have periods for the first time in India, where this topic is frowned upon, we thought it'd be great to share what menstruation is, common misconceptions about it, our experience and knowledge with it as teenage girls, and the cultural differences in India and the US regarding menstruation. Despite the taboos surrounding it, we want to talk about and comprehend menstruation issues. We want young girls to know that menstruation is not a hush-hush topic, at least not anymore, and that discussing it with your family, friends, and even boys and reaching out for help is OK. While this topic seems serious, we hope to make it fun and relaxing for all.

Before we delve in, please note that we are not medical professionals. Our goal is to generate awareness. So please don't treat this book as medical or legal advice. Take it with a pinch of salt, and definitely consult your doctor or medical advisor for specifics.

So let's get started!

Chapter One: Why Talk About Menstruation

We want to discuss menstruation to spread awareness and empower every girl so they can also talk about it openly because it's a social need. As mentioned earlier, the reality is that for most girls, menstruation is accompanied by insecurities and shame. Although we don't see it in the US, where we can openly talk about periods, it's not the same for girls worldwide, especially in underdeveloped nations.

No doubt, many initiatives have been put in place at the global, national, and local levels to raise awareness about the importance of good menstrual hygiene. Likewise, many activists have worked for menstrual rights and fought to normalize menstruation and break down the taboos surrounding it. But the situation is still disappointing and far from satisfactory for millions of girls who menstruate every month.

According to UNICEF, around 500 million menstruating girls, adolescents, and women lack clean toilets or infrastructure where they can take care of their menstruation. In many countries, sex education is not a priority, and many girls, adolescents, and women lack basic education about menstruation.

Menstruation is an issue associated with sexuality that still generates fear and even shame today. There are large gaps in information and access to supplies for the management of menstruation, especially in rural areas, remote areas, populations where there are greater violations of human rights, and in contexts of humanitarian crises.

Each culture, throughout history, has attributed different elements and meanings to menstruation. However, most of them are associated with something negative or dirty. Many adolescents and women who are part of the training processes on sexual rights, reproductive rights, and prevention of gender-based violence point out that it is not common to talk about menstruation. They even give it another series of names to mention it. The taboo and silence associated with menstruation foster gender inequality because it prevents women and girls from experiencing their bodies as a positive element that empowers them.

Furthermore, in some cultures and countries, it is believed that with the first menstruation, girls are ready to engage in sexual activity, making them vulnerable and increasing the risks of sexual violence and child marriage. Likewise, not having complete and quality information on menstruation and reproductive processes limits their autonomy and increases the risk of early and unintended pregnancies for girls, adolescents, and women.

Humanitarian crises create more barriers to obtaining menstrual hygiene supplies and care. The difficulty in obtaining items for menstrual management can stop girls and adolescents from attending school or prevent women from going to work. For example, migrants and refugees who arrive in the country face great socio-economic challenges that force them to make decisions regarding their survival. According to field professionals, women should prioritize access to food and water over personal care items.

For this reason, it is essential to consider educational activities that address myths and prejudices about menstruation and cover basic needs such as menstrual hygiene.

When we researched the topic, we were shocked to see how many indigenous girls and adolescents are still deprived of basic rights and knowledge and how they experience menstruation in their communities.

Because of this lack of knowledge and the misconceptions and taboos surrounding menstruation, many girls, especially teenagers, do not reach out for help and, therefore, lack the necessary hygiene supplies. Also, one of the most disturbing is the menstrual isolation custom, a menstrual stigma used by certain cultures with strong taboos regarding the subject. Thus, the days of menstruation translate into the absence of millions of girls from school. The girls fear getting dirty during the menstrual cycle, thinking they're sick and should stay home.

Through this book, we want to provide our readers with valuable information about menstruation, its associated symptoms, misconceptions, management tips, and everything girls need to know to maintain their health during menstruation. Through this information, we intend to empower girls with knowledge so they can understand their bodies and the menstruation phenomenon and that it's not something they should hide but talk about openly so they can help other girls in the surroundings.

Recent statistics show that two out of every five girls of menstruating age in the world lose an average of five school days a month because they do not have the necessary facilities to attend school during their menstruation. These situations aggravate absenteeism at work or school dropout in girls and women.

A meta-analysis conducted a study among adolescent girls in India on menstrual hygiene status and found that a quarter of the girls fail to attend school during menstruation (Eijk, 2016).

In Bangladesh, however, only 36% of the girls of menstruation age included in the study had prior knowledge about menstruation because there's a lack of education on health and hygiene at the school level.

Another study in Kenya found that the majority of menstruating girls skip 1 to 3 school days, impacting their grades and studies.

The situation may seem a bit better in the US than in the countries mentioned above. But, a recent Procter & Gamble study indicates that almost 1 in 5 girls miss school due to lack of access to period products in the US. You can see that the situation is the same worldwide; the only difference is in the figures.

Why Do We Dedicate a Day in May to Menstruation?

One of our friends told us that when she was in fourth grade, her teacher one day asked all the boys in the group to leave the room. The girls had to remain seated to listen to an informative talk about menstruation. After playing in the yard, the children returned and wondered why they had kept them in the classroom. Neither was able to express the reason.

A message had been established: menstruation was not a subject that could be spoken out loud and should remain between women.

In high school, it was common for someone to drop out of school in the middle of the day or not show up at recess. Getting blood on her skirt was reason enough not to go back to class that day.

No one wanted to explain their absence in the classroom since the classmates already had a wide repertoire of adjectives to refer to menstrual blood, all unpleasant. Although the sneering looks and derogatory comments only reflected the limited knowledge on the subject, they permeated the relationship many girls had and sustained for many years with menstruation.

Many years have passed, but to this day, taboos and misinformation remain about this natural process that half the population goes through.

As part of the efforts to transform the stigma around menstruation, May 28 has been arranged to generate spaces for reflection that contribute to modifying the culture concerning it and improve the conditions of those who menstruate. According to the United Nations Population Fund (UNFPA), Menstrual Hygiene Day occurs on the 28th day of the fifth month because menstrual cycles average 28 days long, and bleeding typically lasts five days.

Menstruation Outside of Scientific Research

Menstruating in dignified conditions is not limited to providing menstrual management products. Although they are essential and must be considered basic necessities, it is also necessary to carry out hard research work for young girls and women, which allows them to build a better relationship with their bodies.

Unfortunately, research on menstruation is not enough. An example of this is the lack of explanations around what has been called "premenstrual syndrome," despite producing different effects on a physical and emotional level. Unawareness of specific causes generated false beliefs about the abilities and behavior of menstruating women during certain phases of the cycle.

Reflecting on this same problem, disseminating statements that imply bad odors or menstrual blood as a synonym for dirt encourages a feeling of shame.

As long as there is no committed interest in learning about the experience of menstruating people, it is impossible to guarantee them dignified menstruation, which in turn causes another series of violations of their fundamental rights.

Recent research studies indicate many menstruating people had little or no information when they menstruated for the first time. Likewise, they did not keep some kind of control or record of the duration of their menstrual cycle, the type of flow, or the symptoms they suffered from.

The findings are disappointing. As girls who have experienced menstruation and are blessed to have all the necessities, education, environment, and confidence, we believe we have a role to play in spreading awareness about menstruation and making girls feel comfortable about it.

Through this book, we aim to:

- Spread awareness about menstruation and everything related to it, from the menstrual cycle and associated symptoms to tips for proper menstrual hygiene and management.

- Help people understand that menstruation is healthy and normal.

- Educate girls who have doubts about what menstruation means, its relationship with pregnancy, and how to manage it well. We want to raise awareness about the fact that the onset of menstruation does not imply physical or psychological preparation to start sexual activities, get married, or have children.

- Break the stigma, allowing taboos and prejudices to be overcome.
- Ensure girls understand their right to hygiene supplies and materials
- To empower girls to manage menstruation and personal hygiene and help other girls.

Chapter Two: What is Menstruation – Learn What is Having Your Period

We remember we were in school when we got our first period. We talked to our mother, who explained why girls get their periods. She also explained what happens to our bodies during this time and how to know if menstruation is regular or irregular. At the time, we didn't understand what it meant because it was quite new and different to us.

However, we gradually grasped the answers, particularly related to the menstrual cycle, which is the period of time between one menstruation and the next and lasts around 24 to 38 days.

As we discussed earlier, every year, May 28 is World Menstrual Hygiene Day, a special day to talk about periods. Too often, girls do not dare to ask questions on this subject. However, the rules are natural.

Periods mark the passage from childhood to womanhood. They are the sign that you can get pregnant, but they only appear if you are not and are sometimes accompanied by confusing symptoms. Appearing in adolescence, they accompany women throughout the fertile years until menopause.

During this period, it is very normal for you to feel like you are on a "roller coaster" because your emotions and hormones go up and down. And largely, it is due to the phases of the menstrual cycle that repeat each month and are controlled by hormones. In this chapter, we will talk about the basics of menstruation.

What is Having Your Period?

Girls most often have their first period around the age of 13. But it can be earlier or later, lasting until around 50 years. Once a month, blood flows through the vagina, lasting between two and six days. The duration varies from person to person.

Pink, red, brown, thick, or liquid, the appearance of the blood also varies.

This was a very simple description of periods. Before we discuss this cycle further, know that it's nothing to be ashamed of. Periods are a sign of good health. They indicate that the body is now capable of making a baby, as discussed earlier.

But the rules are not always fun, right?

It's true. Stomach cramps, headaches, bad moods, pimples, we associate a lot of worries with menstruation. It happens especially in the first years, and, in general, it decreases with time. Some women are not in pain at all. And some experience pain every time they're on their periods. If the pain is really too strong, one must visit their doctor to check that everything is fine.

Now, let's have a scientific explanation of menstruation!

By definition, it is the flow of blood that appears once a month in women. We speak scientifically of menstruation because it is part of the menstrual cycle, a cycle of 28 days, which prepares the body for a possible pregnancy.

Menstruation is a hormonal process that goes from the first day of one menstruation to the first day of the next. It is something completely normal in all women that lasts between 21 and 35 days, and it occurs because the body, every month, prepares for receiving a pregnancy.

Menstruation corresponds to the elimination of a membrane that lines the uterus: the endometrium. Each month, the endometrium thickens under the effect of estrogen, a female hormone, to form like a nest, ready to welcome an embryo.

In the middle of the cycle, one of the ovaries releases a mature egg called ovulation.

If it is not fertilized by sperm, the egg dies after 24 hours, and the endometrium breaks down to be eliminated by the body. This is where period blood comes from. Below, you'll find a detailed discussion about the phases of menstruation.

You have likely heard before that this cycle lasts 28 days, but it differs from person to person. Some of us have more irregular cycles than others, especially in the first years when menstruation comes or before menopause. Therefore, it is normal to speak of a slightly longer period.

Phases of the Menstrual Cycle

Now, we will understand the menstrual cycle phases, what happens in each, and how you may feel while going through them.

Let's begin!

Menstrual or Follicular Phase

It starts the first day your period comes, and it happens when the endometrium of the uterus is shed and you have your period. The duration of the period changes according to each one; generally, it is from 2 to 7 days.

In this phase, you may be much more sensitive, and it is normal if you feel some pain called menstrual cramps.

In this phase, the brain increases the production of follicle-stimulating hormones (FSH), which causes the ovaries to mature their eggs.

Ovulation or Ovulatory Phase

In this phase, estrogen levels continue to rise and cause the body to produce luteinizing hormone (LH), which is responsible for selecting the most mature egg and releasing it from the ovary, thus ovulating, generally on day 14 of the cycle. After being released, the egg travels through the fallopian tubes until it reaches the uterus. Normally, the egg survives for 24 hours outside the ovary; therefore, if it comes into contact with sperm, it can be fertilized, and it will be possible to get pregnant. If not, the unfertilized egg will disintegrate.

During this phase, you feel full of energy and a lot of power. Also very attractive. Give yourself notes reminding yourself how much you love yourself! It doesn't hurt to repeat it to yourself.

Luteal Phase

During the luteal phase, the progesterone hormone is generated, and at this stage, the endometrium is prepared for possible egg fertilization. It lasts 12 to 14 days. If pregnancy does not occur, your period comes, and the menstrual cycle begins again.

At this moment, you begin to feel Premenstrual Syndrome (PMS). Acne could appear on your skin, and you may feel breast pain. We all have different symptoms, and it could even go unnoticed by you.

Premenstrual Syndrome

Premenstrual syndrome brings together a series of symptoms that many women experience a few days before their period. They are sometimes a little unpleasant but let you know that the period will soon be triggered. Here are the most common:

- Temporary weight gain, 1 or 2 kg;
- Nervousness, irritability;

- Slight depression;
- Abdominal bloating or cramps;
- Tension in the breasts;
- Headache;
- Acne outbreak.

For some women, menstruation triggers migraines. It is a very particular type of migraine that announces the period's arrival. In some cases, menstruation also causes constipation or temporary diarrhea.

Keep in Mind!

The menstrual cycle is different in all women and depends on age, weight, diet, stress, genetic factors, and the development of our bodies.

How to Calculate the Menstrual Cycle?

The menstrual cycle is measured from the first day of your period to the first day of the next. In this time frame, you have fertile and non-fertile days. You must have a regular menstrual cycle to know which days are most fertile and which days are safe. If it is not, it is not safe to calculate these days.

A regular menstrual cycle lasts the same each month, and you get your period every month. As we said earlier, having an irregular menstrual cycle in the first years after the first menstruation is normal because the body needs time to adjust to the changes.

How to Calculate My Next Menstruation?

To calculate your cycle, you must write down at least three regular menstrual cycles, that is, for three months.

For example, you should count 14 days from the first day of your period; day 14 will be approximately the day of your ovulation. The most fertile days with a high probability of getting pregnant will be the three days before and after your ovulation. The safest will be four days before your next period; that is, during these days, the chances of getting pregnant are very low.

Remember! If you are sexually active, always use contraceptive methods and visit your doctor so she can explain how your cycles work and how you can protect yourself to have safe sex.

What is the Importance of the Menstrual Cycle?

The most important thing is that the beginning of the menstrual cycle is a sign that the woman is already fertile. What does it mean? That you could already get pregnant. At first, it seems not to be very important, but when the time comes to be a mother and one wants to have a baby, knowing their menstrual cycle well will help one recognize which are the most fertile days; that is when there is a greater probability of getting pregnant.

At What Age Does the Menstrual Cycle Begin?

The female menstrual cycle begins with the arrival of the first menstruation, which is common at 12 years of age. But this can vary from one girl to another. Some can get their first period at 8 while others at 15. Remember that all bodies are different. Don't worry, don't compare yourself.

How Do I Know If My Menstrual Cycle Is Irregular?

The following characteristics indicate that your menstrual cycle is irregular:

- There are variations in the duration of the menstrual period. Sometimes, the cycles are shorter or longer than usual.

- We know an irregular menstrual cycle can be common in the first years after first menstruation. However, other causes can also influence irregular menstruation.

- The absence of menstruation in one of your menstrual cycles may indicate a pregnancy, or if you are lactating, it is normal to have a delay due to your hormonal changes.

- State of Health: Eating disorders such as anorexia or bulimia influence your weight, which, when it increases or decreases, alters your menstrual cycle, and menstruation may even disappear.

- Ovarian Problems: A common disease is Polycystic Ovaries, which affects the regular release of eggs.

- Traveling: Crossing several time zones throws our hormones out of control and, with them, the menstrual cycle.

- Excessive Sport: It only happens in extreme cases where exercise interferes with the development and production of hormones.

Following your menstrual cycle is important because it helps you to know when your period begins and its duration, and at the same time, you can easily identify changes or irregularities, such as the absence of the period or bleeding outside of it, so that you can consult your doctor promptly.

Alterations of the Menstrual Cycle

After telling you everything that could be normal within your menstrual cycle, we want to inform you about some things that are not so common and that, if they happen to you, it is best to consult your doctor:

- Your period stops coming for over three months, and you are not pregnant.

- You've had regular periods for many years; from one moment to the next, they get out of control and become irregular.

- Your period is very heavy for more than seven days. Although periods can last up to 10 days, consult your doctor if they are very heavy.

- You must change your pads or tampons every less than 3 hours because your period is so heavy.

- You present bleeding between one menstruation and another.

- The duration of your menstrual cycle varies greatly from one to the other. That is, one month lasts 28 days and the next 40.

Although none of these signs are likely to cause a serious illness, it is best to consult an expert to be calm and know everything is fine.

Hormones That Interfere With Your Menstrual Cycle

Hormones are in charge of regulating our menstrual cycle. Here we tell you some of the hormones that are part of this process:

- **Luteinizing and Follicle-Stimulating Hormones**: These hormones promote ovulation and stimulate the ovaries to produce estrogen and progesterone, also known as the female sex hormones!

- **Estrogen:** These hormones are produced by the ovaries and are responsible for preparing the body for fertilization and ovulation.

- **Progesterone:** They are also produced by the ovaries, and their main function is to transform the tissue that lines the uterus and prepare it in case the egg is fertilized and a pregnancy begins.

-

Chapter Three: DIY Menstruation Pouch | Period Kit for High School Emergency

The period accompanies us for a large part of our lives, so we must be prepared for each arrival. Schools are the second home for girls and adolescents since they spend approximately 5 to 6 hours. Therefore, it is important that these spaces are safe for them and that they can access products and supplies that allow them to manage their menstruation during the period that they are in class.

However, in any case, every girl should have an emergency period kit at their disposal to always feel safe. Besides having all the necessary supplies, a menstrual kit also contributes to eradicating the menstrual taboo so that girls and adolescents are not afraid or ashamed to talk about it, promoting their autonomy.

We also made a video for our YouTube channel about the DIY menstruation pouch because it is something we have all been needing, and each girl should have it if a menstrual emergency occurs, i.e., when the surprise period comes or a friend needs help. Therefore, we need to have an emergency kit on hand.

In this chapter, we will explain how to make a menstrual kit so that you will always feel safe and free. We also have a very informative video related to this topic on our channel. You can find the link at the end of the chapter!

So let's get started fast before a surprise catches us off guard!

What to Have in a Menstruation Kit?

A menstruation kit is a pack in which you must include the essentials for those specific days. Ideally, you should bring everything you need, but it should fit in a small bag. Otherwise, it will be uncomfortable for you to carry.

Below are the most important products before the arrival of the period:

A Bag or Case

First, you should have a bag to place the towels, wipes, and what you need during the menstrual period.

This bag can be the same size as the one you use for cosmetics. In fact, you can buy one just like that and use it as your menstrual kit.

Menstrual Hygiene Items

Now is the time to choose your menstrual care products. There are several options, the most common being **sanitary pads**. Place the amount you need for a day. This way, you don't fall short.

Depending on the amount of flow, you can opt for various sizes and absorption capacities.

On the other hand, **tampons** are a good option since they last longer than pads. If you're in class and cannot go to the bathroom frequently, it is a good option, but first, you must learn how to put it on correctly.

It's best to start with a mini size until you get used to it, and then you can use a thicker one if you need to.

We advise you to use tampons with applicators, especially if it's your time since having a non-porous surface makes it much more slippery and avoids friction that can be scary.

Finally, the use of a **menstrual cup** is highly recommended. The advantage of a cup is that it is reusable and can store up to 12 hours of menstruation. You have to choose which one is yours since there are various sizes and designs.

Wet Wipes

Wipes are essential for an emergency menstrual kit. They come in handy when you are away from home and cannot wash with intimate soap and water. With wet wipes, you can clean the external area of the vagina. Baby wipes and medicated wipes may be good options.

The best wipes to take care of your intimate hygiene are those that do not have fragrance. Remember, perfumed wipes can irritate the skin.

Extra Underwear

If your period starts unexpectedly and you stain, there is nothing to worry about. It has happened to all of us. But it is not hygienic to continue with the same panties. We recommend you keep additional underwear in case of emergencies.

If your period starts unexpectedly, you'll feel more confident if you can put on clean underwear.

We found period panties amazing. Why should you choose a period panty?

There are thousands of good reasons to adopt period panties.

- The first of them is comfort!
- They are made of a fabric that respects your skin for serene and gentle menstruation.
- The second unavoidable reason is the desire to preserve the environment. With its washable organic cotton towels, the period panties are part of a zero-waste approach. It thus allows you to reduce your waste for a protected planet.

So, there are only good reasons to try period panties.

If your bag is big enough, you can pack an extra pair of leggings or shorts if you need to change clothes.

Resealable Plastic Bags

Keep some resealable plastic bags in your menstruation kit. If you have to change out of your underwear or clothes at school, you may not want to keep dirty things in your backpack. So keep a resealable plastic bag in your kit, just in case. Then, once you change out of your dirty clothes, put them in the bag, seal it, and put it in your backpack. Remember to take out the bag when you get home to do laundry. These bags are usually also useful for storing things that might spill or dirty the fabric, like makeup or a toothbrush.

Treats to Pamper Yourself

Finally, include some sweets in your emergency bag for menstruation. A good option is a small bar of chocolate. This allows you to have energy and, at the same time, pamper yourself. You will see that you will maintain a good mood.

Includes Some Pain Relievers

Painkillers cannot be missing from your kit. Menstrual cramps can make the first day of your period a nightmare.

Some of the best pain relievers are ibuprofen and naproxen. By the way, do not abuse the dosage, and always use them under your doctor's recommendation.

In conclusion, it is important to have essential products for your periods. Remember to update the menstrual care kit so that you have the essentials in each period.

Some Tips To Keep Your Menstruation Kit Updated

- Include two or three sanitary pads or tampons. To avoid making your kit too full and bulky, don't worry about taking a whole box of feminine hygiene products to school. Instead, take what you might need on a typical day. Then, take the kit home and restock it each time you use it.

- Only pack the items you use, such as pads or tampons. However, if you use both options, you can include a couple of each.

- Tampons without an applicator take up less space in a kit but may be difficult for first-timers. Tampons with applicators take up more space but are convenient.

- You may be able to add panty liners for additional protection.

- Choose a lightweight pair of underwear made from a breathable fabric like cotton. Then, fold the underwear or roll it neatly to take up less space in your bag.

Link to Video:

https://www.youtube.com/watch?v=H-BfuAUTaFA

Chapter Four: How to Keep Track of Your Menstrual Cycle | Teenage Period Health

Now that we have covered the basics, let's learn more about tracking our menstrual cycle. You must have heard a lot about this, but do you know why experts suggest that you track your cycle? There are a lot of reasons for this. In our video on our channel, we have talked about this topic. You can find the link at the end of the chapter.

Why Should You Keep a Track of Your Menstrual Cycle?

Tracking your period cycle can help you understand your body better and the standard pattern that your body follows every month. Essentially, it is all about health monitoring. When you understand your body better, you can become more proactive with your health, which is crucial to helping you prepare in advance.

Tracking your period includes everything from how often you get your period, how heavily you bleed, whether or not you have any pain, how you feel emotionally, and so on. Keeping track of your menstrual cycle can also help you understand the different underlying health issues you might be facing. When you keep track of this, it can help you find the root cause of any abnormalities that might exist.

Another vital reason to track your menstrual cycle is to spot any irregularities. A regular menstrual cycle indicates good health because it means your body is working as it should.

However, not everyone has an exact 28-day cycle; some may have slightly shorter or longer cycles, especially during their teenage years. This can be normal, but it's crucial to know what qualifies as irregularities. Irregularities could involve periods that are extremely heavy, very light, too frequent, or too spaced out. Monitoring your cycle can assist in recognizing these irregularities and deciding if they need extra care.

Apart from that, tracking your cycle also helps you manage different menstrual symptoms. This again varies from person to person. For those who have severe symptoms like cramps and mood swings, tracking can help you schedule your activities accordingly and also have some self-care strategies planned out so that you can work towards alleviating discomfort. It is all about promoting overall well-being.

Many young girls do not keep track of their menstrual cycle, which can lead to several problems later on. At a young age, you do not really understand how important this is.

Now, let's move toward understanding how exactly you can track your menstrual cycle.

Tips to Keep Track of Your Menstrual Cycle

Here are a few ways you can effectively track your menstrual cycle. You need to figure out what works best for you, and then you need to follow through with that. The key is to be consistent with what you do and then follow through with that so that it can help you. Only you know yourself enough to know what you can be consistent with.

The Calendar Method

If you are old school and you like to write everything down, then this method will probably work best for you. Every month, when you get your period, note down the date or mark your calendar that day so that you can accurately keep track of it. Also, mark your calendar on the day that your bleeding fully stops. This will help you mark the start and the end date of your period and will help you know the duration of that as well.

To be more apt with what you are doing, also try to note down how heavy or light the bleeding was. Describe what it was like – was it clotty? Was it watery? Was it too dark in color? Descriptions like these can help you understand what your menstrual cycle is like and can help you in the future if you ever need to get in touch with a healthcare provider for any issues you are facing.

It is also helpful to keep track of how you feel during that time period. Some people feel overly emotional. Others feel anxious or depressed. Some feel their body bloating, while some have other physical symptoms like headaches and body pains. You need to see how you are feeling at that time and the pattern that your feelings follow over this time period.

To be more accurate with this, you can even rate your days on a scale of 1-10, depending on how you feel in that time period. Make a note of when you feel entirely healthy and happy and when you feel your worst. Even if all of your days are 10/10, still make a note. This is important to help you understand your body and then take any actions, if needed, to help you feel better.

Additionally, if you are taking any medication in this time period, either to alleviate the pain or to help with some other health issues, make a note of that. Write them down on that respective day. Even if you are not taking any medications and are choosing herbal remedies, make a note of that. This will help you in case of certain side effects or, in the worst case, complications.

Remember, it is always better to be prepared than to have to deal with problems later on.

Period Tracking Applications

Period tracking apps are also a great way to keep track of your cycle. There are so many period tracking apps in the day and age that we live in. Most of them are super helpful and can help you a lot. They can help you predict your cycle, track your symptoms, give you health insights, offer reminders, and so on. Some of them also give you the option of customizing them to help align them with your unique cycle patterns. The personalization makes the tracking experience a lot more accurate and definitely tailored to your needs as well.

So you need to first figure out what will work best for you, and only after that should you make a choice.

Here are some period-tracking apps for young girls. You can check to see whichever you like.

1. Period Tracker by GP Apps

This is a very easy-to-use application for girls, where you can keep track of your dates and also make a note of your moods. This one has free and paid options, so you can choose what works for you based on your tracking goals.

2. Easy Period – Lite Tracker

This is also a really great one that can help girls make a note of their dates. This one has no chat option, which again makes it very safe for young girls.

3. MagicGirl Teen Period Tracker

This is an app that caters to teens specifically. It also has animations and journal functions that make it very functional and fun to use.

4. Flo

This is a very comprehensive application that makes use of AI to provide you with period predictions after detecting trends in your cycle. You also get access to a support network where you can connect with others who are in the same boat as you are.

5. Clue

This app has been featured in many different magazines as well and promises to be of value to people of all ages.

The best way for you to is to experiment and see which one works best for you. These are only a few of the ones that you can use. You can further explore to see which one aligns with your goals, and then you can make use of that one in particular.

Dealing With Period Mood Swings

A lot of girls experience massive mood swings at that time of the month. These mood swings do not only affect them and their activities but also others around them. So, how can you effectively deal with these mood swings? Here are a few tips that can help you.

- **Exercise**

This is one of the most underrated ways you can alleviate your mood. When you get your body moving, your body releases endorphins, which can help combat massive shifts in mood. It is only normal to feel extra tired and fatigued. You might not feel like working out when you are on your period. But that's where the real deal is. Gather up some strength and get your body moving. A nice workout session can greatly help. You need to start off with what works best for you. It could be a nice cardio session, maybe some dancing, or your favorite sport, or even going to the gym. You need to know what will work best for you. How you feel after that will speak for itself, motivating you to exercise every single time, no matter how tired you are.

- **Stay Hydrated**

Drink plenty of water, especially when you are on your period. This will prevent any extra bloating. Try to have lukewarm water to help you with your cramps as well. Ideally, you should be consuming anywhere between eight to nine glasses a day. This will help increase blood flow and will relax the cramped muscles as well.

- **Have Dark Chocolate**

More often than not, we end up going too hard on ourselves. If it is that time of the month and you are craving something, go for it. It is alright to give in to your cravings sometimes if it helps alleviate your mood. In fact, dark chocolate is actually good for you when you are on your period. It helps you with period cramps and also has several other benefits. So go for that favorite dark chocolate bar of yours that you see at the store!

- **Get Ample Sleep**

Getting enough sleep is crucial to help your body get that extra serotonin boost. Ample sleep is crucial for your body to help you feel refreshed and energized. This is also highly underrated. A lot of girls compromise on their sleep for other things that they have to do without really realizing that there is nothing more important than their health.

- **Control Discomfort**

If you have massive cramps, try to control the discomfort by seeing what works best for you. Try some pain relievers after consulting your health provider. You can even try heat pads if that helps you feel better.

- **Avoid Stress**

Try to avoid any stressful situations at this time period. Stress only makes you feel worse!

Try these tips and see what works best for you!

How to Maintain Your Health and Hygiene While Menstruating

Now that you understand why it is important to keep track of your cycle, let's move on to health and hygiene during your period. Your period most definitely does not have to be a source of discomfort for you. If you follow the right methods, you can be healthy and comfortable during this time.

Products and Supplies

Let's talk about period products and supplies – the essentials to help you manage your period with ease. We'll cover the most common options and how to use them comfortably. Remember that the key is to understand how to use these in the right way.

1. **Menstrual Pads**

These are also known as sanitary napkins, and they're pretty common. They come in different types and absorbency levels to fit your needs. With so many different brands in the market, you need to figure out which one will work best for you. They have different features, so you need to see which one you want to go for. With pads being the most commonly used products by girls, you need to do your research first, depending on what brands you have access to.

Here are some details about the types that are widely available.

- Regular pads: Perfect for lighter flow days. They're thin, comfy, and discreet.

- Maxi pads: These are for heavier flow days. They offer more protection and absorbency.

- Overnight pads: The thickest and most absorbent pads, great for nighttime or those super heavy flow days.

How do you use pads in the right way?

- Clean your hands: Always start by washing your hands. Remember, hygiene is key!

- Unwrap the pad: Gently unfold it without tearing it.

- Place it in your underwear: Peel off the backing and stick it in your underwear, making sure it's centered and comfy.

- Secure it: If your pad has wings, press them down to keep it in place.

Remember to change your pad every 4-6 hours or sooner. Even if you feel like your pad is not full, make sure to change it in a few hours. This is important to ensure that you aren't dirty and that you prioritize hygiene.

2. **Tampons**

These are another popular choice and more discreet. They come with applicators, which might seem a bit tricky at first. For those of you who have not used these before, it can seem very tricky at first. But once you start using these, you will eventually get the hang.

Here's how you can start:

- Practice: Try inserting a clean, dry tampon before your period starts. This will help you understand how the applicator works.

- Applicator basics: The applicator has two parts – the outer tube and the inner plunger. When you push the plunger, it pushes the tampon into your vagina.

Tips for comfortable tampon use:

- Relax: Find a comfy spot and relax your body. For a first-time user, this might feel scary at first. But relax your way into it, and don't feel too tense.
- Get the right size: Start with a smaller size if you're new to tampons, and switch to a larger one as you get more comfortable. Once you use the smaller one, you will have a fair idea of whether this works for you or whether you need to make a switch to a larger one.
- Follow instructions: Read the tampon box instructions carefully for step-by-step guidance.
- Mirror help: If you like, use a mirror for guidance during insertion. This can be really helpful at first. Once you get the hang of it, you will not feel the need to use a mirror. But for starters, it's great!
- Change regularly: Remember to change tampons every 4-8 hours to avoid any risks or complications.

3. **Menstrual Cups**

These are eco-friendly and cost-effective. While these aren't a very popular choice, like pads and tampons, they still pretty much exist. Here's what you need to know:

- They are reusable: Unlike pads and tampons, you only need one menstrual cup, and it can last for years.
- They are eco-friendly: Using a menstrual cup reduces waste from disposable products.

Choosing the right size is essential for a comfortable fit. Since this is a long-term investment, you need to do your research and spend some time finding the one that suits you best. This is very important for you. Most brands offer two sizes – one for individuals who haven't given birth vaginally and another for those who have.

Here are some tips to help you make a good choice:

- Size chart: Check the manufacturer's size chart to find the best fit.

- Cervix position: Consider your cervix's position; a lower cervix might prefer a smaller cup.

- Trial and error: It might take some tries to find the perfect fit, but don't give up! Once you find it, you'll have leak-free periods.

4. Panty Liners

These are thin pads for lighter flow days or as a backup with tampons or menstrual cups. While these most definitely don't act as a substitute for pads on your heavy days, you can use these once your flow isn't heavy. A lot of girls with heavy vaginal discharge choose to make use of these on regular days to help them feel comfortable.

Why should you use these?

- Freshness: Panty liners keep you feeling fresh on light-flow days.

- Backup protection: They're handy for added protection against leaks with other products.

How can you use these effectively?

- Choose the right size: Just like other period products, go for the size that suits your needs.
- Change regularly: Swap them out as needed to stay comfy and avoid odors.
- Dispose properly: When you change, wrap the liner in toilet paper or its wrapper and toss it in the trash. Don't flush it down the toilet.

With some sorted hygiene tips, you can make this time period of yours much more comfortable.

As young girls, one of the most important things that you need to understand is that your period is not a disease. It cannot and should not stop you from any activities that you would otherwise do. Try to be as active as you can. All you have to do is manage the symptoms. With ample knowledge of what is required of you and how you can deal with the symptoms well, you can get through this very easily. The female body is very powerful. Your body can do wonders. You just need to never lose faith in your abilities as a woman!

In this chapter, we've talked about why it's super important to keep an eye on your menstrual cycle and how doing this can really help you stay healthy and feel good. We also looked at some cool ways teenagers like you can keep themselves healthy and fresh during their periods so you can totally handle this natural part of life. Just remember, knowing more about your body gives you the power to face your menstrual cycle with confidence and a big ol' smile!

Link to Video:

https://www.youtube.com/watch?v=r0doqNV5Uy4

Chapter Five: The Do's and Don'ts When You're on Your Period

Now that you understand why taking care of your health is essential, let's move on to the do's and don'ts when you're on your period.

As young girls, you might find yourself all over the place when you're on your period. You might not really know what methods to follow or what you must most certainly avoid during this time frame. With so much on the internet, you might not be able to distinguish the right information from wrong. These do's and don'ts will make your life much simpler and the journey ahead much easier for you.

So, let's delve into the details. You can also find a link to our video on this topic toward the end of the chapter.

Do's

Here are a few things we have found that have worked well for us, so we would like to share them with you.

- **Warm Showers**

Warm showers can be very relaxing when you're on your period. They can help you ease cramps and can also help you feel a whole lot fresh. There is a huge misconception in many parts of the world related to taking a shower during your period. Many believe that this can have negative health effects. Research has shown that these claims have no authenticity. In fact, you must try to be extra careful with your hygiene during this time. This helps you protect yourself from diseases as well.

- **Hydration**

Menstruation can sometimes also lead to dehydration, which is then linked to other health effects like headaches and general discomfort. You must keep yourself hydrated during this period of time, with at least eight to ten glasses of water a day; not just that, but also focus on eating more water-rich fruits and vegetables to help you. Staying hydrated can also help you curb your sugar cravings during this time.

- **Changing Your Pad or Tampons Regularly**

Hygiene always comes first. To keep yourself clean and germ-free at all times, try changing your pads or your tampons every three to four hours, depending on the intensity of your flow. The idea is to prevent the growth of bacteria, which can eventually lead to infections. Frequently changing helps keep the area super clean, which is an integral part of your hygiene.

- **Sleeping Well**

Nothing makes up for a good eight to nine hours of sleep. Your body needs ample rest to recover and feel energized enough. To relax your body and your mind, try to have a very good sleep routine. This becomes even more important during your period because it helps you regain any lost energy and makes you better handle any pain as well. It also helps with mood swings, regulating how you feel and eventually helping you overcome any feelings of being low.

- **Eating More Protein**

Health experts recommend that you incorporate a greater amount of protein in your diet when on your period. It gives your body the energy that it needs and also helps reduce fatigue. Not only that, but protein-rich foods also keep you fuller for longer, which means that you are less likely to give in to most of your unhealthy cravings at this time of the month. You possibly cannot give in to all your cravings at this time of the month, but we'll come to that in detail a little later in the chapter.

- **Eating Dark Chocolate**

Dark chocolate has potential health benefits. At this time of the month, it can specifically help you cut down on your cravings and can also lower the severity of your period symptoms. Remember that satisfying the soul is also important, so try and do what you can to help you feel better. Dark chocolate can really do the trick.

- **Exercising**

The proven benefits of exercise are many. But during your period, you might feel a lot more lethargic. You might not even feel like exercising, but giving yourself that push is very important. Try any form of exercise that you like. This could be walking, yoga, swimming, or hitting the gym. Don't push yourself too hard, but try to get some moderate workouts done. This will also help release happy hormones, eventually helping you feel so much better.

- **Managing Stress**

Try to manage stress as much as you can when you are on your period. You need to see what works best for you. Try different stress management techniques, and then figure out which one works best for you. Maybe you could try mindfulness and relaxation. You can even try different yoga poses to see how they work for you. The impact of stress on your menstrual health can be really damaging. So try doing the best that you can to help yourself. You can even do trial and error to see what will work best for you.

- **Consulting a Healthcare Professional**

If you ever feel like you are experiencing extra discomfort, then contact a healthcare professional who can help you out. It is always better to be extra safe. So before it gets worse, consult a professional to help you. They will first get to know more about your symptoms, after which they will thoroughly examine you and tell you if there seems to be an underlying issue.

Now that you know all about what you must do during this time, let's move toward the donts.

Don'ts

Here are a few guidelines that we would like to share with you.

- **Junk Food**

During your period, you will have all sorts of cravings. But what is most important is for you to realize that you cannot give in to all of them. Having a nutrient-rich diet is one of the most important things there is. Your body needs that extra energy to keep you going, so try and make that extra effort to eat clean. It is okay to indulge once in a while, but eating a lot of unhealthy food, or junk food for that matter, will only make you feel a whole lot worse.

- **Extra Coffee**

Some of us just love having coffee, don't we? A cup a day is alright, but if you overdose on caffeine when on your period, then that can alleviate the symptoms of painful periods, only making you feel much worse. Not only that, but it can also lead to breast tenderness, which can be very uncomfortable. Try to avoid coffee as much as you can when on your period, and switch to nutrient-dense foods to help you get the energy you need to keep you going.

- **Smoking**

Again, this is something that heavy smokers would find very hard to do. But the fact of the matter is that smoking leads to even severe menstrual cramps. Nicotine can also greatly contribute to irregular periods and inflammation. So try and avoid smoking at all costs. As it is, smoking is injurious to health, but during your period, you have to be extra careful not to do anything that can make you feel worse.

- **Excess Sodium**

Too much sodium can trouble you a lot when you are on your period. It can cause bloating and can also increase the severity of your cramps. So try to have a balanced diet at all times.

- **Expired Pads or Tampons**

One of the most important things is for you to thoroughly check the pads or tampons that you are using. If you end up using expired ones, then that only leads to problems like itching and can also lead to infections in some cases. So always try to be as apt as you can with the hygiene products that you use.

- **Abnormal Symptoms**

If you notice anything abnormal, like excessive cramping pain or even clotting, then consult a healthcare professional instantly. The last thing that you should be doing is taking your health lightly. There is nothing more important than your health, so try and take that very seriously.

- **Waxing or Shaving**

Try to avoid hair removal as much as you can when you are on your period. Your skin is very sensitive at that time of the month. This means that it can hurt a little extra as well. If things go from bad to worse, then this can even lead to infections. So, try to avoid all kinds of hair removal methods during that period.

- **Breast Examination**

Try not to go for a breast exam during your period. If you are trying to check for some abnormalities, then the results you get during your period will most likely not be accurate. Your breasts will be more tender, and hence, the doctor will not be able to rule out different things.

- **Skipping Meals**

A lot of people tend to skip meals when on their period. If you skip your meals, you will not have sufficient energy, which is not a good thing at all. Replace all unhealthy foods with ones that have high amounts of salt and sugar. This is essential to your health.

- **Heating Pads**

Heating pads can seem to be very helpful. They can help alleviate the pain and can make you feel better instantly. But they are not a really good idea. Heating pads can poorly affect the connective tissues in your body. These tend to soften up due to the heat and can eventually end up making your cramps even worse.

- **Self Care**

You have to take care of yourself as much as you can. Prioritize yourself if you value your health. If you feel like getting a massage or pampering yourself with that pedicure that you have been wanting to get done for the longest, go for it.

Try to make a conscious effort to avoid all of this during your period. This is one of the most essential things to ensure you are comfortable.

Managing Menstrual Pain

Typically, it is a known fact that a lot of girls and women experience massive pain when on their period. The level of pain differs from person to person, but it can severely hamper their day-to-day activities. Managing pain is important for you to live a peaceful life and have peace of mind in this time period.

Here are a few tips that can help you with fast pain relief when you are on your period.

- **Over the Counter Medications**

The most important thing that can work very well for you is over-the-counter medication. These help lower your body's production of prostaglandin. Experts recommend that you don't resort to medication unless the pain is very severe and you find it hard to cope.

- **Adding Herbs to Your Diet**

Adding herbs to your diet can also greatly help with pain. Some of the very useful ones include chamomile tea, fennel seeds, cinnamon, and ginger. These can help you feel a lot better during this time period.

These methods can greatly help relieve pain, making you feel much better on the whole.

Navigating Work and Social Life

When menstruating, we sometimes find it very hard to keep up with the hustle and bustle of regular life. Going to work starts seeming extra hard. Due to the taboo around the subject, women don't even find it very comfortable to discuss certain issues with their managers. The truth is that, in most cases, you don't even get that kind of supportive environment that eventually allows you to get what you want. So what do you do? Let's learn more about how you can navigate your work and your social life when you are on your period.

Communicating With Your Employer

The most important thing is for you to communicate with your employer. This can be challenging depending on how understanding your employer is. But if you don't talk it out with them, then it gets even tougher.

Let's explore some strategies that can help you deal with this in the best way.

- **Choose the Right Time and Place**

Try to be very apt with the time and place. Make sure it is a place where you can have an uninterrupted discussion with them. This can help you deal with them much better.

- **Be Clear and Direct**

When discussing your menstrual needs, be direct but respectful. Avoid vague language or euphemisms. Explain your situation and any necessary accommodations you may require.

- **Know Your Rights**

It is also important that you familiarize yourself with the legal rights that you have. This will help add more value to your conversation. Your employers should know what your rights are and how you want to work toward finding the best way out of the situation.

- **Suggest Solutions**

Always try to find a middle ground when stuck in such situations. If you have a proactive approach, then this makes things a whole lot simpler and allows you both to find a solution that works for all.

- **Keep It Professional**

Try to keep it as professional as you can. Maintain the right balance between sharing personal information and discussing your professional responsibilities.

Addressing Period Stigma

Addressing period stigma in your personal and professional circles is very important. Despite living in the 21st century, there is a stigma that is attached to menstruation. Have you ever thought about how you can fight this situation?

- **Initiate Open Conversations**

One of the most important things that you must do is to talk about menstruation openly with your friends, family, and social groups. When you talk about it normally, it helps people open up to it and also helps you remove the stigma that surrounds it. It is we who have to normalize the situation and learn how to deal with the situation in the best way.

- **Share Experiences**

Share your own experience about the situation. When you openly talk about the challenges that are associated with this, it allows you to encourage others to share their story as well. This helps foster empathy and understanding and allows you to help unfold the situation in a much better way.

- **Correct Misconceptions**

Challenge and correct any misconceptions or myths about menstruation that may arise in your conversations. Provide accurate information to dispel stigma. When people begin to talk about it normally without shying away from it or choosing to do their research properly without just believing in old wives' tales, that is when change happens.

Educating Partners and Friends About Menstrual Health

Establishing a support system around you also helps you ideally deal with the challenges that this brings. So how can you do that? You need to help them have a deeper understanding of the issue.

- **Share Information**

It is very important for you to share information with others about this. What exactly should you be doing? Share articles, books, or videos about menstrual health with your loved ones. This can help them gain a deeper understanding of the topic.

- **Encourage Empathy**

Encourage your partner or your friends to imagine themselves in the other person's shoes. This makes us more receptive to trying and understanding how another person might be feeling. This allows for a better support system to be in place.

- **Normalize Conversations**

Create an environment where discussing periods is normal. This can help your loved ones feel more comfortable asking questions and offering help when needed.

When you try and become as proactive as you can, it helps you deal with such issues in a much better way.

Link to Video:

https://www.youtube.com/watch?v=hFeERW-2CnY

Chapter Six: Common Menstrual Symptoms You Shouldn't Be Afraid Of

Menstruation is a very normal and natural aspect of a woman's reproductive health. Yet, the experience is accompanied by various different symptoms that tend to sometimes cause unnecessary worry. In this chapter, the idea is to shed light on those symptoms to empower girls to navigate through this process with confidence and informed self-care.

Let's understand these symptoms, how you can handle them better, and why you should not be afraid of them. We have also created two videos on this important topic. You can find the links to those at the end of the chapter.

Menstrual Cramps

Your period is often accompanied by menstrual cramps. While some have them very severe, others can sometimes experience mild ones. These can cause discomfort at times and, in severe cases, can also lead to further problems. In this case, you need to take care of yourself and see what works best for you.

Sometimes, girls tend to get extra worried about these symptoms. Remember that this is a very normal part of your period. Most women experience menstrual cramps, but there is no need to be worried about them at all.

Dealing With Menstrual Cramps During Period

When menstrual cramps are very severe, you can deal with them in several ways:

- Apply heat to that area to avoid cramping. Test to see what level of heat helps you. But don't overdo the heating part because that can create further issues. So, try and adjust the temperature and see what works best for you.
- Take a pain reliever: You know best what pain reliever works for you. So go for the one that works best for you.
- Exercise: Contrary to popular belief, exercising can, in fact, help you a lot. So, go for any form of workout that works best for you. Don't overdo it, but try to get in some form of activity that can help you.
- Reduce stress: Cramps coupled with stress make things even worse. So try and see what works best for you. You can try yoga, deep breathing exercises, meditation, counseling, and then see what works best for you in this regard.
- Get your vitamins and minerals: It is important that you get your vital minerals so that you don't feel weak.

Changes in Flow – Normal Variations

Menstrual flow can vary in color and consistency, often prompting questions and concerns. This delves into the spectrum of normal variations in menstrual flow, debunking misconceptions and fostering an understanding of what is considered typical. By embracing the diversity in menstrual patterns, individuals can foster a healthier relationship with their bodies.

Many women and girls tend to get worried when their flow is a little over the regular or a little lesser than that. It is most important to understand that our bodies are very different and can have different patterns based on other health concerns and based on what stage of life we are at. It is important to understand this in the best way possible and then work toward it.

Dealing With Changes in Flow During Period

- Examine your diet: You can sometimes face irregular flow when you do not eat as much as you ideally should. When you don't eat enough carbs, your body can react, and that can show up in different ways on your body.
- Say no to high-fiber diets: When you eat too much fiber during your period, it leads to irregular flow. So always try to be as careful as you can with this.
- Make sure you get enough fats: Consuming enough fats can help you with your hormone levels and your ovulation. Some great sources of fat are salmon, vegetable oils, and walnuts.

Mood Swings

During your menstrual cycle, you might experience mood swings as well. These mood swings happen because of the hormonal changes that your body goes through at this time. To do this, you should try to listen to your body as much as you can. Understand that this is a natural response that your body has, so you have to tackle this in the right way as well.

Dealing With Mood Swings During Period

- Observe and write down: Sometimes, we ourselves don't understand what we are going through. This makes it even more important for us to try and understand our feelings so that we can work toward what we want.
- Do light exercises: Exercising releases endorphins, so you must try and incorporate that somewhere in your routine as well.
- Control the discomfort: Try to see what is bothering you first. After that, try to figure out how you can control that discomfort. That is key to helping you uplift your mood.
- Get good sleep: Try to get a solid eight to nine hours of sleep every night. Sleep is undoubtedly one of the most important things that can help you get the rest that you need.

Bloating

Due to elevated estrogen levels, you might find yourself retaining more water than usual. This can bother some women, and some might even end up thinking that they have gained weight. Understand that this is completely normal and is usually accompanied by your period. Sometimes, women also tend to take this in their stride, which ends up affecting their self-confidence as well. It is most important that you understand how normal this is and how most women face this problem. So, how can you deal with this?

Dealing With Bloating During Period

- Avoid salty foods: When you are on your period, try to avoid salty foods as much as you can. Processed foods may end up leading you to feel bloated. So always try to eat as little salt as you can. Try to target 1500 mg per day, ideally.
- Eat potassium-rich foods: Potassium-rich foods can help decrease sodium levels and increase your urine production. This again helps reduce water retention and improves period bloating. Some of these foods include spinach, sweet potato, bananas, and so on.
- Avoid refined carbohydrates: Try to avoid white flour and processed sugars as much as you can. This leads to greater sodium levels and, hence, more water retention.
- Drink more water: Have a lot of water, especially when you are on your period. A useful hack is not to wait till you are thirsty but to just have water as a routine part of what you do. Try to target eight to ten glasses a day, even if you don't feel the need to have as much.

Breast Tenderness

Breast tenderness also often accompanies menstruation. You may notice some lumps in your breasts, too, sometime before your period. Understand that this is nothing that you should be worried about. There are ways you can deal with this correctly.

Dealing With Breast Tenderness During Period

- Cut back on salt, sugar, and dairy: This can be a leading cause of breast tenderness, so try and cut back on these as much as you can.
- Regular exercise: Exercising regularly can also help lessen menstrual breast pain. Start with moves that you think will help you. You need to figure out what works best for you, and then you must stick to that. No one knows your body better than you.

Headaches and Migraines

Some women also experience massive headaches when on their period. This is usually a result of the many hormonal changes that your body is going through at this time. The key is to understand how you can use different practical strategies to help you.

Dealing With Headaches and Migraines During Period

- Try to avoid stress: Avoid doing anything that leads to stress. When you are stressed, you might find

yourself overthinking. Find the root cause of your stress and then avoid it as much as you can.
- Medications: You can also take medication to help with the pain. Some common medications include ibuprofen, naproxen sodium, and aspirin. If the headaches get worse, then you can also talk to your healthcare practitioner, who will guide you through the process and will help you with your headache problems.

Digestive Changes

Some women also complain about noticing digestive changes in their bodies when on their period. This can lead to constipation or diarrhea. Sometimes, women end up getting super worried, but it is important to understand that this is a very common symptom that affects many.

Dealing With Digestive Changes During Period

- Add more foods rich in omega-3 fatty acids to your diet: Some foods you can add to your diet during this time include salmon, leafy vegetables, flaxseeds, and walnuts. These can really help you with your digestive issues.
- Increase your fiber intake: Try to eat more fruits and vegetables in your diet. This can help you defecate better.
- Avoid fatty foods: Try to avoid all types of fatty foods if you want to improve your digestive health. When

you do that, it will lessen the symptoms of your diarrhea.

Acne and Skin Changes

Some women also notice that their skin breaks out when they are on their period. This is also very normal. There is a deep connection between your hormones and your skin changes, so you need to figure out what works well for your skin during this time.

Dealing With Skin Changes During Period

- Warm and cold compress: This can help ease the pressure by drawing out the pus. It can also help reduce inflammation and ease pain. So always try this to see how well it works for you.
- Use spot treatment: There are so many different spot treatments that you can use. You can consult a skin specialist based on what your skin type is like, after which you can use different products.
- Use soothing creams: Sometimes, your skin is extra irritated when you are on your period, so try to use soothing creams that can help.
- Don't pick: Don't ever pick your pimples. That only ends up making things worse. It irritates your skin further. So, always try and stay put.

Sleep Disturbances

Some people can also experience sleep disturbances when they are on their period. Understand that this is also completely normal. You can experience these symptoms. You just need to figure out what the cycle is like, and then you need to control your symptoms. You need to understand more about sleep hygiene and promoting restful nights throughout the menstrual cycle.

Dealing With Sleep Disturbances During Period

- Have a set routine: Try to have a set routine when on your period. This helps you stay on track and also helps you go to sleep on time.
- Avoid daytime naps: Try to avoid napping during the day if you want to sleep peacefully at night. This is the most important thing, depending on how sound you sleep and what your regular sleeping routine is like.
- Avoid TV before bedtime: Try to cut out your screen time before you go to sleep. Using mobile devices in bed only makes things a whole lot worse.
- Do not drink caffeine later in the day: Caffeine keeps you up for long, so try and avoid it during the later hours of the day so that you can sleep well at night.

Understand that all of what you face is very normal. Most people go through this. The key is to understand your body and your needs and then understand what works best for you. When you do this, it helps you greatly.

Links to Videos:

https://www.youtube.com/watch?v=JJ4hEumjOSk

https://www.youtube.com/watch?v=2Tio7OgKu7s

Chapter Seven: Menstrual Isolation Custom

Menstrual isolation is a cultural phenomenon that has existed for many years. Essentially, it refers to segregating and stigmatizing women and girls who are menstruating. This idea is largely rooted in historical beliefs and norms. It stems from the idea that women are not essentially 'pure' when they are on their period and, hence, should not be doing regular activities. In the olden times, when this belief was more prevalent, people were not as educated about menstruation and did not understand much about it.

But what this really did is that it created a massive stigma around menstruation, disregarding the fact that this is a very normal part of the way that women's bodies function and that everyone should understand this well. Women and girls became uncomfortable in their own skin due to this kind of stigma.

Largely, this stigma is present in a lot of third-world countries because people are not as well aware of menstruation, and they tend to go with what has been popularly believed by people for so many years now. In the context of India and several third-world countries, menstrual stigma is a pervasive societal issue that extends beyond biological processes to become a multifaceted challenge affecting individuals, communities, and public health.

Cultural factors tend to intertwine with socio-economic factors, which then creates an issue that goes way beyond what we think it does. It corrupts an entire society's mindset and tends to make things so much more difficult for women on the whole. When menstruation is viewed through a lens of shame, women find it very hard to break those barriers and live a normal life when they are going through.

When we understand the cultural context of this and why this happens, we can unravel the layers of stigma and work towards dismantling the barriers imposed on those experiencing menstruation. Understanding this is important to help understand the challenges women and girls face at this time of the month and create more awareness around this. This can help promote menstrual equity.

We have also made a video on menstrual isolation. You can find the link at the end of the chapter.

Historical Origins of Menstrual Stigma

The roots of menstrual stigma date back many years. Societies have grappled with understanding and interpreting the natural biological process of menstruation. Across cultures, the earliest historical records reveal a complex interplay of superstitions, myths, and taboos associated with menstruation. Ancient civilizations looked upon menstruation as something mysterious, which was what laid the foundations for so many different discriminatory practices against women.

Women and girls became conscious of their own bodies. Without actually understanding what they were going through, they began to think this was something 'impure,' and they started shying away from it.

In ancient Greece, women and girls who were menstruating were considered impure and were hence not allowed to be a part of different religious rituals. Similarly, in ancient India, Vedic texts referenced menstrual impurity, associating it with notions of ritual pollution. These early perceptions set the stage for the marginalization of menstruating individuals, establishing a historical foundation for the development of menstrual stigma.

Due to the stigma around menstruation, it was considered to be a 'hush-hush' topic for most. This meant that most girls were unprepared for their period. For most, it seemed like something that brought fear, panic, and embarrassment. Many girls were unsure about what it was, because no one really talked to them beforehand. So it came to them as a surprise, which was definitely not pleasant.

A study conducted on the stigma around menstruation in many parts of the world showed how women remembered the first day of their period as one that brought with them lots of anxiety (Lonkhuijzen, et al.,

2023). One of them even recalled that he did not want to go on the school trip because of it, and she thought it was too embarrassing. Hence, she also did not want anyone else in class to find out about what she was going through. Women did whatever they could to hide their menstruation to avoid being stigmatized. One woman recalled her experience, saying, "It never really happened, luckily, but if I would leak through, I would be so embarrassed, and I would be so ashamed. If someone would see me with red stains on my pants. . . Oh no, that would just be super awkward if that happened."

The terms that were largely used to describe this time period also had a negative connotation. Words like "dirty," "disgusting," and "unclean," were used often by both men and women. These attitudes further added to make things a whole lot worse. Amongst the Surinamese people, menstruation is often referred to as a "sick" period, and hence, women and girls are not allowed to cook for others at this time, out of the danger of making the food "impure."

Now we come to the real question: why was it this way? The main reason for this is the lack of awareness about women's bodies. People did not understand the biological function of the human body and hence had negative views about something so normal for a woman's body. The most shocking part is that women still face discrimination to date when they are on their period.

There is still a massive stigma that is associated with menstruation, which makes it all the more important for us to actually understand what women go through during this time. Due to the lack of understanding, things tend to become even worse, creating so many barriers for women even in today's day and age.

Media Portrayal

The media plays a huge role in shaping people's perceptions about things. Throughout history, the media has also portrayed menstruation as something that is looked upon negatively. In the early '80s and '90s, companies like Kimberly Clark released print advertisements for menstrual products.

These advertisements referred to "bandage suspenders" and "combination belts" in an attempt to be discreet and did not refer to their actual function. Advertisements like these reinforce the idea that there is a huge stigma around menstruation. The products were again being shown in a way that people should buy them discreetly "to save embarrassment."

The first commercial advertisement for menstrual products aired in 1975 and was supposedly for "family viewing," but the word 'period' was not used in it. It wasn't until 1985 that the word 'period' was used in a commercial advertisement. A major reason for this was that people themselves were very uncomfortable with watching something like this on mainstream television because they never discussed the topic of menstruation openly at home, ever. It was viewed as a shameful bodily function meant to be discussed by women only in private. The media largely portrayed menstruation as something that should be 'hidden' and not spoken about openly at all.

While the subject is still largely considered taboo, we can see that the situation has improved considerably to what it was some decades ago. The media is also now trying to change how it shows menstruation, which is again one of the biggest steps toward improvement. We still have a huge way to go from here.

Santoshi, a young girl from a village in Chhattisgarh, chose to speak only about her story, shedding light on the taboo associated with this (UNICEF, 2023). She realized that all of this was very much deep-rooted in the system and that it would take a lot of time for things to change for the better. She said, "I cannot change things overnight, but whenever I get the chance, I educate people. I educate my own family, and I can already see some change in them." She realized that change begins with every person taking one step at a time, so she started by educating everyone in the village so that she could do her part to change the way things were.

Dealing With Menstrual Stigma

Period stigma is real and has been there for so many years now. But the real question is how do we deal with this stigma? What is it that we can do to improve the situation? Being a natural way for the human body to function, there should be things that we all should be doing on a baseline level to help the situation. To date, women are accustomed to buying sanitary pads and other menstrual hygiene products in black paper bags due to the fear of the 'shame' that comes with it. Misinformation about periods has always led to women suffering so much over the years. So what can we do to deal with this? Let's understand this better.

The most important thing is to raise awareness about menstruation. All else comes much later. We first need to acknowledge and understand how this is a very natural part of how the human body functions. Developing greater awareness around this is integral to helping us deal with the stigma. It is the women and girls who go through this phase who suffer so much because of the stigma attached to it. So we have to do something to make the situation better. But then again? How do we do that? Here are a few ways we can do so.

- **Encourage Open Communication at Home**

The most important thing is encouraging young girls and boys to start talking about this normally. From a young age, they should be encouraged to ask questions. They should be given information about what menstruation is all about. Not only that, but they should know that they are free to ask whatever they want to. Parents should reinforce the idea that they will always be there to answer any questions that the young minds have. When you start them off early, they are much more aware of the realities of how society works and what their role is here. From a very young age, they should learn to associate menstruation with a very healthy female body and understand how it is a very natural process that every woman goes through. While girls should understand this well to deal with it better, boys should understand to make this time easier and more comfortable for the women around them. Easier access to period products at home is also a great way to dodge the stigma around it. Jen Gunter, a famous Canadian gynecologist, talked about the stigma associated with this saying, "Menstruation is not a problem to be solved, but a part of the human experience to be accepted."

- **Awareness Programs in Schools**

The formative years of a child are very important for their mental development and growth. Young ones should always be fed the right information in school. Schools should make it a point to have different informative sessions where they not only tell students more about menstrual health but also demonstrate the right usage of hygiene products. This way, the focus can be on making this period so much easier for women and men. Jessica Valenti, an American writer, has talked about the taboo associated with menstruation, saying, "The shame and secrecy surrounding menstruation are not just uncomfortable cultural quirks; they actively harm women and girls."

- **No Code Language**

Many times, code language is used for periods, like 'code red,' 'chums,' and so on. The first and foremost thing that should be done here is to eliminate the usage of these words. This can only be done when we understand why there is no need to be ashamed about this. We must understand that this is a very normal thing every woman goes through in her life. Hence, it should be talked about using the right language, which also helps raise awareness about it. The change starts within the home, so it is the responsibility of all educated children and their parents to start using appropriate terms when referring to anything related to menstruation.

- **Accessibility to Menstrual Products**

In many parts of the world today, menstrual products are not easily available in many shops, especially in rural areas. Even if they are, they are not placed on front racks, and there has to be a lot of searching to get to these products. Alone, even talking about these products is such a taboo that women hesitate to ask for help from shopkeepers, too. So, what is the best way to deal with this? The idea is to work towards ensuring affordable and accessible menstrual hygiene products for all. Lack of access can contribute to stigmatization and adversely impact the well-being of menstruating individuals. In addition, we should all encourage and support initiatives that provide menstrual hygiene products to those in need, especially in economically disadvantaged communities.

- **Policy Advocacy**

There also needs to be inclusive and fair policies in place that address menstrual health and hygiene, including provisions for menstrual leave, access to hygiene products in public spaces, and educational reforms that integrate menstrual health. In this time period, women go through many changes in their bodies, and the best thing that can be done for them is the support that they are offered by those around them.

- **Accurate Media Representation**

Media outlets should be encouraged to portray menstruation in a positive light. We should all raise our voices and put forward our concerns with regard to context that perpetuates stereotypes and contributes to stigma. The positive narratives around this should be celebrated so that the stigma can somehow be broken.

- **Empowerment**

Most importantly, women should be empowered to speak up freely about anything related to menstruation. They should be given a safe space where they can discuss any issues they might be facing so that they can get through this in the best possible way. Mentorship and peer support programs should be available so that individuals can share experiences and advice. When women hear things from other women and girls, they can relate to them, which really helps make their own experience a whole lot smoother and allows them to learn more. Promote initiatives that celebrate menstruation as a natural and empowering aspect of life. Events, art, and media campaigns can contribute to reshaping perceptions.

With more and more self-expression being encouraged, the entire situation can change.

What we all need to understand is that change starts today, and it comes from within. When we try to bring about that change from the grassroots level, it helps go a long way. All women ask for is for them to be understood at this time. We can bring about this change if we all play our part duly.

Link to Video:

https://www.youtube.com/watch?v=V99vSQaX7PM

Chapter Eight: Famous Women and Activists Who Contributed to the Menstruation Rights

Several women have spoken about menstruation rights and what it encompasses. These women have played a significant role in trying to educate more and more people about the taboos associated with menstruation, alongside trying to work toward women's rights.

In this chapter, we will discuss the many women who have been advocates for menstruation rights and have played a key role in trying to educate more and more people about what this is all about. To know more, you can also check out our video, the link at the end of the chapter!

Arundhati Roy

Arundhati Roy is a renowned Indian author and activist born on November 24, 1961, in Shillong, Meghalaya, India. She gained international acclaim with her debut novel, "The God of Small Things," which won the Man Booker Prize for Fiction in 1997. Aside from her literary achievements, she has also been an activist for different social and political issues, with menstrual hygiene in India being one of these.

She is known to have broken the silence around menstruation, speaking very openly about the stigma that is associated with this in Indian society. She has largely spoken about how and why it is very important to have open conversations about menstruation so that we can become more comfortable with the idea of discussing the topic openly. The more we shy away from it and make it a hush-hush matter, the more this becomes a problem. There are many myths associated with menstruation as well. She has spoken about how and why we need to look at things from an informed perspective to break this cycle leading to harm.

In her public statements and writings, Arundhati Roy has highlighted the challenges many Indian women face concerning menstrual hygiene. She has pointed out issues such as the lack of access to affordable and quality menstrual products, inadequate sanitation facilities, and the overall societal discomfort in discussing menstruation openly. She has talked about how it is very normal for menstruating women to face multiple issues at this time of the month and how, no matter how much society progresses, it becomes harder and harder to deal with these challenges.

She highlights important aspects of menstrual health and links them to broader issues of gender equality, women's rights, and social justice. She has a vision of seeing a world where women live without any shame or fear about the normal ways in which their bodies function. Her commitment to social causes and her drive to bring about change are commendable in all ways.

They reveal her commitment to building a more inclusive society where women can find a good place for themselves and be very comfortable in their skin. In an interview, she said, "Menstruation is a natural process and should be spoken about in a natural and positive way. It is part of the larger process of reproductive health. We need to break the silence and the stigma surrounding it."

Malala Yousufzai

She is the youngest-ever Nobel Prize laureate. Known largely for her contributions to female education globally, she has also talked about the right to manage menstruation without stigma. She has focused on how sending girls to school is more than just about their education for them to secure employment in the future. It is about how this can raise awareness on so many important aspects that are not largely discussed. It can say so much about how our society functions and how we can further work toward bringing about change. She talks about how there is a need for more activists who can speak about these issues to try and create more awareness about them, which is integral to helping society change at large.

In an interview, she talked about how there is a dire need to make menstrual products readily available for girls in rural areas to help them get through this time without any shame.

She said, "During my trip to Ethiopia in July, I attended a workshop run by Sara Eklund, who founded the organization Noble Cup to distribute menstrual cups and advocate for menstrual-friendly policies in Ethiopia. The girls I met at her workshop told me how difficult it is to manage their periods at school without menstrual products or proper toilet facilities — and how Noble Cup is helping them stay in school. We need to support the work of local female leaders like Sara, who are leading the fight to ensure that menstruation doesn't stop girls from completing their education."

In the same interview, she also talked about how menstruation is viewed as something that women are supposed to be ashamed of despite it being a regular function of the human body. It isn't 'unclean' but rather something that needs to be talked about more openly so that everyone at large understands the idea behind it and can view it as a bodily function.

A massive reason why these problems relating to menstruation persist is because of poor menstrual education at school. Girls tend to believe old wives' tales about them because they receive little to no formal education about what menstruation is all about and how they can deal with it at this time of the month. In fact, so many schools in rural areas have regressive policies like not allowing girls to attend school when menstruating, further reinforcing the idea that women are not clean when they are on their period. Girls and boys alike should know what menstruation is all about and what they can expect at this time of the month.

Arunachalam Muruganantham

A fun fact before shedding light on this person is that he is a man! Yes, you heard it right. We actually have men in the world today who are working for females' rights. Known popularly as Pad Man, his story started in 1998. He was the son of a poor handloom weaver in South India who realized that his wife was using old rags when she was on her period because she could not afford to buy sanitary products. He was shocked and angry at the same time. He wanted to be able to do something to make the situation much better. So, he decided that he was going to produce sanitary pads himself.

So he thought of it as a simple task and started by buying a roll of cotton wool and then cutting it into pieces. He wrapped a thin layer of cotton around it to make it look like the pads sold in the market. But his wife's feedback was not positive, so he thought of where he was going wrong. He started experimenting and tried to come up with the best possible thing that he could. He knew that this was going to be hard, but he also knew that he was determined enough to keep trying so that he could come up with the best product there was.

Upon doing his research, he found out that only twenty percent of females in India had access to proper menstrual hygiene products. This was a huge shocker to him, so he knew that he had to work hard to try and bring about a change. He wanted to develop a way of producing low-cost sanitary pads for girls and women in the country.

So, after a lot of hard work and trying for a very long time to come up with something innovative, he developed a low-cost machine that made low-cost sanitary pads. Many women's groups bought that machine from him, and it instantly became a huge hit. This led to a revolution in his own country and also in many developing countries of the world. He aimed to make sanitary products readily available for women, and he succeeded in doing that.

Aditi Gupta

Aditi Gupta is a social entrepreneur and the co-founder of Menstrupedia, an innovative platform dedicated to breaking the silence and dispelling myths surrounding menstruation. Born in Dehradun, India, Aditi has been a passionate advocate for menstrual health and education. Her main focus behind founding this platform is to raise more awareness about issues relating to menstruation so that women can learn the right things about it. However, the best part about this is that they tried to develop the most engaging way to impact this knowledge.

Menstrupedia is best known for its comic book series titled "Menstrupedia Comic," which serves as an informative and relatable guide to menstruation. The comics use colorful illustrations and accessible language to educate readers, particularly young girls, about the biological aspects of menstruation, menstrual hygiene practices, and the emotional and physical changes associated with the menstrual cycle.

So, while they wanted to make more and more people find out about what menstruation is and how they can take the right steps, they did it in a way that incorporated an element of humor as well so that it would make it all the more interesting for the intended audience. This way, the goal was to present information in a way that is not just educational but also enjoyable at the same time.

The way that she chooses to educate people goes above and beyond comic books. It also allows for having online resources, like a website and mobile apps, so that women can be empowered with the right information, which can eventually allow them to take the right steps as well. The idea was to normalize conversations around menstruation so that people understood more about it. Breaking societal taboos was of utmost importance to her, and she did this in the best way possible, trying to form more positive attitudes around it.

Jennifer Weiss Wolf

Jennifer Weiss-Wolf is an attorney, author, and prominent advocate for menstrual equity. With a background in law and a passion for social justice, Weiss-Wolf has dedicated her efforts to addressing issues related to menstrual health and advocating for greater accessibility and affordability of menstrual products.

Her work focuses mainly on the legal front, where she has tried to shed light on the challenges women face when they menstruate. She has actively contributed to discussions and initiatives to implement policies to ensure that menstrual products are affordable and accessible to all. She has also worked toward removing taxes on menstrual products. So this is how she wanted to help women as much as possible to bring about a positive change, just the type she was seeking.

Another major body of her work includes her trying to raise as much awareness as possible about menstrual equity. Through her works, her aim has been to remove the stigma that is associated with menstruation at large. One of her most famous works is her book titled "Periods Gone Public: Taking a Stand for Menstrual Equity."

For her, the focus has always been on trying to do whatever she can to bring about the change she wanted in the world. Her book has been influential in bringing attention to the cause and inspiring further advocacy. By combining legal expertise, advocacy, and public outreach, Jennifer Weiss-Wolf has played a vital role in advancing the menstrual equity movement.

Miki Agrawal

Miki Agrawal is a social entrepreneur, author, and speaker, best known as the founder of Thinx, a company that revolutionized the menstrual hygiene industry by designing and selling period-proof underwear. Agrawal was always determined to change the narrative around menstruation and the deep-rooted stigma that comes with it. Born in Canada, she has been very vocal about trying to come up with innovative solutions for menstrual products. In an interview, she said, "Menstruation is a powerful and natural part of being human. Let's embrace it, talk about it, and work towards creating a world where no one feels shame or embarrassment about their period."

The first of her many notable contributions was that of forming Thinx. She founded this in 2011, aiming to create underwear that could provide leak-resistant and comfortable menstrual hygiene products. The main ideology behind this was for her to create something that absorbed menstrual flow so that women could be as comfortable as possible at this time of the month. Throughout, she has been a leading figure in challenging the different taboos that surround menstruation.

She aimed to create a shame-free dialogue about periods, trying to encourage women to talk about this as openly. Sharing menstrual experiences only helps more and more women relate to what is happening so that they can try and come to the same page with things.

She also realized how there was so much negative talk about periods. She mainly wanted to promote period positivity here and to do that, she tried to deal with the stigma surrounding that. She wanted to empower females as much as she could so that they could feel more confident about themselves in their own bodies. With sustainable menstrual options, it becomes possible to reduce the environmental impact of menstrual products to make things much easier. Her thoughtful approach toward this has greatly helped with things and has allowed for advancing healthy conversations around menstrual health and female empowerment.

In an interview, she used herself as an example to share her thoughts about how she felt and what was happening at that point. She said, "My judgments usually come from a place of feeling a lack of safety. When I feel unsafe with someone or something, my natural tendency is to protect myself; sometimes, that comes out as a judgment. I do my best to slow down and sit with the person and explain from my heart what I am feeling, and usually, the response is really positive, which only makes me want to keep going with that method."

Amika George

Amika George is a British activist known for her work advocating for menstrual equity and addressing period poverty. She gained recognition for founding the #FreePeriods campaign, a movement focused on ensuring free access to menstrual products for students in schools.

With a strong focus on changing the way things are, she wanted to try and do what she could so that people could access all the right information, ultimately empowering them to make the right decisions in life.

Her #FreePeriods campaign was launched in 2017 when she was only 17 years old. She wanted to raise more awareness about period poverty so that the government would take action to change how things were at that time. She started by providing free menstrual products in schools so that everyone could have access to something that was considered basic. His campaign specifically targeted schools, with the idea being for people to have the right information about it for the cycle of change to start happening. She also organized a petition where she coordinated protests to gain more support for the issues that would address the stigma that young people faced.

Amika George's efforts contributed to increased awareness of period poverty and influenced policy discussions. Her advocacy prompted the UK government to allocate funding for free menstrual products in schools, helping to address the needs of students facing financial challenges.

Gloria Steinem

Gloria Steinem is an American feminist icon. Her body of work shows the commitment that she has to gain prominence as a leader who advocates for gender equality. While she has played a very crucial role in shaping feminist thought and promoting women's issues, she has always also been at the forefront of breaking menstrual taboos.

Her efforts have focused on challenging the societal stigma associated with menstruation and fostering open conversations about women's reproductive health. Being the co-founder of Ms. Magazine, she has time and again resorted to shaping feminist thought and highlighting all sorts of feminist issues. Her speeches have inspired so many women to bring about change and work toward betterment.

Dr. Chris Bobel

Dr. Chris Bobel is an accomplished author, academic, and menstrual activist recognized for her significant contributions to the field of menstruation research and advocacy. She has been working in menstrual culture and activism for a few decades and is known largely for searching for areas where politics, knowledge, and anxiety come together.

She has put together different feminist perspectives, aiming to advance the field and ensure that women have the right knowledge about this because this is all about their bodies. Recognizing largely how there is massive menstrual stigma relating to this, she has done her part to try and promote open discussions about it so that women don't shy away from something as normal as this. Her efforts have helped women understand so much more about their bodies. Not just that, but her efforts have helped shape societal attitudes and have helped create a more inclusive understanding of menstrual health.

As the co-founder of The Society for Menstrual Cycle Research, she has worked toward advancing the understanding of the menstrual cycle through interdisciplinary research, education, and advocacy. It serves as a platform for scholars, activists, and healthcare professionals to share knowledge and promote menstrual health.

Her work has helped bridge the gap between academia and public discourse on menstruation and having a more informed approach toward menstrual health. She has tried very hard to break taboos and challenge societal norms. Her work has had a profound and lasting impact on health and research in this field.

Chella Quint

Chella Quint is a multi-talented comedian, artist, and menstrual educator known for her creative endeavors that challenge societal taboos surrounding menstruation. She takes a very different approach toward such a topic, greatly helping advance the field and create more awareness around it in the best way possible. Her unique comedic approach engages audiences and breaks down barriers associated with menstruation.

As a menstrual educator, her work is mostly related to using her skills to inform people about menstruation and clear any misconceptions about it. She has a very creative way of getting her point across, making it all the more effective. Chella Quint is the creator of "Adventures in Menstruating," a zine and comedy show that serves as a platform for addressing and challenging menstrual taboos.

Through this, she provides a very fresh perspective on menstruation, igniting conversations that are very interesting and entertaining at the same time. She has been very successful in reaching diverse audiences due to the nature of the work that she does.

In 2006, she coined the term 'period positive,' which then gained momentum. She has been touring different places to develop a more positive attitude around periods, which is not seen currently. Her main aim has been to raise more awareness about what this is.

She started researching issues in menstruation education as well so that she could find out how she could do more to help make the situation better. Her efforts have largely been dedicated to counteracting the negative public discourse about menstruation. She has shed light on a very important issue, talking about how the media plays a huge role in shaping attitudes about menstruation. She would like to see a more 'period neutral' world, where people have more positive attitudes about it and where people understand the female body and the way it works much better.

In her words, "The most compelling bits of my research findings are the impact of advertising messages on the fears kids – and adullts! – have reported about menstruation. Their concerns have been of shame, secrecy and leakage fear. There's a history of language use and deliberate marketing in schools that demonstrates a clear link, and it all comes down to two things – secrecy-vs.-privacy, and shame. Privacy is fine – that's a boundary you're setting and it's about safety, choice and consent. Secrecy, on the other hand, is not ok. Secrecy is someone else – whether that's a parent, teacher, advertising message or society more generally – telling you that you need to be quiet about something – or that you need to do whatever it takes to make a part of you invisible. That's no way to be, as anyone who experiences intersectional oppressions or whose gender identity, race or ethnicity, sexuality, or disability is not immediately apparent."

This quote from her highlights how periods should never be a 'hush-hush' topic. She sheds light on the very important concepts of privacy and secrecy. She talks about how it is completely acceptable to have some things count as private, based on how comfortable you are sharing those with others, depending on the type of person that you are and your relationships. But when you are told to take it as a secret, it tells you that you must be quiet about something. That makes a part of you want to be invisible, which is never healthy. Something as normal as bodily function should never be a cause of shame that people shy away from discussing or feel ashamed of. She talks about how this is mainly due to a lack of awareness about it. Both formal and informal institutions should try and talk about this as much as they can to tackle the challenge of dealing with the stigma attached to this. Chella Quint's innovative approach to menstrual education through comedy and art has made her a distinctive figure in challenging menstrual taboos.

Rupi Kaur

Rupi Kaur is a renowned poet and artist recognized for her impactful visual poetry, often shared on social media platforms. Her poetry largely addresses the very central themes of love and feminism. In 2016, she posted a photograph on Instagram of herself lying in bed. While the entire picture is monotone, one aspect that stands out is the red stain on her bottom and the bedsheet.

This gave a clear message to the audience about what she wanted to talk about. Being an Indian Canadian, she was very well aware of how menstruating women are considered to be ritually unclean. So she wanted to give a more period positive message to the audience. As an undergraduate student, she wanted to compare reactions on different social media platforms to her work by testing a theory she had read about, talking about the different ways context influences art consumption.

As part of the caption that she wrote with this, she aimed to educate people about the kind of discrimination that women face on an everyday basis due to normal bodily function.

She wrote, "Some women aren't allowed in their religious place of worship. Out of their homes. To do certain things. And are told they are sick as if the period is a common cold. Yes. This is here in North America. I have been hospitalized many times because of issues associated with my period. I have been suffering from a sickness related to my period. And ever since, I have been working so hard to love it. Embrace it. Celebrate it. Even thought it's given me so much pain in the past few years. And they want to tell me I should be quiet about this. That all of this we experience collectively does not need to be seen. Just felt secretly behind closed doors. That's why this is important. Because when I first got my period my mother was sad and worried. And they want to censor all that pain. Experience. Learning. No. Their patriarchy is leaking. Their misogyny is leaking. We will not be censored."

This gained wide acclaim from all over the world, where so many women were able to relate to what she was saying and felt deeply connected to her message, which was exactly what her intention was before she posted this photograph. With three million views in less than a day, the impact and the message were very clear. But her photo went viral for all the wrong reasons. Instagram attempted to remove her image multiple times to clear its guidelines and messages. However, her professor loved her project.

When asked about her intended message, she talked about how periods are seen as dirty and taboo in many different parts of the world, especially in third-world countries. But she was very proud that she did something like that. The fact that she was able to get that kind of attention only went on to give a very clear message: People found something 'shocking' on the internet, which is exactly what it shouldn't have been. This is a normal bodily function that should in no way be treated in the way that it was. The fact that Instagram later reinstated her photograph showed the importance of confronting censorship and promoting open discussions about menstrual health.

Nadya Okamoto

Nadya Okamoto is a passionate menstrual equity activist, social entrepreneur, and the founder of the organization PERIOD. Her main focus has been ensuring that everyone has access to menstrual products and education. Her activism in this domain has mainly highlighted a major lack of menstrual hygiene products. With something as basic as this, everyone should know what this means and why this has to be something highly accessible for women all over the world.

Her organization, PERIOD, is mainly aimed at fighting to end period poverty and the stigma that comes with it. As the executive director for five years, her organization addressed over 1.5 million periods and registered around 800 campus chapters in 50 states. In 2018, she also published her debut book, "Period Power: A Manifesto for the Menstrual Movement" with publisher Simon & Schuster.

In this book, she explores the history of menstrual equity and shares her own experiences as an activist. Through her organization, she has been able to mobilize a global network of young activists to address menstrual health issues and advocate for policy changes. She has worked toward many different educational initiatives, where she tries to encourage open discussion about menstruation. Her work and her commitment are a testament to her cause, and she has really been able to create a profound social impact, alongside making it to the Forbes 40 under 30 list. Her work with PERIOD reflects a commitment to social justice, equality, and breaking down barriers related to menstruation on a global scale.

Kiran Gandhi

Kiran Gandhi is a musician, activist, and entrepreneur known for her impactful contributions to challenging menstrual stigma and promoting menstrual health. She has collaborated with various artists and performed on international stages. Kiran Gandhi gained widespread attention for her activism challenging menstrual stigma during the 2015 London Marathon.

During the marathon, she ran without a tampon so that she could shed light on menstruation as a regular bodily function and could challenge societal norms as well. She understands how there are so many stigmas related to menstruation all over the world. The need for change is dire, and there also has to be greater awareness around the female body.

Talking about the marathon, she wrote, "If there's one person society won't f**k with, it's a marathon runner. If there's one way to transcend oppression, it's to run a marathon in whatever way you want. On the marathon course, sexism can be beaten. Where the stigma of a woman's period is irrelevant, and we can re-write the rules as we choose. Where a woman's comfort supersedes that of the observer." She wanted to stand in solidarity with women all over the world who do not have access to tampons. Despite the cramping and the pain, basic menstrual hygiene products are not as readily available as they should be, which is a huge problem. Running a marathon like this was a very brave move from her end. Her activism opened the floor to lots of healthy discussions about menstruation and also helped destigmatize periods on a global scale.

Alongside this, she is also a co-founder of "SheTHINX," a menstrual cup company that focuses on providing sustainable and innovative menstrual products. The company aims to offer alternatives to traditional menstrual hygiene products and promote eco-friendly options. Through this platform of hers, she continues to offer sustainable alternatives to women who do not have access to traditional menstrual products.

All these remarkable people have gone to lengths to talk about menstrual health and hygiene. These people have helped transform the world for the better, especially for women, and that is exactly what they aimed to do as well.

Links for the Above-Mentioned Women:

https://en.wikipedia.org/wiki/Arundhati_Roy

https://en.wikipedia.org/wiki/Malala_Yousafzai

https://en.wikipedia.org/wiki/Arunachalam_Murugananth am

https://newhorizoncollegeofengineering.in/aditi-gupta-social-entrepreneur/#:~:text=Aditi%20was%20recognized%20for%20her,trained%20more%20than%2010%2C000%20teachers.

https://msmagazine.com/author/jenniferweisswolf/#:~:text=She%20is%20the%20author%20of,Leadership%20Center%20at%20NYU%20Law.

https://mikiagrawal.com/

https://en.wikipedia.org/wiki/Amika_George

https://en.wikipedia.org/wiki/Gloria_Steinem

https://www.umb.edu/directory/chrisbobel/

https://periodpositive.com/about/about-chella-quint/

https://en.wikipedia.org/wiki/Rupi_Kaur

https://www.nadyaokamoto.com/

https://en.wikipedia.org/wiki/Kiran_Gandhi

Link to Video:

https://www.youtube.com/watch?v=-cz_fzR3EI8

Chapter Nine: Hormonal Acne — An Ally Accompanying Menstruation

Menstrual acne is a very common ally of menstruation. According to a study, around 63% of acne-prone girls and women experience menstrual acne. This can strike around seven to ten days before the onset of the period and then tends to subside as the bleeding starts.

Many girls and women find this time of the month very stressful. When specifically accompanied by acne, it can add to the stress. Ob-gyn Elizabeth Gutrecht Lyster explains the science behind why hormonal acne happens at this time of the month. She says, "In the first half of a woman's menstrual cycle, the predominant hormone is estrogen; in the second half, the main hormone is progesterone. Then levels of both hormones fall to their lowest levels of the month as bleeding approaches." The truth is that you experience these symptoms due to the hormonal changes in your body at this time. While it is not in your control to change the relationship between acne and hormones, you most definitely can manage it better.

A lot of girls and women have the idea that the relationship between acne and hormones is related to hygiene. However, the truth is that it is an internal effect. The good part is that you can manage it if you try. Some women end up getting painful cysts or papules that can take a longer time to go, while some experience mild symptoms. Whatever you experience, it is very much treatable and manageable. Acknowledging the significance of hormonal acne is paramount, considering its potential impact on self-esteem, mental health, and overall quality of life.

We have also created a very interesting video on this topic. You can find the link at the end of the chapter. Do watch it to get more perspective on this topic.

Factors Influencing Hormonal Acne

There are several different factors that affect hormonal acne. Here are a few of the most important ones.

- **Genetic Predisposition**

Your genetics play a very important role when it comes to acne. Understanding the role of genetics in determining an individual's susceptibility to hormonal acne unveils the genetic markers and familial patterns that contribute to this dermatological phenomenon.

- **Lifestyle Factors**

The lifestyle you live is also a key determinant when it comes to hormonal acne. Delving into diet, stress, and sleep patterns, we uncover the intricate web connecting these lifestyle elements to hormonal balance and acne development. Having a holistic approach to health is not just a philosophy but a strategy that we need to master and understand for our own betterment and health.

- **Skincare Products**

The skincare products that you use also determine hormonal acne. You need to use products that suit you best, and you need to follow your dermatologist's recommendations as well. A health practitioner understands your body well and can guide you in the best possible way. Different skin types react differently to ingredients and formulations, making it all the most important for you to make informed choices. Having a sorted skincare regime is one of the most important things to help you have very healthy skin.

Home Remedies for Hormonal Acne

Treating hormonal acne is very much possible. Depending on how severe your acne is, you can make the best possible decision for yourself. If you have painful cysts and it is something that is bothering you too much, then you must visit a healthcare professional who can guide you through the process. But if you think you have mild acne that can be easily treatable through home remedies, then here are some great ones that you can try:

Tea Tree Oil

Tee tree oil is known to reduce inflammation. It has antimicrobial properties that can help reduce symptoms like redness and swelling. You can try and see if this works for you, depending on your skin type and how you want this to work for you.

Turmeric

Turmeric is also known to have healing properties. For years, this has been used to treat many different types of skin issues like redness and swelling. It has anti-inflammatory properties, so you can use it in any form that works best for you. It is a great idea to mix it in any home-based mask and then apply it to your face to see what wonders it does!

Honey

Honey is used in many Ayurvedic products for many different skin concerns. It has antimicrobial properties that can kill acne-causing bacteria. So, you need to figure out what works best for you first. Again, you can use this in any form that you like.

Green Tea

You can also use green tea for your acne. It is known to have great effects on your skin. Since green tea is very high in antioxidants, it can promote good health. The polyphenols in green tea can help fight bacteria and reduce inflammation as well. A lot of women apply it with witch hazel for the best results. You can see what works best for you.

Aloe Vera

Aloe vera has great soothing properties. The leaves produce a clear gel, which, when applied to your skin, can really help make your skin much smoother. A lot of lotions, creams, and ointments. Apply it to your skin to see itseffects. Since aloe vera contains salicylic acid and sulfur, it is great in helping reduce acne.

Lifestyle Modifications for Hormonal Balance

The key to managing your hormonal acne in the long run is to make lifestyle changes to work toward what you want. These changes do not come over a short period of time but appear when you are consistent in managing your hormonal acne well in the long run.

Stress Management

Stress is one of the main factors that can lead to hormonal acne. A study published in Clinical, Cosmetic, and Investigational Dermatology showed a massive relationship between stress and acne severity. But the key is understanding whether stress causes acne to flare or worsen. The "fight or flight" hormone in your body increases in production when your body is stressed. According to the study, "These hormones stimulate the oil glands and hair follicles in the skin, which can lead to acne. This explains why acne can be an ongoing problem when we find ourselves under constant stress." Dr. Truong explains stress acne in one of the best ways. He says, "Usually, it's people who have had acne some time in their life as a teenager or maybe hormonal acne [...], but then they've been pretty well-controlled and maintained on certain acne regimens or acne therapies. And then, all of a sudden, they have a flare-up or worsening of their acne for whatever reason. And it doesn't really make sense to them."

Let's understand how you can manage stress to help you control your hormonal acne.

- Meditation

Meditation is one of the best ways to help you form a strong connection between your mind and your body, which can ultimately help you reduce stress. It directly affects your cortisol levels, helping you calm down and feel much better overall. There are many different wellness programs and apps that can help you relax your muscles and keep your stress levels very low. You can also try guided meditation to help you. You can connect with people who have had personal experiences with this to help you through the process and allow you to manage stress very well.

- Yoga

Yoga is also a great way to help you ease your stress levels down. For that, you need to have a very holistic approach toward it. Start off first by trying out different physical poses for hormonal balance. As a beginner, you must start out with the basic poses first to help you. The corpse pose, legs up the wall, forward fold, and cat pose are all lovely to help you get started. Specifically for hormone-related issues, you can go with hormone-regulating Asanas, and you can also go with stress relief sequences to help you.

- Regular Exercise

You can also try incorporating some form of regular exercise in your daily life. This can be anything you like to do and help you keep active and going at all times. See what works for you, and then start off. Cycling, walking, running, swimming, tennis etc are all great forms of workout. You need to see what works best for you. The idea is to make sure you pick something you can keep going with without actually getting bored of it. Consistency is key to helping you keep active at all times.

- Quality Sleep

This is one of the most underrated things today. You must have heard health practitioners focusing excessively on quality sleep, but very few people actually get to it in the best way. There is a very deep relationship between hormonal balance and sleep. The regulation of the growth hormone happens during sleep, and its impact on cortisol levels is also great. So you need to try to have a sleep routine that helps you be consistent over time. Go for something you can keep up with and that allows you to stay at it while you can. If you have some issues with your sleep cycle, then you could try and get some knowledge on common sleep disorders like insomnia and sleep Apnea to help you understand where you stand. You can also seek professional guidance to help you through any problems you might be facing. Your hormones are generally a lot regulated when you get regular sleep.

Through these lifestyle modifications, individuals can proactively manage hormonal balance, leading to not only a reduction in hormonal acne but also an improvement in overall well-being. It's crucial to emphasize the interconnectedness of stress management, regular exercise, and quality sleep in maintaining hormonal health.

Professional Interventions for Hormonal Acne

Depending on how severe your hormonal acne is and what changes you have made to your lifestyle, you can decide whether or not you need some form of professional intervention to help you with your skin condition. A healthcare professional can guide you through the process in the best way and help you understand how you can navigate the process to get the help you need.

Here are a few professional interventions that can help.

Dermatological Treatments

A dermatologist is your main point of contact for most of your skin-related concerns, more specifically hormonal acne. They will first understand what your skin condition is like; they are also likely to run a few tests first for deeper understanding, after which they can start off with some prescription medications like oral antibiotics or topical retinoids, or they can even so some procedures like chemical peels and laser therapy. It depends entirely on what your skin type is like and what treatment the skincare specialist thinks will work best for you. All treatments and medications can have different side effects, so you need to see what will work best for you based on your skin condition.

Consultation with Endocrinologist

An endocrinologist can help you understand the role that hormones play in acne development. They can run a comprehensive hormonal evaluation first, after which they can go through a testing procedure tailored to your needs to first understand what your skin is like. Once they understand and identify the underlying endocrine disorders that you have, they can help customize a hormonal therapy for you to help you manage your acne well. The role of the endocrinologist is also to promote patient awareness and allow the patient to speak up about any concerns that they might have. By fostering a collaborative and educational approach, patients can gain a comprehensive understanding of their hormonal health and actively participate in their acne management journey.

Addressing Common Misconceptions about Hormonal Acne

There are many misconceptions about hormonal acne. Most people do not understand what goes behind it and what part of that is true. Let's explore this further in detail.

- Myth: Acne is only a teenage problem

Many people believe that hormonal acne accompanied by your period only happens to teenage girls. This is most definitely a huge misconception. Hormonal acne is not exclusive to adolescence. A lot of women experience hormonal acne all throughout, even when they are much older. Emerging evidence challenges this misconception, highlighting that acne can persist well into adulthood, which is why you always need to seek professional help to allow you to get through this phase easily.

- Myth: Topical treatments alone can cause hormonal acne

While in some cases, this might work, it is largely beneficial for you to seek professional help with the issue that you are facing. Sometimes, the issue is much more deep-rooted than you think, which is why you need someone to help you through the process in the best way. Topical treatments can temporarily alleviate symptoms but can most definitely not give you exactly what you are looking for. So try going for something that you think can work best for you.

Importance of Seeking Professional Advice

Many times, people think they understand their skin well and that they can self-medicate and instantly get better. While that might sometimes work for you, it is not the best way out of a situation. It is always best that you consult a professional healthcare specialist who can dig deeper into the root cause of the problem, examine your skin condition, and help you understand what would work best for you. Self-diagnosis and over-the-counter treatments can be harmful in the long run. If gone wrong, they can worsen the condition of your skin, having damaging effects on you in the long run. So it is always best to consult a professional who can first understand your skin and determine the underlying causes to suggest the best treatment for you. They can also craft a customized plan for you to help you get through that easily. Each individual has different needs, so you need to see what works best for you first. Furthermore, this can also prevent potential complications and side effects in the future. A professional can also provide you with the guidance you need to help you further in the future. It is all about how you perceive things.

Link to Video:

https://www.youtube.com/watch?v=mGb8XIOPfvI

Chapter Ten: Period Cramping in College Dorms

Period cramping is quite something to deal with. For young girls living in dorms, it can be quite a dilemma as to how they can best deal with it and create that comfortable atmosphere for themselves at that time of the month when they need it the most. So what is the best way that this can be done? This chapter will help you understand more about period cramping in detail and what unique challenges girls living in dorms can face. We have also created a very interesting video on this topic. Feel free to take a look at it if you want to learn more. The link is right at the end of the chapter.

Understanding Menstrual Cramps

Most girls have menstrual cramps when on their period – the severity varies from person to person. While some have it really bad, others can easily get through it like a breeze.

Causes of Menstrual Cramps

Here are a few of the main causes of menstrual cramps that you need to understand first.

- Uterine Contractions

When you are on your period, your uterus contracts to shed its lining, which is precisely why you bleed. This leads to cramping and a lot of discomfort for many.

Prostaglandins play a huge role in signaling these contractions.

- Prostaglandins and Inflammation

Prostaglandins, derived from fatty acids, serve as local signaling molecules, orchestrating various physiological processes in the body. When it comes to the menstrual cycle, these tiny compounds take center stage in the uterus, particularly during menstruation. Prostaglandin synthesis and release in the uterine lining are strictly controlled, and their amounts change during the menstrual cycle. On the other hand, prostaglandin release peaks during menstruation. Because of their function in cellular signaling, these molecules—which are frequently regarded as hormone-like—induce contractions of the uterine muscles, which starts the process of the lining falling out of the uterus. However, prostaglandins trigger an inflammatory response in the uterus in addition to their own actions. The recruitment of immune cells and an increase in blood flow to the uterine muscles are two aspects of this localized inflammation. This also leads to a lot of cramping for most women.

Differentiating Between Normal Discomfort and Potential Issues

A lot of the time, young girls struggle when trying to understand whether the cramps they are having are normal ones or the ones that signal some other issue. A major reason for this is that everyone has a different pain threshold, which disallows them from fully comprehending the situation. When experiencing normal discomfort, you are likely to experience mild to moderate pain. This lasts for a couple of days or more and goes away without you having to take any measures for it. Most women experience some kind of discomfort when on their period.

However, if you have severe pain that you feel you cannot tolerate, or the duration is extremely elongated, or you have unusual bleeding, then this signals that there is some underlying condition that you are unaware of and that you need to consult a healthcare practitioner who can guide you through the process. You understand your body the best, so you need to be the one to decide things for yourself first.

By understanding the causes of menstrual cramps and differentiating between normal discomfort and potential issues, individuals can make informed decisions about managing their menstrual health. Stress and other lifestyle factors are directly related to menstrual cramping, but since those have been discussed in detail in the earlier chapters, we will not be touching upon that here.

College Dorm Living and Menstrual Health

Now, we come to the main crux of the chapter, which is college dorm living and how you have to address the challenges that menstrual cramps bring with them when you live in a college dorm.

Challenges

Here are a few of the main challenges that girls might face.

- Lack of Privacy

One of the main concerns when living in a dorm is the lack of privacy that you have there. The lack of private spaces can impact one's ability to manage menstrual hygiene discreetly. This can make a lot of young girls very uncomfortable. They might not really be able to understand how they have to find their way through the situation and what they can do to calm themselves down.

- Communal Bathroom Challenges

When on your period, it can get a little messy. Using communal bathrooms at such a time can seem very uncomfortable, which is where maintaining hygiene comes in and becomes ultra important. So you need to try and understand how you can do that and how you can work toward making yourself extra comfortable.

- Roommate Communication

You spend a lot of time with your roommate, who tends to know a lot about you. Open communication is very important at such a time.

- Availability of Menstrual Products

Sometimes, it can be very hard to find menstrual products easily in dorms. This can lead to a huge inconvenience. Many girls might have to ask others for help or might have to travel to farther places to find what they need.

- Laundry Facilities

In dorms, you do not get the laundry facilities that you would otherwise get in the comfort of your home, which makes it even more important for you to understand how you should handle your laundry at such a time and maintain cleanliness at all times.

Now that we understand what the dynamics are like let's move toward the main crux of the chapter, which is how exactly you can deal with all of these issues.

Addressing the Challenges

Here are a few ways you can deal with these challenges in the best way possible.

- Form Strong Connections

Having a support system is very important. When living away from your family, you need to have connections with people who live with you in your dorm so that you all can offer each other the support that you need as you need it. This means that you should be able to talk to each other easily without having to go above and beyond. You should be able to share your problems and the issues that you feel you are facing when on your period with others around you. At this time of the month, you usually have a lot of mood swings as well, so if you have someone who you can talk to, it becomes much easier for you to make your way through. This is especially true if you have an understanding roommate who can help you navigate through your emotions well.

- Improved Privacy Measures

There should also be more privacy measures in shared spaces. If private stalls are introduced in bathrooms of dedicated hygiene rooms, things can become so much simpler for girls going through this.

- Education and Awareness

There has to be greater education and awareness addressing these challenges, which can mainly help destigmatize menstruation in college dorms. It is important to foster healthy discussions so that people actually understand how this is a normal bodily function and what all women go through at this time of the month. With greater empathy among dorm residents, it can become much easier to create understanding and empathy.

- Greater Access to Menstrual Products

College administrations should ensure that menstrual products are easily available in college dorms. Installing vending machines or providing free dispensers in these areas can help make things so much simpler for menstruating women. This is one of the most important things to help make women feel at ease at this time of the month.

- Community Support Groups

Having support groups is also very important. With a strong sense of community, it can become easier for girls to share their experiences with each other and combat feelings of isolation.

- Advocacy for Inclusive Policies

Women's health and hygiene should be of topmost priority everywhere. This means that there should be proper disposal facilities, and hygiene products should also be easily available everywhere. This can contribute positively toward the entire atmosphere there, making things a whole lot simpler for girls there.

With these measures in place, it can become much easier to work toward what is needed. College administrators can foster an environment that promotes the overall wellbeing of all students by addressing concerns about privacy, accessibility, stigma, and disposal facilities.

How to Form Peer Support Networks in College Dorms

Forming peer support networks in college dorms is one of the most important things. This helps deal with period cramping in a much better way. With an inclusive approach like this, it becomes much easier to work through things easily. So, how can you form these networks? Let's understand this better.

- Create an Inclusive Environment

In college dorms, there should be an atmosphere of openness and inclusivity. This means that discussions about menstrual health should be free of stigma. Everyone should be able to talk openly about things and should comfortably be able to share their side of the story. When everyone shares their experiences, it can create a very comfortable atmosphere all around, where everyone feels at ease.

- Host Educational Workshops

The administration should try to host workshops to invite healthcare professionals to talk openly about period-related issues. This can help get the right information about period cramping and can also help dispel myths related to it. When coping strategies are shared amongst people, it can become much easier to work through things in the best way possible.

- Utilize Social Media Platforms

There also has to be the right usage of social media platforms where dormitory residents can connect virtually. They should be able to have open discussions where they can have a space to discuss things openly and share their resources in the best way possible. When people get this kind of support, it becomes much easier for them to navigate their way through tough times.

- Designate Peer Mentors

Designate experienced residents or volunteers as peer mentors who have knowledge about menstrual health. These mentors can offer guidance, share personal experiences, and provide a listening ear to those seeking support.

- Organize Relaxation and Wellness Events

Different events that focus on relaxation and wellness should be done. This includes yoga sessions, meditation workshops, and different stress relief activities. These events can offer different coping mechanisms for managing period cramps.

- Collaborate with Campus Health Services

Collaborate with university health services to plan seminars and events or hand out educational materials. The quality of support that residents of dorms can receive can be further improved by having access to healthcare professionals.

- Celebrate Menstrual Health Awareness Month

Menstrual Health Awareness Month can be celebrated by organizing themed events and distributing information so that there can be ample opportunities created to allow residents to engage in conversations about menstrual health.

By implementing these strategies, dormitory residents can establish a robust peer support network that addresses the challenges of period cramping and fosters a supportive and understanding community within the college dorms.

Importance of Self-Care Practices

It is important that girls themselves work toward having different self-care practices that can alleviate menstrual cramps and enhance overall wellbeing. These practices have to be understood and comprehended well, only after which menstrual health can be managed in the best way.

Introduction to Heat Therapy

Girls in dorms should be introduced to heat therapy so that they understand how this can help them deal with menstrual cramps in a much better way. Heat helps relax the uterine muscles and also eventually helps reduce pain and discomfort. Using hot water bottles, heating pads, warm baths, and heating wraps can help you get a lot of ease.

Relaxation Techniques

Incorporating relaxation techniques into one's routine can help manage stress, which often exacerbates menstrual cramps. Relaxation techniques include deep breathing exercises, mindfulness meditation, yoga, stretching, and so on.

Over the Counter Remedies

Different OTC remedies can help provide the relief that is needed for menstrual cramps. This is usually helpful when you have tried most other things, but they don't really seem to work for you. Some common options include Ibuprofen, naproxen, and aspirin. These can help reduce inflammation and can relieve pain. Herbal supplements are also very useful and can help get the ease that girls might need at this time. With a more holistic approach to things, it can all become so much simpler.

With all of these methods and techniques in place, it can become much easier to understand things better and make dormitory living much more comfortable at such a time.

Link to Video:

https://www.youtube.com/watch?v=jAtmVrkAXXc

Chapter Eleven: Understanding Hormonal Changes: Navigating PMS and PMDD

There are many different hormonal changes that come with menstruation. In this chapter, we delve into the details of understanding those first. We also aim to understand the hormonal fluctuations that lead to different symptoms, and how you can identify them, and seek support.

Understanding Premenstrual Syndrome (PMS)

Many girls and women experience a range of physical, emotional, and behavioral symptoms in the days or weeks preceding their menstrual period, which is known as premenstrual syndrome (PMS). Usually, these symptoms follow a recurrent pattern, beginning in the luteal phase of the menstrual cycle and ending soon after menstruation begins. PMS is commonly associated with a broad spectrum of discomforts that impact multiple facets of an individual's quality of life.

Hormonal fluctuations mainly involve changes in the levels of estrogen and progesterone levels, which are mainly involved in triggering PMS symptoms. These hormones naturally rise during the luteal phase, which happens after ovulation and before menstruation, and then fall. It is thought that the interaction of these hormonal changes affects neurotransmitters, which in turn causes the emotional and physical symptoms of PMS to appear.

There are a few symptoms that you must understand to know that you are going through the premenstrual phase, which can bring about massive changes in your body. Physical symptoms include breast tenderness, headaches, and changes in appetite. Emotional symptoms can include massive mood swings, anxiety, irritability, and also changes in sleep patterns. When you understand these symptoms well, you can understand how they impact your life and then take steps to tackle the discomfort. It is also important to note that different people experience these symptoms in different ways. While some might have them very severe, some face only mild symptoms, which means that this differs from person to person, depending on different underlying health conditions and your own varying degree or how much you can bear.

Understanding Premenstrual Dysphoric Disorder (PMDD)

This is a severe form of syndrome accompanied by your period, characterized by intense emotional and psychological symptoms. It is important for you to understand the difference between PMS and PMDD so that you can take the right steps to deal with it. In PMDD, you can face a lot of emotional disturbances. You must understand what these are and how they affect your mood. This can also hamper your daily functioning, meaning you need to understand accurately what this is to take the right steps to handle it.

In PMDD, there are very intense mood swings. Not only that, but you also have feelings of hopelessness. You get irritated very easily, and you may also experience depressive symptoms. This can majorly impact overall well-being. This condition needs to be diagnosed in the right way so that you can take the right steps and follow treatment strategies to deal with it in the best way. Examining the frequency of PMDD is essential to comprehending its importance within the larger framework of menstrual health. Recognizing how PMDD affects day-to-day functioning also draws attention to the difficulties people encounter in a variety of spheres, such as relationships, employment, and personal wellbeing.

Healthcare professionals use different criteria so that they can differentiate this from other menstrual-related conditions. The Diagnostic and Statistical Manual of Mental Disorders (DSM-5) outlines these criteria, requiring the presence of specific emotional and behavioral symptoms during the luteal phase. It is very important for you to get a comprehensive assessment from a healthcare provider so that you understand what this is and whether or not you have such symptoms.

Keeping track of symptoms is essential to correctly diagnosing and evaluating PMDD. Because PMDD symptoms are cyclical, meaning they appear during the luteal phase and go away with the onset of menstruation, it is important to closely monitor the condition over the course of several menstrual cycles. By tracking symptoms, medical professionals can identify patterns that lead to more accurate diagnoses and easier creation of customized treatment regimens. Differentiating between PMDD and PMS is integral for providing people with the support and care that they need. Since PMDD is much more complex, it is imperative to be much more informed about what this is and how you can navigate through the challenges that it poses.

Coping Strategies

Now that you understand what all this encompasses, it is also very important to have ample understanding of different coping strategies to help you get through this in the best way.

Lifestyle Modifications

Several times in this book, the importance of lifestyle modifications has been highlighted. If you want to alleviate the symptoms associated with PMS and PMDD, then you have to gain a comprehensive understanding of what each of these is and how these can contribute to a more nuanced, harmonious menstrual cycle.

- Regular Exercise

Getting your body moving is one of the most important things that there is. You have to indulge yourself in one or the other form of exercise. This can be anything that you like as long as it keeps you moving. The release of endorphins will help you feel much better. It also promotes overall wellbeing. Once you cater to individual preferences, you can work your way through things and can also incorporate some form of physical activity in your life.

- Balanced Nutrition

It is also important for you to have a balanced diet so that you get everything that you need in terms of having the right dietary choices. Follow nutritional guidelines and make sure that you also have dietary supplements so that your body gets what it requires to function correctly and make the best choices exactly in accordance with the requirements.

- Stress Management Techniques

Effective stress management is one of the most important things that you need. You need to incorporate mindfulness, meditation, and relaxation in your routine in one way or the other to help you keep up. You need to find out what works for you and helps you stay calm. Remember that when you manage stress, it helps you build resilience and helps you keep at ease, too.

Seeking Professional Help

You need to seek the help that you need. A lot of the time, we self-medicate and do not understand why it is important to seek professional help and find a way to navigate through the different challenges in the right way. Getting consultations from professionals like gynecologists or mental health practitioners can help you understand your situation much better. Not only that, but it can also help you come up with the right strategies that suit you and your condition.

Counseling can also help you navigate your way through the challenges that this brings. Counseling alternatives are investigated as useful instruments for treating the psychological and emotional components of PMS and PMDD, such as cognitive-behavioral therapy (CBT) or psychotherapy. A discussion of medication options is also included, with an emphasis on their potential advantages and disadvantages. These options range from hormone treatments to mood stabilizers.

Building a Support Network

To have a support network around you is very important. Communication plays a very important role in helping you navigate through the challenges in the best way possible. When there is honest and open communication, you feel encouraged to talk about your needs and how you feel. This can foster a very supportive environment, which is, again, very effective in helping you cope. Try to have genuine people around you to whom you can openly talk and discuss your feelings. When you have such people around you, you can cope well even in the worst situations. You feel much more empowered, knowing you can openly talk about how you feel without being judged for anything you say.

Tracking and Managing Symptoms

Many times, people struggle when trying to identify different symptoms that they are facing, which, in fact, helps them find out so much about what they are going through. It is very important to understand that well to be able to navigate through your situation and find the best way out for yourself.

There are many different tracking tools and mobile apps that can help you monitor your symptoms after you fully understand what is required of you. That way, you can also have informed discussions with your healthcare provider, who can help you navigate through the process in the best way possible. By being more self-aware, you can definitely monitor your menstrual cycle better and gain valuable insights into the cyclical nature that those have. With a more informed and engaged approach toward doing things, you can monitor your menstrual health in a much better way. Heightened awareness is always a great starting point to helping you understand so much more about your menstrual health.

It is important to explore different coping strategies and then have an individualized coping plan to help you understand your needs and preferences. You need to find a customized coping plan that works for you in your favor.

This can empower you to navigate the different challenges first and then find your way through different situations.

Here are a few links to articles and blogs that have been very helpful for us when we were researching this topic. You might want to take a look at these as well to learn in depth about this topic to enhance your overall well-being.

https://www.health.qld.gov.au/newsroom/features/breaking-the-cycle-a-guide-to-understanding-and-managing-premenstrual-dysphoric-disorder-pmdd#:~:text=Researchers%20think%20PMDD%20may%20be,this%20contributes%20to%20PMDD%20symptoms.

https://www.ncbi.nlm.nih.gov/books/NBK279045/

https://www.betterhealth.vic.gov.au/health/conditionsandtreatments/premenstrual-syndrome-pms

https://www.helpguide.org/articles/depression/premenstrual-dysphoric-disorder-pmdd.htm

https://www.mayoclinic.org/diseases-conditions/premenstrual-syndrome/expert-answers/pmdd/faq-20058315

Chapter Twelve: How Educating Girls Can Prevent Childbirth Complications

In many societies today, the topic of menstruation is still taboo, which means that a lot of young girls do not know what they ideally should know about their bodies and their reproductive health. This lack of knowledge can have dire consequences, making it more important to break the silence around this topic. Especially when we talk about childbirth complications, it is important to understand how this has a very deep link to menstruation and why this needs to be understood well first. We have also created a very informative video on this topic. The link is at the very end of the chapter. Please do watch to learn more about this.

The first and most important step is to encourage open dialogue surrounding menstruation. It is important for menstruation not to be looked at as something that must not be discussed in public or rather as a hush-hush topic. People must be comfortable talking about it publicly and be open to dealing with the stigma around it. When there is a safe space for girls to learn about their bodies without any shame or secrecy, it creates the right atmosphere to allow things to happen smoothly. Furthermore, understanding the cultural nuances is also one of the most important things to help tailor educational approaches, further allowing for greater awareness.

Link Between Menstruation Education and Childbirth Complications

There is a strong connection between menstruation education and maternal health outcomes, making it all the more important to educate young girls about this, starting early. Research shows that women who are educated have improved reproductive health. A plausible reason for this is that they can use important tips and take better safety measures, which in turn ends up helping them greatly in the long run. Not only that, but it also leads to safe pregnancies.

Educating young girls about childbirth complications acts as a protective factor, reducing the risk of maternal mortality. Informed mothers are better equipped to navigate the challenges that come with pregnancy and childbirth. Furthermore, educated mothers are more likely to seek prenatal care at the right time because they understand how crucial it is for the detection and management of potential complications.

Additionally, educated girls also get greater access to healthcare resources, which has a ripple effect on maternal and child health. So, the overall effect of mitigating childbirth complications is definitely a lot more positive. Educated girls are much more likely to attend antenatal and postnatal care appointments, fostering a continuum of care that positively impacts maternal and child wellbeing. They understand why taking care of themselves affects their overall well-being and also the well-being of their child. Access to skilled healthcare professionals at the time when they are most needed also reduces the chances of massive complications. With educational empowerment, women have better access to services and facilities, which is crucial in helping them get what they want.

Another important factor that helps prevent childbirth complications is menstrual hygiene practices. So, overall, the impact of menstrual hygiene practices on menstrual health is massive. It extends beyond just menstruation and affects the overall health of females. Menstrual hygiene practices are very crucial to prevent infections, which can be a leading cause of complications in childbirth. Practicing hygiene properly is one of the most important things here. This chapter will further delve into the details of menstrual hygiene, offering practical tips on how that can help.

Furthermore, educating girls about reproductive health is also very important in helping them prevent childbirth complications. This means that they should know about informed family planning. A nuanced understanding of reproductive health enables girls to actively participate in family planning decisions. This is closely related to them first understanding their own body and then being able to talk about how many kids they want. Breaking down cultural barriers is also very important for healthier discussions around reproductive health. This allowed girls to make informed choices about their own reproductive well-being.

Menstrual Hygiene Tips

Here are a few menstrual hygiene tips in relation to avoiding childbirth complications.

- Use of Sanity Products

Using sanitary products like pads, tampons, or menstrual cups is beneficial. These help you stay clean, prevent infections, and reduce the risk of complications.

- Regular Changing

It is important that you change your sanitary products every few hours, depending on how your flow is. This is essential to prevent the accumulation of bacteria and also minimize the chances of other infections. It also helps you stay much cleaner and makes you feel better.

- Proper Disposal

Dispose of used sanitary products in a hygienic and environmentally friendly manner. This helps prevent the spread of infections, which is very important for reproductive health.

- Hand Hygiene

You must wash your hands thoroughly before and after handling your sanitary products. This is important to promote overall vaginal health. You are not even aware of the germs that might be on your hands, so always ensure that you wash well.

- Avoid Scents

As much as you want to use scents, try and avoid them. These products can disrupt the natural balance of our vagina. Understand how this is something very normal you are going through, which is why you must treat it that way, too.

- Cloth Pad Care

A lot of people cannot use sanitary products and have to use cloths due to underlying skin conditions. In this case, it is important that you wash those clothes properly first before you reuse them.

- Stay Hydrated

As cliched as it sounds, try to drink as much water as you can. Staying hydrated helps you maintain your overall health and contributes to a smoother menstrual cycle.

- Regular Check-Ups

Remember that your menstrual health is more important than anything else. So, you have to ensure that you get regular check-ups done by your gynecologist. This can help you with your overall reproductive health.

Empowering Through Education

This brings us to the focal point of this chapter, which is educating girls to be empowered enough to make their own decisions in line with their reproductive health.

Educational Initiatives

With educational initiatives in place, it becomes possible to equip young girls with the knowledge they need to improve their lives. This can best be done by way of school-based programs, where girls can learn so much about their menstrual health and how this is related to their reproductive health, too. Since the school is where students spend a lot of their day, it is a great way to foster practical tips and allow young girls to interact with professionals and other girls their age to try and understand more about this. Community engagement is also a great way to foster a very supportive environment for girls. This helps break down societal barriers and ensures everyone is on the same page. When girls see others they can relate to, they understand things much better, which is important to help them form that sense of where they are headed. Breaking down societal barriers starts at this phase, which is again very important to foster that sense of what exactly is needed.

Tackling Stigmas

Next, it is imperative to tackle the stigma around menstruation so that girls can be empowered to embrace their bodies in just the way that they deem fit. With collective efforts from all ends, allowing people to learn more about menstruation and have an open dialogue is very much possible. With the stigma around it being much lesser, it becomes easier to educate girls and allow them to share their experiences in a better way. It is not just the girls who need to be made an active part of the process, but boys and men. Engaging boys and men in the education process promotes understanding and empathy and breaks down gender-based barriers.

A Healthier Future Through Education

Girls can become much better equipped to become mothers when they are educated. With their knowledge, the overall impact on the long-term health of women can be massive. Education impacts not just the generation as it stands but also communities and generations to come. It can shape a healthier tomorrow and foster a sense of empowerment in women. Looking ahead to this healthier future, we see that the seeds planted by education now will bear fruit in a future where ignorance about menstruation will no longer jeopardize the health of mothers. Education leaves a legacy that spans generations and provides long-term advantages beyond short-term improvements in health. With collaborative efforts from policymakers, educators, and women themselves, it is very much possible to work toward creating an open dialogue and ensuring that women understand the need to create a safe space for themselves, which can only be done when they educate themselves and allow themselves to know more about their bodies.

Link to Video:

https://www.youtube.com/watch?v=lc919DapD5s

Chapter Thirteen: What You Can Do As a Girl to Empower Other Girls and Women

Having so much discussion around breaking the stigma and allowing for healthier discussions is only fruitful when we have a call to action at the end. It is only helpful when you know how you can play your part. This chapter serves as both a culmination and a catalyst, inviting every girl and woman to become agents of change, breaking the chains of menstrual stigma, and fostering a culture of empowerment.

Here are a few things you can and should be doing as a woman to improve the situation.

- **Shatter the Silence: Your Voice Matters**

Remember that every woman's job is to help bring about positive change. You can only do that when you break the silence and speak up. Your voice as a woman matters. Try and encourage as much open dialogue as you can about menstruation. This is the only way this topic can be looked upon as a normal bodily function, as opposed to being frowned upon as a hush-hush one. As normal as it is, we need to understand that talking about it will help create a safe space for women, allowing each one of us to contribute to help building a strong community of women where we all stand by each other. Change starts with acknowledgment. So, the first step is to understand the need for change and recognize a problem. Share your experiences, engage in open conversations, and encourage others to do the same. By shattering the silence, you pave the way for a more inclusive and understanding society.

- **Educate Yourself**

A lot of the time, we think we know a lot about our own bodies, but the truth is that we are sometimes lacking knowledge. It is important to get the right information by reading and interacting with people who are knowledgeable in this regard. Our entire life is a learning process. It is a process that allows us to understand things and be well-informed. That way, you empower yourself and contribute to dismantling myths. You also get to foster a more informed community that way. Khloe Kardashian talked about the importance of educating yourself about your own body as a woman. She said, "I just think that knowing about your body at any age, whether it's educating yourself on fertility, getting mammograms, going through puberty - whatever it may be, is really important. I just really encourage women empowerment and being comfortable talking about these issues."

- **Be Supportive**

As a woman, you always need to support other women. That way, you create a strong community of like-minded individuals who are there to help each other. Be a sister who encourages other women and girls. Establish a network of solidarity where people can freely ask questions, share experiences without fear of judgment, and receive support from one another. You support a worldwide movement of empowerment and understanding by cultivating a sisterhood that crosses national boundaries and cultural boundaries.

- **Challenge Stereotypes**

As a girl, you have all the power to challenge stereotypes that are associated with menstruation. The best way to do this is to break free from any outdated notions that link feminity to shame. Understand that this is a normal body process. To challenge stereotypes and bring about a change, you need to start somewhere. For that, you must take pride in yourself as a woman and your body. Your menstrual cycle is something that you should be able to talk about easily without feeling any shame of any kind. That way, you pave the way for a more inclusive and accepting world. The world will only become more inclusive when you no longer let things remain within you and when you talk about them openly with others. There is nothing about your body that is shameful.

- **Advocate for Comprehensive Menstrual Education**

Empowerment goes way beyond personal actions. It is not just about what you do but about how you try to bring change at large for society. This means you should advocate for menstrual education in schools and communities. Raise your voice to ensure that every girl, regardless of their geographical location or background, has access to the right information about her body. This way, you can become a catalyst for change. Menstruation is not a source of shame but something that needs to be discussed in the open. It is a topic that women need to be formally educated about to take charge of their own bodies and navigate through the challenging parts of it. Remember that change starts with education. When women understand more about their bodies and understand how and why this is not something that they need to remain quiet about, things will change for the better.

- **Support Menstrual Hygiene**

Take concrete steps to support menstrual hygiene initiatives in addition to verbal support. Offer assistance to groups and projects aimed at giving those in need access to menstrual hygiene products. Promote laws that guarantee these products' accessibility. You can take an active role in removing obstacles that impede menstrual hygiene and health by endorsing initiatives. For example, if you know of some locations where women do not have access to menstrual products, the best way forward is to try to make products accessible for women. Maybe you could join hands with a few others or some organizations that work toward helping women create ease and a safe space for women, who can then work toward creating a more inclusive and safe society for women.

- **Create Educational Initiatives**

Educational initiatives are very important. While you can expect and hope for policymakers to do something better for you in that regard, it is also important that you try and do something yourself. This means that you could try and work toward organizing workshops, seminars, and online campaigns to impart accurate information and address common misconceptions around the topic. When women have the knowledge that they need, things will change for the better. They will be able to take steps to improve the situation for themselves. When every woman plays a part, it will lead to an entire cycle of change that will then make things a lot better.

- **Artistic Expression**

Use creative forms like poetry, art, or storytelling to convey the grace and commonality of the menstrual cycle. Art has a strong ability to challenge social norms and cross cultural boundaries. Depending on how creative you are and the different ways in which you use art, you can bring about a positive change for all times to come. An ideal example of this is Rupi Kaur's photograph on Instagram. She posted a blood-stained photo of herself lying on the bed as a social experiment in an attempt to have more discussion around it. That really did make rounds on the internet and got a lot of people's attention, which is exactly what was needed to stir up conversation. So you could think of all you can do using art to bring about a positive change in the world.

- **Mentorship Programs**

Mentorship programs are also a great idea where older women can mentor the younger ones and create a very supportive environment so that they can discuss menstrual experiences. This can prove to be very beneficial for the younger lot, specifically, and can also help instill a sense of community. With a supportive environment, things can become a whole lot easier.

- **Support Local Businesses**

Promoting local businesses that provide sustainable and affordable menstrual hygiene products is very important. Not only does this help the local economy, but it also helps break the stigma around menstruation. With menstrual products easily available to most people, women can become very comfortable at this time of the month.

- **Involve Men and Boys**

Menstruation is a regular female bodily function, but to normalize conversations around it and to ensure that the stigma is broken, men and boys also have to be involved. This can help break gender barriers and promote a shared understanding of menstrual health. If men and boys also become comfortable with this topic being discussed, then normalizing it in society can become much easier.

- **Social Media Activism**

It is also important to use social media platforms in the best way possible so that everyone can share positive narratives about menstruation. Social media is a very effective platform to help spread the message far and wide and to reach a massive audience altogether. Create and participate in campaigns that challenge stereotypes, using hashtags to reach a wider audience and foster online communities. People should also be encouraged to share their stories with each other online, with the main aim being to understand how women can support each other. With positive discussions around menstruation, things can become a whole lot easier.

- **Lobby for Policy Change**

A policy change can only occur when enough people are working actively for that change. So, a lot of people should collectively be working for changes related to menstrual health. Women should team up and try to ensure that their voice is heard. This could include pushing for free or subsidized menstrual hygiene products in schools or workplace policies that support menstrual well-being. With lobbies being formed, it becomes easier to notice the change that comes about, leading to bigger and better things.

- **Wellness Workshops**

For women to be extra comfortable at this time is very important. This is why wellness workshops can be very important. Different self-care practices can be shared in these workshops so that women understand how they can work toward making themselves comfortable at this time. Other mindfulness exercises can also be shared for this. So this is how these workshops can be made very fruitful. Experienced women and healthcare practitioners can share their experiences, and that can make things a lot better.

- **Celebrate Menstrual Milestones**

Create rituals or ceremonies to celebrate menstrual milestones and change the narrative from shame to pride. Acknowledge a girl's first period as a healthy and normal step towards becoming a woman. This way, menstruation is considered something that must be celebrated. This is something that is very positive and can help create a very positive light around menstruation. Remember that you can create a good narrative around menstruation when you use these tips and try to change the narrative around this.

- **Intergenerational Dialogue**

Encourage intergenerational discussions regarding menstruation. Mothers, daughters, and grandmothers can all bridge understanding gaps and build a supportive family environment by sharing their experiences.

With all of these measures, you can definitely play your part in ensuring that this stigma is dealt with better and that you are on the right track with regard to bringing about the change that it is high time the world witnessed.

Chapter Fourteen: The Environmental Impact of Menstruation

As we comprehend other aspects of menstruation, it is also very important to shed light on the environmental aspect of menstruation and understand the implications of menstrual products on the environment. We are all responsible citizens of the world, and it is our binding duty to make sure that we act in accordance with the due standards, to make sure that we do our best, and also understand the different challenges that we face.

Sustainability of Menstrual Products

With the advent of technology, the way that we view menstrual products has now changed entirely. We can now make eco-friendly choices, but for that, the most important thing is to have the right information and work in the right direction to achieve what we want.

Conventional menstrual products like pads and tampons have a huge environmental cost attached to them. The production of these goods, from the energy-intensive manufacturing processes to the production of raw materials like cotton and wood pulp, adds considerably to resource depletion and carbon emissions. The extraction of these materials also requires a lot of intensive use of water and pesticides. Eventually, there are greenhouse emissions as well, which are very harmful to the environment. In terms of packaging, these come in plastic packaging, which means that there is a lot of additional waste also that has to be catered to. This again goes on to add to the carbon footprint.

So, due to the challenges that are posed by these conventional products, it only makes sense to explore more alternatives that are sustainable and environmentally friendly in all ways. These options make use of eco-friendly products, which also have a smaller impact on the environment as a whole.

- Sustainable Alternatives

Many people are unaware of what eco-friendly alternatives are available and how they have gained popularity over time. These lead to reduced waste, and the impact on the environment is also minimal.

- Reusable Menstrual Cups

This is a very long-term option and is made using medical-grade silicon. Naturally, the environmental impact of this is minimal. This also largely leads to reduced waste and overall cost-effectiveness.

- Cloth Pads

These are reusable clothes made from organic fabrics after taking washing and manufacturing into account. The problem many people find with these is that they are not as convenient in terms of usage as pads. This is why this is something that really needs to be taken into account.

- Organic Disposable Products

Disposable products that are made from organic materials are also a great alternative. They allow for a great balance between convenience and environmental impact.

While all of these are great solutions, it is also important to consider that all of these options are only available to the elite as of now. These options are not as widely applicable right now, so we need to shed light on appropriate waste management techniques. Most people in the world today make use of conventional products. This means that if we take this into account in a better way, we can definitely try and raise more awareness around it as well.

Menstrual Waste Load in India

Taking a look at some statistics will also allow for a greater and much clearer understanding of how things work here. Specifically in India, menstrual waste management is a huge concern that must be addressed correctly, considering the best waste collection mechanisms. There are around 12 billion pads every year that have to be disposed of in India. So, where are these many pads being disposed of? 28% are disposed of with routine waste, 28% are disposed of in the open, 33% are buried, and 28% are burnt in the open. These statistics are quite alarming, which again makes us want to understand more about this to understand the need for stringent policy measures in this regard.

Considering this huge amount, it is imperative to think about the different techniques that can and should be used for this, and it is also important to understand why we need to do this.

Before we delve further into the details, let's understand more about the definition and classification of menstrual waste in India. Menstrual waste is essentially classified as "Blood and used menstrual absorbents, including cloth, disposable sanitary napkins, tampons, and other substances or materials," according to a report on menstruation in India. The Solid Waste Rules (2016) classify this waste as 'solid waste' again, making it all the more important for it to be managed properly and safely. The most important thing is for this to be managed in a way that does not cause harm to the environment and people.

Policymakers have come up with many different approaches to deal with this. They have considered reducing waste volumes, sterilizing waste, and changing the physical nature of the waste. While we do understand the need to do this, it is also important to take into account the fact that there are technical aspects to this as well. For laymen, it is important to understand what they can do to minimize the environmental impact.

How to Dispose Off Sanitary Pads

Let us understand more about how we can dispose of sanitary pads in the best way possible. It is important that all women have some knowledge about this so that they can work toward this in the best way possible and do what is in their control to reduce the environmental impact as much as possible.

First things first – As a rule of thumb, sanitary pads should never be flushed down the toilet. While this is not widely practiced, it is still important to recognize how and why some people might choose to do this. While it does seem like a very convenient option, the impact that this can have on the environment is massive, and hence, this needs to be looked into in the best way possible. Pads or tampons should always be disposed of in the garbage bin. When you flush a sanitary pad down the toilet can clog the drainage system.

Used sanitary napkins are largely classified as medical waste, which means that they must be separated from other recyclables, and hence, the way that you dispose of these must also be very different. In earlier days, used menstrual pads were buried in outside landfills. But this is not the best way to dispose of these either. This way, these are exposed to microorganisms. Alongside that, these also have a high plastic content, which again means that they are non-biodegradable. They can stay there for many years, having a disastrous impact on the environment.

So then, how do you dispose of these in the right way? What can you do that can have the best impact on the environment? Let's understand.

- Have a Separate Bin

The first step is to have a separate bin for your used menstrual products. You must never dispose of these in your regular bin. Have a separate bin with a lid on top so the germs don't spread further. This is one of the first steps to responsible waste management when it comes to menstrual products.

- Disposable Lining

Also, try to have a disposable lining for your menstrual pads. This will ensure that the soiled pads are kept apart from the rest of the trash once you dispose of all trash. Maybe you could even label these bags so they don't get mixed with the other trash.

- Fold and Wrap

Always try folding and wrapping these before you dispose of them. This is important to keep stench, fleas, and bacteria away.

- Incineration

Another way to dispose off used pads is through incineration, where they can be burned to ashes and then those ashes can then be used as fertilizers, which makes them a lot less infectious to handle.

You can dispose of this trash on the last day of your period. We must understand the need to have a responsible approach toward the environment for us to be able to drive change in the best way possible. Jane Goodall, an English primatologist, talked about the importance of menstrual waste management. She says, "Addressing environmental challenges requires a comprehensive approach. Menstrual waste management is an important component of sustainable living."

We have created two videos pertaining to the challenges of waste disposal and management. You might find those very interesting. The links to those are at the end of the chapter.

Innovative Solutions

In the day and age that we live in, it is important for us to have some innovative solutions that allow us to take the best initiatives we can. This exploration aims to inspire a paradigm shift towards a more environmentally conscious approach to menstruation, from businesses supporting sustainable practices to merging technology and design in creating eco-friendly alternatives.

There are so many pioneering initiatives in sustainability that we see now. There are so many different initiatives we now have that prioritize renewable resources and reduce waste as much as possible. There are different innovative materials that many companies are now using. These include bamboo, organic cotton, and plant fibres.

Let's know more about the different innovative products that are on the market. While these definitely come at a higher price, it is important we understand what these products are to at least know more about the different alternatives that we have.

- Fluus

This is the first flushable pad to exist. Made of microplastic-free material, this product breaks down like toilet paper when flushed, which again means that this allows for waste management to happen in a much better way.

- Daye Tampons

These tampons are made from rayon. This material is non-biodegradable plastic, which again can be disposed of easily.

- Thinx

This product eliminates the need to have pads or tampons. This is underwear that absorbs your period easily, which also means that there is much less mess. You can easily wash this up after using it once. On their site, you can learn more about the sizes to see which would work best for you.

These are just a few of the options that you have available. You can explore further to see what options can work best for you. Understand how it is very important for you to work toward what you want and to understand the need to play a huge role in proper waste management of sanitary products.

Climate Change and Menstrual Sustainability

Climate change has a considerable impact on menstrual sustainability. Extreme weather changes mean that there are chances of drought and floods happening. This means that managing menstruation at such a time becomes even harder. There is very little access to water and sanitation facilities in areas distraught by environmental hazards. This means that women's health suffers, which is why it is important to have a greater awareness of this to be able to make decisions in accordance with this. We have repeatedly talked about making menstrual hygiene a priority and ensuring that women have what they need to make this time period as smooth as possible. This aligns with the agenda for that as well.

Barriers to Change

While the concept of the environmental impact of menstruation is very easy to understand in theory, there are some major hurdles that come in the way when we put this into practice. This is especially true for lower-income areas, where the accessibility of basic menstrual products is in question, let alone the access to reusable menstrual products. Very few people in low-income areas of the world truly have access to basic products like pads, so disposing of them in the right way is something that they don't even get to at this point. Educating them about the use of reusable menstrual products doesn't bear fruit as of yet because of the lack of availability of those products in some areas and also because of the financial considerations in this regard.

Say, when we talk about menstrual cups, these aren't easily available everywhere. Not only that, but they are not as affordable as other basic products. So, a huge segment of society does not even think in that direction as of yet. This has very important implications for policymakers, who should definitely consider how and why they can bring about a change when they take into account widespread accessibility. This relates deeply to the concept of period poverty that needs to be taken into account by policymakers to be agents for change.

Another important consideration is that reusable menstrual products don't have the same protocol for usage. To use those products, you first need access to proper water sources. That is the only way that you can use those in the way that you deem fit. The hygiene of these products also largely depends on how you can wash and dry them, which is a huge concern for the environment. This relates to the concern of awareness. So it is only when there is great awareness about this that things become much easier and doable.

Empowering Through Eco-Conscious Menstruation

While there is a widely recognized need in this day and age to reduce the taboo associated with menstruation, the environmental aspect of menstruation largely goes unnoticed. You don't see a lot of people paying as much attention to this aspect as they should. Eco-conscious menstruation initiatives can be a game-changer. Only when people have the right education and awareness about this can they make the best decisions and make more responsible choices. People need to first understand how the wrong disposal methods can affect the environment in deeply damaging ways. With this being understood well, things can be handled correctly and in a much more conscious way.

- The Role of Education and Awareness

The key to changing perceptions of menstruation from a purely biological process to a holistic and environmentally conscious experience is education. People can make more informed decisions by learning about the effects menstruation products have on the environment. There should be more educational programs that focus solely on this aspect of menstruation. Educating people about the value of destigmatizing sustainable menstrual products so they can make decisions based on their values rather than social conventions. It is the responsibility of every individual to make sure that they take steps in the right direction to achieve good things. Ban Ki-moon, the former secretary of the United Nations, talked about the importance of being responsible citizens of the world. He says, "Our planet's alarm is going off, and it is time to wake up and take action! Climate change, deforestation, pollution—these challenges do not recognize borders, and they affect all of us. The environment is not a separate entity; it is our home, and its well-being is directly linked to ours. We must be responsible stewards, understanding that our choices today shape the world we pass on to future generations. Caring for the environment is not just a matter of ethics but a fundamental commitment to the survival and prosperity of all life on Earth."

- Informed Decision Making

People should be able to make informed choices, which can only happen when they have comprehensive information about their various options. There should be transparency in product labelling. This is important so that there is greater consumer awareness at all times, and that helps with driving demand for sustainable alternatives. There should also be sources that are readily available for people so that they can get as much information as they need. That way, they can consider different factors like materials and production processes. Apart from that, the economic aspect of informed decision-making also has to be taken into account.

- Community Initiatives

With community-driven initiatives, especially in the regions where there isn't as much awareness, things can become a whole lot easier. With workshops and awareness campaigns allowing people to learn more about the right disposal practices and what they should use, the situation can improve. People can also become so much more informed that making sound decisions can seem a whole lot easier for them as well. Highlighting the significance of community voices in promoting legislation that encourages the use of environmentally friendly menstrual products, waste management facilities, and more general programmes that support environmental responsibility.

Empowering individuals to understand more about the right waste management techniques is something that aligns with the agenda of removing the stigma around menstruation. With people doing what they should be ideally and being more responsible with the way that they choose to do things, the environment can benefit in the long run.

Links to Videos:

https://www.youtube.com/watch?v=wY5YvtH3vu0

https://www.youtube.com/watch?v=P0lnplg4VWI

Chapter Fifteen: Effects of Menstrual Health on Self-Confidence

Menstrual health is a very important part of a woman's overall well-being. It transcends over and above just the physical aspect. A woman's body changes when she gets her period for the first time, and for her to navigate through the emotional challenges that this brings with it is integral to her overall well-being as a person. In this chapter, the idea is to see the effect that menstrual health has on the overall self-confidence of young girls and women. This is especially true for the ones who have not yet been exposed to a lot of information about menstrual health and are still struggling to navigate through this phase in the best possible way. To ensure quality of life, it is important for a woman to have her sense of self-worth in the right direction, and that can only happen when she is equipped with all the knowledge that she needs to get to a certain standpoint in life.

Understanding the Menstrual Journey

A profound understanding of the menstrual journey is key to helping navigate the challenges this brings as well. The menstrual journey usually begins during adolescence. Characterized by periods of intense physical and emotional development, there is a lot that a girl or woman goes through at this point in time in her life. With a lot of hormonal challenges in the body, the transformation of self-perception and body image is heavy, which is why women need to understand fully what this is all about so that it does not affect their overall emotional well-being negatively either.

The adolescent years of a girl's life are marked by the surge of estrogen and progesterone. These hormones orchestrate the menstrual cycle. Not only do these have merely a physiological role to play, but they also impact emotional well-being and can lead to mood swings. Some women also experience changes in their energy levels, and all of this together can end up impacting their self-esteem in many ways. Exploring how these factors influence a person's self-perception is very important. Especially when we talk about the formative years, in most developing countries, women are not equipped with the knowledge that they need to allow them to work on their self-confidence successfully, which might be affected by the changes happening to their bodies.

The physical changes associated with menstrual health include changes in the body, like breast development and the onset of menstruation itself. This can evoke a range of emotions, depending on the personality of the person and how they think they are being affected. It is imperative to delve into the psychological aspect of this to understand the personal beliefs involved and how they intersect with cultural influences to shape a person's perception of their own body.

Societal norms also play a huge role in shaping the perceptions of beauty and body ideals. Teenagers are exposed to a multitude of images and messages when they start their menstrual journey, which may alter their perception of what is deemed desirable or acceptable. They do not fully understand how their body image, as seen by others, does not define them and that the beauty ideals that are set by society are insignificant in many ways. They tend to take a lot of things at heart, which can negatively affect their image and the way that they view themselves.

It is important to instil values in people pertaining to body positivity and self-love. Understanding the value of fostering a positive self-image, the idea is to understand the functions of education, support networks, and self-care routines in fostering a healthy relationship with one's body. Teenagers can build a sense of confidence in their changing identities and become resilient against harmful societal narratives by navigating the terrain of body positivity. Most people do not understand that the effects of self-perception and body image can be rather long-term and that these have to be understood in the best way to bring about positive changes. As women start their life journeys, it is imperative for them to understand what contributes to their holistic well-being and how they can take care of their bodies in the right way.

Menstrual Education and Empowerment

As discussed earlier in this book, it is important for society to understand the dire need to equip women with the knowledge they need to allow them to embark on their journeys successfully without compromising their self-confidence and mental health. With so much shame and secrecy around the topic of menstruation in today's day and age, there is a lot that has to be understood well first. When women have a sense of control and understanding, things can be catered to in the right way, and the direction in which women choose to take their lives can also change tremendously.

When there is a huge knowledge gap due to societal stigma and society not being able to work a certain way, it can lead to feelings of shame relating to one's own body, which is never healthy. Perpetuation of harmful myths and stereotypes can lead to huge problems. Societal attitudes have to be navigated, but the first step is to bring about a change within, which can only come from education, which is, in turn, empowering.

Education undoubtedly has a transformative potential in our lives. When we truly understand things about our bodies, our lives can change for the better, allowing us to dismantle the barriers of shame. With a clear understanding of things, people can claim more control over their bodies, which eventually also helps build confidence. But all of this is true; it is integral to understand that this comes with policy changes as a whole. Policy change happens over a period of time.

Comprehensive education can transform the way that people look at things. It becomes a very powerful tool that dismantles the massive barriers that exist and can also help provide a very clear understanding of the changes that happen in the body.

Implementing Educational Initiatives

Educational initiatives are a great way to ensure that people are equipped with the knowledge they need and develop very positive attitudes toward communities. This can only happen when there are open and inclusive conversations.

In both formal and informal curricula, menstruation and the changes that it brings to the human body should be discussed. When women understand what their bodies are, how they change, and how menstruation is a very normal part of the human body, their lives become much more simplified. When they are mentally prepared for all the changes their body goes through, their self-esteem does not get affected in damaging ways. But when they do not have the knowledge that they need, then it is an entirely different ball game. Educational institutions should work toward ensuring that there are open conversations about menstruation, which not only helps break the stigma related to it but also caters to a deeper and more profound understanding of the human body.

Addressing gender disparities in this context is also key here. Both boys and girls should develop a robust understanding of menstrual education. When they have a comprehensive understanding of what they should do, then it definitely allows for breaking stereotypes and ensures that communities become healthier and much more supportive. This is how menstruation can be recognized as a natural and shared experience that does not have to be looked upon as something shameful.

Emotional Well-Being and Confidence

Navigating through the emotional challenges that menstruation brings with it is also very important. For this, girls and women need to be equipped with the right knowledge that they need. From severe cramps to mood swings, women need to be prepared for it all. With the right ways to manage symptoms, things can be handled well. If women have the right know-how of self-care practices, it all becomes much easier for them, in turn also enhancing self-confidence to a massively high level.

Some young girls and women struggle when trying to understand the massive mood changes that they face during this time. Dealing with these mood swings becomes even harder when they do not have the knowhow about their own bodies. It is important to have some self-care practices so that things can be handled in the best way. These self-care practices include adopting different lifestyle choices so that those can help navigate the challenges that are associated with menstruation. These practices include dietary choices, exercise, nutrition, and so on. Empowering through knowledge is one of the best things there is. With informed decision-making, stress can be managed better. Encouraging women to take an active role in their overall well-being automatically helps lift their self-confidence.

Tips to Build Confidence

Here are a few tips that can help build confidence when menstruating. These tips are particularly very helpful for young girls struggling through that phase and not knowing how to work their way through the different challenges that it poses.

- Quit the Guessing Game

The first and most important step is to let go of the guessing game. You need to understand your body well. You need to know how long your cycle is, what your dates are, and so on. In the day and age that we live in, things have become very simple. This means that you can make use of period tracking apps as well to help you through this. Make a note of when you get your period, know when the flow of your period is the heaviest, know how long your period lasts, and so on. When you know a lot about your body, it helps you get through even the toughest of phases in the right way.

- Talk About It

If there is anything that is bothering you, it is essential that you talk about it. To know more about your body and how it functions entails more than just doing the guesswork. Talk to others about it. This can be anyone you trust. The best way to go about it is to also talk to professionals who can guide you in the best way and can help you understand your own body very well. If you shy away from this, then you will not be contributing to building a positive change. You have to work toward this in the right way for change to happen and for you to feel better in your own skin.

- Listen to Your Body

It is also crucial to listen to your body at this stage. If you feel tired, then that means that your body needs ample rest. Let your body get the rest that it needs. Sleep as much as you feel the need to. If you think you are experiencing some form of pain, try to use hot packs/cold packs. You can even use painkillers to help if you think that will allow you to calm down. Try to see what works for your body and then follow suit with that if you want to feel calmer and much better in your own skin. To feel better about yourself, you have to treat your body right.

- Hygiene

One of the most crucial aspects is to take care of your hygiene. As much as we sometimes ignore it, it is one of the most important things. This means you must change your period care items regularly. It can help you feel better inside and greatly helps with foul smells. How often you should change your period care items depends entirely on your flow. Also, you must shower regularly using any body wash tha you like. If you feel healthy and clean on the inside, it will surely show up in your confidence levels as well.

- Wear Comfortable Clothes

Wear clothing that makes you feel comfortable. This doesn't mean you have to spend your entire week in your pajamas. It just means that you must wear whatever makes you feel better on the inside and makes you feel confident, too. If you feel bloated, then period pants can help you. Trustpilot reviewed period pants and was all praises for how well they work: "Amazing period pants, have not and will not ever go back to using tampons or pads. I have less pain and more comfort using period pants, as well as the obvious positives for the environment! I never had a leak, and I am more confident sleeping at night than when I used pads. They wash and dry amazingly, and I just wish I had had these years ago! I have recommended friends to use these for how brilliant they are!"

- Relieve Pain

When you are in pain, it shows up on your confidence levels. So, opt for any pain relief method that works best for you. You're not going to be rewarded for bearing all that pain. If you have to, take any painkiller that you want, and you will feel better instantly. You can even try heat therapy to see if it works for you. Prioritize yourself and your body first.

- Exercise

Engaging in some form of exercise helps you instantly elevate your mood and boost your energy levels. The hardest part of exercise when on your period is to get started. You will likely feel lazy, which is also why many people back out. So, choose what you think will work best for you. This can be anything you think will help you feel more energetic. Start with twenty minutes a day, just to help you feel better on the inside. It is all about staying as active as you can.

- Get Enough Sleep

You have to try and aim for at least eight hours a day. No matter how tough your schedule is or what you have planned for the day. You have to try and aim for that time period if you want to feel energetic and if you want to have it in you to be able to do bigger and better things.

With these tips, you will feel so much better, knowing that you have it in you to work hard to remain confident.

In line with this, we have tried to do our two cents and formed an organization named Utpat Foundation. As part of this initiative, we provide sanitary pads to underserved segments in several poor inner-city areas of Mumbai. We have partnered up with several nonprofit organizations for this initiative to ensure that we can help mitigate school absences and help underprivileged girls work on their self-confidence and build themselves up. We hope to do our part in this regard.

To know more about this, please visit our website:
https://utpatfoundation.org/

Chapter Sixteen: Menstrual Health in Educational Institutes and the Workplace

As we near the end of the book, it is important to shed light on how we can work toward having a forward-looking approach. When you are well equipped with all the knowledge that you need to take things forward, you already feel so much more comfortable handling the challenges that come your way.

Menstrual health in higher education institutes and workplaces must be given more importance. The idea is to create a more inclusive environment for females all over so that they can feel included. It is important for cultures worldwide to become more sensitive to this to understand things better and work toward their goals in a much better and much more sorted way.

Menstrual health affects not only one's personal well-being but also one's ability to function in the workplace, classroom, and general quality of life. Menstruation can impact students' participation in class activities, attendance, and level of concentration in educational institutions. Similarly, menstruation may cause employees to miss work, be less productive, and experience discomfort at work. By addressing menstrual health in these settings, we can establish environments that promote inclusivity, support, and respect for people going through their menstrual cycle.

Challenges Women Face in Educational Settings

In educational settings, menstruating women, even in the current day and age, face massive challenges. Let's understand more about what these challenges are.

- Absenteeism

Absenteeism is one of the biggest challenges that women face in educational settings. Due to severe cramping, fatigue, and headaches, some students miss school altogether when on their period. The effects this has on educational performance are largely negative. They miss out on so much that is taught during that time. Not only that, but they fall behind the rest in the classroom. Why is this a challenge? This is because there aren't policies that support women at this time of the month. There is a long way to go before we actually realize what a huge issue this is and how this can be overcome by having the right policy measures in place to do so.

- Stigma

Menstruation-related stigma is another major issue that people in educational settings must deal with. Menstruating students may experience feelings of discomfort and loneliness as a result of cultural taboos and societal conventions that frequently add to the shame and embarrassment associated with the menstrual cycle. Menstruation can be extremely emotionally taxing, and this is made worse by stigmatizing attitudes that can appear as bullying, teasing, or exclusion from social events. Especially when we talk about the opposite gender in classrooms in developing countries, girls are told very often to never discuss anything about their period with the boys around them or to always ensure that there are no stains on them to avoid fear and embarrassment. No one realizes and talks about how this is a very normal bodily function that all women in the world have and that there is nothing to be ashamed of. Change can only come when men are also made to be a part of it, and when talking about it becomes normalized in most societies.

- Lack of Access to Menstrual Hygiene Products

This is also a critical barrier that most women face in educational settings. This is especially true for those who come from low-income backgrounds. They are struggling to get access to menstrual products. But in educational settings, this becomes an even bigger problem. Say if a girl at school gets her period, what are the chances that she will find a pad or a tampon readily available on the premises? Either she has to go home or borrow products from someone else who might have them. This lack of access to products also makes things so much harder for women.

So what is it that educational institutes can do to make the situation better on the whole?

- Schools can implement menstrual health and hygiene policies in a number of ways, such as by

offering free menstrual hygiene products in school restrooms or by setting rules for menstrual leave and accommodations.
- Comprehensive health education programs can be put into place to teach students about menstruation, debunk myths and misconceptions, and encourage positive attitudes toward menstrual health.
- Policymakers at educational institutes should ensure that they create a very supportive environment where menstruating students can feel very comfortable at all times and can discuss their menstrual needs with others to try and get the support that they need at this time.
- Collaborating with community organizations is also a great idea to make it easier for menstruating women to have greater access to menstrual hygiene products.

School environments can be made inclusive and conducive to all students' academic and emotional wellbeing by addressing the issues that menstruating individuals face in the classroom. Phumzile Mlambo Ngcuka, the executive director of UN Women, talked about supporting women at this time. She said, "Supporting menstruating individuals isn't just a matter of hygiene; it's a matter of human rights. We must challenge the taboos and inequalities that surround menstruation and work towards building a world where every woman and girl can manage her periods with dignity and respect."

The Impact of Menstruation on Academic Performance and Educational Outcomes

The impact of menstruation is largely seen on academic performance and different educational settings worldwide. The challenges that come with menstruation mean that women cannot engage fully in indifferent activities that affect their academic success. Understanding what these impacts are is very important to create an environment where students have the right opportunities, exactly what they need.

- Attendance and Participation

We have already discussed how absenteeism can be a huge issue. Let's now also shed light on how girls might not be able to participate in other activities like running around, or any sport for that matter. This can result in gaps in learning and many missed opportunities for collaboration.

- Concentration and Focus

Students' capacity to concentrate and pay attention to academic assignments can be impacted by menstrual symptoms such as headaches, exhaustion, mood swings, and cramps. These symptoms could make it difficult to process information, remember what you've learned, and remain attentive during lectures. Menstruating people may thus encounter difficulties keeping up with their schoolwork, poorer performance on tests, and academic setbacks.

- Emotional Wellbeing

When women don't feel that great emotionally, it tends to have a massive effect on their behavior and performance. This is especially true for the ones who have severe premenstrual symptoms or menstrual disorders such as premenstrual dysphoric disorder (PMDD). They can also experience massive mood changes, which is again linked to their motivation to succeed academically. With a more supportive environment, on the whole, things can definitely become a whole lot easier.

- Time Management and Productivity

When menstruating, women might not be as productive as they might otherwise be. This means that they might not be able to complete given tasks in due time, which can affect their daily routines and academic responsibilities. With self-care and better access to things, a lot can become better.

With policies like flexible attendance, a lot of things can become better. Having educational programs that promote menstrual health can also help a lot of things. When there is a supportive environment around them, women feel much better about themselves and can also find it in them to work better. In one of her interviews, Emma Watson talks about creating a more inclusive environment for menstruating women. She said,

"Supporting menstruating individuals isn't just about providing menstrual products; it's about fostering a culture of empathy, understanding, and respect. Together, we can break the stigma and create spaces where menstruation is no longer a barrier to success."

Educational institutes specifically have a huge responsibility to shoulder. They are continuously working for the betterment of society, and for that, they must realize the crucial role they have to play in the process. Malala Yousafzai talked about this, saying, "Educational institutions and workplaces have a responsibility to ensure that menstruating individuals are supported and accommodated. By prioritizing menstrual health and creating inclusive environments, we can empower women and girls to reach their full potential."

Challenges Faced by Menstruating Employees in the Workplace

Menstruating women face a lot of challenges in the workplace as well. This impacts their overall well-being and their productivity as well. Michelle Obama, who has spoken for women's rights very often, says, "Menstrual health is a fundamental aspect of wellbeing for women in the workforce. We must address the challenges faced by menstruating employees and ensure that workplaces are inclusive and accommodating of their needs."

Let's look at some of these challenges to understand the situation better.

- Stigma

Menstruating employees often experience feelings of shame, embarrassment, and secrecy due to the widespread stigma surrounding their period. Menstruation is stigmatized due to cultural taboos and societal norms, which can lead to discriminatory attitudes and actions against those who experience the menstrual cycle. Stigma can take many different forms, including critical remarks, exclusion from meetings or activities at work, or a reluctance to tell coworkers or supervisors about needs related to menstruation.

- Discomfort

Symptoms like headaches and bloating can lead to massive discomfort, hampering a person's ability to work with full focus. Employees might struggle to manage their symptoms in the best way possible, eventually leading to decreased productivity.

- Lack of Accommodations

Many workplaces aren't designed in a way that meets the menstrual needs of employees. They do not have access to menstrual hygiene products or even comfortable restroom facilities that can give women the comfort that they need at such a time. Workplace policies are also often not accommodating enough, so things must be planned out correctly first. Addressing unique needs like sick leaves for women due to menstrual issues should become a part of the process, allowing for greater ease for women during this time.

Addressing all of this is very important. Here are a few steps that can be taken for this:

- Policymakers should encourage open communication in all regards, especially related to menstrual health, so this can be tackled much better. When there is an overall culture of understanding and empathy at the workplace, it becomes easier for menstruating women to be much more at ease and manage what is going on within.
- There should also be access to menstrual hygiene products in the workplace, like restrooms, so menstruating women can manage their periods discreetly.
- Providing tools and support services, such as access to healthcare benefits, counseling, or wellness initiatives centered on menstrual health, to workers who are uncomfortable or exhibiting symptoms related to their periods.

Promoting Awareness

Here is how you can promote awareness and try to cultivate a mindset in people where they understand things for the better. Most of these initiatives can be taken on a policy level to allow things to be handled much better.

- Awareness Campaigns

Workplaces and educational institutions can host awareness campaigns about menstruation to inform stakeholders, staff, and students. Workshops, seminars, and informational sessions on menstrual health, hygiene, and disorders may be a part of these campaigns. Institutions can foster compassion and empathy for people who menstruate by educating the public about menstruation facts and debunking myths about it. These awareness campaigns can help allow for more open dialogue that caters to all of this in a much better way and also allows for greater comfort regarding things.

- Open Dialogue

It is important for men and women alike to be able to talk about anything related to menstruation without feeling ashamed or uncomfortable about it. This helps create a culture of inclusivity in the workplace. Women should be able to easily share their experiences with others to feel better. Institutions should work toward creating that kind of atmosphere that allows for this to happen in a more seamless way.

- Inclusive Policies

Implementing policies is key here. Most of us understand the challenges, but the key is for these different policies to be implemented to allow for the changes to happen in a better way. Policymakers have to take this into account and have to try to bring about change so that things can happen smoothly. This way, the overall well-being of all the members of the community can be ensured. Malala Yousufzai, an advocate for women's rights, said, "No woman should have to choose between her job and her menstrual health. It's time for workplaces to prioritize menstrual equity and implement policies and practices that support menstruating employees."

- Training

Training programs have to be provided for educators and administrators so that there can be greater awareness. These courses may address issues like understanding menstrual health, identifying symptoms of discomfort associated with the menstrual cycle, and offering suitable accommodations and support. Institutions may foster more inclusive and encouraging environments for people who are menstruating by providing staff with the information and abilities necessary to effectively handle menstruation-related concerns.

- Partnerships

Partnering with different community organizations and healthcare professionals is key to strengthening efforts to promote awareness. With greater inclusivity around this, people can advocate for policy changes much better. When institutions collaborate to enhance their efforts to create menstrual-friendly environments, great change can be brought about in the best way possible.

With changes happening on the policy front, many things can be simplified at large. By prioritizing menstrual health and wellbeing, institutions can contribute to a more equitable and supportive society where menstruating individuals are valued, respected, and empowered to thrive.

We live in the 21st Century now, where a lot of the things that we consider to be massive privileges should be classified as regular human rights, like access to menstrual products. Is this asking for much? Taran Burke, an American activist, said, "Access to menstrual products is not a privilege; it's a basic human right. It's time for governments and policymakers to recognize this and take concrete steps to ensure all individuals have access to the menstrual products they need to manage their periods with dignity and respect." Even though menstruation is a very normal bodily function, women in today's day and age also have to struggle so much to find their place and due rights. With the right policy measures in place, there is room for improvement.

Only when we all work together to bring about some positive change will we see things change for the better? To normalize conversations about normal bodily functions, especially about women, is crucial to creating an atmosphere where women, at the very least, feel safe – where women can speak up for themselves and create greater ease and convenience. If everyone does their due part, things definitely become much easier.

Way Forward

For a very long time, menstruation has been hidden and veiled, which has contributed to the stigma and humiliation associated with this normal biological process. The first step in removing these obstacles and promoting an atmosphere of openness and understanding is to break the silence.

In the day and age that we live in, everyone has to play a part in bringing about some sort of change. While most changes apply to policy levels, it is imperative for each individual to also play their part, work hard, and try to speak up. There are so many female activists all over the world who are trying to bring about positive change by working hard to press for women's rights, but change can only come when we all work hard toward it – when we all play our due parts to speak up to challenge the stigma. We all must start normalizing conversations around menstruation. That is the only way to create that atmosphere, which allows us to simplify things.

The most crucial step of the process is to start educating girls about menstruation from a very young age. Girls must be well equipped with the knowledge they need, allowing them to work toward their goals further. Not just that, but young boys should also have ample understanding of regular bodily functions to contribute toward creating an atmosphere that allows everyone to be at ease. Menstrual health education programs should be worked on at a significant level, equipping people with the knowledge they need to work hard toward what they want.

Stigma and discrimination have persisted in part because of societal norms and false beliefs about menstruation. It takes a concentrated effort to address underlying biases and advance more inclusive attitudes to challenge these norms. Education makes it possible to debunk myths about menstruation that largely prevail. When people learn more about facts, they can correct the harmful stereotypes largely believed to be true and actively bring about change. Chimamanda Ngozi Adichie spoke about menstrual rights, saying, "Menstrual rights are fundamental to gender equality. It's time to break down barriers, challenge stereotypes, and create a world where menstruation is celebrated, not shamed."

Now that you understand most things about menstrual health, have you thought about what you can do to bring about change? Have you thought about what you can do on an individualistic level to be a force for change? A great idea is to list down a few things that come to your mind that can help you understand how you can bring about some form of change. Imagine what kind of a massive change can happen if most people start thinking this way. The idea is to stir up a large-scale movement, which can only happen when everyone works hard.

You could also think about the environmental impact and discuss and start research about the different sustainable menstrual products that are available in the market. When you do that, you can bring about the change that you are looking to see. Investigating environmentally friendly menstruation product options is crucial to cutting waste, protecting the environment, and encouraging eco-friendly behaviors. Menstrual cups, reusable cloth pads, and other biodegradable options are great for you. Think about what works best for you and what you can work with in the long run. That way, you can bring about a significant change and work toward things in a great way. It is crucial to manage menstrual waste properly to reduce environmental pollution and safeguard public health. Reducing the environmental impact of menstrual products requires educating people about efficient waste management techniques. You can also try different eco-friendly practices in menstrual health to do your part to reduce environmental harm as much as possible. Future generations can benefit from a healthier planet thanks to our adoption of creative solutions and advocacy for environmentally responsible decisions.

Participating in community outreach and local initiatives effectively improves menstrual health and hygiene in local communities. People can help create a supportive environment, increase awareness, and facilitate access to resources for menstrual health by actively engaging in these initiatives. Look out for different volunteering options, participate in as many community education and training programs as possible, and reach out for various public awareness campaigns. Different NGOs are working hard in this direction as well. See how you can offer your support to them and raise as much awareness as you can.

Remember, change starts within and is always one step at a time. No matter how small the change seems, you must start with it first.

Conclusion

As we conclude this comprehensive guide on menstruation, the idea is to understand how managing and embracing menstrual health is crucial for women of all ages. From debunking myths to addressing common symptoms, we have tried our best to pitch in and give our two cents on different aspects here. The idea is to help empower women to take control of their menstrual health. We believe that greater knowledge in this arena is imperative to helping girls navigate through this stage in the best possible way.

Throughout this book, we have focused on the intricacies of menstruation, from the biological mechanisms to societal implications. We have also discussed the importance of menstrual hygiene, symptom management, and waste management. We aim to help girls get a more holistic understanding of menstruation as a very normal bodily function. Despite its significance in our lives, there is a massive stigma around it, and we hope to have played a part in helping deal with that stigma better.

Armed with awareness, it is time that we take action and play our parts. Do what you can to encourage open dialogue relating to menstruation, and also try to ensure that you take care of your body in a better way. Let's push for laws that guarantee everyone has access to menstruation products and encourage equity in menstruation. Let's work to establish a society free from stigma and shame, where menstruation is accepted as a healthy and normal aspect of life.

Dedicated to the cause, we also have a YouTube channel (Utpat Sisters), as mentioned earlier in the book. We have videos on several different topics related to menstruation on our channel. Do give it a go and let us know if it has been helpful!

In line with this, we have tried to do our two cents, and have formed an organization named Utpat Foundation. As part of this initiative, we provide sanitary pads on monthly basis to underserved segments in inner-city areas of Mumbai, India. We have partnered up with several nonprofit organizations for this initiative to ensure that we can help mitigate school absences, help eliminate period poverty and help underprivileged girls work on their self-confidence and build themselves up. We are doing our small part in this regard.

To know more about this, please visit our website: https://utpatfoundation.org/

We really hope you enjoyed this book as much as we enjoyed working on it for you. Let's collaborate to progress in our menstrual journey together!

Feel free to reach out to us at utpatfoundation@gmail.com

Before we delve in, please note that we are not medical professionals. Our goal is to generate awareness. So please don't treat this book as medical or legal advice. Take it with a pinch of salt, and definitely consult your doctor or medical advisor for specifics.

Here is a link to our YouTube channel that you can follow. We have put our heart and soul into this channel, where we share a lot about menstruation.

https://www.youtube.com/@utpatsisters

Bibliography

Eijk, A. M. v., 2016. Menstrual hygiene management among adolescent girls in India: a systematic review and meta-analysis. *BMJ Open.*

Lonkhuijzen, R. M. v., Garcia, F. K. & Wangemakers, A., 2023. The Stigma Surrounding Menstruation: Attitudes and Practices Regarding Menstruation and Sexual Activity During Menstruation. *Women's Reproductive Health .*

UNICEF, 2023. *Breaking the Chains of Menstrual Taboos.* [Online]
Available at: https://www.unicef.org/india/stories/breaking-chains-menstrual-taboos

Made in the USA
Middletown, DE
09 June 2024

55328049R00116